THE GOOD WIFE

ELEANOR PORTER

For Chris

First published in Great Britain in 2021 by Boldwood Books Ltd.

Cover Design by Becky Glibbery

Cover Photography: Shutterstock

Every effort has been made to obtain the necessary permissions with reference to copyright material, both illustrative and quoted. We apologise for any omissions in this respect and will be pleased to make the appropriate acknowledgements in any future edition.

A CIP catalogue record for this book is available from the British Library.

Paperback ISBN 978-1-83889-531-0

Large Print ISBN 978-1-83889-530-3

Hardback ISBN 978-1-80162-560-9

Ebook ISBN 978-1-83889-532-7

Kindle ISBN 978-1-83889-533-4

Audio CD ISBN 978-1-83889-525-9

MP3 CD ISBN 978-1-83889-526-6

Digital audio download ISBN 978-1-83889-527-3

Boldwood Books Ltd
23 Bowerdean Street
London SW6 3TN
www.boldwoodbooks.com

To see a World in a Grain of Sand
And a Heaven in a Wild Flower,
Hold Infinity in the palm of your hand
And Eternity in an hour.

— WILLIAM BLAKE, 'AUGURIES OF INNOCENCE'

Were it not better,
Because that I am more common tall,
That I did suit me all points like a man,
A gallant curtal-axe upon my thigh,
A boar-spear in my hand, and in my heart
Lie there what hidden woman's fear there will.
We'll have a swashing and a martial outside
As many other mannish cowards have
That do outface it with their semblances.

— ROSALIND, *As You Like It* 1.3,104-113

1

Again the clay on my tongue. Wet and bitter, and the roaring weight of the slope piling on my chest. If I scream, the sludge will slide through my lips and press at my throat till I gag. But I must scream.

In the blackness I opened my mouth.

'Martha! Martha! My sweeting, my coney! You are safe, safe.' A man's voice, gentle and close by my ear; he lifted his arm from my bosom and stroked my face until the hill retreated and I knew myself. I was in my own bed and Jacob beside me. All the horror of years ago, when Marcle Ridge crumpled and fell on me, was done with. It was only the dead were buried now.

We lay close. I breathed in the scent of the straw and lavender I had packed in the tick; the hay smell of the horses Jacob carried with him. I turned in the darkness and kissed his warm face.

'They will pass, Martha, these dreams, they always do. It is the month, is all. It throws back its memories. It's like the plough unfolding what was hidden.'

The month. February, when even winter was dying. It was my father's worst month too. He would drink till his face scattered in the ale and he did not know himself. Each year, in the weeks after

Candlemas, it felt to me as though the dead stirred; they looked for the bones that had been hurled about when Marcle hill fell down. They came into my dreams and whispered that I should be with them, for hadn't I too been laid in the cold earth, wasn't I the one who had pulled at the land with curses till it tumbled down?

For three days the ridge had roared and then advanced, ripping Kynaston chapel and its yard of graves, pulling the fields along like blankets, with the terrified ewes bleating and ancient trees wrenched like pegs and put down somewhere new. I had been out thieving wood and young Owen, closer to me than a brother, had been shaken out of his bed; the slip picked us and scattered us and covered us over. It was the freezing mud that I tasted again in my dreams, but what came after was worse. Someone, my good neighbours said, must have brought down God's house, torn His hill, struck Owen dumb with terror. I must have lain with the devil. How else would a youth like Jacob turn from a golden sweetheart to embrace a small dark cripple such as me? Eye-biter, they called me, sorceress, Satan's whore, abomination. They could barely wait for the gallows.

'Whenever I close my eyes she's there, Jacob, the night-hag. The mire puddles in my mouth and chokes me. It is as though there is no light left in the world. I'm sorry. I was never afraid of the night before.'

'Come', he said, 'come outside with me. I must be at the stables soon.'

We stepped out from the cottage. The day had been a wet one and at first I placed my feet warily, but there was no need. Above the cleeving field the sky was clear. The stars sparked as though they'd been flung up by the chiselling frost. We laced hands to trace the constellations, the great bull, the hunter Orion with his girdle, the leaping hare, the hounds who chased after it forever. The great dog burned brightest. I liked it that the most flaming star in the whole of heaven was given to a cur. Nobody stirred in the lane, there were no sounds but the owls, and the yearning bark of a fox. We were alone with the vault of stars and all the world round us. I shucked the dread from my shoulders.

'See, Martha,' Jacob said, wrapping my cloak about me, 'there is light even in the blackest middle of the night. All that life is over, gone. We live here now, in Hope.'

It was an old jest between us, but I couldn't help smiling. After the acquittal, he had come to fetch me. He had a position already. He was to be a groom on the Coningsby estate – the clerk of the court had helped him to it out of pity for us both. I should have rejoiced, but I sat on the floor of my cell and looked up at the flies that buzzed in the narrow slit of light from the window and felt I would never leave prison, not really. I was the Witch of Woolhope by then, there was a ballad about me, or so the guards said, although they couldn't whistle it. Wherever I went folks would revile me and call me all to nought. But Jacob sat down beside me in the dirt and took my filthy hand to his lips and smiled. All will be well Martha, he said, you'll see. I am taking you to live in Hope.

Weak as we both were, it took us two days walking. It was the dog days of summer and the roads were thick with heat. As dusk fell I picked loosestrife, corncockle, willowherb, campion and we lay down on a bed of flowers. At Leominster he asked directions and I understood. Hope under Dinmore, in a crook of the Lugg before it falls into the Wye.

The harvest had begun when we arrived. Rain threatened. No doubt my reputation came before me, but when I limped out to the fields to help with the gleaning, the village was too busy to take much note. The women simply nodded me a welcome. At the harvest supper we took our places like the rest and shared the cup, and if people were a little quiet near me, or cast a glance or two at one another, it was far less than I had feared.

I fell into loving Jacob in the unfledged days when trouble seemed a game. I owed him my life three times over. He drew me out of the earth when it buried me; out of the water when I went mad and sought the moon in Pentaloe Well; then out of prison when he spoke for me in the court. The days of my imprisonment are blurred except that one. For days I had given depositions; I felt emptied of words. The cell was all murk, but in the walk between the prison and the courthouse I passed a garden full of roses, pink and red and white. It seemed like a picture of a far-off land. I don't believe I was afraid any more; they hadn't enough to hang me after Owen stepped out of his cottage white-gowned, white-haired like an angel and stilled the mob by calling out my name. The chief charge remaining was that I had bewitched Jacob into loving me. In his fever, I was told, he raved against me and the devil both. They read the words out in the court. He was too ill to testify himself they said; it was thought he might die. It was likely I would receive a year in prison. If I survived that I was free to starve wherever I wished, so long as I was not a vagrant. I felt as lonely as the shrinking moon I watched for through my bit of window, white and cold, with the gaping emptiness of the night round her always.

Then, as all was nearing a close, I heard a rustle in the court-room and stirred myself to look up. Jacob – gaunt as a ghost, pale as one, but walking without a stick. I had not practised on him, he declared, he had chosen me freely, though in defiance of his mother. It was enough to set me free.

I was a wife. We agreed I should not work with herbs and heal-ing. Hearing of my past, people came to me from time to time for charms and preparations, but I put them off, almost always, except when I could not bear to turn them away. It is just a little knowledge I have, I told them, nothing your own mother doesn't know. My fingers ached to be busy, to collect simples again; my skirts brushed seeds and leaves that had power in them and I let it all drop into the mud. I would be Jacob's wife now, not Martha Dynely, prickly and unwelcome as a thistle in pasture. In the evenings, when the work was done, we sat together and I taught him letters on a slate, or sometimes we lay down and I traced them with my fingers on his back, his thighs, or with my tongue in the hollows of his ribs.

It was good to walk the paths and not be known, or barely, even if my history was all about me still, like the echo of a cry. Whenever a child mimicked the roll of my bad leg an older one would whisper and the mocking stopped. I tried not to mind it, for Jacob's sake, because he was determined not to notice it at all. One spring night I walked out to meet him in the grazing fields and he pulled me up on a nag that was kept for the serving men and began to teach me to ride. All my life I had been little Martha. Suddenly I was taller than a bishop in his hat. I felt the strength of the horse beneath me and all the promise of distance and speed. There, he told me, you are not lame, you lack a horse, is all.

Perhaps I could have lived like that forever, for as long as I was allotted, in the turn of the years and the warmth of Jacob's kisses. It was only when the nights were at their blackest and the rains did not let up that the mare-hag came. In Februaries like this, when the land was numb, strewn here and there with bedraggled jags of snow. In the visions I was buried still; even when I woke it seemed to me I was not far enough away from the sucking mud. Often I sought him then, pulling the strength of him onto me, into me, until we both dissolved. You need a child Jacob would say, giving voice to his own longing; then you'll feel whole again. Sometimes I did not bleed for months and we waited and prayed; I collected nettles, feverfew, St John's wort, spoke charms over us both. He turned his face away from the fear that my womb was cursed, but the fear grew; I could see it sometimes, in his eyes. We talked of it less and less. This year, whenever the nightmare stopped my mouth with her clammy hand, he lit a candle or persuaded me outside as he had tonight, until the quiet earth and the stars steadied me.

We stood a long time in the pricked darkness without the need to speak. Slowly, clouds drifted back across the stars. An early cock crowed; it would soon be morning.

'You must shift, Jacob,' I said. 'You said there was more company expected.'

'Yes, tidy me nicely Martha. I'm to dress his lordship's horse today. I had better practise my bowing and scraping.'

After he had gone I saw he'd forgotten the food I had put by for him. No matter, I thought, I could take it up to him myself. I left early, lingering near the drive in the hope I might catch a glimpse of his lordship and the company riding out. I had rarely seen Thomas Coningby and never close up; for the last year he had been in Italy. Folk said he was a fine young man. I loitered behind an elm for a space, but the cold was too much for me. We would have more snow. The frost held, but there was no sun: all was iron grey.

I turned into the path that went round to the back of the stables and as I did so the lords and ladies at last came past in a clatter of shouting, velvet and leather. I pressed myself against the wall so as not to be seen.

Jacob was in the yard. I could see he was smiling. When he caught my eye he ran to me and scooped me up.

'Martha my honeybird, my sweet heart's root, Sir Thomas himself has just been here. He asked if it was I who had taken the stone from the chestnut that had threatened to go lame last week and when I said yes – fearing he had found fault with me – he nodded and smiled and asked my name. "Well, young Jacob Spicer", he said, "if you handle women as you handle my horses you'll not lack for company". Then he told me to wait for him, said I could comb her down for him tonight, that he might have a job for me.'

All afternoon I waited, unsettled as a fly. At nightfall he burst in, brimful of news and pleasure. The young lord was travelling north with his friend Edward Croft on business of the Earl of Leicester. He would need a good groom. They would be gone a month, two at the most.

'Oh Martha,' he said, 'it's what I have dreamed of. To serve such men directly! It will be the making of us both.'

'He will dress you up in livery to match his horse and all the fine ladies will admire your leg.'

He tossed his head back and threw a mocking glance at me and grinned. 'I think so. And they'll tender me their lily-white hands so that I can help them mount. I hear they like that.'

I laughed, although I felt a little queasy. He did not know how fair he was, or see the grace that drew men and women to him. What would I do here, alone for two months with the spring not yet come? I put on as joyful a face as I could. He was right, of course, it was a gift sent by Fortune herself. Who would not welcome it?

That night I did not dream of the hill but of my own cottage, of turning in the night and finding Jacob gone, of an absence like a door wrenched open so that all the winter winds could rush and enter. When I woke I had to put out my hand to feel that he was there, warm and gentle beside me in the bed. I rose and lit a candle; for many minutes I stood and watched the soft rise and fall of his breath and the smile that hovered at the corners of his mouth.

2

There was no moon the night he left. All the frost had wilted and the roads and fields were lined with a grey slubber. I walked with him to the stables and waited while the horses were saddled up and clattered into the yard. Jacob was a fine stableman; I could see why the young lord had picked him out; he had a way of talking that the horses seemed to understand. They bent their heads to him and snorted. In the light of the lantern their white breath smoked about his face.

At last he turned to me, smiling, 'Come here, Martha, we have a little time still.' I followed him up a ladder into a corner loft and sat back against the straw.

'Pinch out the lamp,' I said, 'we don't need that.'

'Don't we, wife? The last time I was with you in a stable loft you near pulled a knife on me, remember?'

'Ah,' I whispered, 'I remember husband, but that was before I had learned to lie with you.'

'Did I not make you an honest woman then?'

'Oh no, our talking always ends in lying.'

'And how does that begin? Like this?'

'Aye.'

That moment – with the smell of horses and mould, with the
horses snorting and stamping below and the men calling and
cursing as they fitted the packs – I think it held the keenest joy I
have ever known. The knowledge he was about to go made the
wonder of it sharper. In the soft darkness there was only his breath
on my cheek as we kissed one another's faces, tracing the contours
and the hollows, pressing the map of one another into our lips. It is
his arms, his holding me, I thought, that keeps me whole; only that.
Without that the sorrows of my life, and my own wild soul will hurl
me into pieces. I will be like the Gabriel Ratchets people tell tales
of, the restless hounds forever howling across the whipped skies,
unable to find my self.

Jacob sat up. 'It is only two months little mouse. I shall be back
before you hang a garland up for May.'

'I hope so indeed!' I said, 'or who will take me out a-Maying and
help me stain my brown gown green?'

'Ha! My Briar Rose still.' He brushed the straw from his hair.

'Jacob, lad,' a voice called, 'have done and come down, they'll be
here any minute.'

He bent towards me, suddenly earnest, 'I don't doubt you. All
the same, be wary whom you trust Martha. You know the Steward's
fondness for making bastards. No, don't take on. If any call you into
their house a healing, make sure there's a woman by. Bolt the door,
nights, and don't walk abroad.'

'I will obey, my lord. I'll not stir from my hearth nor lift my eyes
from the earth for fear of dishonour.'

He threw his head back in his old way, narrowing his eyes. I
placed a finger on his lips before the hasty words came. 'Forgive
me,' I said. 'Don't let's quarrel, I cannot bear you to leave on a quarrel. Come, Jacob, I am tame, you have tamed me quite. You are
much more likely to be tempted than I.' I put my hands round his

face. 'Morning and evening I shall hear the culvers cooing their constancy and I shall sing with them of mine. Be as true to me as I shall be to you.'

'As true as the circling sun, Martha.' He smiled, kissed me once more and leapt down the ladder.

Then all was commotion; the bleary young lords and their retinues came swaggering in. There were shouts for forgotten necessaries, bags added to, orders from the florid Steward and in the grey damp light the horses were led one by one to the mounting block and the gentlemen swung themselves into the saddle. It was Jacob himself held Sir Thomas's bridle. He was barely older than we were; I dare say he looked younger, although his dainty-featured face was golden from his travels. There was a delicate charm in him that spoke of strength, like a jewelled scabbard for a blade. Jacob beamed when his master inclined his head and spoke to him. Sir Thomas did not shout as the Steward and the other lordings did – he garnered attention and spent it generously, sweeping us all in his clear intelligent smile.

The party were about to leave when there was a bustle at the entrance to the stables and flanked by her ladies, the Lady Anne, his mother, appeared. Sir Thomas left off talking to his companion and sombrely dismounted to kneel before her on the bare flags of the yard, his head bowed for her blessing. She placed her hands upon his head and raised him up; then she was gone, but I saw the look she gave her son's young friend and the tightness of her smile as she acknowledged his bow. Ah, I thought, so you do not approve of young Edward Croft, although his father is comptroller to the Queen and he is heir to half the county. I could see why. I think his horse could, jostling against her fellows so that a stable boy reached for the bridle.

'Get back you damned varlet,' Croft muttered, turning on the boy. I think he would have struck him if there had not been others by.

There was some other delay. It was no use skulking in the shadows to bother Jacob for glances. A knot of us straggled to the drive to watch them as they came through. A thin mist had risen from the river and was strewn across the low boughs of the elms like wisps of wool. A ewe bleated; I waited for the lamb to answer. There was an eerie loneliness to the morning; the stillness was beautiful but had no warmth in it. The soft mist would thin into the desolate light of day. At last the cry of the lamb came, but it was far away, over the river, surely; how had it wandered so far? Could it find its own way home? I darted a look at my near neighbour, old Rowland Coggeshill, to quiet myself, but his frown looked as worried as mine. His nephew, John, was leaving home for the first time in his life, working alongside Jacob. I tried a smile.

'What is known of Sir Thomas's companion, Edward Croft, Rowland? He looks a choleric man, not a bit like Sir Thomas.'

'Young Edward Croft? Less known of him the better. Brings all to ruin he touches. Old Sir James, his father, is the powerfullest man I ever seen, near the highest in the land he is, rules the Queen's house and everyone in it, but even he en't got a clue what to do with him. Folks say Edward killed a man out Lingen way, that Sir James had to spend no end of money keeping it in the county. I reckon they're only too glad to lose him to the North for a month or two. Hoping he don't come back I daresay.'

'Then I'm glad he's not Jacob's master, or John's. But I'm surprised Sir Thomas should like him so, or his mother allow him to be one of the party.'

'Well, as to that she don't have much say. Young lord Thomas's a grown man and not in hock to his mother. And Edward Croft may be lively company when drink or his own dark soul don't set him roaring; there's many enough like that, young Martha, great or small.'

'That's true too.' I said, thinking my own thoughts till the coming of the company pushed them aside. The two young lords were out in front, with feathers in their hats, their mares prancing at the bit. Sir Thomas slowed as he pricked past us, deigning a smile on old Rowland, and behind him was Jacob, easy in his own strength, watchful of his masters. He did not need fine cloth to gild him. I held his gaze for just a moment, caught the glint in it, but could not catch the words his lips began to shape, for there was a sudden stir.

It was Master Edward's horse, something had startled it, the mare was rearing all over the road with her rider laying about her, as though a whip would calm her. Jacob rode forward quickly, leaning across to take the bridle, but Master Edward swore at him to hold back and jerked at the bit and brought her in line; the fear still red in her eyes.

'What made her start so?' I nudged Rowland.

'There was a watkin ran across, near under the hooves. Didn't you see a couple of the hounds go after it?'

I swallowed. 'A hare?'

'That's what I said.' He looked at me sharply; he knew as well as I did that to cross a hare at the start of a journey boded ill for the travellers. 'And it don't mean nothing. Don't have to. Leastways not for yours or mine. Best not dwell on it. Look how the sun is trying to shine on them. Give him a last wave, girl, they're nearly through the gatehouse.

I could not tell if he saw me; I think he looked back. Then they were through the gatehouse and the wide road took them.

Rowland patted my hand. 'Come on home. He's a fine steady lad, he'll be back before you know it.'

I smiled and nodded and we turned towards the row of cottages.

The sun was leaking into the edges of the day, but it could not reach the lane. As I neared my own door I felt suddenly that I did not wish to enter my empty home, not yet. I would walk a while, slow as I was, and see if I could lick up some dregs of light. It was a long time since I had wandered gathering simples. I felt a strong wish to do so, if only to banish from my mind the hare's warning of mischance. Perhaps old Rowland read a little into my thoughts because when I made my excuses, he shook his head gently.

'Fortune is as she will be girl. There's a sight more hares waiting in the grass, she ain't riding all their backs. Give it over. There's no use moithering on signs.'

I took a path to the south-west that wound slowly uphill through the woods, curling like shy ivy round and alongside the main straight lane. It was a habit not to want to be seen and besides, I could take what bark and what roots and leaves I wanted with more ease. Not only that – Jacob's leaving had churned up all my old disquiet. If I could, I thought, I would wait here for his return, like a hedgehog in a drift of leaves. Foolish of course; even before I reached the brow a woodsman hailed me from a hazel stand a few yards off. He wished me good day and asked after the company, had they made a fine departure? It soothed me, talking to him; it reminded me that I was simply Martha Spicer, a respectable woman, who kept a clean enough house and was married to a good man, who a neighbour would ask to mind a baby or lend a cup of milk without a blink of fear. It was as Jacob had said over and over – I could let go fearing my fellows. At least for now, I thought, bidding the man good bye.

At the brow, all the tributary paths flowed into a clearing that opened off the Hereford road. Hampton Court Castle was laid out below me, with its square walls and neat stables and embroidered gardens. All the mist had cleared; the light an indifferent white that permitted colour but did not encourage it. Behind the Court the river was an iron bar; it seemed to assent to the great house and offer itself as a fierce girdle. I could not see my own cottage; it was hidden in the hollow. Morning barely reached it before the shadows stretched from the sloping fields to claim it back again. Even our lane snuck down away from the road. For a while, Jacob was stepped up into the world of strong walls and windows, the world of those who could pattern out the earth and even bend the river, who could kick up the mud of the road and scoff at portents. What must it be like, I wondered, to look down on a score of chimneys, on fields and hedges and paths and to feel ownership, to feel it in the pulse of your blood? You could plant your legs so firmly on the earth, look down the middle of the road. Common people would step aside as you approached and you would barely notice.

They would be beyond Leominster by now. I could not make out much of the road, there was too much of a haze in the air and it was too fuzzed about with trees. It was clearer the other way, towards Hereford. I pretended to myself I could see the city walls and the tower of the great cathedral. Owen was there, somewhere, in a scholar's gown, his hair as white as the day he'd stepped out of his mother's house and climbed up to me on the cart that was taking me to gaol. Angel, the crowd had whispered, leaving off their baying and cursing to watch as he called my name and climbed up and embraced me. Who could say I'd witched him after that? My little Owen, who I'd taught to read better than any hedge-priest

He'd be grown now, near as. He was doing well, he wrote; he was going to be sent to Oxford, to the University. When a letter came – it was not often; one year I had seven, one year two – when a letter came I would not read it straightaway. I kept it folded in my gown, feeling the paper with my fingers now and then, the pain and the joy of it – Owen, who was lost to me, who was thriving, who had not forgotten. What I would give to see him! He was to be let in to the world of streets and money, of libraries where all the learning in the world waited for the reaching hand. There was no use my dreaming of any of that.

Would Jacob write? I smiled, it was not likely – or if he did it would not be much. He had mastered the letters quick enough and could read any page of the Bible, but he'd had no need of writing, nor occasion to practise it. For him the world before him, with all its variousness, was enough; he did not yearn for more, nor feel the delight my father had unlocked in me, when the voice on the page opens a door to a world elsewhere. Tell me, I'd said, write to me and tell me about all the places you pass through, the people you meet. He'd laughed. I'll be back before the letter would reach you; I'll put you on my knee and tell you myself – how one town was very like the last, how one master was haughty and another kind and how I tired of kissing the women. He had been fresh come home from the stables with the smell of the horses on him, the energy of their snorts and stamping lingering round him; I closed my eyes and stood still on the road, to hold the picture of him in my mind.

'For God's sake, make way!' a man's voice shouted behind me, beside me. 'What! Are you mad? In the middle of the road like that? You might have lamed her.'

A gloved hand roughly pushed me aside, so that I cried out, stumbled, lost my footing and half fell. I was not hurt, thankfully, but my gown was muddied and the herbs I had gathered were lost. I had let a dream knock away the morning. I hauled myself upright quick and turned to look at the rider. He had turned his horse round and was regarding me and the scattered simples in the mud. My hood was still about my head and he did not know me, but I knew him, I had seen his skinny shanks often enough, checking up on the hands.

The crest of the hill was only a few paces behind. The horse was not breathing hard – it had not taken the rise at a lick then. More like a walk. He might have called out; there had been no need to push me. I lifted my eyes to meet his gaze as he stepped the horse closer. He did not like that; for a moment he raised his whip and leaned as though to strike me. It was enough, I dropped my eyes and bobbed.

'Forgive me, my lord Steward, it was careless of me. I beg your pardon.'

'You are one of our people, aren't you? Pull your hood back.' He put his face down close and peered. I focused on the mole on his chin, the long hairs dangling from it. 'Ah', he said at last, 'I know you, you are the wife of the stablehand Sir Thomas has taken a fancy to. You were to be hanged as a witch once, weren't you?'

'I was found innocent, sir.'

'Yet you rise like a hooded spirit in the woods and frighten my horse. What's that you were holding?'

He could see the herbs as well as I, but I named them for him. What was he, I wondered, near fifty, older? He carried himself like a man who had been handsome. Perhaps he believed himself to be so still, although his cheeks sagged and his belly strained against the doublet. He gave me a reproving stare. 'You should ask permission to pick simples.'

I nodded, returning my eyes to the mud as I ought. An early ramsons bud lay by my skirts, the tissue already peeling back round the tight white flower. The mud was on it; it was spoiled already. I felt his watery eyes on me.

'Are you skilled?' The question startled me.

'Only a little,' I answered, feeling the old tug of fear.

'I think you are. And proud with it, I'll bet. Come and find me soon, you might be of some use to me. Physicians are scoundrels.'

With that he took up the reins again and left me.

Scarce a few hours had passed since Jacob had named him as one to be wary of. He hadn't needed to; every woman within a half-day's ride knew how Steward Boult gobbled girls – and spat them out when he'd sucked the bloom from them. There was more than one fair daughter hereabouts, packed off to marry an old man in another parish when her belly grew big. In my mind's eye Jacob shook his head in warning. But surely, I thought back, it could do us no harm to be useful to someone as powerful as he? Not if I were careful. I was no golden girl, no dewy rose to be sniffed and plucked.

3

Rain set in before nightfall. A cold thick rain that pressed out light and hope. I knelt by my bed and prayed they had found good lodgings and kindness. Even as I did so, I half expected the light touch of his fingers on my neck, his presence behind me. Such foolishness, it was only two months. Nevertheless, I lay awake a long time, long after the cottages were quiet and there was only the odd owl, the rain on the thatch and the drip where it leaked. It was getting worse, the leak. The ridge needed renewing. They had promised it when we arrived. 'Not a bad cottage Jacob Spicer,' they'd said, 'and the Steward's man has promised you a new coating of thatch before winter.' We'd scarcely cared at first, the life here was so much more than we'd dared hope for, but as that winter passed, and the next, we'd grown tired of patching the holes. Last November a storm had threatened to blow half the roof away; we'd had to rope it down, with the gale in our faces. If we were to have another wild night I could not attempt that on my own. Mould spread over our end wall like breath on glass, however often I scrubbed and limed it. If I could be of service to the Steward, perhaps Jacob would come home to a new roof.

I must have fallen asleep at last, for when I woke the birds were loud and the rain had stopped. I opened the door to sunshine, and to Sally Robbins, my neighbour two doors down. Silly Sally we called her, she was always wittering to fill the empty spaces in her head, or else worrying after things she could not help, as though it were only her fretting stopped the sun from falling down. There was no harm in her, for all that; when her sister had died she had taken the children in, though there was scarce room to stand. It had been the making of her, for it gave her a whole houseful who would worry her forever. She was forever clasping the children to her big turnip breasts and weeping at their faults and falls and they loved her for it and strained to get away.

I smiled. It felt good to have another's voice in the house and if I couldn't have Jacob, hers would do, for it lined the emptiness without my having to make much in the way of response.

'Well I didn't see you all afternoon and I said to my Michael, that poor girl – I know you are a grown woman Martha, but you are a girl to me ever since I saw you arrive thinner than a reed in winter – so I said to myself that girl has gone to be alone to weep. And I expect you didn't get a wink of sleep did you, all night long?'

I smiled to think I was near as feeble as she thought me. 'I slept quite well Sally, thank you, although the rain was coming through all night.'

'Yes, you look pale as death itself, poor thing. It's a terrible thing to be lovesick. And you two like pretty doves, if a dove could be as dark as you are dear – if I'm honest you are more brown like mistress blackbird and you have a lovely voice like her too, I've heard you singing. And Jacob your ouzel, but golden. Michael said if you think she's lonely you could send the baby round to her, he'd keep her busy enough!'

'I'd be happy, Sally— '

'—And make you pine the more! Well, maybe an hour or two of

an evening, I have that much to do I barely eat some nights and the poor babe so sick with the kinkcough he whoops all night. But don't you worry, you'll have some of your own before long, there's nothing like a bit of yearning to quicken you up when he comes home – perhaps if Michael had gone away a bit more we'd have had our own. But see, we've plenty.'

'You have, Sally, they're doing well.'

'Are they, do you think so, you don't think Jack has taken to stooping? They are working him too hard in the yards and now with Jacob gone – he'll miss him near as much as you will, always a kind word, Jacob, like a brother he's been—'

'—Sally,' I said, for my patience was wearing a little, 'Roger Boult, the Steward, accosted me yesterday as I was gathering herbs. He wants me to attend to him, I think it must be a sickness of his own, or someone else in the household. Do you know of anything?'

Sally pursed her lips together. 'I won't hear a word against Sir Thomas, he's the best master that ever lived…'

I nodded her on.

'But that Steward is a knave. A bobber and beguiler, that's what he is. Don't have nothing to do with him, if you can help it. Or if you can't, sew up your petticoats.'

'Have no fear for me, Sally,' I said, 'I've known fetters already. There are things worse than hanging – if he touched me, I'd stab him in the throat.' And I showed her my knife to prove it. It was a lie, of course. There was nothing worse than the foetid rat-ridden cell and the slow festering hours and the gaoler's leer and the noose approaching – Sally was an innocent, after all, compared to me. 'He's not after my skirts, or not particularly – there must be an ailment. Do you know what it might be?'

'Well, I wouldn't be surprised if it was his leg. His left leg. Word is, he's a canker on it, after a dog bit him. That'll be what it is. Goes everywhere with it all bound and bandaged. They were talking on it up at the Court, said it smelt foul, that Sir Thomas's lady mother had wrinkled her nose. Should be in his pizzle not his leg, all the girls in the parish would be a sight better off if *that* got bound.'

After she had gone I stood by the door, thinking. A canker. That should not be so difficult to treat, although it was a poor time of the year for gathering fresh plants. My store was meagre, barely more than any good housewife would have. 'Put them by,' Jacob would say when he came home to find me with pestle and mortar thinking up poultices, and I did, more and more, till I mostly forgot how it had been before I married, when every meadow and hedge would sing to me to be picked and used. There was chickweed coming up already that I could boil with vinegar to clean the wound. I went to my simples box: ground goldenrod, betony, fennel seed, horsetail, calendula, hemlock. I had enough.

The first time my grandmother had taken me with her to treat a canker, I ran from the stinking hut to retch. She stood at the door until I was done, then pulled me back in and held my hair to make me kneel and look. It was an old woman, who lived near Putley, with no family or children about her and my grandam sat her in the weak winter sun and stood over me until I had cleaned the wound and pasted it. Then she had me clean the tick the beldam slept on and cook her broth, because, she said, healing begins in the belly.

I doubted the Steward would be needing pottage. I thought of the way his mouth always hung a little open, as if waiting to be fed. I wasn't afraid of his lechery. If he laid his big clammy hands on me I could brew up wolfsbane and quiet him forever. It was thoughts like that scared me, the part of me I had laid hidden in the box, the hungry, outfacing spirit in me that had led me almost to disaster. The spirit that urged me to look directly into men's eyes, into the workings of things, the workings of nature herself.

I took out a root of oak fern I had gathered in November and held it in my fingers. How insignificant it looked, thick and woody with its yellow scales – how easily tossed aside – but I knew how it could loosen the chest, soothe the stomach. Half-empty as it was, my box was full of power to heal and to hurt. If I cured Boult I would be called on, up and down the village, further perhaps. 'It was bound to happen,' I said to Jacob in my head. 'Don't worry, we have friends here, I'll be careful.'

4

Still I delayed any visit to the Steward's house. Quite apart from taking up healing, I had sworn to myself, after the trial and my deliverance, that I would not mess with great ones again, but live quietly among my own sort, a good wife. It should be enough. When Jacob was close by it was, oh more, more than enough; there were summer days when I hailed him as he returned home from the yards or the warrens, and breathless and laughing we turned into a hollow where the grasses and a willow made a green room, and we flung ourselves down and I lay between the press of the earth and his warm body. When we had to mix with the Court on holy days I held myself so quiet I believe I was barely seen at all. It wasn't difficult – what were we but cattle to them after all? We had no books; for a while I had had glimpses of the distances and sights that learning promises and they had thrilled me through, but the mist had come down on the world again so that I must only look before my feet. The village was not short of tales. Sally in especial could yarn out stories as she sat and span, and many nights, if there were gatherings, old men like Rowland told tales of the country, so that it seemed there was a fairy or a witch at every turn of the path.

Jacob was right not to have wanted me known as cunning with herbs. I was too good not to attract notice and we could not risk that, not when we were new here. Each time folks asked me, in the ordinary way of a neighbour, if I had this or that to borrow, my fingers had itched to do more. Surely now we had less need to be so cautious? If I had had a child I believe I should not have felt so restless, although if I wanted a babe it was chiefly for him – to feed the yearning I could see when he watched children in the lane – and to have something, someone from him, that we had made together.

It would have kept him awake nights, the Steward's request. It will mean trouble, he'd have said, you should have prevented it. 'And how could I do that?' I asked him in my head. He could no more have forbad me to go it than I refused, but he would have made sure Sally or another came along with me or, more likely, he would have made occasion to come himself.

It had surprised me to find that Jacob could be jealous. What was I but a cripple, the daughter of a drunk? At home it had been thought proof of my witchery that he'd wanted me at all. Folk were kinder to me here. Last harvest, although I could not dance, I was called on to sing while the dancers rested. I finished 'The Bitter Withy' and Simon Fosbroke, who had clapped me louder than the rest and had had a cup too many, came up close and stood with his tankard raised and shouted a toast 'to the pretty songbird.' Jacob, warm with dancing, had been out to fetch the cider; he stepped back into the barn just as Simon seized my hand and kissed it too long. The smile fell from his face and he darkened with a look I had not seen before. A moment later he made as though he was easy again, laughing Simon further off; though I could see he was angry still. 'It was nothing,' I told him when we lay in bed, 'you mustn't mind it. Think how you yourself whirled Annie Bartlet. I don't fire up at the way she clung to you, or how you laughed together.' He didn't answer for a while, so that I thought he was sleeping, or angry. Then he turned to me and kissed my lips hard. 'Don't talk silly,' he said, 'you know it's not the same. A man is more free, of course he is, but not with a married woman. It felt like a devil had seized me, Martha. For a moment there I wanted to smash his face with my fist. If another man touched you I think I might kill him.' 'What foolish talk,' I said smiling, brushing his cheek. To my surprise, it was wet.

I lay awake a long while afterwards, with his sleeping head on my breast and the rise and fall of my chest following his breath. He was dearer to me than life, and yet there were moments when he seemed strange. I had seen him throw Annie in the air and catch her and I knew it did not matter, it was only the dance and his glad free way of giving himself. How could he be angry at another man's trifling if he believed me true?

I was not permitted to debate my visit to Boult for long. Two days after he knocked me down there was a banging at my door. It was scarcely dawn. One of the Steward's household was outside.

Martha Spicer? You're to come now to tend my master's wound.'

'Now? I must see to the chickens.'

'You can see to them later. Gather up what you need.'

I had the bundle made up already. It was just as well, for he was even now striding quickly down the lane. I had to hirple after, conscious of my rolling gait. More than once he stood to wait, sighing loudly.

'You'd best hurry. He has engagements. He shouldn't be kept waiting by a daggle-tail such as you.' Then he watched me attempt to run, letting a sneer play openly across his lips.

I stopped. Why abase myself? Let the lord Steward wait, and his braided niddicock too. I began to walk at my own pace. 'He could have sent a cart, then,' I said.

He looked a little startled at that and shrugged. 'We have a man in the kitchens, used to work at the Hall in Kynaston. He knew all about you. How you were lamed when you were buried by the hill. Trapped in the earth for days and days until your horse-boy pulled you out. Quite a story.'

I made sure to splash his hose as I lurched up. 'So.' I said.

'Told us more, too. Said he doubted you'd ever dare go back, not there, where people know you, know how it was you that brought down the hill and the chapel, too.'

'I was acquitted.'

'I dare say. In *Ludlow*, I dare say you were.'

Would he have talked like that if Jacob had been by? It was unlikely. He would not have risked his delicate arse being thrown into the mud. But then again, it would be a reckless stablehand who'd raise his fist against a servant of the bedchamber. He was an intimate of his master's shit, too exalted to be touched by the likes of us. I was a fool to think it was over; I would always be exposed. The only safe way was to bide quietly, give no offence and to keep shy of gentry. Yet here I was. If I succeeded there would be talk and envy and customers, if I failed the Steward would resent his weakness in seeking me out. It could not be helped. I shut my eyes to consequences.

For all our rushing, I was left waiting by the scullery an age before a boy nodded me into the house. I smelt the canker from the hall, well before I reached the library where Boult was having his dressings removed. I swallowed hard and thanked my grandmother for teaching me to endure rot. As I entered the Steward was swearing at a man attempting to peel off the bandages. I smiled; it was my guide. Not so lordly now, he picked at the pus-soaked cloth, his face twitching with disgust.

Seeing me the Steward gestured me forward. 'Come on then, you can't do me any good from there, can you?'

I bobbed a curtsey and approached him. 'I'll need hot water, bandages and a good clean knife,' I said to the man, curtly enough.

'Get it sirrah,' Boult shouted, kicking him back with his good leg.

I mixed a draught of nightshade. He drank it off; I was surprised by that. I think the pain from the old cloths was very great. They were matted to the sore. It took me a long time to scrape and clean the wound. I bathed it with chickweed then made a paste of the herbs I had brought and applied it thickly. His skin was very white and hung loosely on his calf. A stick of a leg, with a great round belly above it. He grimaced with pain as I worked but the nightshade kept him placid; he stared at me with his pale, blood-traced eyes and let his fleshy lips hang open.

Above him was a painting of a young woman. I suppose it must have been his wife; Sally had told me she'd died a long while ago, soon after they were married. She was pretty, in a deep red dress with puffed shoulders. A cross hung from a rope of heavy pearls about her neck. I felt as though she caught my gaze and knew me and I looked back so long he kicked me on the shoulder with impatience. There was something poised and ready about her, as though she were about to jump up and escape this dark room with its rank air.

When I was done I stood and stretched myself and looked about me, calling for vinegar to rouse him. There were two shelves of books, all bound in dark leather, titles picked out in gold on the spines. I longed to reach and touch them, but was aware of his gaze on mine and stuffed my hands in my kirtle. It had been so long since I held a book! Since I traced my fingers over the print and felt the words form in my mouth.

He waved me off without a word. I left a draught for him at the kitchen and instructions to change the dressings when they smelt foul, and to send for more of the paste. I felt glad to be done with it all so lightly, but then, as I was leaving the servants' door, a man called me back.

'You are to return tomorrow. In the morning. Early.'

A weak spring sun had risen when I got outside. The smack of the wind, sharp with new-tilled earth, was more welcome than wine.

And so it went on through that week and into the next. Boult did not speak to me, nor I to him, although he grunted with approval each morning when he saw the swelling had visibly reduced, that the dressings were almost dry. He sat at his desk now, with his bare leg stretched out to the side of him. I had grown used to the sight and the smell of it; I was even eager to see the shrinking coastline of the wound, for I was proud of what my skill had done when physicians had failed. Each day I arrived early, hoping to be shown into the library before him, so that I could linger by the shelves of leather-bound books, trace my fingers over the gilt words; but he was always there already, reading correspondence, or running a finger along columns of numbers. If my eyes strayed about the room – the paintings and the books – he was quick enough to prod me back to my task. He took to resting his large hand on my head. My neck grew stiff with the weight of it. Several times I tried to speak, hoping to raise the question of our thatch, but he told me gruffly to be quiet. On the seventh day, his man Richard accosted me as I left.

'My master wishes to know what payment you expect. I am sure you will tell him you want nothing.'

I smiled at the man – he was not in earnest, surely? But of course he was. He raised his eyebrows as though in surprise that I could doubt it.

'Please,' I said, 'please inform him that I would like the new thatch that has been promised us. That's all. And that it should be done before Sir Thomas returns.'

The fellow snorted. 'That's all! You've a nerve. I'll do it, but I won't clear up the mess he makes of you.'

The next morning I was so nervous my fingers trembled as I touched the wound, but Boult said nothing. When I was done he simply nodded and waved me off as before. It could only be, I thought, that his man had ducked delivering my request. Rain glistened on the blackthorn in the hedge. The buds were tight and new, soon the blossom would be thick as shorn wool. Before it finished flowering, Jacob would be home. My bodice felt tight and I paused to pull at it. There was a chance ... but I should not think it, there was so little hope of that. Yet all week how tender and full my breasts had felt. If it were true, if he came home to that news, what would the thatch matter? I smiled to myself and loitered by a bank of primroses, picking a handful to bring the sun inside with me.

As I drew near I was surprised to find old Rowland Coggeshill, Sally Robbins and a few others in the lane outside my door. My first thought was fire, and I threw myself into a lurching trot to reach them, calling to Sally as I came. She waved her arms at me, beaming.

'Well, Martha, look – they've called the thatchers in. Not just any patching job neither but a new ridge and coating. Ever so early they came, Michael and Jack had not long gone when Meg ran in saying, "Ma there's men on Nuncle Martha's roof ripping it down". Years you've been waiting and every month more rotten and leaking. They've come over from Bodenham. You'll be like a queen, Martha.'

It was true, there were four men at least, the ridge was off already and much of the top coating and the end wall where the wind had loosened the spars. I did not know what to say but fell into Sally's soft bosom, holding my flowers to the side.

'Look at you,' she said smiling, 'collecting primroses as though afeard he'll give his heart away! You've no need of them dear, he's true as Robin's arrow. It must be his favour with the master as has done it. Sir Thomas himself must have left word behind. Fancy his lordship stooping to notice. You must bide with me – it's no bother if you don't mind a bit of a squeeze – the roof won't be tight yet a while.'

My mouth dropped open a little at her explaining the favour so happily. I thanked her for her offer of a bed.

'Wait a bit and I'll get a cart from the yard and help you move your things out of the weather,' Rowland said as Sally bustled off. 'You can keep them at mine, there's no end of room in the place while my John's away.'

There was not much that would spoil; only the tick we slept on and Jacob's clothes and stable gear. His chair. My own clothes and my box of simples I could take to Sally's. Rowland said little while we took the things over, but when all was stowed he invited me to sit with him and share a cup of small beer. There was a slow thoughtfulness about him; it was apparent in his cottage, everything scrubbed and regular. I had never seen him drunk or angry, even at harvest or Shrove Tuesday.

I took the mug he handed me and waited while he filled himself a pipe. He was working himself up to talking. 'It strikes me,' he said at last, not unkindly, but walking round to the point, as he was used to, 'it seems to me that it's not likely Sir Thomas's bidding, this thatch. Thomas Probert told me you've been up every morning to the Steward's house, doing healing work...'

I looked up; I must have frowned, for he shook his head.

'There's no mischief in Thomas, or not a purpose. I seen you myself a couple o' mornings, walking with your mouth a set line, before the dew has settled. Steward Boult's canker's all but healed. Thomas thinks you must be a marvel, that the Good Lord has lent your hands a little of His grace.'

I shifted uneasily, staring into my pot of beer.

'The power of healing is a holy thing and there en't no harm in a cunning man, nor woman neither, that helps nature along some. I don't say so to the vicar, but there's ministers of God and ministers of nature and as long as one sticks to the soul and t'other to the body then all's well and holy. But you've no family here and young Jacob is away and so I said to myself it was up to me to counsel you – I trust you won't take it amiss. You better be careful, that's all.'

'I did not dare refuse him Rowland. He sent a man to fetch me.'

'Aye, right enough, but I doubt you wanted to refuse, did you? Not really. You wanted to try what you could do?' He leaned forward and looked at me, still friendly, but keenly too. 'There's a power in your fingers asking to be let out, that's what I'm thinking. And maybe you can stop it and maybe you can't. But ...' and he paused, knocking out the ash and looking at me, 'there'll be things he's likely to ask which you had better say no to, if you want to be happy with your bonny man.'

I coloured and summoned a temper, but it would not work. 'He is not interested in that, Rowland. In any case, I can protect myself.' Rowland patted my hand.

'Be ready. Remember how the look of things matters, whatever the truth is. You know that already.'

I nodded and he smiled. 'Good,' he said, 'and if ever you need help child, ask me.'

5

I was guarded when I approached Steward Boult the next morning. For the first time he was not already at his desk but standing at the shelves. I followed his eye along the gilt titles as it came to rest on a handsome volume: *In Praise of Folly* by Erasmus. I knew it; Miss Elizabeth, the great lady of my own village, had put it in my hands to teach from when – because I could read and nobody else was cheap enough – she had paid me to learn the village boys their letters. I was as honoured as if I'd been asked to greet the Queen herself. Day after day, in a room above the stables, the boys twisted on their benches clutching slates and I wrote out lines to copy. She thought she was saving our souls; I thought her all that was great and good. She picked me out, she promised to protect me – and then disowned me in a trice. The last I saw of her was her gloves at a window when the rabble came for me and she shut her door.

The village boys didn't care for Erasmus and proud as I then was, I didn't care for them. I blushed now, remembering how I had belittled Jacob when he came to join the boys and learn, how he had kicked a bench and left. Boult looked at me slyly.

'You like the gold, don't you? You people always do, drawn to glitter like crows. Be glad you don't understand it. Give thanks you can live a simple life, girl. The poets are right, it's a blessed state. Free of the cares that bedevil our sleep. We envy you. As long as you are hale you can sleep soundly.'

How useful that we villeins must lower our eyes. There is so much we can avoid revealing. Some of the passages from Erasmus's book Owen and I learned by heart. Anyone who loves extremely, Erasmus says, lives not in themselves but in the object of their love, and the more they can move out of themselves into their love, the happier they become. I am not here Jacob, I thought, I am with you, wherever you are.

'I will sleep much more easy now, sire, with the generous gift of your thatch,' I said, bobbing.

'Ha! Surprised you, didn't I? Thought I'd send you packing for your insolence. You've got a bit of spirit, girl. I like that. Raise your eyes.' I looked up at him, taking care to shut my mind tight. 'Yes, a bit of spirit is good. But not too much, eh?' He stepped back and sat heavily in the chair, sticking his leg out. 'Roll down my hose, will you?'

I knelt and did as he asked. The stockings were flecked with skin. I noticed how a vein bulged out below his knee. His skin smelt old, sweet, like lice. On other days, when I had rubbed behind the wound to move the blood, he had been indifferent, but I felt now this had changed. When I began to chafe his thin shank his leg tensed; without looking up I could see he had turned to me. All at once he thrust his hand beneath my cap, rubbing at my hair. I stopped.

'Go on,' he said, his hand holding my head from rising.

'I must not,' I said, 'it will bring too much heat to the sore.'

'Oh, very well,' he said, releasing me.

He let me alone, then, and I finished up as quickly as I could. 'I think, sire,' I said, as I prepared to leave, 'that you have no more need of me, the wound is so nearly healed.'

He was staring at the papers on his desk. 'I will decide that, girl. Come tomorrow.' He waved me away. When I had my hand on the door he spoke again, so quietly I was not sure I had heard aright. 'Whatever you may have heard, mistress, there is no cause to fear me. I do not force.'

* * *

That night I lay awake and thought about our home, with the thatch undone and the rain feeling its way into our room. How easily we could lose all that we had. Houseless we would be nothing: afraid of the morning, like the dew snails that left their moon threads over the floor at night and in the morning were gone. Might the thatching be left half done if I refused him? 'I do not force,' he'd said, moving his finger down the rows of figures. Yes, I thought, it's buying he's after. It wasn't belly flame that moved Boult, not much; he was slack and spent. No, it was the pricing up, finding what his gold could do, how much might bring a girl to yield. Well, he'd find I cost more than a few bunches of longstraw. I could do my own reckoning. 'No, Jacob,' I said, as though he'd sent his spirit to upbraid me, 'you are not here. I must manage how best I can.'

It was good of Sally to take me in, though the bed I shared with the little ones was cramped enough. Mary slept like a dormouse, warm and still, but Meg wriggled down the bed until her feet were level with my nose. Meg was my favourite of the children; she had a lively eye and wit, where her brother was only dull. She called me 'nuncle' because, she said, she used to think I was a boy dressed up. It was a tender joke from such a chit, and everybody laughed at it, even I, until moon after moon my belly failed to quicken. I wondered if I was not made right. But that was changed; as I drifted off she flung a leg across my chest – how full my breasts were! I felt a smile curling in my heart but I would not own it, not yet. I lay and listened to Sally and Michael snoring, Jack turning in his sleep, the snuffle of the baby and, nearer, the soft outbreath of the girls, gentle as a wind that stirs the leaves. Across the bolster Mary's face in the moonlight was so smooth, so round! I reached out and touched the petal down of her cheek and in her sleep she smiled.

In the morning as we broke our fast Michael grinned at me, pushing his tongue through the gap in his teeth.

'Off to the old lecher again are 'ee Martha? That's what's put a bit of colour in your cheek is it?'

Sally gave him a friendly clout. 'Don't take any notice, Martha dear. Pretty girl in the house and he thinks he has to play the wit. You be off to work Michael.'

'Are people talking, Sally?' I asked, when he and Jack had gone.

'A course they are dear,' she beamed. 'But it's mostly on account of your healing him. You'll have no end of business now. As for the other, folks know he'll be trying it on, but nobody's foolish enough to think you'll fall.'

I leant towards her and laid a hand on her arm, 'I'm afraid of rumour, it almost put a rope about my neck. It's why I've not liked to offer my healing.'

Sally put a finger to her lips. Hanging talk was unlucky, especially in front of the children. 'Mad tattle that was. Dark house and a whip they needed for talk like that. Wouldn't happen here, that kind of nonsense. Not with a master like Sir Thomas. But you'd best be off.'

I'd had faith in a great house to protect me and keep the world on a just course, once. Almost to the last I thought Miss Elizabeth

would save me. It pleased me that Sally could have lived so long
and not grown bitter. She'd had her share of hardship, but her
world had never fallen out of joint. However she liked to gossip,
Sally would walk a sharp mile barefoot before she'd believe malicious tales of me. I had cured the Steward and no harm was done.

It was a beautiful day, blue and young, with a fresh wind
tumbling the clouds across the sky. In the wet lane the puddles
from yesterday's rain shone like metal. I lifted my face to the sun
and felt as strong as the morning. I will tell him, I thought, that I
can no longer come. A reason will present itself to me.

As I reached the house I saw the Steward's horse was being
made ready. My heart lifted. I was shown into the library as usual
and, as I'd hoped, he was in travelling clothes.

'You are late,' he said, not looking up from the scrolls on the
table. 'You were right yesterday, I don't need you.'

'Thank you sire,' I said and smiled inwardly. I turned to go.

Did he catch a wisp of the smile? At any rate he strode across
the room and caught my arm. 'Stop,' he said, oily now, 'I did not
give you leave to go.' His pale eyes were only inches from mine, his
lips hung open in a loose smile. 'Wait while I pack these documents. I have to go to Shrewsbury on business. Not sure how long –
several days perhaps. I have told the thatchers they must be done by
the time I return.'

'Thank you sire, I – and I speak for my husband, too – ... it is
very good of you.' That smile again. He lifted his hand to my face
and regarded me slowly, until I shifted foot to foot. 'Your husband,'
he said at last, 'who is very far away. You can spare me a few
minutes, I think.'

He turned back to packing scrolls into his bag. Presently he
shouted for his man. 'Where the devil is my Ovid? Richard, have
you packed it?'

The manservant rushed over to the large desk and both began

looking, uselessly lifting the same piles of books and scrolls. The book was on a chair beside me; I had seen it as I prepared to leave. A little pleased with myself I picked it from the cushion, and held it out. The leather was soft beneath my fingers – how I yearned to open the covers. My father had talked of these stories, he had read them at school in Latin. Of all they had had to study he had loved them the best, he said; pages and pages of stories, of girls becoming trees and stars, of a boy flying too near the sun; falling.

Boult was looking at me with narrowed eyes. The manservant, too, was staring. It struck me what I had done.

'Well,' Boult said, 'so you can read, too, can you? Bring it here.'

'O...Only a little,' I stammered as I came forward. I did not like the look he gave me.

He opened the book at random. 'What word is that?' Daphne, I thought, but shook my head. 'That one?' He pointed at another, a couple of lines down. Apollo. I shook my head again. He took my chin between his fingers and regarded me. 'Liar!' he said. 'I can see how your eyes skim the lines.'

I twisted to face him, bold, reckless. 'I can read,' I said, 'My father taught me.'

He looked at me suspiciously and then, abruptly, he smiled again and placed the book in my hands. 'Leave us,' he said to the servant, who bowed and left.

'Go on then,' he said as the door closed. 'Read it. I shall pack my bag a moment.'

I opened the book and read.

'Aloud, girl!' he shouted from the table.

'"Of shapes transformed to bodies strange",' I read, '"I purpose to entreat"'. The meaning of the words tumbled into and through me. Shapes transformed, I thought; my father was right, it is a book of dreams.

'Before the Sea and Land were made, and Heaven
　　that all doth hide,
In all the worlde one onely face of nature did abide;
Which Chaos hight, a huge, rude heape ...'

Chaos. I had felt that once, the earth, churning itself undone. I could imagine a beginning of the world like that, at strife, all things waiting their proper shape. As I read it felt to me as though the Steward's walls had thinned, and I was looking out at wonders. I thought I had dulled this hunger for words, for stories, but it came roaring. Then, as I turned the page, his hand was there.

'Hand it back,' he said.

I swallowed, but I closed the book, and placed it in his hand. He left it there between us, the gilt caught by the sun through the window. 'Unless,' he said, 'you would like to borrow it awhile, a few days?'

I nodded, half in a trance.

'Then kiss me. One kiss, that's all.'

His face hovered near mine; he was smiling, but there was the hint of a sneer on his fleshy lips. His breath was of sour wine and meat. I glanced at his blotchy skin, the hairs growing from the mole on his chin. Outside the window horses were being brought round to the front of the house. Quickly, I leant forward and pecked his greasy cheek.

He grinned with all his mottled teeth. 'Have you never been kissed, girl?'

With a lunge he pressed his lips on mine, pushing his thick tongue into my mouth, twining it, as a toad puts out its tongue to catch the fly. His free hand grabbed my breast roughly. I willed the wall behind my back to swallow me, but it merely pressed me back into him, so I tried to reduce myself to the fingers still clutching the soft dry leather of the book. Then there was a knock on the door and it was over. He gave me a quick look, up and down, his eyes merry with triumph, and dismissed me.

'Wait,' he called, grinning, as I pulled at the door, 'any soiling and you will have to pay.'

There was more laughter behind me when I took my cloak by the servants' door – was it written on my face, I wondered, had one of the men glanced through a window? But perhaps not, perhaps the cackling was not thrown at me at all. I hurried out and filled a cup at the pump to rinse my mouth – over and over I did it; until I reflected how I could be seen.

The taste of him lingered as I walked away; it made my gorge rise so that more than once I bent over the verge to retch into the grass. My bosom, too, was sore. I felt sure that if I were to strip, the mark of each finger would be there upon my breast. If they should stay! Jacob coming home would see the bruises of another man's hand upon me! I had heard of such happenings, the mark of guilt on the body. There was a murder years back – a miller down at Eardisland – where nobody suspected the pious brother weeping at church, until it was noted that at a certain time of the afternoon his hands turned bloody. Nothing he did could prevent it: even though he plunged them in the millstream an hour together, the blood ran down his nails.

For the first time since we had come here I had done something that would anger my husband; that could cause bitterness between us. He would not take it lightly; it would rankle and fret. How could he, in all his simple goodness, understand the desire I had felt, with the pages in my hand, to unravel those stories? It had seemed such a nothing to give, at least till Boult's fat tongue wormed within my mouth. That taste! There was a coppice hard by, thick already with wild garlic. I picked a skirtful and sat down in a patch of sunlight, stuffing handful after handful into my mouth until its fresh bitterness cleaned through to my throat and I felt rid of him.

I sat very quiet and still in the sunlight, though I could feel the damp through my dress. There had not been such a warm day yet. The trees were busy with it – as I sat and listened it seemed the leaf-buds, pressing to unfurl, sounded a high thin music. Above me on a branch a blackbird sang full-throated to his mate. All the world was quickening. I placed a hand on my belly – but any mystery there was hidden. If it were true, how Jacob would smile and smile. Unless ... no, I would not think it. Damn the Steward. It had only been a moment; I lifted my face and told myself the kiss of the sun on my lips made everything new. It may be that Jacob would never find out; that I would never need to tell him; that nobody had seen. I looked at the bag beside me. There, wrapped in the cloth I used for my simples, lay the book. I took it out and opened up the pages to the light.

At first my hands shook and I felt too giddy to read steadily, but skitted from page to page. Then a name caught me. Ceres, I read, goddess of the corn, who drew plenty from the earth as we draw water from a well. I closed my eyes and the spring sun glowed through my lids – golden, like ripe wheat in the summer. Ceres had a daughter, Proserpine, who swore she'd never marry, but liked to play with her fellows in the woods, gathering flowers. It was always spring and she filled her skirts with violets, lilies – perhaps wind-flowers too I thought, looking about me at a bank of anemones, bright as stars on the wood floor. One day the Lord of Hell came thundering into her glade behind his great black horses. He plucked her from the ground and carried her away. How she must have drooped in his fist! If only her mother had been by – however the horses reared and stamped, Ceres would have held them; she would have prized apart Hell's fingers one by one to release her child. But she was far away and didn't hear her daughter's cries. All that was left were the scattered flowers, dying.

I had never known a book like this one. It was thick with stories like the ones my grandmother told me, of spirits and gods who were fairies; ungodly, wicked stories the minister had called them. Yet they were taught in the grammar school. I wondered how the Church could allow them. One tale was plaited into the next, twisted together like a fine rope or a woman's hair. Surely a book like this one was worth a bit of sullying? What was a moment of bile in the mouth compared with this? Jacob would not suspect me of foulness. This winter, when he came home weary and the candle had burnt down I would have such stories for him, folded beneath my tongue.

It was only when I noticed the grey cast of the sky that I considered how much time had gone by. Such sluggardness would not do. Until I was back by my own hearth I resolved to keep the book close. Sally knew I could read a little, but not that I could unravel such a text as this; besides, even she was sharp enough to suspect there'd been a price for the loan. What would she think, I wondered, if she discovered what I'd done? Sally wouldn't understand the fierce longing that had gripped me when I held the book, to peel back the edges of my world and follow where it led me. She'd be uneasy, she would think it a wildness in me, she'd fear my ruin. My neighbours, good people all, would take a simpler view; skittish they'd think me, weak-willed, hankering after what wasn't proper in a woman, what was unnatural. Or else they'd look straight to the kiss; I was a wanton, a trollop, after what I could get.

I would take it to the church and read it there. The vicar never locked the door in daylight, nor entered until his luncheon had been well slept off. If he saw me at all he would take it for the prayer book. I placed the volume back into my bag and set off home. After a little way I glimpsed Jack Robbins and another lad following on behind me, mimicking my gait. I turned very quickly so they knew they were seen, but then I smiled; Jack turned redder than a robin and sheepishly asked if he might carry my bag. Sally was right; he had taken to stooping a little, afraid of his own scrawny growth. It could not have been easy, losing his parents and his home.

'Stand up tall Jack,' I said. 'You've a right to look at heaven as much as any other man.'

6

I dreamt Jacob stood over me as I lay between Sally's girls. He bent, smiling, to kiss me, but as his candle caught my face he frowned and shook his head very slightly. I raised my lips, but the mouth that bore down on mine was wet and greasy and tasted of meat.

I must have gagged as I slept, for I woke to little Meg pounding my back.

'Do you need the bucket, Martha?' she asked in a whisper. I turned towards her; her hair smelt of warm hay, it restored me.

'I'm well Meg, don't mind me. It was the mare-hag visiting. You sleep now.'

I could see her wide dark eyes in the gloom, gazing at me without blinking, as young children will. At length she nodded. 'You can hold my hand if you like. She doesn't come when you are holding hands.'

'Has she come to you then?'

She nodded, solemnly her dark eyes on mine. 'Ma always held my hand when she came. She daredn't creep up on me when I was holding Ma's hand.'

I took her warm hand and held it.

'My ma died,' she said. 'Baby Peter ripped her. She was so worn in holes with bearing us Ma Sally said that the devil had only to breathe and she burned all up.'

'Peter's not to blame,' I said.

She nodded again. I pressed her hand to my lips. I thought she had gone to sleep, then, but a while later she put her hand out and touched my cheek.

'Are you crying about my Ma?'

I shook my head, but perhaps I was, a little. On the other side of me little Mary made soft whimpers as she slept. The girls were so warm and new, how could it be that their mother had been taken from them? A few feet away the baby began to cry and Sally, from somewhere in her sleep, began to croon to him. He had been her sister's seventh child. I put my free hand on my belly. These last years I had longed to feel the hard knot of a life beginning, had dreaded each return of blood, Jacob's suppressed sigh. The bleeding had not come this month, not yet – it could be nothing; yet my breasts were still tender ... By the time he returned I would know, I would be certain. Meg had fallen asleep at last, her hand still folded in mine. Perhaps, this winter, I would have my own baby beside me. If I lived. I pushed the thought away. I had survived a hill falling on me – but a life, gathering its body from my bones and blood, pushing its way out of me, would I survive that? Would I have to survive it again, and again, my body losing its own shape, its fastness, with always the sour piss taint in my skirts because I could not help but leak? I thought of the stories in the Ovid book, where girls were wrenched into new bodies with no power to say stop, let me be as I am: Io, turned to a white cow and watched by a herdsman with a hundred eyes, left to graze and waddle, unable to call her father by his name. Little Mary cuddled against me in her sleep as though listening to the story in her dream. Then she let out a long gurgling giggle. I couldn't help but grin: there was not only loss; a child's joy, their petal-freshness, there would be that, too.

It was good to feel Roger Boult gone from the village, to have the morning my own again. I helped Sally with the children and prepared and sowed our bit of ground ready for Jacob's return. Word had got out about my healing work, as I had known it would. Sissy Probert came the first morning. I was busy with a bit of mending when I heard her outside with Sally. Soon enough there she was, Sally behind her, nodding and smiling over her shoulder.

'Now Goody Spicer,' she said, as though I were one of her grown-up children late for church, 'my Thomas tells me you've cured the Steward of his canker that stank worse than my privy.'

'It's mending,' I said, 'it's not gone, but it shall in time, God willing. I helped nature along a little, that's all.'

'Well nature was taking her time about it. And it's often enough she doesn't step in at all. It strikes me it's like starting a fire from the sun. Sunshine alone won't do it, however dry your kindling – you need that bit of glass to marry the two together.'

I smiled, a little warily. 'I used to do a bit of healing in my own country,' I said, 'but that was before I was married.' I hesitated, not sure how much was known of my history, not sure how much to tell. 'My husband does not want a cunning woman for a wife.'

She waved her hand as though pushing a fly away. 'I've heard you had some trouble from idle tongues. That's no matter.' She stood up and as though delivering a sermon added, 'It's a sin to stay the hand that might give succour.'

Behind her Sally sighed and nodded piously. I raised my eyebrows at her.

'Sally agrees with me, Martha. You can't say a good heart like Jacob's would wish to let a neighbour suffer. My mother groans so with her sores I scarcely sleep.'

It was true, he would not wish it, but neither would he be happy that I was called on. 'I'll come along with you,' I said, 'and if I can be of any help at all of course I'll try.'

Each day brought a new supplicant or two, hanging by the hedge, till Sally spied them and ushered them in, talking me up no matter how I tried to hush her. 'There's such grace in the girl's fingers,' she'd say, 'curing Boult when the Court had given up his leg for worm's meat. It'd have been the knife for him if it hadn't been for young Martha. To think we had a regular Merlin in our midst and we all thought her such a little brown mouse!' And people would smile and nod and a part of me drank in their admiration and a part of me quailed. Not Merlin, I'd say quickly, just a little learning I got as a child.

It was as though a part of me was waking and my neighbours too were seeing me freshly. Such a happy sleep, with my head on Jacob's shoulder and my breath rising and falling to the rhythm of his chest. Never mind, I said to myself, when he comes home all will be as before – or nearly so. Even as I was called to a neighbouring parish to see to a fever-ridden child I said it, even as I walked back exhausted, happy, the next morning, scouring the unfurling verges for what they might yield.

At the same time I was hungry to be reading. I began to take the book with me when I went visiting. I said it had belonged to a physician that my father had known, that I read in it for my cures. Then one morning – I was back at Sissy Probert's – old Rowland happened by where I sat reading by her mother's bed. Sissy pointed to the book, it had no end of cures, she said, reaching back past King Henry's time, all laid down by a doctor of divination. Rowland took the book gently in his hand; I watched his eyes follow the lines and understand them and my chest tightened with apprehension. Then, as I was sure he would, he leafed through the covers. There, in black ink, Boult's name. Rowland looked at me. 'It can be perilous, to get and have possession of a book like that,' he said.

Nothing else. He didn't need to. I reddened to the ends of my hair. I had presumed too much on my neighbours' ignorance; Rowland wasn't alone in knowing his letters. Another man would take the question to the alehouse. *'Young Martha Spicer's got a pretty book of the Steward's, keeping it close, says it's charms or some such. What do you reckon she paid for that, eh?'* How could I have been such a fool? Rowland passed it back to me and I put it quietly away. I was more careful after that.

The Steward had spoken the truth when he said the thatchers would be done before he came back. A part of me had been sure that the minute he was gone they'd be off – they must have other business pressing – but I was wrong. By the Monday after Palm Sunday they were done, my house shucked tight with thatch, all cut and trim and gleaming in the morning. After the tightness of Sally's cottage, where every patch of floor had a child upon it, where I could not move in the bed for girls, where all evening Michael filled the room with his fug and talk, worse than a baby hungry for the nipple with his need for women to feed him with attention, after all that my house felt as large and free as the Court itself.

Old Rowland borrowed a cart from the stables again to bring back the things he'd stored for me. I sat beside him, awkward in my heart from not knowing what he thought I might have done for the book.

'A fine morning,' he said.

I stumbled into talking. 'You can read, Rowland.'

'Aye, it's not such a magic as people say. Thirty years since I was first made a warden in our church. I figured that if the word of God was the way to heaven I had better get and learn it.'

'Boult saw me looking. In his library. He offered me the book to borrow just for a bit, while he's gone, if I take good care of it.'

'And he didn't ask payment for the lending of such a pretty book?'

'A kiss on the cheek like a bird at the grain, nothing.'

'A nothing kiss, eh?'

'Yes, a nothing.'

'And your Jacob, he'll think it nothing?'

The words boiled in my throat. I looked down at my lap and was quiet.

Rowland patted my knee and smiled. 'I'm not about to whistle up strife child. But a man like Boult, he'll expect payment, full payment. And you're getting about a bit now, with your healing, into people's minds and mouths. It won't take much to be wondering at that thatch of yourn. My advice is you be clean and straight with your young man when he comes home. He'll shout and puff at you a little like as not, but it'll let his mind settle back easy.'

I looked across at him as he stared out at the pony. 'I'm afraid he'll shape it bigger than it is.'

Rowland nodded. 'He will,' he said, 'there'll be a bit of mending to be done, but better to root out any rot before it spreads through the house and brings the frame down on your heads. And Jacob's not home yet. The Steward will be asking a little more I warrant, before the travellers return.'

I shivered. 'I'll give him nothing.'

Rowland made as if he didn't hear. 'And when the Steward does come asking, if you need help, you come and see me. I said it before and I meant it. Whatever happens or has happened I won't judge you.'

'You'll have no need to,' I said. 'But thank you.'

It was easy to put the conversation out of my mind in the days that followed. Boult was still not back. It was as though I were a carefree girl again – better, for as a girl I had never been this fortunate or this free. I limped through the lanes for simples and felt all my knowledge flowing back into my fingers. Sally rooted through the neighbours for pots to put my preparations in. I was paid for my healing in food and candles; Sissy Probert promised me a piglet when it was weaned. In the evenings I sat in the quiet of my bed with a candle and read until my eyes ached and all was quiet except the lonely call of an owl or the bark of a vixen in the fields. Soon Jacob would be home again and he would cup his hand round my breast and feel how full it was and say Why Martha, my sweeting, you are become a woman.

I had begun to be sick in the mornings. It had been coming on a while. Even at Sally's I had felt queasy when the bread was broken at first light. Now often as not I had to lurch from my bed to the bucket. Then for two or three hours together I could barely take a morsel – my body would revolt and I'd be retching. At least I am alone and nobody to notice, I thought, but it did not take long for Sally to mark it. She had a way of coming in with barely a knock and on the Thursday morning she walked in to find my head in the pail.

'Oh you poor love,' she said darting to help scoop and hold my hair. 'What have you eaten, are you sick?' I did not need to answer. She stroked my back with her free hand. 'I saw you out gathering, I have no doubt you have eaten some of your roots and they have made you ill, you should be careful, my dear. There's no end of cunning folk have made themselves crop sick. There's Meg at the door. Meg go and fetch Aunt Martha a mess of pottage from the fire, to restore her.'

'No, no,' I began, but Meg cut across me.

'Shall I Nuncle? Or will it make you sick again. Isn't it just like at our house when you were pale and swallowed over and over and gave me your bread? She always did that in the morning, Ma Sally.'

I stood up and let go of Sally's arm. 'You're right, Meg, I don't want food.' I turned back to Sally. Her face was filling with smiles, words would spill out soon enough. 'Please,' I said, 'I'm not sure, yet. Please don't talk. Not till he comes home.'

'Oh you can count on me,' she said, shooing Meg away. 'I won't say a word to a goose. Oh, what a homecoming he'll have, a new baby and a good sound house and his wife the marvel of the parish with her healing and no end of favour with the Steward. Oh what a spring you're having and no mistake. You had better sit down. I'll comb your hair. You can have baby Peter's things of course, he'll be big by then and the crib, Michael can mend it ...'

'But you won't say a thing, Sally?'

'Oh no, not me. An October baby then, that's a good month, it can get good and strong before the winter sets in, and then you can sit all through the dark months and feed him into a regular little king by the spring. Peter was February of course and my poor sister sick with the cold and rain before she even came to bed. Have you plenty of milk? I've a little butter, you should eat butter you know.'

She sat beside me and I let her prattle on. She could no more stopper her mouth than a pot could cease itself from steaming when the fire is lit, but she was a good soul; year after lonely year she'd longed to feel a life quicken beneath her ribs and been given only her old parents and her husband's parents to nurse, then on a sudden more mouths than she could feed, but there was no bitterness in her. I took her hand and felt her joy bubble into the air. I could not but be happy too, but all the same I felt these days of luck were fragile, that I was tempting Fortune's wheel to roll. I must not be like my father, I thought, waiting to be flung down into the dust. Or perhaps the Steward's tongue had introduced a worm into my happiness.

That night I read about the sun god's child Phaeton who sought out his father and asked him for a gift. 'Of course,' his father answered. 'Then,' the child said, 'let me drive your chariot across the sky.' Apollo tried to warn him off, showed him the stamping horses, the terrible strength they had, but the boy would not budge. And so he let him mount into the chariot alone. The horses of the sun felt how light the boy's hand was that gripped the reins and they ran wild through the compass of the sky until the earth was charred and Jove struck the boy with a bolt of fire and burned him too.

The story rippled through my dreams. The earth was thick with the bones of those who overreached, who could not hold the reins of life, and fell.

7

Our vicar was a feeble preacher. He laid his plump hands on the holy book and intoned the sermon sleepily, with a gaze that lingered round his fingers as if through every holy word he longed to be picking at his meat again.

It was Good Friday, the most terrible and wonderful day of the year, when our Lord climbed the hill of Calvary and embraced the pain of death and the pain that leads to death so that we could live again. I thought of Christ nailed to the cross by his hands and feet in the slow glare of the day until God put out the sun and there was darkness all over the world. After Phaeton fell Apollo, in his grief, would not ride the sun across the sky; he let it be hid, until the earth cried out for light. We knelt in the church and prayed, but outside the woods and fields knew already that He would rise again and were busy with the business of becoming. Tomorrow, as always, we would deck the graves with flowers for Easter Eve.

Meg came by with little Mary to collect me in the afternoon. We did not need go far for flowers, despite the earliness of Easter. We began up the same path I had followed on the morning Jacob had left, but not far, for Mary toddled every which way and then grew tired, so that I had to put her on my hip. As we filled our baskets I talked to Meg about what leaves and roots were good for healing and how they might be used. She listened with a serious expression and her head cocked to the side like a blackbird.

'When I was a little girl like you,' I said, 'my grandam took me collecting and taught me how to read the verges and the woods for remedies.' It was hard to imagine myself so young, chifchaffing at my grandam's side.

'And now you are teaching me,' Meg said. I nodded, laughing, and put Mary down among the primroses.

'Ma Sally says you are with child. She says it'll be a girl, that's why you've been so sick. You can call her after me if you like,' Meg said.

It was likely half the parish knew already. I was about to ask Meg more when Mary began to howl. She had wandered almost as far as the road and fallen. A party of horsemen were advancing at a canter from the direction of the village; I scooped her up and stepped back into the shadows of the trees and crooned her quiet while we watched. They went by so fast I could barely see their faces; gentlemen clearly, on fine mounts, one finer than the rest. I had seen him before, I knew it; the sight of him made me uneasy although for the life of me I couldn't place how I knew him. Then Meg called me and I left off staring after the riders.

There were groups already across the graveyard, most from the village, some from other parishes, returned to deck family graves. As the afternoon wore on and work was finished with, more and more came, all bearing knots and clumps of flowers. The sun was warm yet and the light turning golden for evening. I chose a quiet corner where three or four old crosses leant towards the hedge as though unsure of their fellowship. None of my people were buried here and although I did not want to stand aloof I felt more at my ease at the margin. I knelt and cut the turf with the knife Jacob had given me and heeled in daffodils, violets, primroses. Children ran from grave to grave hanging chains of blooms over the mounds and crosses. The custom was stronger here than it had been at Kynaston where I grew up. It was as though the parish sought to conquer death with petals.

As the light faded people lingered still, till the blooms began to gleam palely in the twilight. I stayed for a long while, breathing in the scent of damp earth, listening to the choir practise anthems for the morrow's service. At last Meg found me; she said Sally had sent her to get me, declaring that I should not breathe the cold spiritous air. We walked home together, her small warm hand in mine.

It was with the same easy forgetfulness that I went to the corn-showing Easter Day afternoon. It was expected that all who were hale enough would go, for as well as the luck it brought the harvest, we picked the cockle that sprouted up between the corn. I could have stayed at home for all that, but it was another fine clear day with the frost already shrinking by the hedge banks by the time the bells were rung for service. I wore the fine new girdle Jacob had given me at Christmas and, truth be told, I felt young and pretty and wanted to be out with the others in the glistening field, every-body wearing something new about them for Easter Day and laden with cakes and wooden bottles of cider; the parish full of song and laughter. Roger Boult was not there for the service, so I believed myself safe from him and indeed, although it's usual for a Steward to lead in the corn-showing, he was too grand for such a country custom; every year I'd lived in Hope he had left it to the farm bailiff to lead the blessing and the march.

I followed behind Sally, holding Meg and Mary by the hand, and as we rounded the arc of the field to join the gathering we could not help laughing at the sight of John Cook the Bailly, cider bottles bouncing at his hip and his big arms wrapped round a half dozen plum cakes as red as his Easter doublet.

'Why,' Simon Fosbroke said too loud as we drew near, 'Martha Spicer, you're more pretty than a primrose, than a bank on 'em, regular blooming you are. If you was my leman I wouldn't go dallying round the country, not though the Queen herself demanded it.'

I must have looked all confusion, for Sally patted me and told me not to mind him, he was a gawping dolt who should mind his tongue or he'd be chewing on his own teeth. 'But,' she said, grinning, in a voice not so soft as she thought it, 'there's no hiding the bloom on you child.'

I squeezed her arm, but it was not Simon who set me colouring, it was the man an ell behind him who'd turned at his words and regarded me with a slow leer. So, Roger Boult was returned. I did not meet his eye. If I could have left without attention I would've done so, but it was not possible. I removed myself to the back of the crowd while they buried the cake; we spread out to step the field and bless it and to scrabble out the cockles.

> 'Every step a reap, every reap a shear
> And God send the master a good harvest'

We sang, stooping and peering, but it being such an early Easter the soil was near bare. Polly Tonkins was corn maid and she walked ahead of us all so the man who found the first cockle could claim his kiss. It was Boult himself who found it, though more likely it was passed to him. He strode up to the girl with his arm aloft, the root squeezed in his fat fingers and he caught her round the waist and off her feet while the men cheered and her mother looked doubtful, but the kiss he gave her was chaste enough. Then he stood still and scanned the line, his hand up for silence.

'A kiss for the maid,' he boomed, 'and another for the matron who charmed my wound away. Where's the little witch hiding? There you are! Mistress Spicer!'

He strode across the field to me and clasped my shoulders; his thick moist lips bore down on mine, his tongue pushed at my clenched teeth. Then he unstoppered a bottle and took a long draught of cider, making as though to toast me. The men cheered, if a little uncertainly, and the bottles were slurped along the line. I should have laughed. I should have smiled and ducked a curtsey, made light so that others too made light, but I felt the blood drain out of me and could only stand like wax. His voice was at my ear, 'You'll kiss me back next time, hussy.' He would have said more, but Rowland had appeared at his side.

'With your leave, sir,' Rowland said, 'has there been aught of the travellers?'

Boult left off his leer but he continued to stare at me, though his words were for Rowland. 'They do well enough, Coggeshill. They will be back in a month. There was some little trouble in an inn; Sir Edward was obliged to leave the party. It was nothing of any consequence. Fortunate perhaps.'

He stared at me but I was barely sensible. After a moment or two Rowland cajoled him back to the line of folks stepping the corn. Perhaps it was only a moment; I could not move. There were crows wheeling above me and ahead of me the line was loosening with cider and singing, the yellow March sun licked at my face and shoulders, but within I had frozen. He had called me a witch and marked me as his strumpet. It was Meg who roused me, pulling at my skirts.

'Are you taken bad again, nuncle, are you going to spew?'

I dropped to my knees on the wet earth and hugged her. She patted my head and little by little I was restored to myself. Nobody thought me a witch. Not any more. Boult might seek to throw it on

me as a halter, but I was not his beast nor anyone's. I was not a girl
any more. I would not be tripped so easy.

'I don't like the Steward,' Meg whispered in my hair, 'he sprays
spit like a wheel in slurry.'

'Yes, Meg, yes he does.' We picked our way back across the field.
Other groups of women were leaving now, only the men left
carousing and many of them too, the soberer ones, beginning to
peel and go. When I reached the cottage and kissed Meg goodbye I
felt myself recovered and lifted the latch quite sanguine.

My first thought, when I saw the neat package lying by the hearth,
was that Jacob had found some way to send me a trinket; or perhaps it
was Owen, who had not written in months, remembering his old friend
at last. I was all delight as I pulled at the wrappings. The fancy box put
me right fast enough. Jacob could never afford such velvet, nor Owen
neither, unless they'd dug up a pot of gold. My guts heaved and I flung
the thing from me and the letter beneath it, with its lump wax seal.

I sat on the floor and stared at them for a good long while, till
the sun sank behind the hill and the lane outside was in shadow.
Now and again I heard a man or two carolling home; a wife's tart
responses. At last I opened the letter.

> *I am in Ludlow. There was a necklace made for you here I'm told. Here*
> *is another, much more, I trust, to your liking. You owe me a book; I have*
> *an offer for you. When I return we can discuss accounts. Don't think*
> *yourself too high, mistress. We all must wear a chain at one time or*
> *another. Be merry, you have swapped rope for gold. You have a pretty*
> *neck.*

When he came, I thought, I would make him take back his filthy
gift. I would stuff it into his mouth and make him choke on it. I sat
on the floor without a fire or a candle while the sun went down on

the Resurrection and I cursed my healing hands and my knowledge of letters. The cottage felt so very empty; I had given too little thought to my life's riches – the pleasure of hearing Jacob's hand upon the latch, of choosing to stay bent over the pot as he entered, knowing he would softly step up behind me and fold me in his arms and kiss my neck. I had felt so safe with his arms round me. It would be four more weeks at the least before he came home. Until then I would have to rely on my wits.

It was no good moping. I lit a flame and paced the dark cottage, to and fro. Then I thought of Boult's book; its form-shifting and escapes. I could not hate it, for all the trouble it had caused me. The Steward proclaimed me a heifer he could buy and use, but the book let me believe things could be otherwise. I took it out and sat down to read; its pages unfixed the world. In the yellow moon of my candlelight, girls and men and gods changed shape and when I lifted my eyes to the darkness that pooled beyond the flame it seemed a world waiting to be born. I sat half waking, half sleeping, and the snuffle of Sally's pig carried in it the snorts of a man entranced and the lonely call of a tawny owl was a god gliding over the wood.

8

April began clear and bright. One morning, not so long after Easter, I stood at my window scanning the empty lane, as I did so often now. I knew well enough it would be a good few weeks yet, but I could not rid my mind of the fancy that I should be looking out at the early mist when a man would appear out of the gloom. As he drew near he would begin to run to me and I to him. It was a piece of foolishness, but it fed me better than breakfast. I would never, I thought, let him go so long again – and then I smiled at myself – as if I would get to choose! I touched my belly; next time, God willing, I would not be alone. The days and the nights, too, would not be empty if I had a baby to coo to, or a child at my knee. Would it be a girl as Sally said? When he first met little Meg, Jacob threw her in the air until she squealed. I smiled thinking how I would tell him, how each morning and evening he would rest his hand on my belly to feel for the flutter of its quickening.

I stood at the window idly waiting and dreaming till the grass outside was licked with sun. The lane stayed empty as usual, but all at once I heard the cuckoo, the first of the year.

'Did you hear it?' Meg asked me a little later.

I nodded.

'I hope you were outside. I was. I was on my way to the privy house. My pa used to say that it was bad luck to hear the first cuckoo from within the house. Whatever you were doing you'd be doing all the year.'

'That's a silly tale Meg,' I said, 'there's no fortune attached to the cuckoo's call.'

'There is though,' she answered me earnestly. 'My brother Samuel heard it in his bed and scarce ever got up again. Ask Ma Sally if it's true.'

'Well, it doesn't touch me in any case,' I lied, 'I was outside praising God for the beauty of the morning.' I wasn't though, I thought, I was by my window, yearning. I did not like to think what that might mean.

The season brought much to be done and I helped willingly. I was not so sick as I had been, or else I had grown used to it. Nothing was said to me openly of the Steward's kissing me at the corn-show-ing, but I knew that didn't mean it wasn't talked of. I prayed some other business would push me from his mind and it seemed my prayers were answered for a while, for he was back and forth to Croft Castle, to Sir Thomas's great neighbour. It was talked of that Edward Croft had fallen out with Sir Thomas and had returned under some cloud or other. I remembered how he had raised his whip when his horse was started by a hare, how quick he was to curse; Sir Thomas was well rid of him. Beyond this and the hope it would speed the return of all I did not think; I was merely grateful Roger Boult was occupied.

I had in my mind to talk to Rowland about the letter and the chain, to lay everything before him and ask his advice: how I should act. I found him in the yard by the great barn, grinding at the shears, although it was weeks till they'd be needed. He would not see sixty again but there was no one, in our parish or beyond it, who could match Rowland for shearing. For a while I stood in the shadow of the barn and watched him work; he stroked the blade back and forth along the grinding stone, back and forth, with a smooth roll. If he noticed me it did not interrupt the sweep of his arm.

There was no one by, but the words were as awkward in my mouth as pebbles; every way I thought to come at it the necklace called me out a harlot. At last I coughed.

'I was asking myself when you'd likely begin Goody Spicer. You're worse than a sparrow that won't settle to peck. Words ain't blades, be they ever so sharp.' He pulled himself up and regarded his shears. 'And if they were blades, it were better they were keen; it's the blunted hacking every which way which does most damage. It's about the Steward, I'll warrant, his being so free with you at the showing. Now I can't say as folks didn't notice, and you a pillar of salt at the touch on him. You'll have to bide a bit of wagging.'

'There's something else, Rowland. When I came home—' but Rowland had with a glance beyond me shown me I should stop. It was Meg's brother, Jack Robbins.

'I been sent to fetch you Aunt Martha, the Steward hisself has come to inspect the thatching. He wants you to report on it.'

I returned the look old Rowland gave me, what he said in it I couldn't tell, but I was sure he meant it kindly.

'He's inside,' Michael Robbins said as I scurried up, not bothering to hide a leer.

I nodded and stepped into my cottage, leaving the door wide open. Boult was seated across the room in Jacob's chair. I tensed all through at that, but nevertheless I bobbed him a curtsey and waited.

'Ah yes,' he said, 'I had forgot you were lame. Aren't you going to thank me?'

'Thank you, sir,' I said, 'it is very fine thatch.'

He stood up and quietly walked past me to close the door. 'Not the thatch, girl. Where is the chain?'

'You are very kind sir,' I said, 'but I cannot accept it.' I went to where I had hid the box under the tick and came back towards him, holding it in my outstretched hand. He did not take it straightaway, but stood without moving, only a curl of his lip showing he had heard. Then he lifted it slowly from my palm.

'I want to see it on you,' he said quietly, his eyes on mine. 'You shall put it on.'

'No sir,' I said, backing away a little.

All at once he lurched and grabbed me. His face was red, but he was smiling. 'No manners at all. I only want to see it round your dirty neck. That's all. I don't force, I think I told you that already.' He had his hand on my smock. I must have glanced past him at the door, for he added, 'If you want your husband to have a position to come back to, you will do me the courtesy of trying it on. I doubt you'll brook another scandal.'

I swallowed and nodded, lifting my chin to bare my neck but averting my face from his.

He came closer and, drawing the chain out of its box, lifted it up before my eyes. It was a dainty, delicate thing; the sun caught it and it glowed. A single pearl hung as a pendant. He moved round so that his face was before mine.

'Are you sure you don't want it? Think how the pearl will warm against your skin.'

'I'll none of it, sir, thank you,' I said. 'It is too fine. It would not suit me at all.'

'That, Mistress Minx, is for me to decide. Stand still, while I thread it round.' I had no choice but to let him circle his arms about my neck and fasten the chain; I twisted my neck so that I didn't have to look into his face. His breath was warm on my skin.

'Brown as a hazelnut above that collar. How does it look, I

wonder, on whiter skin?' The sense of his words didn't reach me, not until I felt his fingers fumbling the laces of my kirtle. I tried to pull away, but his hands were at my smock, snatching it from my shoulders. I should have screamed out then, I should have kicked him. Anything. I don't know. But I could no more have moved or cried out than a tree can scream when the axe cuts into it.

'That's better, that's better,' he said, looking down at my naked chest and nodding. For a moment I thought he would just look me over as though I were a horse he must assess, and let me be. But then, all in an instant, he looked up at me, and leered, and pressed his mouth against one and then the other breast, sucking hard on the nipple, so that I winced with pain. Still I said nothing, did nothing. It was as though even my breath was choked. I looked where the hair was sparse upon his head and there was scaling on his pink smooth scalp and I thought of the knife in my pocket, Jacob's knife, how clean and ready the blade was. His lips kneaded at me. I felt his slaver grow cold on my skin and I stood rigid with revulsion and fear. It is not enough to say I hated him, that came before and after – when suddenly about my day or lying in bed I felt again his pawing hands and his mouth and to quell the cold sweat and the horror I pictured driving the knife into his neck.

What could have happened next, I don't know and I won't think, but what did happen was a knock at the door. He released me; I staggered away, pulling my clothing about me.

'Goody Spicer, Martha,' a familiar voice called. It was Annie Bartlet, from up the way. 'My father, he's had a fall, working the barn roof, his leg is cut bad and broken. Can you come? Can you bind him?'

'I'm no bonesetter Annie,' I called out, but then I relented; it was a deliverance. I must take it, even at the cost of a leg. 'You go on,' I said, 'I'll come straight.'

She waited for me where the lane meets the high road, too pale and shaken herself to notice my state. A second after I reached her Boult strode past. She ducked him a curtsey and trancelike I copied her.

'I have heard about your father Annie', he said, 'I will pray to God for a swift recovery. You must apply to me if you require help.'

As she bowed her head in thanks he met my eye, lifting his brows slightly as though we were plotters, as though we had escaped together. Although it disgusted me I knew in part it was true; he had pulled me into an intrigue. I was glad she had not seen, that in her fear for her father she did not question how, with the lane empty behind us, he had heard about her father.

I gave Tom Bartlet nightshade for the pain and set the bone as well as I could. At first my fingers shook so much I had to pause and pinch myself, but little by little the work calmed me and I felt my breathing steady in my chest. There was a ragged wound on his thigh where he had fallen against a plough. I cleaned and bound it, stopping the blood, mixing a poultice. Annie and her mother bustled round me as I directed, lit candles as the light faded. When we were done we knelt to pray together. As long as no fever set in he would mend well, I thought, and said so.

Annie ducked out of the cottage behind me and walked a way back. The evening was cool and empty with the moon palely rising. As I said goodbye she put out her hand to my neck. 'A golden chain and a pearl too. I en't never touched a pearl before. When you were praying alongside me the flame licked along it so pretty and the pearl all white like a moon.'

My hand followed hers. I had forgot it, quite, the chain. 'It was my mother's,' I said quickly.

Annie gave me a long slow smile. 'You a lady in disguise then? Is that why the Steward likes you? You don't let the grass grow Martha Spicer.'

'Annie, please, I love my husband. How could I prefer the Steward?'

'Course you love him, but he en't here is he? Preferring ain't got nothing to do with it. Get what you can I say. Even if Jacob finds out he's not like to do much. Huff and puff. Knock you about some maybe. He'll be glad of a new roof same as you when the rain comes.' She patted my cheek. 'Don't look so affrighted, I won't tell nobody.'

I looked at her, luminous in the soft twilight, twirling the chain round her finger. Even if I could persuade her I was true, what was my innocence to her? I'd merely be a fool to pass a treasure by, that had been left for me to take. And in any case, something like guilt was gleaming round my neck. Her face was fresh and downy as a newly opened rose. Who was the more simplehearted, I wondered, her or me?

9

It dawned through the village everywhere at once, like sunlight. The party was on their way back. Two weeks. Less if Sir Thomas wished it. I was glad and fearful all at once and angry that I should be afraid. Now when I pictured his homecoming – his arms opening for me on the road; later, at home, his mouth covering me with kisses; his hand resting with joy on my belly – now when I saw all this in my mind's eye I saw him hesitate, then draw back and frown at me with a doubt in his eyes I could not bear to see. A voice at my left ear whispered to me that if I seemed a child to Annie Bartlet, Jacob was greener still; he could not tolerate guile or strategy; he loved freely, wholly, or he did not love at all. But another voice sat at my right and told me not to hearken to such folly. He had cleaved to me when all the world had called me wicked, his own mother foremost among them. He was not such a lamb that he didn't know how clever the wolf could be. Hadn't he warned me, just before he left? Ah the first voice said, yes, he warned you, remember the thickness in his voice then; how he fears you will give him horns.

I slept with Jacob's knife beneath my pillow. In the day I got on with the work of the opening year. There was planting to be done and Sally's hives to be unwrapped of their winter coverings and scoured. Every day near enough I went collecting, but I was careful to take Meg with me.

'How that child loves you,' Sally said to me one morning when I came for her. 'It's good of you to take her off my hands. She's big enough to be helpful but she has a way of loitering at your feet. That, or she's found herself the tiniest nook she can and is there crouching, picking apart a stem or such like.'

It was true, I'd often found her just beside the wood, all tucked up, her brown hair like a piece of oak bark. 'Yes,' I said, 'she likes small spaces.'

Sally glanced behind to check we were alone and then leaned into me. 'Do you think she's right-minded, Martha? I swear sometimes she's a fairy looking out at me, her eyes all glazy. I have to shout in her eye for her to hear me.'

'I think she's full of thinking, Sally,' I said, 'and sometimes the thoughts are so bright in her head she gets lost in the patterns they make. I knew a boy like that in Kynaston. They made him a grammar school boy.'

'Go on with you,' Sally said, but I could see I had pleased her, though it was nothing but the truth. The thought came to ask to have Meg stay with me, just till Jacob was back. The nights would be less lonely and if Boult did come I would not be on my own.

It felt strange to be putting a child to bed in my own house. The first night there was a wind that banged the shutters and whined under the eaves; I woke to Meg's whimpers. It was not such a big storm, but nothing would quiet the child, till I brought a candle stub and sat up with her head on my lap and told her a story. Every evening after that she wanted another; sometimes I plucked one from the book, sometimes I gave her one of my own. It was all one to her, clever fox or sun god. Often I would glance down and she would be asleep already, the shadows flickering her face and hair as fast as dreams. The next day, out gathering, or at our work, she would beg me to take up the thread again, ravelling out the beginning to me almost in my own words.

'Tell me about your mother, Meg,' I said once; we were scrabbling in the wood for pignuts, 'what was she like?'

'My ma? She was big and broad-looking. She had a blue ribbon, she let me tie it in her hair at harvest. She was always working and groaning, like this,' and Meg put her hand on her back and moaned.

'That was because she was tired Meg, from the baby in her belly.'

'Peter ripped her all to ribbons,' Meg said, rubbing at the earth on the root, 'that's what Ma Sally says, but they pulled up the blanket and wouldn't let us see. It was stained red. I don't think it was right, to say she was like ribbons, do you Martha?'

'It's just a way of talking Meg, it means she bled too much, that's all. Was her hair curly like yours? It must have looked pretty when you put a ribbon in it.'

Meg paused and frowned. 'I don't think it was very curly. Maybe. I don't remember. Can we talk about something else now?'

In my thoughts her face was pale, worn thin from bearing and suckling, and her eyes that had been like blue ribbon were shot with red. But what did I know of her? She was fading even from her daughter's mind. I took the pignuts Meg handed out to me and kissed her bonnet. It was not her fault. What did I remember of my own mother, but moments which fled before I could grasp them and that other picture, the vision of the gallows tree that I spent so many years refusing? How little time we have to thread ourselves into the fabric of the world, especially if we are women. I thought of all the girls in Ovid's book, becoming trees and stars. It seemed a lonely way of lasting. Would I choose that, just so I would not be forgotten? It would be better, surely, to live in people's hearts and tongues. If I were to die when the baby came, Jacob would talk to her of me, perhaps people would tell her how I healed them; perhaps that should be enough. I took Meg's hand, sticky with soil.

Meg smiled. 'Sometimes I held her hand,' she said, 'when she looked sad like you, and she held mine, too, when I was afraid.'

When we got back to the cottage Annie Bartlet was at my door wanting more physic for her father. She raised her brows at us as we drew close.

'Wasn't expecting you from the woods Martha,' she said with a wide grin, 'or not without leaves in your hair. Pignuts is it? You could be dining on finer fare than that afore long. You oughta let yourself eat gravy.' She all but nudged me in the ribs and I flushed, despite myself, at Meg's confused look.

'Don't Annie,' I whispered. 'I don't want to hear it and I won't. From him or you. I sent the chain back, days ago I did it.'

She bent her head confidentially towards me, pursing her lips as you might to reprove a child. 'More fool you then, Martha Spicer.'

It was a lie; I had not sent it. Every night I had resolved I would do it in the morning and every day I had put it off. The thought of seeking him out disgusted me – and what if he refused to take it, or assaulted me again? A slight fever had taken Rowland to his bed or else I might have asked him to take it; there was no one else I trusted for such a task. But I could no longer put it off. That evening I did not take down the book when Meg asked. As soon as it was light I rose and wrapped it as carefully as I could, folding the necklace in paper and placing it within.

'Come,' I said to Meg, who was still rubbing the sleep from her eyes. 'The world's all fresh laundered. We'll do an errand before breakfast.'

It was true; all smelt new washed. The road glistened. In a brake a thick clump of windflowers drooped as though the dew had made them weep. I would return the book and the chain and there would be an end to it – I would rid myself of this dread, I thought, so that I could feel fresh and clean for Jacob's homecoming. Any lingering murmurs I could outface, because I would tell my husband everything. Everything but the kiss or how Boult had put the chain about my neck and touched me. I smiled down at Meg.

'Nuncle?' she said, 'do you think the flowers pray? The windflowers look like they are praying.'

'Yes child,' I said, 'they surely do. Every night they bend and pray and every morning too, until the light of day comes and releases them.'

The world was innocent and new. I felt the familiar sickness rise in my belly and welcomed it. I would soon be able simply to rejoice in the gift I carried. A breeze riffled through the flowers and grass as we rounded the spinney where I had first sat and read the book. The garlic was coming into flower now, feathery white, but today the sky was thickening into cloud. Despite its promise, it would not be a day for lingering after all. By the time we came in sight of the Steward's house all the light was gone grey. Meg dragged on my arm as I began a lumpen run to outpace the shower.

It was little use our having run before the rain, for they left us standing outside the door. I had intended to give the package to the first I saw, but I thought better of it when the grease-gleaming scullery boy thrust out his hands for it.

'I cannot hand it to you,' I said, 'I'm to give it to his man, Richard.'

The boy frowned but shouted over his shoulder, 'It's the cunning woman from the village. Says she's got a package, urgent like, for Richard to give the master.'

'Well let her give it him herself,' a man called back, 'we're at our breakfast.'

The boy jerked a thumb over his shoulder. 'Through there,' he said.

Richard was in Boult's hall, busying over the table. I stood at the back of the great dark room and coughed. Meg hid behind my back. He curled his lip when he saw me.

'What is it?' he said. 'You've been paid, haven't you?'

I held the parcel out. 'I beg to return this to your master,' I began – and stopped. Richard had stood, up, his face suddenly all officiousness.

'Well, well,' a familiar voice said behind me, 'what pretty maid is this?' He pinched Meg on her cheek. 'Richard, take the child to the kitchen and tell them to give her some cake. Then bring food for Goodwife Spicer, she will break her fast with me.'

'No need to hem and haw, woman,' he added over his shoulder as he strode down the room ahead of me. 'Think of this as business.' He pulled out a chair for me across from his own and stood behind it as I sat, as though I were a lady. It had a high, carved back; he rested his hands upon it, either side of my neck and waited until Richard returned with a laden plate and a cup of ale; then he settled himself in his own seat, shook out his napkin and signalled for us to be left alone. 'Eat,' he said, 'I have a mind to watch you.'

The bread was warm and soft, but though I chewed and chewed, it was almost more than I could do to swallow. I felt nausea suck at me; I was afraid I should vomit, on all that dark wax-shiny wood. He leaned back in his chair and watched me. The beer was better, when I raised the cup it hid his face.

He did not eat. He said nothing; I began to wonder how long this would go on. Presently, he reached across the table, picked a crumb from the corner of my mouth with his finger and put it to his tongue. I gripped the wood with my fingers.

'Sir,' I said. 'I ask for forgiveness if I have misled you. I must ask you to take back the gift you gave me, and the book.' I placed them on the table.

He lifted a finger. 'Remember where you are, madam,' he said. 'I will take them back when I have a whim to do so and not before.'

'My husband,' I began.

'Your husband,' he put in, taking a slice of bread, 'is a churl, a villain, a thing of no consequence. You may put him out of your thoughts. I have asked people about you, Martha Spicer. "You mean Martha Dynely", people said, "the little witch of Marcle Ridge." You're not very far from your past. Less than a day's walk. Could you not get further than that? You were not even married in a church, girl. Let me be frank. I want you to come to my bed. I want you to do it willingly.'

It is strange how anger can clarify the air; every detail, from the threading of the veins on his cheek or the legs of the fly, dozy with good fortune, that had settled on the meat, stood out with precision. So, I thought, it is laid out clear as a lease. I half expected him to take out a paper I should sign; the clauses numbered, what I had to gain, and lose. How easy it would be to extend his fat fingers and pinch me, like the poor fly on the beef.

'Never.' I said, hearing my voice high and brittle. Even as I spoke I realised he expected, perhaps wanted such an answer. It was sport for him, this hunting me down. I was not a woman, only quarry. 'Never,' I said again.

He stared at me, almost smiling, then he stuffed the fork into his mouth and his jaws worked at his breakfast. 'We will see,' he said at last, gesturing with his fork for me to go.

I stood and started for the door, but he called me to halt. 'Take them,' he said pointing to the package.'

'Take them,' he said again, 'or the whole parish will know that's my bastard you're carrying.'

I froze and he started laughing, great guffaws that spat the food from his mouth. I picked up the cloth-wrapped book. 'Tell Richard I need more beer,' he called after me.

Meg was pink with cake and petting when I took her from the kitchen.

'You're holding my hand too hard,' she said when we got to the lane.

I let go. 'I'm sorry Meg,' I said.

'Are you well, nuncle?' she said, 'you look poorly.'

I nodded, 'Let's get home, Meg, out of the weather.' It was no sweet April shower after all, but a steady rain and a wind that battered the branches above us and tossed the windflowers back and forth as it wished. How silly, I thought, to tell the child they prayed. They cowered, that was all.

10

The mornings turned back towards winter, with a dripping light that lost itself in mist. Our boots and hems were sticky with cold clay. I woke earlier every day; if I lay awake the knot of waiting tightened till I could hardly breathe, so I tucked Meg gently in and left. Always I found myself wending towards Leominster, because they would be sure to come that way, although I knew there was very little chance they'd arrive of a morning and even then, not early, but I could not help it. The expectancy was present in the pulse of my blood, in everything I saw and heard. It seemed to me sometimes that I could sense Jacob coming closer – the rise and fall of his breath on the moving horse. He would believe me, surely. I would lay out all before him and he would take me in his arms and say 'Martha, heart's breath, I am here now, he cannot touch you.' And if he believed me true, and if I told him all, what might he do, then, in anger? Might he put his own sweet life in danger?

'You won't speed them with your loitering Martha,' Sally remarked one morning, seeing me limp home from watching. 'You're looking that downcast lately, I'm getting worried about you, venturing out o' mornings to feed on nothing but foul night vapours. Have you the green sickness Martha? It's not just yourself you have to think of now, eh my girl.'

I smiled as heartily as I could and promised I would not tempt the drizzle and the lingering mists. After that, when I rose I tried instead to steady myself with reading. The paper and the binding might belong to the Steward but that was scarce the stories' fault. They danced free. Soon, when I lifted my eyes. Jacob would be there, as familiar as the hearth. 'Go on,' he would say at my ear, 'tell me, what happens next.' Maybe he would merely wave away all Boult's importunements with a shrug and all would be easy and good between us.

Later, Meg's babble and the work to be done helped the hours to pass by; often I was called out to treat a neighbour, but afterwards, as the day wore on, I would find I could not be still in the cottage. Sometimes I took Meg with me, sometimes she went home to play an hour or two with her sister or mind little Peter; either way I would find myself limping over to the slope behind the church, where there was a good view to the road, and I would wait there until the light muddied and the sheep loomed white against the grass.

Then, one noontime, Meg and I were returning home from Sally's when we were overtaken by a cart in the lane. It was one of the thatchers from Bodenham. He'd come to fetch me he said, to see to his mother out by Saffron's Cross; her leg was a running sore. I fetched my things and sent Meg back. As we rode the sun shifted the clouds and for the first time in nigh on a fortnight it felt warm. The thatcher was young and awkward at first, frowning at the reins when I addressed him, but when he fell to talking he grew easier. His name was William, he said, the youngest of four brothers, three of them working now at the thatch like their father and uncle. 'And the other brother,' I asked? He shrugged and was quiet a while. 'London,' he said. That was the last they heard of him. He'd fallen in with bad company, taken up with a doxy out at Leominster fair. He'd come back once, dressed half in velvet like a gentleman; told them he lived in London now, at a place called the Blackfriars. He was a player. Broke his mother's heart when he left again. He squinted up the road as he talked.

'You'd like to follow him?' I said.

He glanced at me quickly. 'No, not me. In winter sometimes, when the idlers in the malthouse are past bearing and the candles all stubs. But the coldness of that road prevents me – that and the harm it would do my mother.'

He stared ahead as he spoke, at the sunlit valley open before us and the meadows bobbing yellow with cowslips.

'Not only in winter,' I said.

He glanced at me and smiled. 'No, not only then.'

We were quiet a while then and I felt a whisper of his yearning for a world elsewhere, for the city. I had told myself often enough it had been killed in me, by the rank closeness of Ludlow gaol, but there were days when I glanced at the road with longing. I touched my belly; that kind of thinking must be put aside now. How would Jacob be, I wondered, now that he had seen the world? Might he have discovered a restlessness within himself, for throngs and talk? I laughed softly to myself, what nonsense was I thinking! He was less than two months gone; had I begun to forget him already?

'My husband,' I said into the silence, 'is with Sir Thomas's party that are returning from the north. It's a lot of miles he's travelled. I haven't seen him these two months.'

He whistled. 'Then we'd best hurry. They were at Croft Castle two nights ago I heard. The lords are at odds again, I hear. Young Edward Croft returned pell-mell two weeks ago, rode on to London. Sir Thomas stopped to make peace with old Sir James. He'll be on his way again by now. There was ever bad blood between the Crofts and the Coningsbys.'

Oh, I thought, they might be arriving now, already. Jacob opening our cottage door, calling me and finding me nowhere. What would he think when he found I'd gone out of the parish healing, against all his wishes? Would I come home to find him angry, even before I told him of the Steward? William talked on about Edward Croft and the trail of wrongs he scattered behind him, but I could not attend. What did I care for a cossetted lord? Nevertheless, when we reached the cottage I found I could still myself and look to his mother. It was as though I stepped into a different face; my heart was all in tumult but in the foul air of the cottage with the poor woman before me, I could forget myself. My voice was clear and smooth; I explained the making and applying of the poultice to her son's wife and waited and repeated it until she did not fumble over quantities. It was only when I stepped outside into the afternoon to wait for the cart that my breath caught in my chest with impatience. There was a problem with a wheel; it took an hour to sort; I was on the verge of walking when the cart trundled up with an easy roll.

We did not talk much on the journey back. I kneaded my hands in my lap until I saw William glance at them. He smiled. 'You're impatient to be home. That's natural enough. I wish I had a girl to pine for me like that.'

The light was still clear but it was taking on the slant of evening. How I wanted to be able to take a switch to the poor old nag that bore us! As we reached the edge of the park a man passed us; a gamekeeper on the estate, I knew his face and called out to him. Had he heard if they were returned?

'Oh aye,' he said, 'two, three hours since. No end of commotion and comings and goings.'

Two, three hours since! I heard the words, and I was reeling giddy, the air itself was reeling. Oh dear God! I felt the sun itself would pause from sinking. The very birds trilled it. Then we were crossing the gatehouse with the long view of the drive; empty. 'Take me by the stables,' I said; I got down; scarcely nodded to William's thanks; there were the horses, rubbed down, clean-bedded, snorting; he was not there. I began to run; over the grass to the bridge; to the orchards; there was old Rowland with his John, waving, waving; what were they shouting? It did not matter! I waved back; panting now, my heart splitting, my face splitting with the joy of it. There was Jack Robbins, kicking stones on the lane. 'Good day to you Jack.' I cried, but the poor clown turned in a mumbling sulk. No matter; I reached the end of the row, my new-thatched cottage, my own door; my hand on the latch, lifting it; pushing the door wide; calling out, 'Jacob!'

'Jacob?'

The room was empty, just as I'd left it that morning; no bag flung down, no footprint, no bread torn from the loaf. He has gone to find me I told myself. I was not here and so he has stepped out to look for me; I'll sit and wait for his return. I sat down in the chair then straight stood up. I could not sit and wait in such a flutter. There was a great blackness gathering at the edges of my vision and I felt if I could just look straight ahead, if I could just avoid all but the very centre of my gaze, it might just go away. The door opened; my heart stopped. It was Sally with tears at her eyes and the blackness rose up from the floor and I fell.

* * *

Sally was very kind. She sat by me an hour telling me over and over that all was well, he was just delayed was all, I was foolish to take it too hard. He was following after; I could ask Rowland Coggeshill's nephew. Meg came and crept up on my knee and stroked my face with her hand. Perhaps they were right, I thought. I should try to take heart, but then I remembered Rowland and John waving to me as I rushed by. John had begun to run toward me, old Rowland catching at his arm. It hadn't been a greeting, of course it hadn't; he'd been trying to warn me.

'I must see John Coggeshill,' I said to Sally. 'Will you come?'

11

When I think back to that time I see the darkness that rushed at me from the floor; I hear a silence that is like roaring. Time unhitched itself. There were minutes and hours, light and dark, and I was present in them, but apart as well. I was in the silence; it had always been there, under the bustle of life, waiting. Lucky people never glimpse it, or deny it, but I had known it already – and felt it call to me. What was it, the roar of hell? The roar of God forsaking me? Of the night without God, with only darkness; the whisper of my prayers just the sound a mouse makes in the grass that only the listening owl attends to.

I could not see John Coggeshill that night, for he had gone back up to the Court when we called. On the way back Meg gripped my hand very hard. All night as I lay beside her the soft sough of her breath calmed me. In the morning I rose early and left Meg sleeping in the cot. There were voices already in Sally's cottage, raised voices; I paused outside.

'I never said she went with him. You saw the kiss he gave her at the corn-showing – that didn't come of nothing. Arh! Why do you strike me mother? I'm only saying ...'

'Well don't. Any more talk like that, Jack Robbins, and I'll take a stick to you. Proper turtle doves Martha and Jacob, I've never known married folk love so.'

'Not married folks, maybe,' put in Michael. 'Seems like she couldn't do without it.'

'That's enough from you and all,' Sally cut in. 'It's no time for jests. Poor girl! And her with no family at all.'

'They say his own mother swore she witched him,' Michael began. I stepped carefully away, feeling sick in my stomach. I scarce dared glance down at my feet, in case I saw the earth splinter madly beneath them like a sheet of ice when a rock is thrown. The ground was getting ready to shift again. What good was Sally waving her apron against such a slide of rumour? I would never be rid of the shadow of the gallows tree. Only Jacob's open, honest face kept people's faith in me. A sharp shower lashed my face as I walked and I was glad of it, for it kept the lane empty.

Rowland opened his door almost before I had knocked. 'Been expecting you this half hour girl,' he said. 'Sit yourself down. John's out the back.'

He gave me a cup of beer and as John talked I stared into it, watching the image of my face that wobbled and reformed. 'It was in the week before Easter it happened,' John told me, then stopped.

'Has nothing been said? Has the Steward not spoke to you?'

I shook my head and said nothing, gripping the cup. John glanced at Rowland who nodded at him to go on. 'I don't know all,' he said, leaning forward on his stool. 'It was late. Sir Thomas himself called Jacob out with a message for Edward Croft. I heard the name of a tavern where he was like to be found. "Be sure to find him", the master said, "and bring his answer." There was little love lost by then between the two of them. I believe Master Croft owed Sir Thomas money. I offered to go along, but Jacob laughed. It'd be easy enough to search Croft out, he said, he'd only to listen for the sound of baying and brawling. Oh, if I'd only gone along with him!'

He put his hand on my arm and I looked up. Great fat tears were running down his face. I knew then what was coming; it was as though my blood were draining into the floor, all of it, draining out, till I was left whole and empty as a cast adder's skin. I thought for a moment I would choke, but someway I swallowed, and then I was able to pat his arm. 'Peace, John,' I said. 'What happened?'

He shook his head. 'I don't know,' he said. 'I went to my bed. At dawn Sir Thomas's man, pale as plaster, shook me awake. Jacob had been surprised by rufflers in an alley next the inn and though he called out and Master Edward and his men themselves heard and came running, they were too late. He was stabbed Martha; they could not staunch it.'

Old Rowland leant towards me. 'I'm sorry, child,' he said.

I heard the words, all of them, and heard what they meant, but I could not reach them; it was as though they were at a distance, far off, like a skein of geese beyond bowshot, not the crow that flaps over the thatch and calls out death.

'What was done with him? Did you see him?' It was my voice, although I did not expect it.

'In faith I tried. He was took to the tavern, they told me. I feared they might bury him unready so that he went hot to hell like a brawling rogue. I swore I would not let them. First thing I did was to buy bread and beer to pass over him for the sin-eater to consume away his sins. Street to street I went. There was no one to be had. They have Romish priests to do their sacraments and do not have the custom. Folk scoffed at me for a country clown. And the more they jeered the more it came to seem the only thing of weight in the world, that he should pass clean over, without any wrongdoings dragging him downwards. He was the best friend that ever I had, Martha. That he should die so, in the dirt of an alley, him who could soothe a foaming courser with a touch of his hand, so it would let him lead it into hell if he asked it—'

'—Don't,' I said.

'No. Forgive me, you're too full already. Anyways, at length I found a Welshman, from Monmouth he was, and I brought him back with me to the alehouse and ...' John fell silent and studied the floor.

'And what, tell me, did you pass the bread over him?'

'They would not let me see him,' he said at last, rubbing at the floor with his boot. 'There were men there, two of them, they barred the room and declared he was a malefactor and not fit for holy ground, but that his master had interceded for a parson.' John stood up and turned away. 'I went straight back, thinking it was some mistake, it could be soon sorted, but when I opened my mouth Sir Thomas's man struck me, told me Jacob's name was forbidden, that he'd betrayed the great love and favour the master had shown him. He would be decently buried, but that was all, we were not to talk of it. The next day we left.' He had begun to sob. 'Don't believe it Martha, he had no harm in him, none.'

'No,' I said at last, 'I don't believe it.' I stood up very slowly then, placed my cup on the floor and stepped outside to the lane. John and old Rowland, glancing at one another, followed after. I had only gone a few steps when the bile rose and I began to retch. I gripped my hips with my fists and bent to the ground and felt the rush of vomit again and again and the throw of it spattered the whole stinking tale onto the earth.

When I could stand again I wiped my streaming nose and the bitterness from my mouth. John and Rowland, I realised were holding me by an elbow each.

'Leave me alone,' I said, but they would not; rather they took me back to Sally to fuss over me. I sat in her small house while all the people of the village came and condoled with me and left again. I remember the faces appearing before me and my hands taken and stroked and some of the women were weeping, some of the men too. The grip of their hands was a comfort, pulling my soul back into my body, but I scarcely heard what they said, beyond their hope, glancing at my belly, that before long I'd have some comfort, that I'd find then he was not altogether gone. I do not believe I spoke a word. At last I was given strong spirits and put to bed in my own house; sleep rolled over me like a fog.

When I woke the darkness was so heavy I thought myself still sleeping. For a moment – it can have been no more than a moment – I was aware only of a formless dread. Then I remembered. They had told me he was dead. I tried to form the words on my lips but could only say his name. Jacob. Over and over in the dark I said it, because it brought his face close to mine. Jacob; his name ended with a kiss. Had I known that always, I wondered, breathing the image of his face against my lips? Next to me Meg sighed and turned; I rose and left.

The moon was big, but it was sinking. I did not have much darkness left, so I headed into the woods, where only the hollowness of the air led me along the paths, one foot after another. Only in utter darkness, it seemed to me, could I keep from thinking, or rather think as I ought, as I wanted to. After minutes, but I was not sure, it could have been an hour, I tripped over a fallen branch and fell headlong into a soft bank of old leaves, twigs and long damp bluebell spears. Instinctively I put my hand to my stomach, but there was no need, I was not hurt at all; I did not bother getting up, but sat with my knees hugged to my chest. About me, things crept and scuttled so quietly I caught only the whisper of a moving stem. Before me a great oak tree inked itself; a blot of darkness so swollen it must have begun its dying long ago.

We first made love as man and wife under branches in the crook of ruined walls long open to the sky. Here, in the thick black calm of the night, I could call the thought of him to me so that he seemed as real as a breath of wind against my cheek. 'Oh my sweetling,' he said, unlacing me to kiss the brown mole on my shoulder, 'how foolish you are, how could you think I would let this go?' I closed my eyes and felt how big his hands were against mine, all the life beneath his ribs. It was not possible that I could breathe like this, push my fingers into the crumbling wood rot and he be gone from the world; from the whole living world and the cold clear stars in their spheres. 'Listen,' he would whisper close in my ear on summer nights when he had led me out to the fields, 'do you hear the music, do you hear the music the stars make? Sometimes I think I hear it.' And I nodded, because it pleased him, but I didn't hear it; I only heard the warm rhythm of his pulse against my skin.

I opened my eyes and looked up; night was fading and if there were any stars the ragged clouds obscured them. If heaven was there I could not find it. What use was heaven to me now? I did not want it. I wanted his body, his voice; I wanted to go back and find him by our hearth, pulling on his boots, poking at the fire, cursing the slowness of the pan to boil. The light had grown now so that even if I closed my eyes it pressed through them. He had not and would never come home. I hugged my knees and rocked back and forth as the bright horror of the day lit on me. There was no comfort, none. Weeks hence the promise in my belly might bring me some kind of solace, but not now, not yet. Above me birds trilled to their nests and each other. He'd used to copy them; waking me with the woodpigeon coo '*I love you honeysweet.*' No, no, I must not think of that. The pain pressed at my ribs, my belly, and though I moaned and rocked it did not ease the tearing at my heart. 'What kind of bird am I, then,' I asked him once. 'You're a wren, Martha.' 'No, surely,' I said, 'let me be bigger than a wren.' He darted kisses over my face and neck. 'You're a wren, small and brown, with your tail cocked at all the world and a voice stronger than any.' My heart would burst. How could I not break open?

If I'd had his knife in my pocket I believe I would have stuck the blade into my leg, have let the free flow of blood relieve the strain in my chest, but I did not have it. There was a dense patch of nettles by the path; I went over and drew my hands and wrists across the saw-edged leaves. The stings burned. I jerked off my boots and walked into the clump barefoot, holding up my skirts so that my legs were seared, over and over; until I flamed. I grabbed the young plants, crushing them in my fingers, against my neck, my chest, my face – but tearing at the plants was no good way to get the hurt from them. The scalding tempered the worse pain however, turned it somewhat, so that in the stinging I found a way towards anger. That he had been left so, like a thrown shoe in the road and I not told and all that was his not brought to me!

When I reached the cottage Sally was there, and Rowland; Sally all in a pother that I had done myself mischief in the night.

'We were that worried, Martha. Roused every house in the village we did after Meg crept into me that you were gone in the dead of the night. Oh if anything had happened, I could never have forgiven myself that I did not sit up to watch you. In your condition, too. "Who knows what she might do in the grip of her grief," I said.'

'She sent our Jack to Master Boult's house,' Meg said before Sally could shush her.

'Just so as men could be sent to look,' Sally said quickly.

I felt my heart tighten and took little Meg's hand; the child had been crying, her face was stained with tears.

'Forgive me, Sally,' I said, 'and don't worry, I would not offend God.' I turned to Rowland. 'Would you come with me, to the Steward's house? There are questions I need answers to; I think I should be much stronger with you beside me.'

* * *

Boult was striding through his gates whistling as we approached. He stopped when he saw me and put on a doleful face.

'Yes, you had better come in. You can wait if you wish, Rowland.'

'If it's all the same, sir,' Rowland said, 'I said as I'd stand with her and I shall.'

Boult frowned at that, but pointed back towards the house, showing us into a small office that I had not seen before, with a single chair and a desk.

He sat down and pressed his fingertips into an arc, regarding us a moment as we stood, awkwardly, before him. 'It's my duty, Goodwife Spicer, my painful duty, to let you know the truth. As no doubt you have heard, your husband did not die an honourable death. Nevertheless, out of his compassion and generosity Sir Thomas left instructions for a minister to bury him decently.'

The stinging was fading from my arms and legs, but it was enough; my voice wobbled but did not give way. 'John Coggeshill has told me what little he knows sir, but not the particulars of his death. How was it dishonourable?'

Boult eyed me sharply. 'He tried to force a girl in an alley. She cried out and a brawl ensued.'

My legs buckled. It was only old Rowland's arm that held me upright.

'No,' I blurted, 'he would not,' but I collected myself. 'What is the name of the man who killed him, sire?'

'What does it matter? He drew a knife first. There can be no doubt. Edward Croft's men witnessed it.'

'Edward Croft's men.'

'Yes, girl. Master Croft's men. Jacob had come to an inn hot with liquor– sack-sopped, wrangling with every comer, with the fly that buzzed before his nose. When he reeled out they followed, to prevent any trouble in the town. They saw it all.'

I could not speak; I stood staring stupidly at Boult who for his part stared back at me. There were scales behind his eyes, weighing and counting. It was Rowland who broke the silence.

'In what parish, sir, is the boy buried?'

Boult consulted a letter on his desk. 'Ah yes, the parish of St James. What does it matter? He was given a Christian burial. Be grateful for that; it's more than he deserved.'

When he spoke again it was in quite a different tone. 'As you know, you have no claim on the cottage without your husband Goodwife Spicer. Indeed, it will be needed. But Sir Thomas is merciful, it may be that some arrangement can be made. He has left the matter entirely in my hands. I have no doubt I can find you suitable work in my own establishment – and more convenient accommodation.'

He glanced at me pointedly to be sure I had his meaning. It wasn't hard to guess. When he spoke again his voice was oily. 'You should not suffer for your husband's crimes Martha Spicer, nor should the child you carry.'

Rowland held my arm as we walked back. 'I lived in Lancaster a week, more, as a young man,' he said.

I frowned at him, surprised, impatient. What was that to me?

'Unless I'm much mistaken, there's but one parish church – St Mary's, there en't no parish of St James.'

12

That Boult was lying was clear enough, but what lay behind the lies I had no idea. I was not such a fool as to think that he would tell me, however agreeable I made myself to him, but I nursed my anger because it kept despair at a length. Hour on hour I fed it. With innocent Meg beside me I lay and fancied myself conjuring a monster out of darkness, a giant who ripped men's limbs and chewed their bones. I sent it striding down the lanes to mangle the Steward in his goose-feather bed. At times I half believed he had contrived Jacob's death to have me a harlot in his house to own and use at will.

Jacob was loved. No end of folk brought their gifts and sorrow. There seemed no sly allusions, no round suggestions I had found another bed, although I knew well enough that was a nod to decency, no more. The visits kept the days busy and for that I was thankful. More than that, they drew me back from madness. To each I repeated that it was not true, the story put about, it could not be true. And if it were not true, a voice within me whispered, if the manner of his death was falsely told, perhaps he was not dead at all. It was Annie Bartlet who voiced the secret stirrings of my heart.

She sat down across from me after handing me bacon and good wishes from her parents. I was weeping again and she waited for me to stop, or perhaps for her own eyes to settle. 'I know you did not wish for this, whatever the Steward might have in hand,' she said, more honest than her neighbours. 'Convenient for Boult, though en't it? I can guess what kind of rent he'll be after.'

'I'll make a doll,' I said, 'and stick it till his heart's blood dribbles from his mouth.'

She nodded. 'You don't want to let folks hear you saying things like that. Especially you, with the past you've had, and the noose missing you once already.' Her slyness was all gone and she took my hand. 'Have you thought, Martha – if how he died en't true, maybe he's still living?'

I stood up and leaned my forehead on the wall. 'Of course I've thought of it, Annie. A hundred thousand times. If I had any cause, any cause at all to hope it might be true...'

'Well, it's only an idea, mind, but it's St Mark's Eve tomorrow night, when the year's dead troop into God's house. You might watch from the church porch to see if Jacob is among them. If he stayed within then you would know. If he's ill but not dead, and not going to die, he'll come out the church again, that's what folks say.'

I must have looked askance for she went on, 'Not all do see, of course. My mother watched time and again for my grandmother, she was such a creaking door, biding with us year after year, but she didn't see a thing, even the year Gran was took. I'll come with you if you like.'

I knew the practice of waiting to see what souls were called. I'd even tried to sneak and watch myself as a child, the year my grandmother took ill, but my father had cuffed my ears and told me not to be softheaded. 'Yes,' I said, 'tomorrow night. St Mark's, why not? I'll do it, Annie. Thank you. But alone, it will be better alone. And please, I beg you, don't tell a soul.'

It was not forbidden, but not approved either. There had used to be a place, purgatory, where dead souls suffered before they were judged clean enough for heaven; it was close enough to the waking world for the spirit to step back through, to warn, or to punish, or to beg for justice, but that was all done with now. Our souls, we were told, jumped into fire or light at the moment of our death and the spirits men saw were devils' business. Perhaps in church we believed that to be true, but not at night, when the lanes were dark and the owls called, or the fire flickered and shadows jostled at the house eaves. We knew how the dead yearned, how they were knitted into hearths and hollows. How they lingered. Jacob would not consent to heaven without leaving me a sign. Didn't my own heart lodge in his? I would have felt the tug of his crossing. And if he lay yet on the shore with death creeping like the tide his spirit would show me that, too, whether he was doomed to go over or return.

The next night, therefore, as soon as it was dark, I set out for the church. Sally had wanted me to keep little Meg by, but I could not risk her fretting again, or following me. It was a damp night, and cold for April, and the low mist that hung above the graveyard seemed an exhalation of the dead. There was not a soul about. I pulled my cloak tight and sat under the yew to wait among the graves. A man coughed on the lane below and cursed and spat; then there was nothing but the owls and the distant shriek of a vixen. The old porch loomed blackly. Now and then the clouds thinned enough for the wan moon to bleach the stone and pale the mounded graves. I leaned my back against the rough trunk and cursed myself for a fool. The dead lay all round, young and old, why shouldn't Jacob have joined them? What was I doing, acting on the words of a giddy girl like Annie? And what if I were to see him among the lately dead of the parish, or those that were to die this year – could I bear that? I should haul myself home to bed now, I told myself, and pray out my folly on my knees. But telling myself made no difference; I did not move, though the minutes slipped into hours and my bones ached with damp and stiffness and the silence drew its folds about me.

A sharp breeze blew off the hanging mist and the moon stared bleakly down at me with all her stars about her. Let me see him, I begged her, even if he is to die, even if he has been cold in his grave for weeks, let me see him come. Let him haunt me every day of my life. It felt to me that for these few hours God leased the white-cast world to the moon; within the church He reigned with book and cross, but out here in this bare world of silver and shadow, stone and death, the moon was allowed her rule. But night would soon be over and nothing had happened. I huddled into myself, part of the darkness of the yew.

Perhaps I blinked, perhaps the dread and the cold confounded my wits – all at once it seemed the moonlight thickened. Shapes, human figures, appeared before me; it was no dream, I would swear it on the Bible. There was the vicar, or the spectre of the vicar, holding the Bible, the graves and the holly hedge quite clear through his surplice. Behind him a cluster of familiar forms, shuffling silently, each wrapped in a white winding sheet. My heart caught in my mouth, for there was old Rowland, with a dark stain above his eye; Annie Bartlet's mother, so thin and spare her collar bones were ridges beneath her sheet and – oh sweet Lord – there, taller than the rest, his thick curls glistening, Jacob. I could not move. I could not call to him; even the motion of my breath had paused. He was as bright and real as the moonlight on the stone; there were hollow rings round his eyes and he stooped as though even spectral steps exhausted him.

The group entered the church and from within there came the hum of prayer. I was caught between life and death, unable to feel, to move; I was reduced to the vision I had sought. The moon shone on, insensible. For a long while nothing happened; if I had been capable of thought I should have lost all hope, but then a woman – I knew her – Sarah Pugh, a grandmother, issued from the church; she was made of moonlight as before, but dressed now in her own clothes. After her, nothing, at first nothing, then a man, a young man, leaning on a staff but looking about him as though new awakened into life. Jacob, unburied, alive, and yet no more himself than a painting. He did not turn to me, but passed on, out of the churchyard gate.

How long I remained there I don't know. At length I became aware of two black eyes watching me – a badger, paused in its saunter to the hedge. Its gaze was quick with life. I hauled myself upright and it turned away unhurriedly, sniffing through moonlight and shadow alike. What were spirits to the world of rich rot and loam, to the whispers of earthworms? The strange stupor which had fallen on me lasted into my dreams for the few hours till morning, but I woke with a fierce new conviction: Jacob was alive.

13

There was the question, of course, of what to do. A week slipped by, then another. May began, and all the young people, and most of the old, rose before the dawn to gather flowers – and some returned with green-stained gowns, smiling into the morning. 'I shall be back before you hang a garland up for May,' he'd said before he left. I drew the shutters and sat with the green ring Meg made me, shredding the petals. I must be like the beaver and build a dam that could hold and check my sorrow. He was alive, the vision said – but he might be ill, grievously ill yet. How long might it take him to recover himself and reach me? He was likely lying in a fever in some filthy lodging house, where the rats were loud in the walls and there was no one to care if he lived or died. If I could only reach him, if at the least I could send him word he was to be a father! I had last had my courses late February; I was at the most only three months gone. By July, I told myself, he must be home by late July when the baby, mothlike, would begin to quicken.

Slowly the attention I had been given fell off, until only Sally and little Meg and old Rowland checked on me daily. Young John could hardly bear to look at me and more than once I spied him crossing the orchard or a field to avoid an encounter. As if I would hold him to blame!

I was careful to tell no one what I had seen, not even Annie when she came calling the day after, saying only I had dreamed he was alive. In part this was because I did not trust myself to lie about the others I had seen making their doleful way into the church – or not to lie well, so that it could not be worked out of me. Pious folk might say it was a visitation sent by the devil, but that was not true, I could not think it, for what would that mean for Jacob? Rowland had lived a long full life, but if any man were truly good, it was him – I did not want to think he had only a few months left to live and Annie's mother too, though I did not know her nearly so well. Knowledge of what will be is a heavy burden, it left you yearning. In my healing I had always turned from conjuring work; I did not want it now, except to know the truth about my husband. How could so many have been so rash as to risk the vision, I wondered, till I remembered my own case and the urgency I felt that had leapt all risks and would leap them again and again. Whenever I saw Rowland his ghost hovered like a shadow in my mind's eye, with the black gash in its forehead.

'You've picked up well, young Martha,' he said to me one morning. 'I'll admit I was fearful for you, but your eyes have got their boldness back, or some of it, leastways, if you don't mind me saying.'

I could hold my peace no longer. 'He's not dead. I am sure of it.'

Rowland frowned. 'I feared it might be some such tale. Better than the other. Ah child, is that likely? Boult may be a rascal, but would he lie a man into his grave? Think Martha, what purpose would it serve?'

I hesitated.

'No, not for that even. How could he, at such a distance? I agree that not all the truth has been told, but you must not rot your mind with fancies. There'll come a time, soon, when you'll need to look about you.'

Rowland hadn't said what he meant by better than the other, but I knew clear enough. Boult had lingered for me after church on Sunday, saying loud enough for all to hear how when I was ready he would send a man to help me move my things, that there was work in the dairy and two good rooms above it. I was not blind to the looks and the nudges behind me while I bobbed and begged for leave to stay till harvest. He did not answer. It was not to be borne, but I did not know what was to be done about it. I knew that once I had left the cottage and my good neighbours, I was lost. My black ribbons would not protect me; if I could stay put till I grew big, surely then, I thought, he would not lay hands on me. I did not reflect, goose that I was, how he used my pregnancy against me. I carried his bastard the murmur said. He had breathed the rumour into being; he had now only to blow a little for it to grow like a wave at my back. I could not hope to halt it; I would be washed up at his feet.

Meg came back to stay with me, because I was afraid. Other people, even Sally, skirted round Jacob's name as though to say it would set back healing, but Meg did not know this. She liked to ask me questions when we lay down to sleep.

'Are you still sick from the baby?'

'No, not so much now, Meg.'

'But is it Jacob gave it you or Master Boult?'

I turned towards her. 'What have you heard Meg?'

'Oh, my Pa says it'd better be the Steward's now and Ma Sally says however could you say so and Pa says if she's got any sense in her head she'll get herself set up because it don't matter what the truth of it is, everyone believes it's the Steward that's knocked out the apple.'

'What do you think Meg?'

She was quiet so long I thought she'd gone to sleep. 'I don't like the Steward, nuncle.'

'No,' I said, 'and nor do I. I wouldn't let his baby grow in my belly.'

By and by, hesitantly at first, folk came again to ask healing of me. Perhaps, I thought, if I could keep my home, I could get by till Jacob returned to me, working charms and herbs for my bread; after all it could be any day, morning or evening – a cart would rumble by and stop. I told Meg to be listening out for wheels. But the days went by and he did not come.

It was almost more than I could bear, to go about my days, thinking of him without friends, or money, ill to the point of death; I would go to him, I thought, but then buckled at the distance and the difficulty. What if we missed each other on the road? Even if I knew where to find him it was so far – if he were ill when I set out he would be either well or dead by the time that I arrived. And the road was no place for a woman, let alone a woman with child. I had more than myself to think of now. Better far to trust in his return. But again, what if he could not travel? If they had left him a cripple and declared him dead for ease's sake? The more I reflected the more it seemed the most likely story. I remembered the cell in Ludlow and the trial and how he had broken out of a sickbed and a locked door to recover me from death itself. My belly might not show for two months yet, maybe more so's anyone would notice, and we could be back in Hope by then. Back and forth I went with my thinking, like a scrabbling hoe, and more and more I returned to the thought of leaving.

Twice I saw Boult face to face. The first time I was at the river where it drops down into a washing pool. Meg poked me in the ribs and pointed across the water. Boult was standing in the dappled sun on the farther path, watching me. I bent my head and said nothing, rubbing grit into the wool to shift the dirt. At last he passed on. The second time I was returning from weeding peas. There was a group of us, but I was a little apart, less because of my hobble than the cloud that hung about me. It was a golden afternoon and the girls all wore circlets of lady's smock, herb-robert, buttercups. I trailed a rope of goosegrass I feigned not to have noticed Meg sticking to my back. If it stuck till I reached home, I thought, it would be useful for the trouble old Margaret was having with her waters. Boult rounded the corner on horseback, all smiles and courtesy. He lifted his hat to Annie and the other girls.

'What ladies have we here? Queens of the May?'

They giggled and curtseyed. I hung back, hoping foolishly that he would not see me, but he drew alongside and bowed low towards me.

'Mourning becomes you,' he said, low enough to pique the listening ears. 'I am growing tired of games, madam. The rent quarter begins at midsummer. You must be in my house before then.'

As soon as he'd gone Annie slipped back, and threaded her arm through mine, arching her eyebrows.

'He is a toad.' I said.

She nodded, 'He's very like a toad. You must find your way to the jewel in his head.'

'I will kill him. I will mix hemlock in the cream and drip it on his fat lips.'

Annie paused then and squeezed my hand. 'Don't be a fool, Martha. You must ask a high price while you can.'

I shook my head. 'Jacob is alive,' I said. 'I feel sure of it. He will come home.'

The next morning Boult's man, Richard, arrived at my door with a skirt of fine blue lawn and a collar of lace. There was a letter too.

Mistress

*After I saw you yesterday I could not rest. You are as far above the
rabble that you live among as the falcon is above the mouse. Do not
deceive yourself you hate me. That will not last. Think. Your husband is
dead, you have no family. Come to me and I will cover you in gold. I will
provide for you and for my bastard child. Mine, I have said it. Such pride
in such as you, a cripple, with the scars of irons on her legs! Gather your
things, I will send a cart after the shearing. Fie madam, have a care, I
will not suffer humiliation.*

Richard was leaning against my door, watching me with a grin.
He gestured at the room with his chin. 'Nice cottage this. Shame
you won't get the benefit of that thatch. Still, you'll be tucked up
nicely at the house. He'll poke you ragged for a while then he'll tire
and get another one. Best not anger him.'

After he had left I put the letter to the fire. A kind of stupor took
me; I willed myself to consider what to do. Would he truly put me
out of the house? The question was an idle one, he had said so. I
watched the flames lick and mumble at the wood and saw a future
unfolding. For a brief while I would seemingly be cossetted; during
the days I would dress in silk and bathe my hands in rosewater; if I
charmed him long enough my child might be sent to school. Every
night I would lay myself out for use; his damp pink flesh, the rank
smell of his sweat in the sheets, worse, I would be expected to chaff
his damp limp piece to action. Countless women had endured this
since the dawning of the world; I knew I was no better than they.
This was not the worst, however. Boult would tire. It wouldn't take
long; it would begin perhaps as soon as he rolled off me, aware of
my disgust and the darkness that waited just beyond the lamplight.
Then what? The pox and poverty and a child I could not feed.

'Jacob,' I said bitterly to the embers, 'what good are you alive,
and far away? It's here I need you. Here, now.' It was still two weeks
till the shearing. Perhaps I could buy a little time, bargain for my

cottage; perhaps Sally or Rowland could take my part? But what could they do, what had they to offer? All it would do was bring them trouble and anyhow, there was little chance he would let me stay in my house if I denied him what he asked. If Sir Thomas had been at home I could perhaps have thrown myself on his mercy, pleaded the love he had once borne Jacob, but he had stayed barely two nights at the Court. There was no hope there. Every way I cast it I could not see my way free. Tell me Lord what I should do, I prayed, but God did not answer. I sat so long that when a neighbour came by for a salve my pottage was cold and the fire all ashes.

All that day and the days that followed I let the hours unfurl. I was a leaf, existing for the sun. I knew a storm was coming that would blow me to the mud, but it seemed to me I was fixed and powerless to help myself. All might yet be well – wasn't the world busy with beginnings? We had days of soft warm weather, light breezes where it seemed the woods were swishing skirts. The earth was merry with burgeoning. I abandoned myself to soft thoughts and silly fancies – conjuring over and over Jacob's look of glad surprise as he put a hand to my belly, imagining myself big already, my stomach hard and strange like the moon. Other times I would drift into absence, my hoe raised to the earth, a ladle poised above the pot, looking into nothing, tears I had not noticed coursing down my cheeks. 'What could be more natural,' people said, 'than that she weeps?' When she was by, Meg would put her hand up to my face and wipe it dry.

'Come back, nuncle,' she would say and I would shake myself and smile and hug her hard, all the terror that awaited me returning.

In the small hours of the night when the world had shrunk to the close quiet of my room, I determined I would leave – soon, tomorrow, the day after tomorrow – I would take only what was needful and find a cart going north. There was time yet before the baby came; we might be home by harvest. Or if not, if I had to wear out my shoes searching, why then I would not be the first great-bellied woman to find herself roofless. Our Mother had not flinched, not even when they led her to a stable in the dead of winter, when the trough water curdled into ice and the ox breath steamed. In the morning the confusion of the world leaked through the shutters and I would hesitate again. Go where? And if I did not find him, if he was cold – oh but I could not think of that. Next to me, warm and tangled, Meg would begin to wriggle, and then she'd sit and smile, pink with sleep and I'd stroke her hair. Not today, I'd think, I cannot bear to leave. I'll wait another day; he might come home.

* * *

The good weather held for the shearing. Light fell in yellow folds through the great barn doors and dust motes sparked gently upwards. Below, all was bleating and sweat; the men knelt on the threshing floor, holding down the ewes to cut them. We women passed round the cider, gathered fleeces and tied them. I was careful to stay close with the others. Old Rowland could not stay long on his knees and so between shearing himself, he minded the others, chiding them for roughness, watching that they did not nick. On the last day I was refilling the jug from the barrel in the brown back reaches of the barn when Boult strode in. He poked about at the tied fleeces and then came up to the second shearer as a fresh ewe was hauled to him. I watched her terrified striped eyes as he held her fast and clipped the fleece from her shoulders, so that it splayed back like a shawl. Boult leant in to watch.

'You ought to go in closer,' he said to the shearer, 'you're leaving half the wool on her back, she's all in petticoats when she should be stripped.'

'Ain't possible to go in no more,' the shearer answered, undaunted, 'without I make her bleed.'

He let the ewe go and she stood up surprised and naked, before a boy took her to the pen to be tarred with the Court stamp.

'Hey, bring the jug,' the man called, and I had no choice but to start forward.

Boult saw me and thrust out a cup and drank it off then wiped his mouth with his hand and smiled, looking at me all the while.

'Tell me,' he said to the shearer, grabbing my elbow as I was about to move off. 'Why do you start here?' He put down his cup and put his finger to my neck.

The man stood and stretched, signalling the boy bringing a shearling to wait. 'Open her up steady at the neck and collar and she'll let you undress her all the way to her tail.' He clapped his knee and grinned and the others laughed.

Boult pulled my elbow so that I was forced to bend back beneath him. Carefully, he took the jug from my hand. Glancing round he put two fingers to my bodice, and mimed the descent of the clicking shears. The men laughed again, but did so, some of them, nervously. Then he let me go so suddenly I fell down to the straw. My head must have hit the flags beneath – for a moment the air was knotted with stars – and then his face appeared among them as he leaned down to haul me up. I tried to bat him off but he grabbed my wrist and smiled; his lips shaped the word 'tomorrow'. It was all over in a moment. He turned his back and I brushed my skirts down and picked up the jug.

I could not get out without walking the length of the barn so I retreated to the barrel and pretended to be filling my jug till the voices and bleating told me I was forgotten. Then, glancing to see that no one observed me, I slipped behind the baskets of new shorn wool to let my heart grow calm. The heat here was thick and rich with the wool oil and would have sent me as giddy with sleep as a drunk fly if I had not been so agitated. Little by little it soothed me and I picked up some scraps which had fallen down, remembering how I loved to push my fingers through Jacob's thick locks and press my face into them to breathe their horse-hay scent. How at night he would rise through his dreams to turn to me and press his lips against mine.

I shook myself. There could be no more of this see-saw off and on dreaming. Jacob had not come home; I could wait no longer. Tomorrow, Boult had said. By nightfall I would be houseless – or his whore. And what use Jacob returning then – to find his wife a harlot, his child an acknowledged bastard? Better that he thought me dead than that. Better that I was. I was not a mare to be ridden till I was broken meat, good only for the hounds to chew on. I would leave tonight, before first light, while the village slept off the shearing feast.

A man's voice, close by, started me up. 'Where's she gone?' it said, 'the lame girl who was handing out the cider?'

'She's no girl, Martin Bright,' Sally's voice answered, 'you've been coming here to shear long enough. She's Jacob Spicer's wife. Or widow I should say, poor thing.'

'I remember him well enough. So that was her. Seemed a good man to me. A shame for a man to end like that.'

'There's more to it, I'd swear it on the Bible, though Sir Thomas himself bore witness to the truth of it. She's taken it hard, as any wife would and them so much in love, it were a delight to see, I tell you. It weren't right of the Steward to use her so and urge the men on to laugh at her, her with her husband barely cold in his grave.'

'From what I heard, he's been making use of her a good while now,' a younger man put in, 'popped a bastard in her belly.'

'Why! How dare you say so, how dare you spread such mischief.' Oh Sally, I thought, don't defend me with so shrill a voice.

'I've a good mind to throw this cider in your poxy snout. See if I don't.'

'Peace woman!' Martin, put in, 'we could barely set foot in the village before hearing how Spicer had gone to a brawling death and his wife become the Steward's jade. The jostling leaves in the orchard whisper it. Maybe she's not the Steward's whore, not yet. He's as good as shown she will be. He might as well have tarred her with his stamp like one of the ewes.'

'Then shame on all of us,' Sally said, '"Thou shalt not go up and down with tales among thy people; neither shalt thou stand against the blood of thy neighbour", that's what the Bible says. Good day to you.'

There was silence for a while then, so that I thought they had gone and I might be able to edge out, but then the bell was rung and they sighed and spat.

'Well I pity the girl,' the older one, Martin, said, 'if she doesn't wish it, but who's to say? Maybe she fancies lying on feathers, even with Boult's sour breath in her neb.'

'It en't fair though, is it? She looks like a fierce one, wouldn't mind blunting my edge on her myself.'

'You're a coward, Thomas Pike, and cowards don't get to die like that.'

They laughed and moved off back to the work.

I waited till the barn was quiet. At the further end men were pulling tables for the supper, but they did not mind me. My heart ached at all I was leaving – the soft light falling in chords through the wide barn doors; the dappled orchard; the familiar toing and froing of my neighbours in the lane. It was no use weeping; there would be time enough for that.

14

I took very little with me. Near the whole village was at the shearing supper, but it would be understood, expected even, that I should not go. Before she left for the feast, Sally had knocked at my door with oatcakes and cheese, and clasped me to her ample bosom, stroking my hair.

'What is it Sally?' I said, pretending ignorance, hoping she did not notice my blotched cheeks, my breathlessness.

'Just remember, Martha,' she said, 'you're not friendless. You're my kin, just as much as if we shared blood.'

I felt myself falter then, wrapped in her warm clasp with her love about me. It was at the edge of my tongue to talk, to utter some folly that would hint at my leaving: *Bless you Sally* I wanted to say, *God be with you, think well of me, forgive me.* The words pressed in my throat so hard I thought that I would sob, but I hugged her and said nothing.

When she was gone I gathered what I had of value. It was good, after all, that I had not returned the chain. It would sell for a good price. The book troubled me; I resolved to leave it. After all it was not mine and to take it would be to brand myself a thief. Jacob's knife I put in my satchel along with my purse and the chain. Even without the book my bundle was heavy enough, what with simples to sell and candles and the blue kirtle and all the food I could carry on the road. I waited while the moon rose and the first revellers returned, letting the dark gather round me. The years in this house with Jacob had been the happiest I had ever known. They were pinned to this place. As soon as I stepped away the memories would loosen and begin to fall out of shape. I walked round the cottage brushing my hand over its surfaces – our bed, his chair, the dimpled wall, as if to take the knowledge of them into my palm, my fingers. If our life were only a book that I could open and read at will, every time the same with the same words clear on the page! But perhaps we should find a way of returning. Perhaps we could be just as we were that March morning when he said goodbye.

At length I went out to see from the height of the moon how far into the night it was. Before me, very still on the path, a pale shape hovered, for all the world like a fairy child.

'Come, Meg,' I said. 'Whatever are you doing up so late? Couldn't you sleep, child?'

'I dreamt about you, nuncle,' Meg said.

'What was your dream?' I said, drawing her into the house.

'Well, rightly, it warn't about you, but uncle Jacob. He was sitting on a big wooden chair with a smile all over his face and a baby on his knee, dandling it up by the arms, so.' And she raised her arms up high. 'Then I woke up and thought to myself that the devil must have sent the dream, because uncle Jacob's in his long home and en't never coming home.'

Her lip trembled and I hugged her head to my bosom. It was a sign, of course it was, that the child should dream of Jacob living and happy now, just as I was preparing to leave. 'That wasn't the devil, Meg,' I said. 'Would the devil send you such a picture of joy –

and innocence? An angel sent you that dream. I'd swear it. It means Jacob is living.'

Meg stepped back to look at me, although I hadn't lit a candle and there was only a thread of light, where the shutters were ajar. 'You know he's cold, nuncle. They said prayers for him in church.'

'That doesn't make it true, Meg. Why would you be sent a dream like that if he were under the earth? I don't believe it.'

'That's doubting, nuncle. Ma Sally says that she's afeard for you, because doubting is like to turn your wits.'

'Does she so?'

'Yes, she says it all the time.'

I turned then and lit a candle, and sat down, drawing Meg before me. 'Listen. They wouldn't let Rowland's John see his body. They left with too much haste. Who knows but that he might have got better. Do you understand?'

Meg solemnly shook her head.

'Never mind. Listen. I am not brainsick, Meg. I am going to find him and bring him home. I will be gone awhile; you must have faith. When they miss me you can tell them that I've followed his path to bring him home. It's an adventure.'

Her eyes were large in the candlelight. What a foolish thing to tell the child. She would be sure to rouse them. I ploughed on. 'But don't tell them till tomorrow, till the sun is sliding down again. You can keep my house clean for me while I am gone.'

Suddenly, she smiled. 'Can I come with you?'

'No, no darling, it's too far and Sally needs you. But I shall bring you home a present. A doll from the fair, should you like that?'

Meg nodded. 'Good girl,' I said. 'And Jacob will sit and dandle his baby like in your dream.'

It was like a cloud gone from the moon; she was all bright excitement and pride at the weight of a secret to carry. When finally I persuaded her to go back to bed she waved at me from the door of

Sally's cottage and put her finger to her lips and giggled. It was all I could do not to rush and hug her to me and cling to her, but I merely raised my hand in farewell. I had little faith she would be able to keep her knowledge from bubbling out, but all the same I was glad to have told her; I had said goodbye. It might be put about I had gone mad, but in her heart she would know it was not true.

However, there was no time to lose. If I lingered till she babbled I would be prevented. I took one last look at my cottage. The book was lying on the tick. Without letting myself think too hard I picked it up and placed it in my satchel, then bound the bigger load to my back. After all, I might not be gone long.

My first thought was of Owen in Hereford. He might know people who could help me, who could send ahead. In the last letter he had written to me he'd talked of finding great favour with his teachers, said he was bound for orders and the University. But Hereford lay due south and what good could a grammar school boy do me? It would be wrong to ask it of him. I turned along the road the party had taken in March. It was a bright night that promised a good clear morning. The roads would be dry and sound and nobody would notice a pedlar woman stooped under her load. I could be at Leominster by breakfast time, perhaps even Ludlow before nightfall. I shivered at that. When I had last seen Ludlow my wrists and ankles had shackle sores. I was the Witch of Woolhope, who had scattered the graves of the dead and the chapel walls, who had brought a hill down on her own head. I tried to shake the fear off; it was doubtful I would be recognised, and if I was, what of it? I had been acquitted. Jacob had delivered me and walked me home; us both so weak we advanced like caterpillars feeding on sunlight and when we were weary of walking we lay in some dappled shade and unwrapped one another with our lips and hands till we were butterflies.

It was no use; I could not bring myself to go to Ludlow. In any case, I told myself, if I were to be followed or asked after it would be in Leominster. There would be nothing so easy as overtaking me, the slowest old nag in the stable could do it. Boult would stand me before him; perhaps he would lay out my choice – cunt, or neck – and he'd pull out the book from my satchel and the thin gold chain. Perhaps he would not bother even to do that; it'd be too late for choices.

I turned east towards the glimmering dawn and took the road to Worcester. The night held past Bodenham, where the restless thatcher lived. At Pencombe I startled a pedlar out of a ditch. We eyed each other warily, for the light was too grey for ease. Soon after, cottagers began to emerge for the day's work, but I was beyond my own lands and although some turned to stare after they said their good days, there was nobody to know me.

For hours I walked; the track climbed and fell and I did not mind it. After the days of indecision it felt good to move; I welcomed even the pain in my shins, the dull ache of my ankle. Whatever the road brought, whatever dangers it had in store, it was better than Boult's rank bed. It was months before I'd grow too big for walking. I would not think about that, yet. My father had a silver medal of St Christopher with the Christ child on his shoulders, striding the stream; he wore it on a chain about his neck. It had been his own father's and he kept it for that, he said; he had no truck with charms or trinkets, but I saw how he touched it, without fail, on setting out. One night on a drunk he gambled it away. I wished I had it still, next to my chest, to ward off evil. But no matter, I thought, I could pray as well without it and I knew how to pick luck from the hedges and lanes. Here was mugwort, tall as my chest, that St John wore as a girdle in the wilderness. I twined myself a bracelet that I tucked under my cuff; the scratch of the stems lessened my loneliness.

Near noon an old carter passed me and offered me a ride as far as his master's farm. I told him my mother had died and I was joining my brother in Worcester. He nodded as though to say he expected as much and gestured to the parcel at his side.

'Reckon you'll be hunger bitten if you've walked all from Bodenham this morning. Hereford born you say? I been there once, when I was more of a one for striking out.'

He dropped me at the top of a long steep hill and pointed out the way. 'You'll reach Bromyard easy enough. You bide there tonight lass. There's all kinds of rogues on the wastes beyond, it wouldn't do for an eyesome wench like you to be wandering uncompanied over by Bringsty. Promise me? I won't sleep tonight without your word on it. Bad enough you travelling alone at all.'

I promised and thanked him. It was a good sign to meet such kindness on the road so soon. I leaned a little on a gate at the brow where he turned off. The sun was high and warm and before me the world dropped away in embroidered shades of green and then rose like piled clouds as far as the Welsh hills. Despite all the sorrow of the past days I felt my heart lift at the promise such distance offered. Somewhere beyond the mountains the sun licked at the sea. Perhaps one day I should see it. In Boult's book I had read the story of a queen called Dido, but I had not returned to it because it was so sad. When her lover left her she built a pyre high on the hill above the sparkling bay and gored herself upon a sword. Oh Dido, I thought, looking at the blue-grey horizon, why did you not go after him? The wind off the waves must be something indeed. I swore I should not be so weak; I would wear out iron shoes and still I'd search. High on the hill all the world was open before me, all the roads I had never known.

15

Heeding the carter's warning, I found a dry hollow in the split of a double hedge about a mile before the town. A badger or a fox might sniff me out, but no man would find me unless they were hedging by moonlight. It was such a dry night there seemed little point in paying for a bed or risking chatter; I was weary with walking and all the watchful hours of the night before. On either side the tangled dog rose and field maple walled me in. The small birds ceased their fidget prayers and a fall of crows some way off cawed themselves into silence. Above me the sky greyed into night and then, slowly, stars winked out. I searched out the northern star that never wavers. That way, I thought. Somewhere perhaps he was star gazing too, lifting his finger to thread the constellations. I lifted mine to touch his. 'Come look at them Martha,' he would say on nights like this, taking me with him to lie down together under the moon. 'They're the light from heaven coming through. It's like the Lord himself poked the screen with nails to give us just the glint of it.'

'So then,' I'd answer, 'when we die, will Saint Peter whisk the cloth back, to give us the dazzle whole?'

'Maybe,' he'd say, shifting onto his side next to me, and pulling at the laces of my bodice, 'but I think he'll rather let it happen slow; like this,' and he would tease open the fustian and push aside my shift, so that my chest gleamed naked, 'St Peter will give me a glimpse of heaven and I'll crane close, like this, and rest my finger-tips, so, on the cool white stone and burn so to enter that my lips will make the alabaster blush.'

'Blasphemer!' I'd laugh at him, lifting his head, 'You make me into an old carved image in a church.'

'Oh my honeycomb, I could kiss you till my lips bled.'

I shooed the dream away. Why did I torment myself so? 'You will not let him sleep softly in the earth,' Sally would have said, 'you'll make his soul restless with your grieving.' But I knew why. The ache it stoked and left me in was only partly pain. At first I told myself that if I could only have his ghost then I would cradle it, draw it so close I could breathe it in. But if he was living – ah, then, there was a promise in it too.

I slept better that night than I had in days, although I woke up stiff and wet with dew. My first thought was to sell the candles in my pack. Bromyard was too small a place to profit well and without suspicion on the chain, but there'd be a chandler or two and the candles were heavy. I was shown a locked narrow door just off the square.

'You wait there,' my guide said, 'he'll be up by and by, if the ale hasn't turned his guts.'

It was a slow town for waking. I sat down on a post under the market house and watched the door. The morning was fine, but there were rags of cloud. I should not linger if I wanted to reach Worcester before dark and avoid a drenching.

When the door finally opened it wasn't by a man but a young woman with a baby on her hip. She laid out the candles carefully on her counter and gave me a good enough price.

'You from far?' she asked, as I carefully counted the coins into my purse.

'Hereford,' I told her, 'to join my brother in Worcester.' The story came easier today and when she smiled I was encouraged. 'My father was an ironmonger,' I continued, 'had a fine shop that I helped him in, but he died and all was owed and taken. I'd been near despairing till John, my brother, sent word to come...' Then I stopped, affronted – the woman was grinning at me outright.

'You'm not so good at lying, are you lamb? You'm never worked in a shop, or you wouldn't peer at the coins so, as if they were magic counters. It's all right, don't take on, it don't bother me none what your story is.'

I looked up at her. She had bold, quick eyes and though she was laughing at me there seemed no malice in it. I smiled back.

'You ain't from Hereford, neither. Never been to town on a market day I'm guessing.'

Not as a free woman, I thought. 'How do you know?'

'The way you wear your purse for one. Where any passing fool could grab it. Keep only the money you might need at once to hand. Stuff the rest in your boot or some such. Are you going to Worcester in truth?'

'I am,' I said, 'I'm looking for something.'

'Someone more like.' She leaned over and patted my cheek. 'Forget him.'

I gave her a tight smile at that and turned to leave, but she called me back.

'It's a bad road.' Her shrewd eyes were weighing up my chances. 'A dell like you is easy pickings. It's not safe for a woman.'

I nodded. 'I've been told so.' Again, I turned to go.

'Wait,' she said. 'My father is taking a load to the city. There's a few of them going, there'll be men alongside. You seem a sweet wretch to be wandering the wastes up there. I wouldn't want to hear of a fool found dead or a girl badly used when I might have prevented it.'

'God bless you,' I said, 'but—'

'—No buts,' she said sharply. 'You'd better learn to take help. You'll need to, if he takes a while finding.' She gestured to me to follow her. 'Come through here. You can help me hitch the horse while the old sot eats his dinner.'

I held the baby for her while she covered and roped the baskets. She was a widow, she told me, her husband had died a year before, soon after the baby was born. I was sorry for that, I said.

'Oh,' she said, 'it's a pity, and the child not having a father. He was a good man all in all, my William, never raised a hand to me, but he was a dull hick all the same. A mite too fond of a cockfight and a prey for any passing doxy caught his eye.'

'You'll marry again, surely? You've such a pretty face.' It was true. Her cheeks were scarred with pox but she fell into smiles easily. They belied the sharpness of her glance.

She pinched my cheek. 'I thank you for saying so, stranger, and truthfully there's one or two have been calling to tell me the same, but I think they fancy the business as much as me. Why would I marry and give over my body and my bed again, aye and my gold too, when it can be all my own?' She took back the baby and rubbed her nose on his so that he giggled, then glanced down at my hand. 'It's a fine thing to be a widow.'

Perhaps she was two, three years older than me, but she made me feel a green girl. I blushed. 'If he has died,' I said simply, 'I think I cannot go on living.'

'Don't be a goose,' she said. 'Mind the baby while I fetch the horse.'

Her father said barely a word to me when he came out, merely jerked his thumb at the board after he had climbed up, all the while muttering to his daughter that she should keep her charity for works of her own hands and not be asking him to do it for her and had she packed him food enough?

'I have,' she said, 'and mind you share it with my friend. You are my friend now,' she said to me as we left, 'and I'll pray Fortune smiles on you.'

It was almost noon by the town clock. I assumed the rest of the party must have gone long since, but it turned out they were as slack as my benefactor; we were kept another half hour for a dozen cheeses to be added to a farmer's wagon. Besides the chandler and the farmer and his wife there was a draper with an over-laden nag, another man whose business was never made clear to me, but whose mount was fine enough to do the journey twice over in the time we would take, and five or six walking – two of them labourers with staves whom I was told would leave us once we were safe over Bringsty.

Not far past the town the road began to climb. Soon the fields gave way to furze and broom and high ferns. The old man had not said a word to me since we had left, although he had acknowledged the others with a surly nod, telling them when they asked that I was some waif his Mary had picked up. I noticed how his hand trembled a little on the reins and remembered my dead father – the bitter mornings after the brave nights. The road was packed and hard, but uneven as a river bed and he had to judge a course nicely through the half-patched holes, and ruts and ridges.

'This is a road that would have given my father no end of business.' I said, forgetting to lie. 'He was a wheelwright out near Woolhope.'

The old man nodded without turning his head. 'A good wheel is a beautiful thing,' he said. 'You'd best walk now a while; it's too steep for passengers.'

I got down and walked. The sun was hot and the air was growing heavy but there was a lick of breeze as we climbed. Behind us the land rolled in warm green waves westwards, before us and on either side lay the manor wastes and downs; it was as though the world was a great bolt of cloth rolling open. High, high above, a pair of forktail gledes made slow circles.

'Bloody carrion eaters,' the man beside me said, following my gaze.

'What a view of us all they must have,' I said. 'All the earth open below them. We must seem like mice scurrying hither and thither.'

'They only look to see what they can eat,' he replied. 'En't so different from us on'y worse, if you asks me, like lawyers. They're after ripping and feeding off the dead.'

I glanced back up. 'All the same,' I said, 'it must feel good, to glide on the breast of the wind as they do.'

The gentleman on the fine black prancer had crested the hill and now stood outlined on the brow waiting. The carts toiled and we sweated after, too hot for talking. At the top we waited for our breath to catch us up.

'Look,' my companion said, laughing, 'your gledes have followed after us.' I glanced where he pointed and laughed with him. The thought darted at me that I was happy; the world was wide and free and the people I had met were good and kind. The next moment I felt ashamed and I rubbed at my wedding ring.

'That's not good,' the draper was saying, 'carrion birds keeping by us, I don't like that one bit.' He shook his fist at them.

'Oh peace you old dawcock,' the chandler said, 'they're thick as grass up here.'

'And we're past the common now surely?' I asked, climbing up again.

'Past it?' my companion said, 'No, wench, it's over beyond the manor lands.'

'Is it so bad?' I asked.

The chandler turned to me. 'Don't be worriting about it,' he said. 'Been quiet these past months. It's an unkempt place is all; all kinds of rogues and hedgecreepers hid there in Queen Mary's time, but it's nigh cleaned up now. These folks,' – he gestured at my companion and his stave – 'talks it up to screw a bit of money from us poor traders.'

I smiled. We'd be well past the common by nightfall, even if it seemed we'd not reach Worcester till tomorrow. They were local men; they'd know a place to bide tonight. We'd need it, for the weather was turning: the shreds of cloud had knit into a mat that pressed the sticky heat into faces and our backs. It was a pale grey yet, but if it darkened we'd need shelter quickly.

Soon the land dropped into heathland that rose and fell beside the road in knolls and hollows. The great wide views were gone. There were dense thickets and paths that wound uncertainly into bramble and bracken and furze. At our backs the sky had still some blue but ahead it was thickening. Despite his words, I noted the chandler began to peer about him and he gripped the reins hard. One by one our conversations fell away; the horses stepped with pricked taut ears. But round us the birds were louder than ever – there was the high shriek of a buzzard and a song thrush trilled from a hazel tree. Close by, a cuckoo called and another answered it.

The chandler froze.

'Get down,' he said to me in a hoarse whisper. 'Hide yourself.'

It was too late. There was a man at the bridle. There were men everywhere. A wagon had been drawn across the road. For a second the sun flared yellow against the stacked slate cloud. The scene was still as a painting; the light picked out our open mouths, the black horse rearing, the farmer's wife with her arms lifted up as though in praise; the song thrush singing. Then the wife screamed and all was noise.

A man pulled me roughly off the cart onto my knees, seized my wrist and began to wrench my wedding band from my finger. It was too sudden for thinking – I remember the look of concentration on his bony face, his two brown teeth; he barely seemed aware of me at all. It was the insensible focus of the fox; I felt a rush of fury and fear and bit hard into his thieving hand. He cried out, surprised, then grabbed me by the hair and kicked me, sharply, in the belly. It knocked the breath from me; the pain was jagged and yellow and sudden as the lightning that cracked the sky apart.

I could not breathe for pain. I felt it, I felt my belly break. I curled and fell onto my face in the baked mud, clutching at my middle as though to hold my rent womb whole. In the same moment I saw he crumpled too, with blood leaping out of his neck. I didn't see who killed him, I didn't care; I crawled through the confusion of shouts and legs into a fernbrake. Nobody stopped me. I followed a badger's path into a growth of alder until it rolled me into a pit behind. I was being split in two. I tried to haul myself up to my knees and it set me retching. Behind me there was shouting still, then the sound of a man close by, groaning.

A single drop of rain fell on my hand and burst. Another. Then thunder ripped heaven open and its rivers poured down. I crouched on all fours like a dog in the alder bushes and the rain plastered my clothes to me and I wept for the pain searing through my stomach and for what it meant. For a while the ache would lessen and I would fool myself that all might yet be well and then it would return worse than before, like a knife that turned blade edge then blunt then blade again within my belly and all the while the rain washed down until a stream opened up a few feet in front of me. At last I was able to drag myself forward to where a lip of earth made a shallow cave. My satchel hung under me like an udder. The hollow beneath felt almost dry and I pressed myself into it, drawing my knees tight up to lessen the pain. It did not take long for the bleeding to begin. Again and again I thought of Mary the chandler's daughter rubbing her nose against her baby's nose and I thought of little Meg and the soft warmth of her hand and I sobbed and sobbed.

Not four months, not even that. Weeks back, I had half expected it to fail, to wake bloody and bereft, but not this, nothing like this, to lose the child out of my own doing. I could have bided safe, endured Boult's pawings and cradled the promise in my womb. Like a butterfly's wings, women said, when the child begins to quicken, like the flutter of silk wings within you; I had not felt it, it was only a dream yet. For years I had not thought I wanted to be a mother, had believed that what we had was enough; oh but now, at the point of loss, what a fierce longing tore at me! The rain hammered on the earth and on the trees and I moaned and rocked. Then the pain came so strongly that I could not think. I stretched out my legs and screamed and the clotted blood was warm and then as cold as the dripping earth and I scuffed it from me with my boots.

It was only much later, when the rain had stopped and the clear moon picked out the fringe of dripping grass that hung over the bank above me, it was only then that I could bear to think of Jacob, and how I had woven the joy of our meeting with this gift he had yearned for long before I had learned to welcome it. 'It was for you,' I said, 'that I put myself in jeopardy, that I risked all,' but the words felt insubstantial. Would he hold it a judgement on my striking out alone? 'Oh Martha,' might he say, 'why could you not bide a quiet good wife? Look where all your learning's brought you, your hankering after books and doctoring.' However soon he softened and forgave me something would be changed between us; we could never be carefree as we were.

I hugged myself and whimpered at the cold indifferent moon and it offered me no comfort, none at all.

16

The morning was bright with innocence, as though washed of all knowledge of crime. At some point, perhaps, I had slept, I don't know, but at length I became aware of the light and the need to move. The pain of last night was gone, or rather I was left with only its echo, and an ache of desolation as though my heart had been carved out with a spoon. It seemed to me I should go back to the road to discover what was left. It may be my companions had prevailed, but there was little chance of that. Villeins with staves were no match for such a band; they would have been cut down like corn. I shuddered. Perhaps it was not so desperate; perhaps they were merely stripped and bound. I had to hope so. I staggered back through the sopping grass and beaded scrub, crawling where I could not walk. When I reached the road, I stowed myself behind a thorn brake where I could watch unseen.

Half a dozen men were gathered by the farmer's cart, hitching a nag to it. At first I shrank back with alarm, thinking them the wild men of yesterday, but from their garb and manner it was soon apparent these were townsfolk sorting the wreckage. A little further off there was a dray pulled up and two men were clumsily lifting a bundle onto it. I swallowed. A body; there were two more already on the wagon. Three dead. More perhaps. I thought myself numb to pain, but the sight made my eyes well up. Such good people. What kind of a world was this where men would cut you down for a bit of cloth or candles or cheese? The flame of a life pinched out in a moment. I remembered how the chandler had tried to save me, his daughter's long-suffering affection. Had she woken fatherless?

When my heart was steady I forced myself to look again. There was no sign of the chandler's cart or any of the horses. All had been taken then, to the last jot, my own poor bundle among it. The outlaws would be long gone by now. Had they spent last night counting and carousing, did they wash the blood from their hands before they tore into their meat and ale? I spat at the ground: 'may your flesh fester and fall from your bones,' I muttered, 'may your wounds canker, your teeth rot in your gums, your eyes cloud into sightless jelly.' I looked down at the ruin of my skirts; what good was cursing? It could bring nothing back, not the life I had begun to kindle, my spark, my flicker of a child. I had nothing now.

The dray ambled off and the road was left empty under the blue sky. I should have stepped out and hailed the men as they left, let myself be taken back as a witness. It was the good and Christian thing to do, but I could not do it. In my head I watched myself call after the cart, saw the men halt and wait, saw them figuring to themselves what had been done to me as I drew close and they saw and smelt the blood. They would find me a blanket and place me upfront where I should not have to see the dead. In the town there would be pity and questions and a clerk would be sent for to take a deposition. Even if I bore all that it would be days and days before I could head north again. What little I had left would all be gone. Worse, for sooner or later my story would tumble from me and a message would be sent to Hope. I imagined Sally weeping over me, Meg burying her head in my bosom, but it was too late for that. It was not them I would return to, but to Boult.

I could never go home. Not until I had found Jacob, likely not even then. Somehow, I began to understand what I had done. I could not go back. As softly as I could I withdrew further into the common, where no passing traveller on the road would see me.

I had nothing left but my satchel, that held the book and the chain and Jacob's knife. Worcester lay only a few miles off; I could rest there and buy new clothes. 'Collect yourself and go,' I told myself, over and over I said it, but my legs buckled at the thought of faces and greetings and talk. To think, only two days since, I'd looked across the waves of hills and believed I could cross oceans! How could I have thought myself fit to chart a course across the country? Jacob was right. I was proud and restless and it had ruined me. I had thought myself brave, but I was prey for any passing rogue; I was easy meat; even the gledes, the red kites circling above me knew it. At least in this wilderness I could be alone awhile; I turned into the thickets and tangle of the common and gave myself up to the meandering paths of outlaws and of beasts. I knew how foolish it was, how little my life was worth in such a place, how I might simply starve. I think I partly wanted to die, or at least to hand my fate to fortune and take what chance was given me. It seemed in some mad way a reparation.

It was a strange country, of sudden empty hollows and dense briars, thick spinneys that it seemed a weasel could barely thread through and then a sudden spreading oak. More and more my vision rolled and blurred and I had to pause for the earth to steady itself, until I began to doubt whether I was in some other world. Near noon I found myself stepping into a blazing clearing with a weed-grown cottage set back against a bank. There was a deer standing in the open door and birds sang in the thatch as though it were a fairy house drawn from a tale like those my grandmother wove for me; made by the little people to trick the traveller into their kingdom under the hill. But the deer pranced off and inside it was real enough, with a pot of oats in a corner. I ate a handful of them and the weevils too, reckless of the gripes they might give me; at least retching would keep me from thinking. Then I lay down in the sun and slept.

I dreamt that Meg pushed at my cheek. It wasn't a dream; something had touched me; a shadow had fallen across my face. I sat up and the horse, for that was what it was, shied away. We stared at one another. There was no mistaking it – the fine black mare from the day before, with its saddle and bridle, but nobody on its back. At first, when I stood, she started back. Jacob, I thought, help me and I felt, I saw, how he would stand with his hand outstretched, letting the beast take its own time. So I waited for her to come to me and when she ate the oats I offered her I leaned my head on her neck as Jacob used to do with nervous horses and breathed soft and long, until I felt her blood quieten. It felt like a gift had been given me.

We stood like that a while and then I led her gently towards the trees at the clearing's edge so that I could loop her bridle over a branch to prevent her leaving. All at once I felt her nervousness return. 'It's all right,' I said, 'you are safe,' but she was not happy. I followed her gaze. There, stippled with shade, was the body of a man, a youth, round his chin the black scarf our assailants had worn. I nudged him carefully with my boot. Dead. He must have been thrown; his neck was just a little askew. It seemed too easy a way to die after the violence on the road and the tempest which followed it. I crouched down. 'You don't deserve my pity,' I said to his staring eyes, but when I lifted the scarf I saw by his hairless chin and the roundness of his face that he was just a boy. I closed his lids and stood back. He lay among the foxgloves and the ragged robin as though he were a pretty elf asleep. He was beyond any anger now. My first thought was to leave him resting where he was, but then I had a picture of crows sitting on his corpse, hopping up towards his eyes; I hauled him out to the open space before the hut. The horse watched me, her ears back against her head, but I talked to her softly and she went back to cropping the damp grass.

The effort of it dizzied me. I sat down in the shade of an elder tree and looked at him. He was slight, with a long face and yellow straw hair; his lips were curled as if about to smile. Perhaps he was sixteen, perhaps a year or two more, or less. I wondered if he had a mother living who looked to his return, who prayed each night for his soul; it was likely he had done things in a few months which would cost him an eternity of burning. Perhaps if I had seen him do them, perhaps with that smile at the edge of his lips, I would not feel the pity I felt now for his frightened soul, but I had not been present at his sins. There was only the skinny boy, dead on the turf. Poor knave, I thought, we all of us make mistakes. Hadn't I let that dribbling lecher kiss me for a handful of tales? My sleep-starved fancy twined a rope from the dead boy to Boult's slobber and my own misfortune. I could have waited, virtuous at my door for my sweetheart's return, with our baby safe in my belly. 'I am so sorry Jacob,' I said wringing my hands and addressing the boy who was nothing like him. His mother would be weeping too, weeping and waiting. Why was it always our lot to sit and wait and suffer loss? Was he her only child perhaps, ripped from her before he had learned how to be a man? 'I was alone, Jacob,' I said out loud, 'what could I have done? Could you not have sent me word, one word by your own hand or another's?' I conjured in my mind to find him wherever he was now, feverish abed perhaps, or not himself, raggedly haunting some distant town, but none of my imaginings rang true.

A cloud passing across the sun roused me; it showed the boy's pallor. His soul was tugging to be gone. I would have to bury him; it was the only decent thing to do. At least after last night's drenching the earth would be softer than before. I got to my feet to find something to dig with. My kirtle and petticoat stuck bloodily to my legs and stank of iron in the heat of the afternoon, although I was still damp down to my smock from the downpour. Moving at all was irksome. Before I dealt with the boy I needed to address my own misery. I glanced back at him. Although he was damp he was not bloody anywhere but his head. He did not need his clothes now. I said a quick prayer and set about stripping him. There was a look of Meg's brother Jack about him, I tried not to think of that. The obstruction had barely begun to stiffen his limbs. There were no sores or marks of contagion on his body, I rolled him over to check. His shirt and hose I hung on a branch in the sun to dry and I covered his nakedness with plates of elderflower.

My first thought had been to wash myself clean and scrub my clothing before dealing with him, but now I had touched his cold body I knew that I would not be happy caked with the dirt of the grave and would need to wash again. Much better to lay him to rest first. Round the back of the cottage I found a rusted axe head that made a fine spade and after seeing to the horse and my own hunger I began to hack a long trench. The turf came up easy enough, but it was hard going to scrape out enough earth for a body to lie in, even such a meagre one. I took the axe head in both of my hands and, kneeling, drew the blade towards me as though I were scouring hide. My shoulders ached and my head swam with faintness, but I kept at it, watering the wet earth with useless tears, for it felt in a way I did not wish to peer into that I was digging a grave for my own poor baby who would never be born, that I was scouring my own soul and body of hurt and pain. My brain must have been giddy still, or I would have worried that I would be surprised, but not once did the thought of it occur to me. Perhaps it was in part a fairy house and a fairy glade; we were alone in it, the boy and I. Nobody could come near.

At last I decided I could do no more, though it was more a furrow than a pit. The sun was gentle again, throwing long shadows to the east. There had not been a human sound all day. Death locked him stiff now, so that it was hard to arrange him in the earth with his face toward heaven, but with some indignity to us both I managed it, and I covered him over with flowers and earth and then the broken turf again, saying as I did so, all I could remember of the service, being all the priest and congregation he could have. "'We brought nothing into this world,'" I said, "'neither may we carry anything out of this world.'" I felt a guilty twinge then, scattering earth on his stripped body with his clothes hanging just behind me in the warm evening sun. "'Man that is born of woman has but a short time to live,'" I went on, "'and is full of misery. He cometh up and is cut down like a flower; he flieth like a shadow and never continues in one stay. Let us eat and drink for tomorrow we shall die. That which you sow is not quickened except it dies: so is the resurrection of the dead. It is sown in corruption; it rises again in incorruption.'" There was more, much more if I could remember it, but I trusted that would be enough to bend an angel's eye to him. 'Please God,' I said, 'he was some father's, mother's son as the dear Christ was yours; if he has not won it on his own, let their sufferings be enough to lend him grace.'

I stood up. Who could know if he was saved – or damned either for that matter? His things were very nearly dry to the touch, I could go now and wash. I walked across to the stream that wound and fell just beyond the spot where I had found his body. As I clambered down the bank I noticed there was a leather strap hooked to a branch, and beneath it a bag. Why had I not thought to look? Fumbling it open I took the loaf that poked down one side and ate a piece of it slowly, chewing till the sour dough turned sweet in my mouth. Too much at once would knot up my guts; I replaced it for later.

There was a hole where the water came up to my thighs. I watched the water swirl about my smock and then I took that off too and rubbed at the crusted blood; blood leaked from me still, as though my body could not stop its weeping. If I let the water calm itself I could see the thread of it curling away from me. Beneath my toes the mud was soft. "'Hear my prayer, O Lord,'" I whispered, "'hold not thy peace at my tears, for I am a stranger with thee and a sojourner, as all my fathers were. O spare me a little,'" I said, 'please spare me a little, "that I may recover my strength before I go hence and be no more seen".' Softly, softly the clay and the blood washed away and were picked up by the wandering flow of the stream.

My petticoat and my kirtle were madder red and the blood quickly rubbed from them, leaving only an edge line that would fade over time. I slung the boy's bag over my shoulder and returned to where his dry clothes hung. Then I dried myself carefully and, under the gaze of the nodding horse, became a boy.

It was not by design. I donned the shirt and leather breeches, surprised at the justness of the fit, their ease for moving. Then I buttoned up the doublet and noticed bitterly how little a woman I was; even my still ripe breasts could scarcely be noted. If you could see your nuncle now, Meg, I thought, you'd think he'd found his proper self. It did not matter, I thought. There was nobody to see, and it was only till the things were dry. A few hours and then I could be my dullard self again, a dell on the high road, as Mary the widow had said, fruit for the picking. On display, for any passing lubbock to paw at, for any gang of loiterers to mock. I put the boy's cap on my head and pulled down the brim. Who would know? Scrawny lads were everywhere on the lanes and roads, hither and thither alone and nobody marking them. In the flush of decision I took out Jacob's knife and sawed off the great rope of my hair.

It lay at my feet like a horse's tail. For a moment I was appalled at what I had done. I saw Jacob's confused, stricken face; he would never approve such rashness. 'I am your good wife still, Jacob,' I said to the vision, 'but I must shift how I can.' I gathered it up and threw it into the scrub. Then I thought of my body alongside his, the breadth of his hand when I placed my palm within it – how he could bend and carry me as if I were a bag of corn. How could I be a man? But men's bodies were not alike, any more than their minds; if I could play the swaggerer the weakness of my fist and shoulders might be a jest, but that was all. 'Have at you,' I said to my shadow, punching like a bully fighter, kicking my leg high because the breeches said I could.

That was too much, perhaps that would come later. I crumpled down again and rubbed at my traitor eyes. 'No more weeping,' I said aloud. No more dwelling on what was lost. I must have courage and if I couldn't find it in me I must counterfeit. What was I after all? Not much of a woman, I had scarcely played that well. It was vagabond boys who roamed the roads to find their fortune. I would be a boy; it would help me to forget myself, forget all this, until I found him.

The bag held ample recompense for the bundle I had left in the cart. There was a pretty dagger and a half dozen lengths of woollen hose, a whole cheese and a wrapped lump of ham. The hat the gentleman had worn. Two rings. A silver cross. There was money in four different purses. I emptied them into the hat. Two held only farthings and pennies but the other two were richer – one had four shillings and a half groat alongside its pennies; the last took my breath from me so that I had to stand and stare at all the winking gold. The king and all his court – a sovereign with his crown and a host of angels besides. It was more money than I had seen in all my life. It made me suddenly afraid and I began to pace my patch of turf, darting glances at the trees and bushes. Were there eyes watching me even now? I had been too tangled in my own misfortune to consider that the wild men of yesterday might return to find their comrade, or for that matter that the townspeople and constables might comb the common after the outrage, but now, with the tussock-strewn mound beside me and the gold lazily gleaming in the evening sun, it struck me that no band of cut-throats would let this lie. If they thought him absconded they would be after him; I had to hope they thought him taken, for then they would make themselves scarce. Still, I should not linger. Tomorrow, at first light, I would have to go.

'And what to do with you?' I said to the peaceful mare. Jacob would have known how much she was worth in money; I had no idea. More, much more than my life would be valued at. The saddle alone was a beautiful thing. But I could not sell her. She would be known at once as stolen. There was likely a reward posted for her. If I knew where and how to look, there'd be dealers who would take her anyhow, but even if I knew how to find them they would play me false as soon as winking. The proper thing no doubt would be to return her, but that was as risky as the other – there would be too many questions; I should be seized long before I could show myself to be honest. However much it pained me I would have to leave her to her own fortune.

I did not dare sleep in the cottage, but made myself a bed of fern a little way off, where I would not be seen. When I woke the sun had risen. For a while I lay awake and staring, unsure where or what I was, the clothes unfamiliar on my limbs. On a fallen trunk across from me a flecked dunnock lighted by a fledgling, passing food from beak to beak. The sight pierced me with sorrow; at once I was myself again, remembering. Or not myself quite – my short hair bristled at my neck and my legs looked long and thin in the breeches. I stood up, stiffly. I should have left already. It struck me how far there was to go, how little ground I had covered. What was I doing lingering here? Even now my husband could be rising from his sickbed, calling me.

A half dozen trails led from the clearing, deer paths, boar tracks, as likely to lead me to a briar mound as any human road. How far had I wandered yesterday? I had no idea. Not far, probably, I was too weak to cover much ground and as aimless as a blown leaf. Worcester lay to the east, that I was sure of, almost sure. Beyond that I had no idea which way to go, nor how far the wastes extended. I stowed the money about me and packed my own clothes in the boy's bag and tied it to my back; the valuables I placed in my satchel. Then I went to the mare and unhitched her bridle and leant my forehead on hers to say goodbye. In a way I did not understand her coming had offered me comfort, even strength and I was grateful. Perhaps she felt the same. At any rate when I turned away she followed me, pausing puzzled when I told her to go back, and then approaching, nudging my shoulders softly with her nose.

At length I yielded and took her by the reins. I would take her as far as the road, I thought, it was better so, she was not fit for the wilderness any more than I. Now and then she inclined her head to me or nickered for affection or for oats. After an hour or so of hesitating this way and that, but ever making east towards the sun, we reached a holloway that climbed from the common into oak woods. I could have left her there, but in truth I'd found her a good companion. My pack pulled at my shoulders, why not fasten it to her back a while, I thought, at least to the top of the rise? The lane pitched so steeply; with every step my legs grew heavier. I felt drained of blood, weaker than a day-old lamb. Barely a third of the way up I had to pause to lean against the bank. At this pace I would not reach Worcester by nightfall. I would grow sick.

I glanced at the soft saddle. As if she understood me the mare shuffled alongside the bank. A rock poked out like a mounting block. I hesitated, then swung myself stiffly up. Jacob had taught me how to ride – on tired nags and broad-backed shires, never on a stirrer such as this; I felt the power of her back beneath me, but she moved as smoothly as a gliding swan. Over the crest our track joined a wider road sloping gently to the north and east. All the country was laid out before me and a gentle breeze whispered to my spirits to lift; the mare picked up her pace.

We ambled down. The slightest pressure from my legs and she fell into a trot, but the lilt was easy. By and by we passed a straggle of farmhands who doffed their caps and made way and did not meet my eyes, but swept their gaze approvingly across the horse. It was only a crumb in my mouth, but I knew the taste of power from it – to be above the herd of men, with all that sleek strength beneath me, any moment ready to break free of the caterpillar pace of days and hours, throw the miles like grit behind us. No wonder men grew giddy with it and forgot that it was only borrowed might. 'A little further,' I said to the mare, 'a little further yet and then I'll walk.'

The high road when we reached it was wide and easy, meandering with the Teme to the city. There were more travellers now and eyes more ready to appraise me as I passed. However much I liked the elevation I knew I must get down and walk again and find a means to give her up. I'd passed farms and two fine manors with parks rolling down to the road, but I was wary of stopping. By noon, however, I judged I must be within a few miles of the city and could wait no longer; every furlong risked discovery. There was no help for it; I would have to leave her by the road.

We stopped in the shade of a spreading elm; I was debating with myself whether to loop her to a branch or leave her be when a shadow touched me. I turned round. It was a woman of middle age, in a costly black riding dress and a high-brimmed hat with a red plume. There was a weary looking man behind her, leading a grey palfrey. 'You, boy, is that your master's horse?'

Fear bloomed in me and wilted just as fast. She was pointing her crop at me, but had eyes only for my mare.

'Madam, it was my guardian's horse,' the words tripped out freshly, like water from a spring, 'but he died on Easter Day. I am to sell it in the city, tack and all, to pay my mistress's debts.'

She pursed her lips. 'You may sell it to me now and save yourself the trouble. My man, William, has had a fall. Horse just buckled underneath him. I want her checked out. How old is your mare?'

William had already begun assessing the mare, pulling up her lips to check her teeth.

'She's seven years old.'

'Twelve if she's a day,' William answered. His eyes did not leave mine; they were half closed; he did not need to hold my jaw to know me for a liar.

I turned away from him to the lady. 'Madam, forgive me, but this is hasty,' I said. 'My mistress said to go to Worcester, to find out a dealer she knows.'

The woman drew herself up and pointed her crop at me. 'I am Lettice Cowarne of Lulsley Court. Lulsley Court, tell your mistress that.' She looked over at William. 'I will give you three pounds for it. Pay the boy, William.'

'With your leave, Mistress,' William said, stepping up to me and leaning his face close into mine, so that all my uneasiness returned. 'What was the name of your guardian, boy?'

I was not such a fool as that. I had read the name stamped on the saddle, but I flinched all the same. They might be neighbours for aught I knew. 'George Overton sir.' I tried to sound indignant.

'And what was he and where was he?' He pointed a finger at my chest. I could barely breathe.

'A respectable man, sir,' I squeaked, 'as any that tread ground. He was a draper.'

'Come, come,' the lady put in, to my relief. 'Don't play the constable, William, it doesn't become you. And no man should look a given horse in the mouth as they say. The boy has an honest face. He'd hardly parade the beast on the highway like this if he was a common thief. We have company tonight; I must get home.'

I bit down on my eagerness as William counted out the gold and I caught myself before I bobbed a curtsey. I could not bear to look at the mare as he led her off. Till they were almost out of sight and the road curved round a hill he turned and stared back at me. If he wheels her round, I thought, I'll jump the hedge and run. Did he know me for a girl, was that it? Or was it that he guessed the horse was pilfered?

Either way, by two in the afternoon I was within sight of the walls of Worcester and then its beautiful six-arched bridge. There were people coming and going all about me. I mingled myself among them, marvelling at the towers and walls. I was a free man, and rich to boot. Within a yard or two I had companions.

'Young sir, do you need a bed? I know an inn.'

'Here, sir, I think you dropped this?'

'A fine young fellow like you must be wanting work?'

Coney catchers, one and all. I gripped my bags close and ducked them, blessing Mary of Bromyard for teaching me to hide my gold.

17

When I was a girl I had longed for the city, but in my mind it was always Gloucester, where my father had first been rich and then been ruined; where my mother had been hanged. Later, when the gallows sought me in my turn, I was taken to Hereford and then to Ludlow, but that was not a time, of course, for looking about me; on such a journey you see little but walls and faces and the filth of the gaol. Turning away from the crowds now I found myself in a damp, close alley where the reek of piss and rot recalled the cells. I had to steady myself on the grimy wall. As soon as I had found my way back to the light I set about getting a bed and safety.

There was a widow, I was told, in a narrow house near the corn-market, who would let me a room for as long as I had money in my pocket. She looked me up and down as though doubting I knew the feel of a penny, but when I paid her a week in hand she grew civil and led me, wheezing, up the tightening stairs, to a narrow box with a bed and shutters that gave out on the street. 'Would I be wanting my dinner brought up?' she asked me, with her hand leaning heavy on the latch, 'or would I share with the others in the parlour?' 'The parlour,' I said quickly, to her evident relief.

My fellow boarders were apprentices, full of gripes and chatter. At first they eyed me with open curiosity and tried to tap me for talk, but they soon decided I was a sullen fellow and let me alone. The pottage was good enough, but my stomach was knotted and I could only manage a little. I went back up to the room and turned the key.

I flung myself on the bed to think what I should do, now. Rowland's John had told me Jacob was attacked in Lancaster, but was he there, still? Lancaster, the north, they were only words to me – a place where wars and rebellions were born. What kind of monsters lay between here and there? A city was too broad a goal. Dear God, he might have left already! To travel so far and find he had left before me – I should be lost, my heart would wear away. What if all my wanderings proved bootless and Jacob returned to an empty cottage wondering what I had become, called a horned man wherever he went? I prayed for some vision to show me where he was, but nothing came. There were only the flies jagging above me, turning lazily round and round as though spinning on the axis of my breath, or the fruitless circles of my thought.

Had I brought this on myself? In the village they would say that I had lost the child because it was born of sin; it could not stay, the poor thing, with a maimed soul; my losing it was proof enough I had lain with the Steward. The room was stiff with heat; I could hardly breathe. Even with the shutters open the air barely moved; I kept so still I fancied myself like the dead boy I had covered over with soft earth and flowers. Perhaps I deserved rest less than he – hadn't I taken his wrongs upon me when I filched his things? I was like the sin-eater who passes the bread over the corpse; the boy had gone into the earth innocent and I had dressed myself in all his sins.

The chandler who had been kind to me, the farmer and his wife, the draper – what right had I to any of their pennies or their gold? Instead of taking off like a rustler I should have returned the money to the constables, discovered if my companions had been left stripped and trussed like swine – or if their throats were cut. Would you even know me Jacob, lying here in breeches stuffed with stolen gold? Your thinking was never muddied with dishonesties as mine has always been; when a path was tangled you hacked at it to make it clear, you did not seek to go round or under as I did. In my place you would give back the money as best you could – but you would not be in my place; you would have stayed and fought with the rest even till your throat was cut. And that is not fair either, for what good was I at fighting and how, being a man, how could you know my fears or the bleak understanding when my womb was torn? 'You have no right to judge me,' I said to his stern face.

At last the baked air cooled and the shapes of things softened in the twilight and I drifted into sleep. It was not Jacob, but the others who leaked into my dreams. I saw the farmer's wife, lying in her bed, shaking with fear at every shadow that leapt from her candle; the draper's hand trembling over the cloth, worse, cowering behind his door when the creditors came knocking; Mary, the chandler's daughter, forced to marry from the loss of stock. In my visions they became mixed up with my father, drunk in the gutter, stumbling through the dark to his bitter bed, cursing Fortune's wheel that cast him down and crushed him like a fly in the dirt; at dawn once again dragging himself upright to the workshop, spitting the crabbed flux from his mouth. There were mornings when I brought him ale and bread and watched him in the shafts of light that fell through the open door sitting at the spoke horse or bevelling the angle of the felloe ends without barely a need to measure. He answered Fortune with the work of his hands as though he could not let alone what bruised him, seeking the beauty of the wheel's roll when it was true and just.

I woke to the sound of rain on the tiles above me and a creeping dawn. The thatch I was used to did not patter so; I liked the sound, being warm and dry beneath it. The bleeding had stopped. I sat up; it did no good to laze and mope. What was done was done and after all it was not I who had pulled a knife or threatened any Christian soul, nor taken their goods – the horse aside – and I pushed that out of mind; they were none of them such gudgeons as to stuff all their wealth in their purses as I had lately done. Below me the sounds of voices and wheels, dogs and chickens began to thicken. Even if I had not known, the bustle would have told me it was a market day.

From the window I watched the people on the street. The men, especially, how they walked and bantered. All my life I had lived with men; my father, Jacob, and yet it seemed to me that I had never noticed how they moved – the swagger in the walk, the spread stance talking, even the way they flung words into the air struck me as different. I thought of Jacob walking. He did not swagger, there was a gentleness in everything he did, but when I stood and walked along the room, positioning my gait to his – as much as my lame leg would allow me – I felt how his stride, the easy poise of his hips and chest spoke of a strength, a confidence that the world was there to be embraced. Whereas I – at even my most defiant – had learned I was allied to shadows, to stooping, to the circumference of a skirt. 'Look,' I made his spirit say to me, positioning his hands upon my shoulders, 'this is how to stand now you are a man, this is how you hold your chin.'

I ventured out and bought a length of soft lawn to bind up my breasts and some good linen drawers. I had my hair cut short and close. I practised pushing my voice from the back of my throat so that it grew harsher and deeper. Then, directed to a draper, I bought a whole set of clothes to appear as a sober scrivener or clerk, top to toe, slops and doublet and all. I was lucky, for he had a set that fit me and I did not have to risk standing for his measure.

The boy's things I kept, all but the doublet. The draper swindled me on the price, but I was glad to be rid of it; it held the scent of him so keenly each breath felt like a haunting. The streets were busy with buyers and sellers, to advance at all was to weave a dance in and about – a woman with a tray of pies, a man with a load of pins, a gaggle of apprentice blacksmith boys who snickered as I tripped out of their path. It made me pause – did they mark my counterfeiting? I stepped into the lee of an inn gate to let my cheeks cool. A butcher's man crossed near me with a brace of fowl, into an onion girl, upsetting her and her load both.

'Look where you go, you stinking jade,' he shouted, shoving her aside, although it was he who'd usurped the path. Every way I looked men forged ahead and women dodged them and although the lesser man gave way for the greater, all in all each sought to go straight like an arrow or a knife. Even bowing a greeting there was a stage laid claim to, a pageantry of air, so different to our dipping. I must be like a bull calf I told myself, bred to plough straight, be the earth cledgy or frozen.

That night, after my landlady's broth, I found a tavern where I could sit near the back of the low room and watch the company. The market had brought fiddlers, or perhaps they always played, and one after another men and women too stood up to sing. I knew many – who doesn't know the jest of Robin Hood? – others were new to me, but not to the company; they raised their cups in readiness when the singer began 'King Lear and His Three Daughters' or 'Henry Martin'. I drew myself into the gloom of the wall to listen. One of the minstrels stepped forward.

'It was a gallant knight,'

He sang.

'loved a gallant lady,'

And his voice was so deep and mournful I was afraid I would betray myself by weeping.

'My love believe not,'

The abandoned lady pleads with her knight.

'Come to me and grieve not, wantons will thee
    throw.'

'Oh, it's a long one that,' the girl said, bringing me another pot of beer, 'he'll be at it a quarter of an hour.'

'Hold your peace,' I said, losing the story and straining to pick it up – the lady abused, abandoned, but so constant that when he is taken falsely for a murder she offers her life for his. He is condemned to walk before her to the scaffold but he cannot lift the sword to strike her; it is only their loving embrace, her thousand kisses at the scaffold that moves the ruffians to pity, so that the cruel harlot is exposed. The words were weak enough, but all the pain and pity of love was in his voice; when he had done my eyes brimmed. To lay down her life so piteously! I would do it too, I thought, if only I could. To my surprise the girl was back watching me.

'Look at you,' she said, not unkindly, 'have you never heard a bit of heartbreak before – or is it your own case you're sorrowing after? I don't care for that one anyhow. It's always the whore gets hanged. Give me a tune with a jig in it, less of your maudlin ballads. You need to go easy,' she nodded at the beer, 'not used to it, are you? I'll bring you some pie.'

She was right, it wasn't like the ale at home, the room had gone dizzy, it rocked a little as though a wind had caught it. When she came back I grabbed her hand.

'Will you sit with me a while?' I asked.

She laughed and glanced back at the bar. 'It'll cost you,' she said, plumping herself down.

I tried to remember what it was I had to say.

'You've a nice hand,' she said, turning it over, lifting my wrist to her lips. 'Are you lonely?' Her voice was cooing, soft. 'I don't go with men, you know.'

'Nor I with women,' I said, smiling. The pie was good; it had begun to clear the fog from my vision and I turned to look properly at the girl. She was younger than I, although it might have been the dancing candle and the dimples round her mouth. There was a flush on her cheek. I pressed my hand to her neck, to feel for the King's evil. She caught at my hand, laughing.

'I have a room,' she said.

'Do you sweat at night?' I asked.

She stood up affronted. 'I've a mind to slap your chops and have you thrown out on your backside.'

'Sit, sit,' I said. 'Forgive me. You mistake me – I was apprenticed to an apothecary – I cannot help searching out ailments. Please, sit down and talk to me.'

I placed a coin on the table. Two. She sat again, but a little stiffly. 'There en't nothing wrong with me.'

'No,' I said. 'No, course not, you're as pretty as a daisy. My name is Jabez.'

'I am Mercy,' she said. This was better. The fiddlers started up again, a reel this time and some started pushing back chairs for dancing. 'Jabez,' she said, 'That's an old name for a beardless youth.'

'My mother bore me in sorrow,' I said, giving her chapter and verse, 'and I pray to God to bless me and let His hand be with me and He grants my prayers.'

She tilted her head a little. 'Does He so? What's your business young Jabez?'

'I'm looking for someone,' I said, for there seemed no need for lying. 'My brother. Not here – in the north, in Lancashire. My family think him dead, but I believe him living still. I mean to find him and bring him home.'

She looked at me more closely. 'Before he's hanged, you mean? No wonder the song caught at your eyes. That's a long road, even for a ready youth like you, you'd best find company if you don't want to fall prey to some ruffler or wild rogue.'

'You've seen men like that?'

'There's one, an upright man, notorious, my father said, came in bold as brass, sat picking the blood from his nails before he ate. We'd have called the constables if we hadn't been afraid. But it's not what I've seen, it's what I've heard too. Less than a week back there was a party snared at Bringsty, stripped of everything they owned and one, a draper, John Norris, stabbed through the heart.'

I was fully alert now, the singing seemed far off, in another country. Sweat broke out on my forehead. I leaned further back from the candle. 'They were travelling at night?'

'No, no, broad day it was, just before that storm that washed out the bridge at Bransford. A lawyer of Coventry – Overbury? Overton? – walked as far as Sapey Bridge in his underclothes like a dripping ghost. Before he left town he said he'd give two pounds to the poor for every man who swung for it, five for the youth who seized his horse. They've mustered men.'

I swallowed. 'Some good may come of it then,' I said, 'the common will be cleaned and the poor assisted.'

She stood up and leant forward, kissing me lightly on the lips, 'Oh you are a woodcock,' she said. 'I like you. It's not likely, is it, unless they find a lad whose neck will do as well as the other. They'll be long gone, halfway to Wales before the lawyer had new hose on his legs. They'll not be caught. An' if they were, he'd forget his promise in a wink, though the mayor himself had signed it.'

I got up to go then and thanking her I pressed my way through the tables to the street and all its stars.

The next morning I woke with a sore head, cursing myself for malingering. Days had been wasted. If, once I had climbed on the mare's back, I had simply turned her nose to the north perhaps I should be almost at Lancaster by now. Over breakfast I became more forgiving. I was only half newborn. Across the table the apprentice boys ribbed and railed; one pushed his neighbour playfully in the chest, another rubbed at his hair with the heel of his hand. From the corner of my eye I watched them. They were talking of a merchant's wife, who had lost a gold ring and had it found.

'It was that scryer, Talbot. Him that's come down from Oxford.'

'Scryer ...' I almost started; it was as though I were being given a message. In our first years in Hope there'd been a famous scryer who lived alone in the hills above Wormsley. He had a great water bowl whose still surface, at his incantations, offered up revelations. Whatever had been lost was called on to appear and had no choice but to show itself. There was no evil in it, for he took no payment but prayers and the gifts people left at his door. There were others too, of course, less holy; Jacob said you'd see them any market day in Hereford; men who'd profess to find a vision in a pond, a puddle, in a cup of ale. Mountebanks abounded, but that didn't make the practice false – we don't lose faith in music because a piper cannot play true. It was a kind of natural magic, a tuning in to Nature herself. My grandam told me she had dabbled a little in the way of it, till she became afraid, being a woman, how it might be used against her.

The boys were excited. I listened more carefully.

'Come down from Oxford? Came back more like. He's no more a Talbot than I am. He was born in Doldey Lane, plain Edward Kelley. John Kelley's youngest son. My master says how he doubts he was ever at the University at all. Says last he knew he was grinding poultices for old Sterton, till they threw him out for dealing with magic.'

'Well he talks like a University man. Got the devil's own wit. Fred Bains says he's after learning how to talk to angels in their own tongue.'

'He's learned sommat that's for sure. I heard Mistress Tusser was so frantic for that ring she'd have let him swive her daughter to get it back.'

'And have a go with her while he was about it.'

'He don't look like he's particular.'

'"Well, Mistress Tusser, if I'm to find your ring I must be shown your jewel."'

'"Oh but sir, why don't you try it on?"'

They were rising to go. I broke into their foolishness. 'He found the ring?'

At once they stopped laughing and looked at me, as though surprised that I could speak.

'Oh yes,' the first one said. 'He looked into her mirror and said the words and it appeared to him straight. There ain't nothing hid from him.'

They began to file out. I gazed vaguely after them. It was an answer to my prayers. If this Talbot could show where Jacob was, how much time could be saved, how much mischance averted! 'Where can I find him, this Talbot?' I called after them.

They paused in the doorway. One shrugged. 'Show a bit of gold in the street,' he laughed, 'an he'll find you.'

'Oh, he's been forgiven,' another said, 'he's back on Angel Lane at the drugger's. Sterton married his mother, you know.'

It was barely a five-minute walk. The shop was tiny, squeezed between a milliner's and a fulker's. The shelves were lined with neatly labelled jars and at the back a grizzled man stood over a mortar. He narrowed his eyes when I asked for Talbot, looking me up and down till I began to shift from foot to foot.

'I don't know any Talbots.'

'Edward Kelley, then.'

'And you'd be wanting him for?'

'There's someone I'm seeking,' I said. 'My brother.'

The man pressed his fingers together; the tips were stained brown; he continued to survey me.

'You have a tidy shop, sir,' I said. 'My poor mother was something of a herbalist, she would have relished the use of an establishment such as yours, but being buried, as we were, in the country, she had to make do. Do you have, by chance, any ointment of lesser celandine? She swore it could heal the King's evil.'

'She was right,' he said, lifting down a pot, 'If caught early. I have the roots. I could make an ointment up.'

When I came back a little later to collect it and pay, his manner, though still wary, was more forthcoming. 'And if I were to cross paths with young Master Talbot, whom shall I say was asking after him?'

Jabez, I said, realising I had only half a name. 'Jabez Foxe. I am lodging at the widow's house next the Bull and Bear.'

On my way back I weighed up how long to wait. If this man Talbot could, by some good magic, show me where Jacob was, and in what state – oh how it would ease my mind! For the first time since miscarrying our child I felt hope stir. All would yet be well. An afternoon returned to me, a summer's day, a year or more ago. We had begun to believe I had conceived, my courses had not come in months, but then returning early he found me washing out some bloody clouts. He'd said nothing, but turned and headed back to the stables and I'd waited, till the stew was spoiled and the ragged sun had sunk. When he came home he held me tenderly and kissed the tears from my cheeks and we did not talk of it. The words formed in my mouth, but I did not dare utter them. 'Jacob,' I said now, 'I am not barren. I lost a child, by God's grace we can have another.'

I spent a fruitless afternoon tramping the city. Talbot's reputation grew or crashed from street to street. He had found a pig, a stolen gown, a truant boy, a baby. He spoke with angels, they whispered in his ear; he had conversations with the dead. He was a swindler, a brawler, a gambler, a forger and a thief. A tavern owner on the Sudbury road asked if I was the foreign gentleman come to pay his bill. All were agreed on one thing – he'd not been seen these two days past. I turned back to the widow's and flung myself on the narrow bed to count the flies. A headache hammered at my temples like an iron bolt. I should have asked the apothecary for willow bark and yarrow. It came of too much loitering. Tomorrow I would rouse myself at dawn and leave.

For an hour or more I lay on the bed, with half-made plans drifting in and out of my head, all the while berating myself that I couldn't seem to stir. Just as the bell for supper rang up the stairs I heard the cry of a pedlar outside my window. My bones were stiff with walking but I wrenched myself up and seized the bundle of my women's things. He was already turning past St Martin's Church when I halloed him. They were good clothes, but as he held them up to the evening light the line the blood had left showed up like a tearstain on paper and he gave me only a shilling. Returning, I felt strangely lightheaded and desolate, and my cheeks burned as though my honesty were tied up in my skirts.

I had thought to leave the ointment for Mercy in the morning, explaining it was for the swellings I had noted on her neck; but as I climbed back up the narrow stairs I decided to take it to the tavern tonight. It would be better to give it into her hands – to do otherwise would invite questions of her. Also, I realised suddenly I could not bear to be alone. It would be good to talk to my ale wench and to dull the ache in my head in thick sweet beer. I felt a hollow, empty thing. I missed Jacob, it was a wound I fretted at, that would not close, but I missed the others too, little Meg most of all. Did it cause her pain when people spoke of me, or worse, when they avoided my name? I thought of the dampness of her hair in the morning on the bed, the way her gaze had not yet learned to swerve and dodge as adults' did, but held you, moment on moment in serious study.

When I found the tavern open and Mercy not there I thought I would go home. My head beat so that I could barely think, but the landlord set a cup before me and it worked as well as willow bark. I drank it off; he set another. Before long I found I had companions and there was Mercy sitting on my knee. I was losing at dice.

'This is Jabez,' she said to the big bearded man next to me. 'He's in quest of his brother who I think must be a rascal and not worth saving, to leave such a pretty youth as this.'

'At your service sir,' the big man said.

'I think he should stay here and get himself a sweetheart,' Mercy said, pouring me more beer. The room was a rocking boat; I held tight to her to keep from falling.

'You'll be needing a guide,' the big man said.

'You will,' a scrawny grog-nosed man put in as he scooped up the ha'pennies I'd laid out.

'I must go to bed,' I said, but the words would not form properly in my mouth.

'Shush,' Mercy said, tipping the cup to my lips and kissing the drops that dribbled down my chin. 'Such smooth skin – I think a maid passed dough across your face and now you'll never grow whiskers.'

I patted her face away but it came back, with her eyes swimming in her head. 'Don't, I beg you,' I said.

The dice spattered over the table. With a great effort I pushed Mercy from my knee and scraped my chair back. The room was full of eyes turning towards us. I'm drunk, I thought, glancing from Mercy – wobbling in and out of view, laughing like a tumbler's bell – to the two men across the table. They seemed to have two heads apiece; it was very funny.

'You owe us money,' the scrawny one said. 'A groat.'

'A shilling,' the fat one put in.

'Two.'

'He'll pay you, he'll set you right, won't you Jabez?' she said; then her voice cooed at my ear, 'you better pay, dear, Hugh's friend here sliced off a man's ear that crossed him in a game.' Somewhere, I saw that the big one was balling his fists and I was afraid, but they seemed so like players on a cart and poor ones too – rogues aping menace with their masks all loose and the doltish audience mooning round. What did it matter anyway? The pain in my head was returning, like a rope twisting at my eyes. I squinted a grin.

'You're a pair of piss-hosed cozeners,' I said, reeling back against Mercy.

'And you sir? I know what you are,' Hugh, the scrawny one, began, poking my chest. I looked down at the finger, so giddily pleased it was not a little lower that I began to laugh.

'I know what you are,' he repeated, putting his hand on his knife. But I had begun to laugh, I could not stop; they took me for a fool and they were right, but no worse than they, we were a ship of fools deceiving one another into hell.

I would have undone myself quite, for the big man lumbered forward, and seized my doublet and I still laughing. Then all at once one of the listeners came into the light and seized him by the ear so that he yelped and hopped.

Scrawny Hugh stepped back. 'Let him go, Ned,' he said. 'This en't your quarrel.'

'Oh,' said the stranger, 'but you see I've decided that it is.'

A moment later I found myself outside, with my head thrust under a pump and a cold stream of water rinsing my brain clear. The sun had not quite finished going down.

'Thank you, sir,' I said, as the stranger pulled my head up between thrusts, 'please let me go, now. I am not feeling well.'

For answer he lowered his head to mine and grinned, then held me under the flow just a moment longer before he released me.

'You need another name young Foxe,' he said. 'The hounds would have you in a minute. I think you are more a cock pheasant – easy game, and not a little pretty.'

I looked at him. His saving me gave him the right to condescend, but for all that he was barely older than I was, and not a great deal taller, although thickset as a bear. His bulk sat oddly with his voice; he spoke like an educated man. 'It was my good fortune that you were by, sir,' I said, forming the words carefully in my mouth, as though speaking were new to me.

'Not fortune at all. You have been calling my name up and down the city all the afternoon. I came to the tavern to decide whether to be found.'

I turned to him in surprise and opened my mouth to speak, but could think of nothing of sense to say. Beer and pain puddled my vision, and my teeth chattered with a cold that came not from pump water but my bones.

The man was peering at me beneath his dense eyebrows. 'God's death man,' he said, 'you are falling. Let's get you to your bed.'

19

I had wit enough left to refuse to let him help me undress. The widow fussed into the room behind him.

'He's only paid one week,' she said. 'I won't bear the cost of a funeral. And what if it should be plague? I've heard the new law, I'll be boarded up, finished. This is a good clean house, I don't want sickness in it.'

'Madam,' Talbot boomed – for though he was a short man he had a voice that could silence a cockfight. 'There's no question of plague, or of dying. The boy has a fever, brought on, no doubt, by dirty linen and poor food. I, Edward Talbot shall be his surety.'

'What's that to me?' she said, a little quelled nonetheless, 'Whoever you are, he's not staying here without I have another week in hand.'

Talbot told me after that I sweated in and out of sense all night; that I recoiled when he approached, clutching my belly and screaming so loud it brought my fellow boarders to the door. In the morning I felt well enough to send him off – and to button my shirt up to my neck. Then the fever mounted again. For three days I began clear, burning but in sound mind, able to piss and drink,

even to eat a little. Then from noon the fever gripped me. By nightfall I felt close to death, babbling and weeping. My limbs ached as
though they were slowly turning to stone or clay. They were too
heavy to lift. I was the dead boy covered in elderflowers and
foxgloves with the turf piling on my chest and face. Or else I was in
the cave again with the rain a curtain before me and my belly
frayed cloth. My mother came to me with the rope round her neck
and cold lips; my father too, and that was better, he was making a
doll for me, he would cover it in lace; 'don't you worry Meg,' he said,
'I will bring you a doll to play with.' 'Aye, but can I trust you?' Jacob
said. He was always leaving; I could see his shadow in the doorway;
he was loping through the orchard; I heard his voice in the street. I
tried to heave myself up to go and reach him. Only once, in the
heaped confusion of my visions did I believe him with me, lying
naked with his leg over mine and his head on my chest. I drew my
fingers through his hair. We were both sated and weeping. 'Forgive
me,' he was saying, over and over. And I was answering, 'No.'

There were intervals of reason. Sometimes the widow appeared
briefly, to empty my piss pot and bring me drink, shaking her head
slowly or making the sign of the cross above me as though I could
not see. More often Talbot's ugly face leaned over me with a foul
brew and I cowered, thinking him a constable, or sent by Boult, or
worse, one of the Bringsty outlaws. Soon the visions shrank and I
drifted in and out of sleep, half grateful to give over any thought of
action or intent and simply let my body sink into the cot.

Then one morning I woke to the smell of warm pottage and felt
my mouth run with hunger. Talbot was standing by the bed with a
steaming bowl in his hand.

'This tick stinks,' he said. 'Get up. I'll make the flint-fisted hag
change it while you eat.'

I felt a little dizzy, but my head was clear. I dressed myself
slowly, listening to Talbot bombast the widow. He seemed a man

who was either very quiet or very loud. When he returned I looked at him warily. 'I am in your debt, sir,' I said.

'That's true.'

'Why did you help me?'

'If I said I was prompted by the tender mercy of our Lord, would you believe me? No, I thought not.' He chewed on a piece of bread and frowned. His eyes were wide-set and watchful as an owl's and his brows, too, as bushy as a horned owl's. 'Well then,' he went on. 'I'll tell you the truth. I did it on a whim. You interest me. It's a sap-brained clown, but a witty one, who falls to laughing at a man about to skewer him. When the fever took you, you wailed I was the Gorgon, petrifying your cold limbs inch by inch. Odd, to find a bumpkin bubbling Ovid. I thought to put you to bed and leave you to get better or to die, but the old woman seemed likely to throw you out to the parish and my conscience got the better of me.'

'God bless you,' I said, 'for your charity.'

'Yes,' he smiled, 'and well, it suited me these last few days to have a place certain fellows did not know of.'

My brain seemed still a little loose in my head and I had to place words like careful steps, for fear my tongue would begin running willy-nilly where it would. 'I trust you will let me pay you, sir, for your trouble.'

'As to that,' he said, 'there is no need. You have paid me quite handsomely already.'

His words made me uneasy and the smile he added, more so.

'Come,' he said. 'You're as pale as a robin's egg. Let's go out into the sun.'

We passed my landlady at the foot of the stairs. She waited for Talbot to go past. 'New bedding is extra,' she said to me.

'What?' he shouted back to her, opening the door to the street. 'And do you charge extra too for rats and fleas? I believe you are farming them – the walls seethe.'

She shook her apron, 'Go to, go to. You are a devil Edward Talbot.'

* * *

My legs felt feeble and I was glad of his arm at my elbow as he propelled me down to the river.

'So, Jabez Foxe,' he said, as we sat down by St Martin's Gate. I started at the name, then remembered it was mine. He paused, amused. 'You could have chosen better – but we'll let that go. You are seeking someone.'

I nodded, glumly, watching the Severn swirl south. 'I have lost days and days.'

Tears leaked out of my eyes and I turned my head to hide them. 'Martha, Martha.' I said to myself, 'remember your doublet and hose.' Swallowing, I turned to him. 'Tell me sir, was I raving?'

He nudged me and winked. 'It's lucky for you I am not a judge. You as good as paid for the rope – it was well I kept the widow off those first two nights. Hour after hour you sobbed that your whole body was clotted with blood – cried that you were sorry and yelped if I came near you, as though I were a constable. I'm not very particular, Jabez, and we all have sins to atone for, but I hope if you murdered a man you had good cause?'

I stared at him in horror. 'You could not think I would kill?'

He snorted. 'How could I not think it? I barely know you. You're a fresh young thing, but I'd wager it's an overheated conscience made you ill. And you're no stranger, I think, to a gaol cell.'

'I talked of that?'

'No, not to any purpose, but your ankles are marked by shackle scars.'

I lumbered myself up away from him and stood watching a barge unloading bales of cloth at the water's edge.

Talbot walked up behind me.

'What else do you know?' I said. I didn't turn round. If he had seen my ankles, what other parts had he seen? 'Do you know what I am?'

'What you are? You are Jabez, or George, or Barnabus. The name's all one. I know you for a thief.'

I forced myself to turn round and look him in the eye. The same amused, keen stare. So, I thought, that much he knows. Enough to ruin me; yet he has not done so.

'Come, come,' he said, 'shake hands. We are already in business anyhow.'

I raised my brows in a question.

'The widow was ready to throw you out and so I paid her two weeks' rent. Naturally, I had a little look around for reimbursement. Stop jittering, I left everything where it was, all but a dagger – and a little silver cross that has proved most merciful to both the widow and to me. There is a little left over, enough to pay for the first leg of our journey...'

'*Our* journey?'

'You mumble like a rotten-toothed mummer at a country show. You wish to travel north; you have money but are in need of a guide to help you find what's lost. That is my business. It also happens that it suits me to go north, but just at present I am short of funds. You may be my assistant.'

I sat down again and stared at the wide brown water and tried to take in what he'd said. It would mean protection; I would not have to face the road alone again. I'd have a guide, one who knew not only how to unfold what was hidden, but how to thread a route together. All this flashed before me, but I was wary. It was too sudden. 'No.' I said. 'I am grateful to you Master Talbot, and would very much like to engage your services as a scryer before you go, but as to travelling north with you, I would rather trust to myself.'

He grinned broadly. 'I like you more and more Jabez-George-Barnabus – Master What's-your-name. You don't trust me. I don't either, and the devil take me if I trust you. If you come with me I'll scry for you, but only if you come. There's a queue of creditors at my door and I find I am too nice to relieve you of the rest of your loot. With you or without you I'm off tomorrow. But have it as you wish. If you change your mind you may meet me at the Foregate by eight o clock. I won't wait.'

He clapped me on the back and turned back towards the gate and the city walls. It was only then I noticed that he too had a slight roll when he walked.

20

There was a fine early morning drizzle and so I waited under the jetty of a new-built baker's shop and watched the stream of people passing in and out of the city. How many, I wondered, wore false faces for the world as I did, as to a degree I'd always done. Being a boy now I could squat on my haunches on the public road and did not have to find a stool to prop me. In the grey light what I was about to do struck me as far beyond folly – me, a married woman, putting my trust in a man half the city thought a trickster. Was I a gull, flattered by his interest? No, I told myself, it wasn't that; he had been open in his bargain with me. I waited.

A clock struck a quarter after eight; there was no sign of Talbot.

After he left me by the river the day before, I had gone back to check my possessions. He had told the truth about that, at least. Nothing was gone but the dagger and the silver cross. It seemed apt after all I had done that I should lose them. I spent part of the afternoon sewing the rings and the chain severally into the lining of my shoes and doublet; the sovereigns I distributed likewise. Then I wrote a letter to Owen at the Cathedral school in Hereford, sketching my story, or the parts that would not accuse me if another read them. It seemed important that at least one living soul knew what I was about.

Talbot was right at least that I should be moving. The widow did not shed a tear at the news, but followed after me up the stairs, grumbling about the fresh bedding wasted, that she would never have let me a room if she had known I was confederate with that rascal Talbot.

'I've enquired after him. He's a courtesy man. None of the respectable inns will let him at the door. And when he's not fleecing the coat off a stranger's back he's taking gold for conjuring and such like. He's the devil's kin. You'll part with him boy, if you love God and hate trouble.'

I sat on the bed and waited for her to cease. It seemed she would rattle on till Judgement Day with her tiresome prattle, but after all a coin quieted her. There was some justice in what she said. He'd as much as admitted he lived like a seed that waited for the wind to blow him where it would. There was a restlessness about him, a recklessness – I had marked that much already. Perhaps, he had seen an echo of the same in me, but it was only an echo surely, of a voice in me long since quieted. Jacob had stilled me; he was a clear deep pool where things retained their proper shape, only purer, rinsed by the clarity of his gaze and thought. In his eyes I could settle, I was not forever shifting, yearning. Talbot would unfix my thinking. Even as a boy it would not be proper to travel with him. I could feel how he would wrap me round with words; he would tempt into doubt and risk.

I drifted into sleep with a decision made; in the morning I would find a boat going north to Shrewsbury. Once there I would hire a horse and find out if there were another scryer who could help me, and if all failed and Jacob was gone south again, I would follow after. And if, a whisper did not need to say, if he has left on the journey to his long home what then? Then I will be like

Orpheus, I thought, and cross the black river into hell itself to peti-
tion his release and I would not look back, but trust him to plant his
footsteps in my own till we were safe on our own ground again.

I dreamt that night that we were back in the apple orchard that
slopes down from the stable yard towards the village. It was a day I
remembered, not long after we had moved to Hope, when our days
were gilded with newness. We had no ladder so when we had
picked the fruit within reach Jacob bent for me to climb up. All the
summer blazes were in the red-flecked apples and the air was thick
and sweet; drunken wasps licked out the windfalls. Hold steady, I
said, and pulled myself up so that I stood barefoot on his shoulders.
With his hands circling my ankles and a bough to brace my waist I
tossed the apples one by one to a boy who hopped at Jacob's feet to
take my place. Someone got out a fiddle and Jacob tapped his foot
to make me sway and laugh. I am at home, I thought, delighted; this
is what it is like to be happy. Then, perhaps it was the boy, perhaps
the mush of apple on the ground, but Jacob lost his footing and my
feet slipped. It can only have been an instant, he wheeled round to
catch me as I fell – a second too late; I slipped through his arms and
fell forward on the grass. The fiddler stopped at the sight of the girl
falling out of the tree; I heard the sudden hush – but there was
nothing broken. I laughed and clambering up, brushed down my
skirts; Jacob pulled me to him and kissed me on the mouth and the
pickers cheered.

I woke with the scent of apples still around me and the touch of
Jacob's lips so present that I closed my eyes to sleep again and find
them, but the dream had gone. There was only the sounds of the
street and the boarders lumbering down the stairs for breakfast.
The dream was clear – this was a smaller risk than venturing alone;
it was a chance to leave at once. I would meet Talbot after all, I
thought.

The half hour sounded. It seemed Talbot had thought better of

it. I waited so long the baker cursed me for deterring trade and I
was obliged to buy a pie. Carts and carriages came through the gate,
but no hobbling scryer. I would have to go alone, after all. When, at
last, the rain let up I stepped out and turned to wave a farewell to
the city. He was there, in the shadow of the gate, watching me, on
the back of a piebald mare. From his stillness I think he had been
there a good while, too. Seeing that I marked him he gestured at the
chestnut by his side.

'Get up,' he said.

'You have horses!'

'We are both of us lame, of course I have horses. You owe me a
gold sovereign. It would be more, if I had not been lucky. They
belong to an associate of my brother Tom.'

I was astonished at this confidence that I should join him, when
only yesterday I had refused his company, but I already knew him
well enough to keep silent, being sure I would get only riddling
answers. Once again, I wondered at my being alongside this man; a
look would tell you that he was no gentleman, but not a poor man
either. The lace at his cuffs and neck sat oddly on him; it was altogether too dainty for his face. He looked at people on the road with
no regard to rank; whoever caught his eye he met their gaze and it
was they who looked away. I remembered how he'd twisted the
bully's ear in the tavern. What must it be, I thought, to go through
life without cowering? I was done with being fearful.

It felt good to be in the saddle, ambling through the suburbs
above the smatter of mud and the hawkers and the mingling
thieves. A lady went past on a white palfrey; her clothes were as fine
as a countess's and her servant wore livery. Ah lady, I thought, you
might have a silk feather in your cap, but your legs are crooked up
sideways while mine rest either side of my horse's easy flank. I
smiled warmly at Talbot as he stared after her, appraising her
worth.

'What is my horse's name?' I asked.

'Juno, which makes her a jealous mistress.'

'Which makes me Jove,' I said.

'The king of the Gods, and not yet a whisker on your chin. Come, we will stay in Bewdley tonight, at the house of a friend of mine.'

'But that is barely more than a dozen miles. Can we not go further?'

With a quick lunge he seized my reins, pulling poor Juno to a jolting halt. All his good humour was gone; his face had an angry flush.

'I plucked you back from death, peasant. Remember that. And a word to the constable while you lay sweating about the glimmer in your bag and those fine legs would have been in chains again.'

He put his horse to a trot; I waited a moment, watching his square back, his thick neck. I must, I thought, be careful.

* * *

We stayed in Bewdley for four days, at the house of a ropemaker – John Smallbone – a rough man, whose wife had died two years before. He had two male servants, as gruff as himself; neither he nor they concerned themselves with the children, a boy and a girl, as filthy as the rushes we slept on in the hall, scuttling under the feet of the men and boys running the sisal along the rope walk. When he noticed them, Smallbone bawled at them for being idle, useless things; they took care to keep a distance from his hands. One afternoon the boy was not quick enough; Smallbone discovered him sat with his book among the peas he'd been sent to pick. The clout sent him reeling onto the dry earth and split his lip.

Smallbone turned to Talbot. 'Sometimes I think his mother must have opened her purse to a mincing player. What are you,' cuffing at the boy's tears, 'some little whoreson, got by a milky priest? One thing I can't bear the sight of, that's effeminates.'

Talbot smiled narrowly and I said nothing, standing behind Smallbone's immense back. I'd seen how his lip curled at the span of my hand when I took his in greeting. 'Got yourself a catamite, Kelley?' he'd whispered, so that I could hear.

'Why does he call you Kelley?' I asked later as we were lying down to sleep in the hall – there was no spare chamber.

'It was my name.' Talbot answered, offering nothing else.

The second evening they were locked in conference. Other men arrived. Through the crook of an open door I saw Talbot arranging papers on a table, Smallbone holding a candle over them, his small eyes gleaming. Afterwards they went to the tavern. I was not asked, nor did I want to be; there was a whiff of conspiracy about it. It was a market day and the streets were busy; both men came back with skinned knuckles, Smallbone a bleeding cheek, both were loud with ale and the breaking of noses. I had seen such giddiness in men at a cockfight; it was no better than the slaver of a dog. However long I spent in breeches I would never learn it.

Early the next morning I left Talbot to his snoring and walked out over the arched bridge to the other side of the Severn to look back at the town climbing the hill on the western bank. Every street laid out to view, as though it held no secrets. The sun rose behind me and threw its glitter on the houses so that for a brief while it seemed that they were made of gold.

'It is just that the place is new,' Talbot said at breakfast. 'A score more years and it will be as stained as a drab's skirts and its golden mornings as tainted.'

He rubbed at his cheek; it was swollen. 'You were fighting last night,' I said.

'It was a choleric night.'

'What?' he said, when I made no reply, 'do you disapprove? Are you my keeper now?'

'I am eager to be gone, that's all. If you are bound over for brawling ... Never mind. It's none of my business.'

'No,' he said. 'It isn't, Jabez-George-Barnabus. Perhaps I have changed my mind anyhow; perhaps I may stay here and go into business with our gentle host. Smallbone is a clod and a stinking one at that, but he knows how to turn a profit. He says he has a merry widow of a sister with a comfortable purse.'

I didn't laugh at the joke: tavern talk, cunts and money. I looked at him across the table, there was something disproportioned about his face – it was as though his eyes had been mistakenly fitted to a ruffian's nose and jaw. He watched me now with a kind of gleeful cruelty to see how I would respond.

'I wish you joy of her,' I said. 'And your fine noose-maker of a brother.' I stood up.

'Where are you going?'

'To prepare Juno. There is no use in my delaying if you are staying put.'

Before he could answer a servant appeared at the door and gestured to him. 'My master wants you,' he said.

As he followed the servant out of the door Talbot turned to me. 'The horse isn't yours to take,' he said.

The horses at least were tranquil and well-rested. I had half a mind to seize my possessions and saddle up, but then I noticed the ancient manservant watching me.

He grinned with all of his four teeth. 'Thinking of flitting with the horse, was you? Wouldn't if I were you. My master would pound you to a paste and Kelley, Talbot that is, would put a curse on you to make you hobble on both legs.'

'I'll go when I please,' I said, but my voice had a quaver in it that betrayed me. The truth was that I did not feel strong and the prospect of following the road alone frightened me. I pressed my face into Juno's warm flank and smelt Jacob's hay-rich smell. Oh, how I missed him! Every lonely day. I was a fool to think that I would find him, and this was a fool's journey, but what could I do? I could not go back now if I wanted to, and I didn't want to. Could I ever live so quietly again? First I must find him; there would be time enough then to think about a future. I must find him. I would tramp north until the mists and the mountains dissolved me into a voice, crying on the wind.

By the afternoon I had recovered myself. If Talbot had resolved to stay I would buy Juno from him; he would not refuse gold. I sat down under a walnut tree and for the first time in days I read the book I had taken from the Steward. The stories twisted together like Smallbone's rope. I read how a king of Crete's wife made love to a bull and bore a monster that the king, Minos, shut away in a labyrinth more finely wrought than a spider's web, feeding him young Athenian men until Minos's daughter Ariadne fell in love with one of them; she showed him how to leave a trail of linen behind him to lead him out of the maze. I leaned against the crevassed bark and looked up at the sun playing through the leaves. Poor Ariadne, who saved her prince, but had no safety rope to help herself when he was fickle. I didn't notice Talbot approach until his shadow fell across my legs.

'What are you reading?'

'About the minotaur.'

'Ah,' he said, 'Ariadne, waiting for her lover to come back to her, only for him to cast her off with nothing but the salt wind and the gulls for company.'

'Yes, I don't like to read that part, where he abandons her.'

'Left her weeping without a second thought, although she had saved him from a wandering death, from wasting away in darkness.

But Bacchus found her and comforted her and set her in the stars. So it ends well, I suppose. I've often wondered though... '

'Yes?'

'All those mortals made celestial. It's a desolate kind of glory.' He flung himself down on the grass beside me.

We sat in silence for a moment with the thought. It was strange to be talking to another soul like this, about a book, about ideas. Even more so to be talking to a man who, however he had come by it, was learned as I could never hope to be. He spoke to me as to another student, almost as an equal. How fine that was! If only for that I would have pardoned his coarser side and kept company with him, but I would not tarry. 'Master Talbot,' I said softly, 'I cannot stay here. Will you sell me Juno?'

'You should have given him a thread to follow, little Jabez. Not that it will make any difference, of course. The minotaur has probably had him, and if it didn't, he'll go where he chooses. One way or another we're alone.'

The words seemed more pitying than cruel and his voice was flat. All the spiteful energy of this morning had drained from him. 'Have the horse,' he said. 'I paid for her with your loot. Or wait for me a day and I'll come with you.'

'You're not staying?'

'My head aches. The gold that should purify us turns us into rotten meat. Sometimes I hear devils whispering at my ears and when I pray to God's ministers to defend me a battle begins inside my own head. Did the devil ever send you visions little Jabez?'

There was an urgency, an intensity in his eyes that I could not help responding to, if only because he appealed to me as someone who could understand. 'Perhaps,' I said. 'But I have had a vision sent by an angel too, it saved a boy from dying in the snow.'

'I am at war with my own soul. Satan draws me to the tavern and sets my mouth watering. He makes me a whoring knave and a brawler and then I have a thirst for darkness so thick no stars will pierce my soul with remembrance of God...'

I grasped his hand in pity, 'You should kneel and pray—' I began, but he pulled away and interrupted me.

'Spirits take me by the hand and tell me angels will reveal all to me and sometimes I think they serve God and sometimes that they serve the devil. A worm has crawled into my head.'

'Please,' I said, taking his hand again, 'pray.'

For a moment he looked at me with that strange, suffering gaze and then he shook himself, patted my arm and pulled himself up. 'I will,' he said, lumbering off towards the house.

I supped with the children that night, for Talbot declared himself fasting and Smallbone was about the town somewhere. Although I tried to win them over with smiles and chatter they stared at me warily and would not speak. At length the girl asked me if I should like to see her doll, Nan, who had a lace collar. As she passed her brother she pinched him so hard he cried out and ran straight into his father who swore and shook him for a blubbering wretch. I would be glad, I thought, to leave this house.

21

The next morning, at first light, Talbot was shaking my shoulder. There was water dripping from his hair and he smelt of clay.

'Come,' he said. 'I am ready to look for your 'brother'. I have purified myself in the river. Follow me.'

He led me east, over the bridge and up onto soft downland towards the town of Kidderminster. Though his pace was quick I found I could keep up; I was relieved but at the same time it seemed wrong, almost, how soon my body could heal and forget. After less than a mile we encountered a small round pond.

'Here we wait for the sun,' he said.

I lay back among the cocksfoot and the quaking grass. Now that midsummer was come the land was turning hay golden. A cloud of coppers danced above my head; I lay so still some lighted on my waistcoat. The air was thick with wings and bee-rich humming. I could almost forget myself and be happy, I thought, lying here with the sun warm on my face, even with the want of him, like a tear in my chest, reminding me of the keenness of life. I was a little nervous at what I might see, but more excited than afraid. It seemed impossible to hear of ill tidings with all this flutter of life all about me.

'Why do we wait?' I asked, pulling myself onto my elbow. Talbot was kneeling.

'For the sun to rise until the mirror of the water can drink down its light and speak to me.'

'What do you mean speak? Isn't it a picture that we'll see?'

'All things send forth threads. Creation is a cloth in which all is woven – nothing material or immaterial exists of itself but is woven into the whole. The world is spun from light.'

He frowned – it was clearly an effort to speak; it interrupted his prayers or enchantments. It seemed as I watched him that he was weaving a door of air to step from the swaying grasses and the butterflies, towards the light itself. He bent his head and crossed himself many times and then, taking me by the hand he rose and drew a circle round us on the ground next to the pool. Last of all he took a talisman from about his neck, a triangle of beaten gold inscribed with symbols and muttered over it, but I could not understand the words. It felt to me that the air was charged with spirits and I prayed in my heart that what we did was holy.

'Tell me the name of the man you seek.'

'His name is Jacob Spicer.'

'Now,' he said, 'look upon the water.'

I looked. There was the blue sky with clouds like rolled fleeces; our own two faces at the water's edge. Nothing besides. I had feared a horror, but not this. Jacob, I thought, don't be lost to me. Dead or living show yourself; even if you lie in the earth and your eyes are sunken holes and the worms crawl through your mouth I must see you. Nothing. We waited. A chill crept down my spine; it had not worked. The cloud passed and the water gleamed with sunlight; and there – suddenly – in the golden mirror I saw a figure tossing with fever. My Jacob, his cheeks flushed and the curls on his forehead wet with sweat. A hand placed a cooling cloth on his face. Bless that hand, I thought. Then it seemed the vision blinked. I saw gaunt grey fells and stone houses; he was standing there on the road with other men and the wind whipping about him. He turned towards me, stretched out his hand and smiled.

I fell to my knees, shaking. Talbot laid his hand on my head as though to bless me. 'I saw him,' I said, when I had got back to my feet and recovered breath enough to talk. 'He was ill, but now he is strong again, he was on a road with bleak hills all behind him. Did you see the same?'

He shrugged. 'I saw the slate grey north and a young man praying in a room with the shutters thrown open and the sound of children in the street.'

I felt drunk with certainty and hope and seized Talbot's face and kissed his forehead. 'Oh, you have saved my life!' I said, 'If ever I can, I swear I will save yours.'

'Bold words, little Jabez,' he said, a little amused. 'You must be ever so fond of this brother of yours.'

'Yes, I am. The world is all darkness without him. But he is alive, he's waiting for me. I saw him stretch out his hand to greet me. We could set off this afternoon.'

Talbot frowned. 'At any event, it appears he is alive still. Stop jigging so, I need to rest; my brain seethes. We will go tomorrow.'

On the way back he barely spoke and then only to tell me to let him alone. He had a headache, he said; he had work to do for Smallbone. I left him to it and strolled about the town buying necessaries. At a butcher's shop I collided with two girls with baskets on their arms. The nearest cast me a look up and down.

'I'm sorry I'm sure,' she said, giggling and cocking her head at me. 'You a 'prentice?' I blushed; she was flirting with me; even as a girl I was not used to flirting.

At supper Talbot had revived his energies but not his humour; he had the malicious glint in his eye I had seen before.

'You should stay here with me,' Smallbone said, thrusting his fork at Talbot's chest. 'That's a tidy bit of money you've made me and I could put more such business your way. Let the boy follow his goose chase on his own.'

Talbot wiped Smallbone's spittle from his doublet. 'I would go mad,' he said.

For a moment Smallbone stopped chewing and his small blue eyes narrowed; the air wavered nervously. Then he leant forward and clapped Talbot on the back. 'You're a mad bastard already.'

Talbot drained his cup of wine. 'Come John,' he said, 'Let's get drunk.'

I walked with them as far as the tavern door, then wandered up and down the few streets in the dying summer evening. I passed an apothecary's shop. The girl had taken me for an apprentice. What kind of a life might I have had, I wondered, if I had been born to breeches? Could I have run away to the city, learned a trade, become my own master? It was not impossible. Men remade themselves all the time. And why not women, too – or at least why shouldn't I? I thought of Talbot, how he grasped at life and talked of books as easily as bacon. There was a wildness about him but also a freedom in his thinking that drew me. I could learn from it.

In the close heat of the night, as we lay side by side, listening to rats in the walls, I asked him what business he had been doing with Smallbone.

'I copied documents for him.'

'Oh,' I said.

There was a silence; I thought at first he had fallen asleep, but he began again, 'I copied leaseholds and altered the terms in ways favourable to him. I am a forger, a counterfeiter, Jabez, I make false claims.'

I was silent. I knew what he was saying, but it was not altogether true, for I had seen Jacob myself, woven from the rays of the sun.

He moved nearer me, his sour breath on my face. There was enough light from a high casement to cast a glitter on his eye. I did not want to argue, so I said nothing. 'Do you judge me?' he said, seizing my shirt at the neck. 'You, with other men's rings sewn into your shirt, other men's gold in your hose. You are like Gestas, pinned to the cross next to our Lord, reviling Him.'

'You are drunk,' I said. 'Go to sleep.'

'No.' he said. 'I ask you again. Do you judge me? Think, Jabez, how easily I could kill you.'

His hand was at my throat, but oddly, I did not feel afraid. One of the verses my father loved came into my mouth. '"Whoso is partner with a thief hateth his own soul.",' I said. '"He heareth blasphemy and telleth it not forth." It is you, Talbot, you judge yourself.'

'Yes.' His grip loosened and his head fell on my chest and he was sobbing. 'Spirits talk through me,' he said, his face pressed to my shoulder and the thin blanket. 'I am like a mirror and I throw back the image of this world or the other, the spirit world that lies beyond, but I do not know, sometimes I do not know, if it is a demon or a minister of God that speaks through me and throws its images onto my mind.'

'How can it but be through God,' I said, 'if you find what is lost and mend what was broken, and if you pray, as I have seen you do, and fall to your knees and beseech God's angels for their help, as I have seen you do?'

'I think I am like glass,' he said, balling my shirt into his weeping face, 'and I have no form or colour but by reflection. You cannot know what it is to see into the world of light, to long for it, body and soul both, but be unable to step through into it.'

'I know what it is to love,' I said. 'That sounds like love.'

He lifted his head and propped himself on his elbow, his face very close to mine. Somewhere above us a board creaked and a man was snoring. 'It is beyond love, it is the light of God, the promise of a union with the light.'

'You're right,' I said, 'That is something else; I do not think I want it, not yet. I want earthly love.'

He was a looming shadow, and then suddenly his mouth pressed down on mine, softly and then harder, more urgently, and I did not know what to do, for a second, because I was a boy and because I pitied him. He rolled onto me, heavy and lean and his hands were stroking at the bindings on my chest. I felt him grow hard through the thin linen of his nightshirt and for a moment, just for a moment, I thought how easy it would be to close my eyes and make-believe him to be Jacob and take him in, to feel the good hard reach of a man inside me. But he was not Jacob. I pressed my palms against his chest and pushed him gently off, back into the dark.

'You want this,' he said, kissing my neck so that I kindled despite myself. I pushed him harder.

'No.' I said, 'I'm sorry.'

He groaned and rolled so that he lay with his back to me. After a short while he groaned again. 'Good night,' he said. He was soon snoring.

I lay on my back and stared up at the pale slip of moon which had risen above the casement. 'Jacob, forgive me,' I said up to the moon. I had erred, more grievously than before perhaps, because I felt in truth no revulsion and no shame. I saw again the vision from the pool, Jacob in the road with his hair blowing and his hand stretched out in greeting. 'You left me in spring,' I said to his smiling face, 'and now it's gone high summer and the green leaves are not salad-pale any longer but coarser, darker, from being in the wind and rain. There will be scars, dearest Jacob, when we meet again; we must be careful how we touch them.'

22

We left while the town was still mostly asleep, or eating its breakfast. Neither of us mentioned what had passed in the night. He knew I was no boy; that was clear enough, but though I wrestled back and forth with how to broach it I couldn't bring myself to speak. He was surly, sore-headed, but had made no move to expose me before Smallbone or, after we had turned north, to separate.

The good weather of the last few days had broken and a steady rain was falling; if it lasted the farmers would be anxious for the harvest, for the grain was already tall and yellow in the fields. But I was grateful, for we could pull our hats down over our eyes and avoid one another the easier. Before noon we came to Bridgnorth with its steep-sided castle bedded into the hill; beyond it a street stretched north with such galleried houses the downpour fell like a curtain through the middle of the street and we were able to dismount and avoid it. Talbot hadn't said a word to me for the fifteen miles from Bewdley, but now we were elbow to elbow; I on the outside, where every cart spewed up gutter water over my hose.

'It amuses you,' I said, noticing his face lighten each time I was smattered.

'It does.'

We neared a grubby-looking tavern, but the man who stepped out from the yard gates and offered to take our horses and dry them down while we ate looked decent enough.

'What are you doing?' Talbot said, as I handed the reins over.

'We need to eat,' I said. 'I will buy you your dinner.'

Talbot grabbed the man by the shoulder and snatched the reins back off him. 'Get you gone, pizzle-nose,' he said to him, 'before I kick your arse.' He turned to me. 'You are green indeed,' he said. 'Anyone could see he was a prigger. He might as well have been branded. Do you think a hovel like this would have an ostler waiting at every corner?'

The man had melted into an alley and my indignation with him. 'Juno,' I said to the mare, 'I apologise.' I turned to Talbot. 'Thank you.' I said. 'Forgive me. Can we not be friends?'

He spat at the ground. 'You're a skinny wretch and you make a better Jabez than a Jane,' he said, but his tone had lost its edge. 'Have it as you will. Your harlot purse is less delightful than your gold.'

It was slow-going, but at least we were no longer at odds. The road curved round old woodland and through cornfields stained with rain. At last the pelting stopped and the cloud rolled back; we were rounding the Wrekin. It loomed above us, triangular as the talisman Talbot wore about his neck and tangled with woods and ominous. Talbot told me it was dumped by a Welsh giant intent on drowning all the men, women and children of Shrewsbury by dropping his spade of earth in the river. It was a long road and the giant grew tired of walking; finding the town still out of sight he asked a cobbler directions. The old man was clever; he showed the giant his sack of worn-out shoes. Shrewsbury was such a distance, he said, he'd worn the leather of each pair through on the journey. The giant groaned and dropped his spadeful of dirt and went back home.

'Why did he want to kill so many people?'

Talbot shrugged, 'He was a giant, it is what they do. Or perhaps,' he went on, 'looking down from his cave in the mountains the giant saw the noise and filth of man and longed to wash the earth clear and clean.'

I thought of the people, going about their haggling in the marketplace and then noticing a shadow fall, thinking the sun only gone behind a cloud perhaps, but looking up to find earth sliding from the sky and the water already bubbling over its banks towards them, and the giant peering down at their panic and their scurrying as a boy watches an ants' nest he has kicked. It didn't happen, but the townspeople still look anxiously at the sky; there are always giants.

I had never ridden so far in my life; I was so weary I thought I might faint in the saddle, but I felt how any expression of weakness would please my companion and said nothing, until I could bear it no longer. We stopped in the town of Wellington at a friendly place, more alehouse than inn; it had a room above the buttery with two soft beds and a thick stew for our supper.

'You are a Talbot,' the landlady said, brightening as she set down his beer, 'you are of the family at Albrighton?'

'Distantly,' he murmured.

'Well no matter how distant, it's an honour to have you sir,' she said. 'You call if there's anything I can get you.'

'The Kelley branch, is it?' I said when she had gone.

'Quite,' he said. 'Jabez-Jane.'

'Did you know already, before last night?'

'Of course. I had to shut the door to your landlady, or the whole house would have heard your raving. You make a good youth, I'll give you that. I should call you Iphis – look him up in that book of yours.' He leaned forward over the rough table and took my chin between his fingers. 'A little androgyne. A royal child.'

'What do you mean?'

'I am a student of alchemy, I search for the philosopher's stone.'

'I've heard of it. I've heard the devil keeps it in his pocket.'

He ignored me, 'In the union of sun and moon, mercury and sulphur a child shall ensue who is an androgyne, a new creation, neither male nor female. How do you like your doublet and hose?'

'I like it very well. I can sit astride Juno; the doors of the world are open to me and I may stride through and say, "where is my seat?" Only ...'

'Only?'

'I am my husband's wife. I am afraid I will forget how to walk in skirts.'

'But not how to lie on your back. I don't think you will forget that, Jabez-Jane.'

I said nothing, but applied myself to the stew. It seemed impossible to me, now, that I could have imagined welcoming his touch, even for a moment. I was no androgyne, I was the cold inconstant moon and bright, golden-curled Jacob was the sun.

Talbot was talking again, half to himself, 'Sometimes in visions I see spirits; there is a hawk flies out of the sun; as he swoops he becomes a man, bright as Hermes, and then, when his bare feet touch the soil, he becomes a girl, beckoning me after. All is flux and change. Separateness is corruption; if I am to bend matter to my will I must learn how to undo identities. When I saw what you were I knew it was a sign.'

'A sign of what?'

'A sign that I should take you with me.'

Before I could think how to answer I noticed how his intensity, or our newness, was drawing attention. 'A drink for our friends here,' I said to the landlady, gesturing at the three men who'd been weighing us up from the next table, muttering to each other in Welsh. They could have been shouting and it would have been all the same to me, but the beer worked, for they grinned and stepped over to us to raise the Queen's health and our own.

As he banged his cup with theirs Talbot shrugged off philosophy for mirth; he called for more ale and, with a sly glance at me, led the talk towards ever greater lewdness, till it reeked like a sow's midden. The landlady brought jugs and frowned.

'Your Wrekin,' I said lamely, to bring some air, 'it's a fine hill. We were told the story of the giant.'

'Ah yes, a fine clot-brained countryman of yours,' Talbot said, 'I believe it; the hill is shaped like a shovel of dirt.'

'That's a poxy tale,' one of the men growled. His fellow said something to him in Welsh. I'm a fool, I thought; now we have offended them. I should have left them all to their boasts of cunnies and water-gates and quims. I spread my hands to pacify but there was a gleam in Talbot's eye. In a moment, I thought, he will blurt some spittle that will end in a bloodied nose. And us with fine featherbeds I've paid for.

'There's another version of the tale we prefer here,' the landlady said, coming between the men and offsetting their squaring up with her plump round body. 'Though I daresay it's less pretty, even, than the other. There were two giants making the Wrekin, but they fell to arguing, and then to fighting as men like to do. One took a swing at the other with his spade but his fellow ducked it and sent a raven to peck out his eyes. Bound and blinded he got stuffed under Ercall.'

'That's right,' one of the men said, wiping his beer-frothed mouth with the back of his hand, 'they say you can hear him weeping November nights, when the wind is high enough.'

'Aye, if you've had enough ale,' she said. By the time we retired we were all easy and friends again.

It was as yielding a bed as I had ever lain on; I listened to Talbot turn fitfully in his sleep. Before we snuffed the candle I had challenged him over the way he had goaded the men, but he'd simply shrugged. It seemed to me he had a fascination, a thirst even, for disaster; he could not let things be. He was after the unravelling of things and perhaps that was a search to comprehend and seize hold of essences as he said, but I did not think that's all it was. I remembered once coming along the lane in Hope on a high hot day, Jacob beside me, when we saw an adder curled on the warm stone near our feet, a puddle of coiled gold and black pinking. We stopped a moment to watch, as still as the snake; and the air, and the lane and the sunlight held its breath. Then Jack Robbins came up behind us and, seizing a stick, poked at the creature to pick it up; it slid into the grass. There was a smear of blood on the stone where Jack had wounded it. Talbot sought to understand creation and to be master of it, too.

It was not the giant, but Talbot's talk of androgynes that filtered into my dreams. I was a housewife once again, in my woman's clothes, and yet I was a man, I had always been a man and nobody knew, not even Jacob, for didn't I wear a petticoat? Every night I put off his caresses so that he could not know me, what I was. Then I was on the heath again, where I had seen him in the pool, there were butterflies all around me – coppers, and gatekeepers and marbled whites. The trees beside the water crawled with caterpillars, their branches dripped with chrysalids that shone like leaves of gold. 'See,' Talbot said, putting out his hand for me to alight on, 'you are newborn, a painted lady and a male.'

I woke after a while and could not sleep again and so I sat at a chair and lit a candle. It was not yet dawn; through the shutters the rain had given way to a thick mist. I opened my book and read the story of Iphis, whose sweetheart believes her to be the boy she pretends to be. Oh poor Iphis, I thought, as I read how she fears she will fail her darling on their wedding night: *'amid the water'* she says '*we shall thirst.*' Talbot is wrong, I thought, he wants the sexless world of souls, but Iphis and I, in our breeches and out of them, long for our lover's arms. Our bodies burn and we cannot put out the fires they begin, no matter how they started. I blew out the candle and waited for morning to put aside such idle thinking.

If Jacob was indeed alive, I thought, it might only be a week until I found him. How would we explain ourselves, what would we say? I opened the shutter a crack to see how the dawn went on, but there was only the paling mist; across the road a great linden tree loomed, like a giant crouching.

23

When the mist burned off the day proved fine, but the horses were weary and I so sore it was a relief to walk. Talbot, by contrast, was spry and eager, despite the quantities of beer he had drunk. He fair skipped about the horses as I trudged. That night we slept in a wood by a fresh brook. The next day we rode again, through pasture and marsh, past a fancy new palace a pedlar told us was Corbet Castle and so on to a flat heath called Prees where the butterflies were near as thick as in my dream. We bought bread and cheese from a farmer's wife and sat among the grasses with the horses cropping contentedly beside us, the sound of their munching regular as a shearer's stroke.

Round my head red fescue and sweet vernal grass, silky bent and wavy hairgrass, spiked or drooped in the windless air. This is the world of the harvest mouse, I thought, lying back and looking through the forest of stems; the common is all England to her. Distance was only a question of perspective; every day I was drawing closer to him.

Talbot interrupted me. 'We know why you are travelling,' he said, lying on his back a few feet away, '– you come to pluck your beloved from the warm thighs of a northern whore – but you have not once asked me my motive. Do you think I am drawn by your charms Jabez-Jane? I hope not, you are miserly enough with them.'

I rolled onto my stomach and watched the slow progress of a beetle. Go to, I thought, with your bully words, you are not so brave, you forget how you wept on my shoulder in the night – but I said nothing.

'Well,' he said, 'your interest is so keen it pierces. You know I was at Gloucester Hall, at the University...'

I know you say you were, I thought, *but I wouldn't vouch you wore a gown and not an apron.* I nodded.

'I met a great many people there, men who shared my desire to know the secrets of things. I studied the work of Plato, Plotinus, Agrippa, Hermes Trismegistus – but these names mean nothing to you...'

'You have called me a clotpoll and a peasant. I know no Latin, what could they mean to me? I have heard the name of Plato, perhaps.'

'Yes, you are thick with clay and a girl to boot and one as flat-planed as a plank, which is to say hardly one at all. Why do you interrupt me so? At Oxford I impressed many – important men too – with my ability to draw aside the curtain of matter. I received many requests to scry, including one from a great lady, Elizabeth Stanley of Hornby Castle. Finding myself at liberty I decided to travel north to take up her gracious invitation.'

I sat up, the common stretched away before me; beyond it lay Whitchurch, Cheshire and the north. The road was strewn with labourers, some with a scythe over their shoulder like a stem of hanging sedge. Already the hay was piling in the fields. It would very soon be harvest. Was Meg picking my peas, I wondered, were the beans come yet? Did Sally hold Meg's hand and glance together at the road for me as I had done for Jacob? Did they lift the latch sometimes of a morning to check I was not come home, with a fire burning and a pot bubbling? I dabbed at my eyes; these were shallow, watery thoughts; I had made choices. If I had stayed there would be lace at my neck as heavy as an iron collar, Boult's harlot, his common woman, decked in gaudy, scorned. The other thought, I tried to swallow down, I did not want to think it, did not want to touch my flat empty belly, but my hand betrayed me.

Talbot was looking at me carefully. 'Why, what is wrong with you? You are a boy remember. Is it your ignorance, is it that?'

'Yes,' I said, 'only that. I am a country mouse. It will be an honour to meet your great lady, if you'll take me.'

'You can clerk for me, if your hand is good enough.'

I nodded and he seemed satisfied with that.

I had never had a great deal to do with horses, except in the ordinary way of things, but I began to understand, with Juno, how it was that Jacob loved them. Talbot's horse, Erebus, was a piebald, dark and light like her coat – and her master – but Juno was sweet and strong as honey. I held Jacob in my mind's eye and stepped into his image to hold up each hoof to check for stones; I spread my hand in his hand over back and belly to feel for swelling or rubbing. When we stopped I gathered mint and rosehips and meadowsweet to put in their feed at night. Juno liked the mint especially, pressing her nose into my arms as I carried it in.

It was easy, sandy country north of Whitchurch. We passed the pale of the Earl of Shrewsbury, Blackmere, named for its dark pool. There was a greater mere a little further on at Ridley that a carter told us was so thick with pike, bream, tench and perch a fisherman could catch a meal in his cap for breakfast. At Bunbury there was a tavern that took guests. It called itself an inn, and had garish painted cloths on the walls; Talbot spat when he saw our room, and inspected the beds for fleas before he flung himself down.

I went down to the stables. The stablehand was a big, rough lad with hair that looked like bedding straw. He watched me as I went to talk to Juno and I didn't like the way his eyes roved over me, but he said nothing, and nor did I.

Erebus had a swelling and a graze on her foreleg. I challenged the boy that he hadn't noted it, but he simply shrugged. 'En't nothing to fuss on,' he said and wandered off.

It did not take long for me to find comfrey and yarrow for a poultice. Juno could carry the bags tomorrow, I thought, my own weighed nothing. I became aware of a presence behind me as I applied the paste to the muslin; a man uncomfortably close and silent. I paused; Jacob's knife was tucked into my belt, but I doubted I would be quick enough to use it well.

'No, don't stop. Go on.' I sighed with relief; it was Talbot. 'I've been watching you Jabez-Jane. I was curious. "Doesn't the fool know I was an apothecary?" I said to myself. "Why didn't she ask me?" But then I saw how quick and sure your fingers were. You are a healer, I think, and not a common one. Perhaps you are a witch.'

I turned to him, too abruptly, startling the poor horse. Had my colour risen? It would not escape him; Talbot noted everything. 'My grandmother knew herbs, she taught me a little of what she knew.'

Talbot raised his brows. 'So. You are more wrapped round and pasted than my horse. I think there must be a deep wound still healing. Did your grandmother tend your shackle wounds with comfrey too?'

'She was dead by then, praise God,' I said, remembering how night after night in the warm gloom of our cottage in Hope Jacob took strips of petticoat and spread them with the cool herb paste to swathe my swollen ankles. *'Is there not treacle in Gilead,'* I would whisper, kissing his head as he worked. *'Is there no physician? Would God that I had a cottage somewhere far from folk.'* 'You have treacle, sweeting, you have a physician, you have a cottage far from folk,' he answered me and the pain of his gentle fingers on my wounded shins was a keen, keen joy. Did we blaspheme, I wondered, taking the Bible so, is that why we are punished now? I did not believe it. Our Lord was not some mincing fop to be so easily offended.

After supper Talbot and I attended evensong in the village's ancient church. It was large enough to seat two hundred, although there were only thirty; all along the nave the pillars seemed as fine as threads, spinning arches up to heaven. It was hard to believe there could be narrowness of thought in such a place but I found it too grand for prayer. Talbot lingered; it was a relief to leave him. I wanted to breathe my own air and rid my head of his voice for a while, so I left him kneeling and wandered on to find a mere a half mile distant where, I'd been told, clouds of starlings swooped down at night. It was a large pool, fringed with reeds, that were echoed now in the water by the sinking sun. There was nobody about – the haymakers had gone home and beyond the rows of heaped hay there were only lowing cows. In the distance a shelf of hill stretched in sunlight and shadow across the horizon.

There were the starlings, gathering and scattering over the sweep of the pastureland. I had never seen so many. They were a great cloak folding in and blowing out again; a black wind rising; the whirlwind of God rolling the dry chaff off the mountain. I flung my heart out with them; over and back they turned, as loud as a working mill, roaring and squeaking too as they came nearer. You could think them a spectre, I thought, a black spirit advancing over the worked land, except that they thrilled with life. If anything was holy it was this, this free flight together. Jacob would smile and take my hand; he understood, he had a feel for the poetry of living things; I could almost believe he stood beside me as I watched. The mere waited; a grey iron plate in the twilight. At last the birds turned as one towards it and blew into the reed beds like tossed autumn leaves.

Dusk was thickening as I turned from the water back to the

village, slyly felting the edges of things. Just before the village I heard a twig snap and glanced back, expecting to see Talbot's thickset shape, but it wasn't him. In the gloom I made out two slight figures. Boys, I thought, my hand moving to my knife. This was too small a place for mischief, surely. I quickened my step a little, aware that would only make my limp the more pronounced. Then a youth stepped out in front of me. My head came only to his shoulder.

He grinned. 'I like your doublet,' he said. 'You may step aside and give it to me.'

I began to pull out my knife, but in an instant he had my wrist. A hand reached from behind me and clapped my mouth, dragging my head back.

'He's a fancy type,' the hand's voice said, 'I'll swear he's got gold in his drawers.'

'Plugged up his arse more like.' I recognised the voice. The stablehand.

They began to drag me towards a hole of darkness at the side of the road. Oh God, I thought, they will beat me and strip me and then, oh God, I saw again the man on the common, the concentration on his face as he pulled at my wedding ring. I was at the lip of the road. The darkness was an absence, perhaps a well, perhaps the pit of hell; I could not breathe. Then loud uneven footsteps sounded from the village. The hand at my mouth slipped enough for me to bite down hard enough to make the youth scream.

'What's this, what's this, friends?' Talbot's voice sounded amused.

'En't nothing, stranger,' my attacker said over his shoulder. 'Local business, you'd best be getting back.'

Talbot had no light, he seemed patched out of darkness. Please be clever, I thought, or they will kill me. I could feel the boys tense. The one holding me flicked my wrist back hard and took my knife from my hand. Oh dear God they will kill us both, I thought, for they are three to two and I am less than one.

It all happened very quickly. The boy had the knife and then he didn't; he began to turn and then his head was wrenched back and Talbot had a blade held to his neck. The other two grabbed me.

'You have a choice,' Talbot said over my head to the boys holding me. 'Release my man and disappear into the dark. I'll let you all be, even this one,' he prodded at the neck of the one he held with the point of the knife. 'Or make trouble and listen to the sigh of a cut throat.'

For one still second they hesitated, then they pushed me to the side and ran off.

Talbot still held his blade to the first youth's throat.

'What do you think Jabez, shall I kill him? Or shall we rouse the constable, and give the ropemaker some trade?'

I was bent over, my heart battered at my ribs so that I could hardly breathe and behind my eyes all was lights and squealing as though the starlings were swirling in my head. When I was myself again I saw Talbot had put the blade away and the youth was on the ground groaning, reaching out to grasp the knife, my knife, that lay dull as a stone on the road where it had fallen. Talbot waited for his fingers to stretch round it, before he stamped on the hand, picked up the knife and handed it to me.

'What is your name?' I said with the knife in my hand.

'William,' he said, snivelling.

In my head I saw again the body of the boy I had buried and whose shirt I was wearing now, the lockram stiff with sweat. 'Leave him,' I said to Talbot. 'I am none the poorer and I know the shadow of a noose too well to wish it on another.'

Talbot looked at me and nodded, then he kicked the man hard and took my arm to walk back.

'That was cruel, surely, to kick a man who lay grovelling at your feet.'

Talbot clapped me on the back. 'For a thief and a juggler you are an unsalted fresh fool. Did you want him to come sneaking behind us with a sharp greeting for your gentle heart?'

He sounded happy. Blood excites you, I thought. Once again, I wondered if this was what it was to be a man, but then I checked myself – tonight, at least, I should be glad of it. If Talbot were less of a wolf I would be lying in a ditch.

'Thank you,' I said. 'I should give you something in return. My true name, it's not Jabez, it's—'

'—Don't tell me your name,' he said.

In the morning when we came to depart, our horses had not been got ready. Talbot raised his brows at me when our landlord bustled through to apologise that the stablehand was gone.

'He's my sister's boy. I don't understand it. He fell in with a bad sort a year or so ago, but all that's behind him, not missed a day's work in six months and her that happy that he's keeping to the stony path.'

I was glad. I did not like to think of his oafish hands on the mares.

24

It was a bare ten miles to Northwich. Talbot was eager to get there; he had decided to scry in the market for money. The dirt of the road weighed on him, he said, and his spirit called on him to use his sight; besides, he wanted gold. I thought he was merely bored, and told him so, but after he had come to my aid so well I felt I should not cavil overmuch. If he chose to sell his gifts like a common lotteller then so be it.

Three miles after Bunbury we entered Delamere forest. To our right was flat heathland, but to our left the land was wooded and hilly. We were told that the place was rich with fallow and red deer but we saw none, till at the skirt of a wood, two bow shots away, five or six red hinds appeared with a great horned stag among them. It was a beautiful creature, its antlers reaching out and up as though in celebration. It made me think of old Robin Hood the outlaw, living freely under the oak boughs, but Talbot scoffed at me. 'There's not a hide, but it belongs to someone – every pike, every bream in one of these dark pools is counted and the loss to be paid for.'

'There is no freedom, but in wealth,' he said.

'Is that true?' I said, 'Do you believe that to be true?' We had entered a stand of trees and I looked at the sun filtering through the great elms and oak and dancing on the brook that ran across the road. We dismounted to let the horses drink.

'There is freedom in all this,' I said. 'Look at the light, how it ripples through the leaves and bounces on stone and water. I don't need gold to feel the joy of this.'

'You need food in your belly,' Talbot said, 'and no dog at your heels. But you are right, in part. The history of the world is a falling off from light. This world of rocks and trees and beasts was created when light splintered into pieces. It shattered as a crystal does, into infinite intricate forms so that everything in the universe has order and harmony in relation to everything else. Do you understand?'

I shook my head.

'Think of it like this,' he went on, 'have you ever looked at a dandelion and noticed the arrangement of the petals, ring upon ring, or seen the lacework of a flake of snow? There is a pattern in creation and it is the pattern in the mind of God. That is what I search for in the stone. The language of God, that when it is mastered will restore base metal to gold and the human soul to godhead.'

He was staring at me intensely, with a fire in his eyes that excited and appalled me. 'Do you understand?' he said again.

'You wish to rival God,' I said. 'I do not think it can be right to poke into the mind of the Creator and seek to change what He has made.'

'Matter and men's souls are never at rest, Jabez; we are so far corrupted that the last days are at hand. I seek to understand the architecture of creation, its arithmetic – do you see? To step into the harmony and number of creation and so shed sin. The greatest mind in our land has said this: "And in our soul number beareth such a sway, and hath such an affinity therewith that some ancients hold man's soul to be a number moving itself."'

I turned to Juno's quiet dipping and drinking in the stream. The architecture of creation, it was a beautiful phrase. I thought of the high pillars of the church in Bunbury, how they made an airy lightness out of stone. Sometimes when Talbot talked I felt myself on the edge of revelation, if only I would let go a little more and follow. But something held me back. There was such a strange opposition in Talbot, with his brawling, his bull neck and yet his power to weave pictures on water out of light itself. He was a belligerent, greedy man, but he saw things others could not see.

'So is it real or spiritual gold you seek?' I said at length, 'I don't think you can be after both.'

He had been stooping to look directly at me, on a level with my eyes. Now he stood and swore. 'Never mind,' he said. 'How could you hope to understand? Listen. Do you believe in spirits?'

How could I not, having seen them? 'Yes,' I said.

'There is the world of spirit and the world of flesh. And although we are forever dying, the spirit which animates us, that does not die.'

'Yes,' I said. 'That's true.'

'So it is with gold; it is both the massy element and the spirit of purity.'

'They are at odds,' I said, climbing back on Juno to prevent his response.

How I have changed, I thought, discussing alchemy in a strange forest with a cutpurse philosopher and not only that, but venturing to disagree. Was it the doublet and hose that let me face the world instead of sitting askance like a lady? It wasn't only that, I thought. It was partly Talbot, too. He cared so little for the customs of the world.

A little further on the trees thinned and we started a skylark from the grass. Up and up it spiralled, as though threading a necklace of the sky; each note a blue bead. I watched it till it was no more than a speck of dust in heaven; yet such a quantity of song – bright plaits of it.

Talbot paused, following my gaze. 'See?' he said, 'how it makes its melodies of air? The whole world is a lyre, if we could but listen. All separate things within it are strung in order and harmony. If the lark can play it, why shouldn't I learn the fingering?'

I smiled. I liked the image – rocks and trees and humanity itself rippling with song. Far better, I thought, that creation be made of music than of minted gold. My soul vibrated with the tiny bird's roundels. We watched until she dropped herself down and down into the heath. There, hidden by the furze, in a leaf-lined hollow, lay her nest. The thought of it gave me a foolish pang; good luck little mother, I thought. I hope you fare better than I.

A couple of miles before Northwich, Talbot's mare Erebus cast a shoe and we thought it best to walk, despite Talbot's wish to hurry. The road was busy and I found myself next to a woman with a basket strapped to her back and a baby tied in front that wailed piteously. Her husband fared no better, clanking with pots and tools and a scrawny boy on his shoulders. Ignoring Talbot's hissed objections, I put the boy on Erebus and the woman and her infant on Juno. When I gave them bread her blessings and thankings made me uncomfortable.

'I'm no gentle sir, madam,' I said. 'I've been as poor as you, albeit without the babes to feed. My master here is a scryer, he is bound for the market to cast visions.'

She gave him a nervous glance but soon fell talking to me, over the cries of the infant. Her name was Ann and they had grown up on a manor near Tarvin to the east, but over years the commons and the wastes were shrunk and hedged till there was nowhere to graze their cows and then no cows to milk. 'Been making cheese in my family since Noah went to sea,' she said, in a voice that sounded surprised at her own story. 'Whole village came together to make it and sell it, had always been so, sent it off to Chester. Now there's only the master's cows and the master's cheese; barely a soul left in Aldersey where my mother was born and raised.'

I glanced at Talbot. 'Your gold at work in all its purity,' I said to pique him.

'Aye,' the husband said, as though I had spoken to him. 'It's gold right enough; rich men hold it in the hand and watch it breed. The master's house grows faster than a molehill in the night and he dresses his daughters in satin. There's nothing left of my father's house, not the old elm tree that whispered me asleep in summer and creaked like the moon was splitting in a storm, not the shippen where we kept the cows. A man can't wander as he would, or catch a fish for his dinner, but he's hedged and hemmed about till he feels he must trip on his own thoughts. And they call it bettering and improvement.'

While he talked I looked more closely at the baby. Any fool could see that it was sick. 'What ails the child?' I asked.

'Oh,' said Ann, beginning to weep, 'her guts – this last week she has had such a gurry on her, I am afraid she won't last.'

'Have you tried fennel?'

'Some, but there is none to be found.'

'Wait,' I said, stopping Juno and searching through my pack, 'I have some and more, that might help her.'

Talbot came up behind me. 'Will you start doctoring every child that has the skitters on the road? God's truth Jabez, we will never advance an inch. I will lose the market.'

I frowned at him for an answer and searched out my bag of simples. 'Here's more,' I said, 'and chamomile and bloodroot – that will help her most.'

Taking them she began to weep in earnest. 'We've nothing to give you,' she said.

'That's of no consequence.' I said. 'What will you do?'

'I've a cousin at Northwich in the salt trade,' the man answered. 'We can bide with him a while and get work, God willing. They need no end of hands, my cousin says.'

They stopped to see to the child and as Talbot was keen to press on we mounted, but Ann called me back.

'You might tell your friend,' she said, 'to go careful and avoid the market. The sheriff and the aldermen are godly men and won't have players in the town, I doubt they'd suffer a sorcerer.

They looked a piteous sight when I looked back to them to wave. I should have given them money. If Hope was barred to us we should be like them; houseless, hungry, hoping for whatever work we could find. Perhaps, I thought bitterly, it was as well that I had miscarried; better that than watching the child starve. I had thought so much of finding him and not at all of how we would live, then. It was so easy to become like chaff, winnowed out, cast aside. But we were young, we would find positions. Perhaps even here, in the saltworks; there was plenty of work the man said.

25

We smelt Northwich before we saw it: woodsmoke and brine and the middens left by the fires. It sat bitter on your tongue and in your lungs. For all that, the town beyond the brineworks was pleasant and prosperous looking. Talbot took his horse to be shod and I wandered for an hour down to the river Dane and the saltworks.

Off Seath street a great brine pit fed the wich-houses. Channels led to vast barrels in each house and these were used to fill half a dozen pans in which the salt water was set seething by the fires beneath. I stood in the swirling exhalations and felt the sweat run down my face. A shrivelled old woman showed me how she and the other wallers leaned through the vapours to scoop up the salt and set it in wicker baskets to drain. 'Our backs are planks of pain,' she said, 'from the stooping.' Each breath scorched; when I coughed I feared I should never have the strength to breathe again; the walls and the bodies ran slick and wet; the salt stung my eyes and raked my skin. Only the drying crumbs in the barrows gleamed white and sinless, belying the foul fumes that begot them. 'These are the last days,' Talbot had said; maybe he was right. This was as far from the golden threaded music of the lark as Satan's burning caves from heaven. All about me curses, limbs marked by burning, red-rimmed eyes. They must have no fear of hell, I thought, for this place is hell already. The beldam accompanied me out and when I gave her a silver penny she cackled through all her yellow teeth and bobbed me a curtsey as though I were a lord.

'My lad Thomas had a look of you, till the mustering men took him,' she said. 'Years now. He en't coming home, though please God he's living. It's no good for a woman on her own.' Then she brightened. 'Plenty o' work here for a lusty boy like you.'

I nodded, though the likeness in our stories made me shudder. Here was work indeed, but the thought of Jacob taken from the good fresh air to tend a fire pit was more than I could bear to think of. I wished I had not come.

Talbot, when I found him, was in as much a hurry as I was to be gone. 'Your charity was to some effect, Jabez. I don't know if you stopped the child voiding, but I think you may have saved me a whipping.'

That night we lodged in Manchester, a busy town with a single parish church rebuilt only half a hundred years ago. I went to bed, but Talbot was restless and declared he was going out to find a jade who would let him read the fortune reflected in her eyes – and if he could not, to play dice.

At some point in the evening I opened my eyes to find him on his knees by the bed feeling at my clothes for money. When he saw me staring he grinned at me and held up a ring.

'Put that back,' I said, 'it isn't yours to take.'

'It's a pretty thing, don't you think?' he said, turning it in the light of the candle. 'Did you pull it from a dead woman's hand, or was she alive to watch you?'

Deep into the night I heard him fumble at the door and stagger in. He lurched into the bed cup-shotten and stinking. 'Jabez' he said, clumsily grasping my backside, 'let me use you like a boy; it would not be adultery; you've such a pretty arse.'

I spread a blanket on the floor and slept there.

The next day was a Sunday. I would have gone on, after the service, but the horses needed rest and Talbot was seized with holiness. I was woken by his loud repentance.

'You should ask forgiveness of me, first,' I ventured. Piety gripped him like a pair of tongs. He glowered at me but did not stop. It appeared I was a portion of his sin.

'I had never heard how ale could bring a man to holiness,' I said, as we walked to church. 'If only the rain were beer we should all be saved.'

He glared again. 'Don't you fear damnation?' he said.

I opened my mouth to say I feared truly, when it struck me I did not. Once upon a time I had flung myself into water to cleanse the world of my wickedness. It seemed so long ago. If God loved me, as the scriptures told me He did, I could not think that He would hurt me. Hadn't He, even then, sent Jacob to pull me from a slimy death into his warm arms? 'Care not then for the morrow,' the gospel said, 'for the morrow shall care for itself.'

In the sermon the minister suited himself to Talbot's temper; he was all about judgement. '"And whosoever,"' he declaimed, '"was not found written in the book of life, was cast into the lake of fire."'

I could not listen; in my mind I heard the skylark playing on the lyre of creation. The verses in my head were flowers: '*Consider the lilies of the field,*' the gospel said. Yes, I thought, I will.

At supper in the small dark parlour of the inn Talbot's mood lifted, although he was still as sour as bad ale. It was a warm night, but he shivered and said he was cold. I fetched a blanket for his shoulders and gave over hating him.

'Do you truly believe we are in the last age, as the minister said?' I asked him.

'Yes,' he said, 'I do. The signs are apparent. Even in whatever dunghill you have crawled from you will have seen them. The comet that blazed last winter.'

'I saw it. It was like a chariot, like the story of Phaeton careering through the sky because he could not manage the horses of the sun.'

'Why, how you gobble Ovid. I am not talking about pagan stories, Apollo's bastard son, but this world, now. There was the comet, that was a sign. Five years before that there was the star.'

'The star.'

'Yes, dammit, a star in winter, a new star, the first since the birth of our Lord. I tell you I felt it tug me. I gave over grinding leaves like a common drugger and set out for Oxford. It is the stars that rule us Jabez.'

'I pray to God, not to the stars.'

'You wouldn't understand. How could you? You are like a snail thinking it can understand a castle because it carries a house upon its back. Know this. There is a divine order, that falls from the Creator, through the angels and the stars, even to the stones beneath your feet. Each has its place and influence.'

'Strings of the lyre,' I said, 'I understand. The note sounded by a star vibrates through us.'

'Yes!' he said, his eyes flaming, 'I am called to step through worlds; to talk with daemons and angels; to learn the notes of our first Maker, the pattern of Creation.' He leaned across the table and seized my wrist. 'In the days of destruction I will be one of the golden makers of Jerusalem.'

Was he brilliant or mad? I was not sure then and am not now; there was a dazzle in his thinking, but it was threaded through with wildness and perhaps that drew me just as much; the license he offered to defiance. I felt that if I scoffed, now, he might well overturn the table, kick the plate and punch the boy who hovered at the door. He strained towards godhead with both fists clenched.

'So,' I said carefully, putting my other hand over his, 'being called so, chosen so, why are you not glad?'

He threw his head back and laughed, too loudly. The other diners, a milliner and his family, stared a moment; then the good-wife pulled her children's faces back to their dinners. Her pains were wasted, for in the next instant Talbot let out a great groan. The father coughed in disapproval; the dish boy jumped.

'I am wrenched apart.' Talbot cried, heedless of the attention he garnered. 'I am a door; an angel and a devil stand either side to throw me wide open to their visions. And sometimes they take one another's clothes and sometimes the visions, the visions blaze across my mind's eye so that the stench of my own seared flesh chokes me.'

The children stared with open mouths; the parents, crossing themselves, began to bustle them out.

'Please,' I whispered to Talbot, 'calm yourself, or you will have us clapped in irons.' I turned to the family, 'Forgive my master,' I said. 'He is not well.'

The woman lingered after the rest; with the stout authority of a merchant's wife, she stepped forward and prodded at my chest. 'He's not fit to be abroad.'

'Not fit!' Talbot seemed to wake from his trance. 'Not fit, madam,' he said quietly, with a nasty levity, 'the day is coming when Beelzebub will spit you, arse to snout and turn you on his fire and your children will smell the fat and their little mouths will water.'

'Enough!' I said, bundling Talbot from the room while she stood stock-still before him, slack-jawed as though waiting for the roasting rod indeed.

Our dishes lay barely touched on the table.

In the room Talbot flung himself down on the bed laughing, but I shook him by the shoulder.

'Will you have us arrested? Arraigned as heretics? Have you no sense at all? You forget I know what it's like to sit on a cart with a crowd jeering at me, with their fists twitching to fasten the rope. Do you want to suffer, is that it? Do you think it will redeem you? You can damn yourself but you won't damn me. Tomorrow I'll go on alone.'

I expected him to blaze at me, perhaps to hit me. I was so angry that I think I did not care, but he said nothing. When I'd done haranguing he cupped my chin.

'I'm sorry little Jabez. I burn things, I burn those I love. Myself most of all. Those people are nothing. See – I blow them away,' and he blew over his hand. 'Don't leave me yet.'

I was pacified, but I was still uneasy. All night I lay half awake, listening for any disturbance in the road, any warning footfall on the stairs. Talbot muttered and snorted beside me. I doubted she would let it pass; what would befall me if we were taken, my doublet and hose plucked over my head, my treasure discovered? We should have left at once. At some point in the night I went to the window to open the casement wide to the air. I was growing used to the sounds of a town at night; the rustle of a rat, a horse moving in its stall, the odd moon lurker or drunk – and later the subdued voices of those who rose before dawn to work. Above the houses opposite the stars were clear. I sought out Cassiopeia, where the new star had sat.

'Come, look,' Jacob had said one night in December, taking me outside. I had thought he meant me to notice the rime of frost that fringed each reed of thatch, and lay like down on the still branches, but he pointed up to the heavens.

'I heard them talking of it at the Court,' he said, 'a new star,

there, do you see? It is the first, they say, since the star at
Bethlehem.'

Later, curled together in the close darkness, I asked him if he
feared the Judgement Day. 'No,' he said, 'or only as other men do.
My heart is not angry as it once was. I have my wife in my arms, and
a good master and, God willing, soon a child – or two, or three – to
fill the house with laughter.' I nestled in the dark and smiled,
because it was barely a year since we had settled and I did not
dread my courses as I soon would, but I was not altogether easy,
even so, and when I roused him with long kisses and drew him into
me it was partly for his sure weight along my body to steady my
disquiet. Then I felt him pulse within me and the rush of joy came
for us both; the shadow unhooked itself a while and I was free. Oh
Jacob, I thought now, I need the circle of your arms; how else will I
avoid hurling off into the shrieking winds? And the thought came
back to me that this was not so true as it once was. I could not step
back into the shape I was, and perhaps he too would have changed.
That though I loved him just as fiercely I was not so afraid as I used
to be.

I turned from the casement and looked back into the room,
where a candle stub flicked monsters on the walls and the wrong
man grunted in his sleep. I was merely painting my mind with
doubts. When I found him, all would be simple once again.

Before sunrise I took our bags to the stables. The ostler was
asleep in the straw, but a half-groat had him up and cheery too.
Waking Talbot was more difficult. We were so near my journey's
end now I had half a mind to disregard my promise and leave him
to whatever his insolence brought on, but only half, and a lesser
half at that. While he dressed I crept downstairs and into the
kitchen for bread. How I blessed my hose and breeches – pilfering
was never so easy in a skirt! When I reached our room my ostler
was there.

'You'd best go by the other stairs,' he said, grinning. 'There's folks asking for you in the hall and one o' them's a constable.'

If I had not been a boy I should have seized his dirty face and kissed him. I shook his hand and we followed him by the backstairs and a laundry door into the yard, where the horses stood waiting. Before we left I pressed another penny in his hand.

'I like you,' he called after me as we ducked onto the cobbles, 'come back soon and marry my sister.'

26

The day began overcast and grew worse; a soft rain set in that whispered its way through all our clothes and dripped gently but remorselessly from our hats. Talbot had forgotten his affection of the night before; he complained of a headache, then cursed me for losing him his breakfast. I let Juno fall back, to be out of sight of his face.

Much of the land either side had been enclosed for pasture and arable long since, but there were also wide wastes and mosses where the grass was broken by black scuffed patches that I was told would rarely bear a man's, let alone a horse's weight, but would suck you slowly down. The more you struggled the faster you'd be swallowed. Even the green heath had a brown bleakness to it that struck me with its foreignness. The sharp dark smell of the peat was alien in my mouth. As we climbed the wind whipped the rain into our faces and we rode into cloud, so that only the highway before us stood out clear and stony. Each step brought me closer to the city where Jacob lay, perhaps sick, perhaps a prisoner in some lightless cell. I tried to stop the excitement bubbling in my chest and the anxiety, too, that left me troubled in the midst of hope.

The vision Talbot had conjured in the pond recurred to me over and over. A stony road, like this one, and bare moor rising behind him. The wind was blowing on his face in the sunshine and he held out his arm in greeting. If he was so free why had he not come home?

Of course the vision might lie, or it might trick. This happened again and again in my book of tales – where fortunes were given but not understood. It could have shown him months, even years hence. I might have years of wandering ahead of me, or years of waiting, a prison widow, for his release. How would I live till then? I looked ahead at the mist-cloaked road for inspiration but could see only my hands on Juno's reins. My hands, I thought, yes. I would find somewhere I could live cheap and earn what I could as a healer and a scribe.

Talbot called me back to the present. He had dismounted by a broken cross to talk to two men. I could barely understand them, but it appeared we had been misled by the cloud and ventured too far east, almost to Wigan, but the road now was plain north, we couldn't miss it, even if the fog hid our own noses. We urged the horses on to go as fast as the road allowed, which was not much, rutted and streaming as it was. My companion seemed recovered and determined to ignore my wish for solitude.

'Fine fellows,' he said. 'They told me the story of that cross. I think we were led to it; it concerns you almost point for point. There was a gentlewoman – there I allow it differs from your story – whose husband left her for the wars. How she pined for him, how she wailed when he did not come back to her! Do you see the likeness?'

I frowned and turned my face away.

'When he did not return she married a Welsh knight, just as you will marry me, and they carried on handsomely, swiving and singing till the day her husband returned indeed. Dressed as a palmer he came to her castle and she wept, for he looked so like her dead lord and the false knight whipped her for weeping.

'It is not my story at all.'

'Oh but listen, it returns to you. Her lord made himself known to his peasants and the false knight fled, but he was overtaken and slain. The gentlewoman was enjoined by her confessor to walk bare-legged to this cross once every week to beg forgiveness for her smooching and slabbering. Now, you see, how it touches you?'

'I do not,' I said, 'and if it does, what about you? You cast yourself as the false knight whose throat is cut on the road?'

'Yes,' he said, 'no man likes horns. Could you not steal wisdom with the gold you took? You are more green than June grass, more silly than a prodded hen. What do you think your bold horse boy, your centaur will think when he learns we've shared a bed from Worcester? Will he nod and say, 'Oh, no matter, she was a boy then.''

The horror of it struck me. I recalled Jacob balling his fists at poor Simon Fosbroke, then I looked at Talbot and remembered how deftly he handled a knife; they must never meet. 'Jacob must never know,' I said.

He trotted off. 'I'll not tell him,' he called over his shoulder, 'cast the thought away.'

I tried to, but the thought of Jacob's jealousy fretted my thoughts with presentiments as unformed and troubled as the mist that swathed the road ahead. Talbot bounced forward whistling. I urged Juno on to catch him up.

'Don't presume too much on my gentleness, Edward Talbot Kelley. I know things about you too, remember. Enough for you to leave this world by the steps and string. Why do you take such delight in provocation?'

He grinned and looked at me closely. 'Why Jabez, I think you could be dangerous. I like you more and more. I meant it, by the way. You will marry me, by and by.'

I snorted and fell back. You roll your fellow man like dice, I thought, to see how we will land. One day, perhaps years hence, perhaps tomorrow, you will pledge too much in the game and be required to pay.

The afternoon at last shrugged off the cloud to reveal a long ridge to the right of us; it hung there for miles, like a wave waiting its time to fall. It was already almost evening when at last we neared the town of Preston. I was worried about Erebus, after the swelling a few days since, but it had not worsened. We stood the mares in a flowing stream before we approached, letting the water cool their legs. Then we clattered over the five arches of the Ribble bridge and so into the town. Talbot evidently knew the place and turned into an inn yard. When it came to pay however, he had but pennies in his purse and I must needs broach a sovereign.

In the morning Talbot announced he had business in the town; I was glad enough to stay a night for it seemed to me that if Jacob had come south he must have passed through here. I spent the morning loitering my way through alehouses and poorer lodgings but although it cost me a fistful of farthings I learned nothing of any use or note. Even as I opened my mouth to question a potboy or an innkeeper I could hear what a goosish fool I sounded and the words curdled on my tongue. How could they remember such a one, each told me, with all the folk who passed through? And as far back as April – the cuckoo had come and gone since then. I might as well have asked the swifts bedding in the house eaves, or the sparrows skipping round the stalls in the market square. I could have wept, if it would not have betrayed me. Yet for the first time on the journey there was the echo of his presence in the air. At every corner I felt – as I had in those days of expectation in the village – that I might turn and find him standing before me. The hope and the dread of it gnawed my guts.

Talbot lingered another day, insisting I went with him to the house of a rich clothier.

'What has he lost?' I asked, as we waited by the gates for a servant who evidently wished us to know, by his slowness, how little he regarded us.

'His son,' Talbot answered, bowing extravagantly to the liveried man, when at last he let us in.

We were shown into a parlour with fine oak panelling and polished brass sconces, which were all lit, although it was the afternoon, so that the room was suffused with a stuffy radiance. The family – the clothier, his wife, and a grown girl – were waiting for us. Beside her husband the wife looked grey and insubstantial as though without the abundance of her skirts and ruff she would fade like a cloud into the air, but the girl eyed Talbot angrily. A large mirror was placed on a low table, before a painting of a fair young man who seemed caught in the act of smiling at himself. Talbot called for the doors to be closed and then he prayed and began his incantations, sweeping his arm across the mirror. Either side of him the parents sat rapt and staring. I watched the girl.

'I see a city, there is a wide river, he crosses it, he knows his way. He is going to a tavern, he has friends there—'

'—Which city, which city, man?' the clothier butted in.

Talbot looked up, as though surprised to see the room, 'Why, Deptford, London,' he said. 'You should not interrupt.'

Shock and fury washed across the girl's face; as Talbot bent again to the mirror she let out a small scream and fell forward, pointing. 'There is a devil on his shoulder! I can see it, I can see it Mother. It is whispering into his ear. Oh deliver us all from evil!'

She lay on the floor shaking and moaning. Her mother let out her own scream and jumped to her daughter's side.

'What are you sir?' the clothier cried, seizing Talbot by the collar. 'Dear God, what have I let into my house?'

For a moment Talbot looked nonplussed; he glanced at me.

'Quick!' I said in as a commanding voice as I could muster. 'An evil spirit attempts to possess her, to prevent the finding of your son. Go mistress, please,' I said, pulling the mother's arm, 'bring peony and betony to expel it. Don't wait for the maid but go – it is assailing her. Please sir,' I said to the astonished clothier, 'pass me the crucifix hanging behind you, it will protect her. We must pray.'

To my surprise he at once let go of Talbot and handed it to me. Talbot recovered his wits enough to begin a loud prayer. I bent down to the girl with the cross and whispered. 'Go to, mistress, recant or I shall reveal all, aye and suggest they search for the letters.' It was a gamble, but the glance she shot me showed that I was right. When the mother came back with a man behind her bearing the herbs the girl allowed herself to be garlanded and girdled as though asleep and then did a fine play of waking into sense.

Talbot could barely keep from hooting when we'd left the house. He clapped me so hard on the back I almost fell.

'My little Jabez, what a rogue you make. Admit how you enjoyed it.'

'Very well, perhaps I did, a little. I wonder what he ran from. Did he look happy in Deptford?'

Talbot's face fell. 'No, truth be told, he looked ragged.' He paused to face me. 'She might be right of course, for all she was his confidante. Perhaps there was a devil on my shoulder.'

'The devil would have lied. I do not think you are a good man, Talbot, but I believe you have a gift: you see truth.'

He searched my eyes and nodded. 'Yes. This is why you must marry me.' he said.

I laughed. 'I have a husband.'

'An' if you don't? Think, Jabez-Jane, what we could do together. What I could teach you. I will be famous. I could take you to Paris, to Bohemia, to Rome. You could breakfast on hypotheses and peaches.'

I looked in my turn for mockery in his eyes, then frowned, for he appeared to be in earnest. 'I have a husband,' I said more firmly, 'and I will find him.'

'We'll see,' he said.

He was well enough recovered from the morning's agitation to haul me to the tavern after supper to meet other 'friends' he had been dealing with. One was a lawyer, about thirty, whose fancy collar belied his sombre black. He had a sneering way about him and could not bring himself to notice me. To Talbot he spoke with an affected roughness as though to bulk his codpiece. I had met his kind before, both men and women, who mime a swagger but are always early for a hanging. The other was a slight man, a clerk of some kind, who had a habit of repeating the phrases of others like a gnat about the ear.

The lawyer leaned confidentially forward. 'So, Talbot, the deeds, all is in order, I trust? We can leave nothing to chance.'

'Oh, no, nothing to chance,' the little man put in nervously.

'Gentlemen,' Talbot said, 'you could trust me with your lives – nay better, with your wives.'

'Oh yes,' the lawyer said, 'I'll drink to that.'

'Do you think it might be wise,' he added, dabbing at his mouth with a fine handkerchief, 'to hire a man to ride with you? There's Cockerham sands before you reach Lancaster and if you should be waylaid?'

'Yes,' the little man spluttered over his cup, 'if you should be waylaid?'

'Oh,' said Talbot, 'as to that, there's no cause to worry. The letter will be in cipher by morning. As to the rest – I have my man Jabez here. He might look like a slender reed but he's already slipped the gallows once; he'll find a man's pulse quicker than music. He'd sooner let out your life's blood than show mercy.'

I took out Jacob's blade and put it before me and kissed it.

'Aye,' Talbot said. 'He's after a man in Lancaster, aren't you Jabez, and you mean to have his heart.'

'I do,' I said, looking Talbot in the eyes, 'and neither God nor man will prevent me.'

The lawyer turned to me then with a look that was both perplexed and gloating.

'What is your business with these men?' I asked Talbot later as he sat over the desk translating a letter into a labyrinth of signs.

'I tell you Jabez-Jane, they are base metal. I am turning them into gold.'

Later, in the dark, I wondered again how to fit together the parts of this man snoring like an ox beside me, whose fingers were dirty with corruption but who talked of angels and called down visions from the stars. And then I wondered at myself still more, at the thrill I had felt in my own invention in the face of risk. When we were young, before he had made peace with being in love with me, Jacob had shied away from my recklessness; he was right to fear it, for it had almost led me to the gallows. I must tamp down again. And yet, and yet, the bright world was so full of possibilities, there were so many thoughts to be spun out of air, so much to be known and learned. Talbot had offered me courts and cities, but I could never marry him, nor did he want me, not really; it was the story of his future that he loved. It was very well for Talbot, for any man. He could fashion himself a new fortune ten times over; I could not. I did not want to. I had a husband more dear to me than all the gorgeous spectacles the world could offer. I would give away the moon, and the stars, too, just to trace a finger along his collarbone and kiss the hollow there, below his neck. Somehow, together, we would build another life.

27

When at last we left Preston I was so nervous I could barely hold the reins: today we would reach Lancaster at last. Juno breathed in my restiveness and pricked and started at every fly. Over the smudged blue fells to our right the summer dawn streaked lilac. The air held the quiet expectancy of heat, but a freshness hung above the water as we crossed Savick brook and then the River Brock. By the time we reached the Calder, the slopes were washed with yellow light and shadow. Already heat licked at our necks.

'Abate your burning little Jabez,' Talbot said, swiping my cap from me, 'the day will be blazing enough without it.'

The bright sun took away some of the bleakness of the place so that I could believe it beautiful after its fashion, black moss and marsh; the secret stillness of the reeds and the lonely horn of the bittern. After Garstang there was scarce a field of wheat. It was a pretty village, but we did not pause, for we wanted to reach the sands before the tide advanced, and only stood a little in the Cocker to let the horses cool their legs, before we pressed on.

Strangely, it was not the sea I noticed first, but the birds: a great multitude on the expanse of gleaming mud and sand; from a distance they moved and glittered like the water that dwindled in streams and pools all round them. We rode to the guide post and stood awhile, waiting for a man to lead us past the quicksands. I could see the birds more clearly now, but many were new to me and it was only later that I learned their names. Most were streaked brown and grey like the shingle on the sand, but there was also a jostling crowd of black and white oystercatchers and here and there, white and slender as the crescent moon, a tall egret. As I watched, three curlews landed near to us, and picked their way delicately to a shining runnel in the sand, their beaks improbable, drooping, until they jabbed sharply at the mud.

Soon the guide appeared, coming at a jogtrot towards us on a rough dark pony. A few birds lifted in alarm, like the scurf of a wave and then the bay erupted, flickering, shrieking until the air was a ripple of wings. This is a day for marvels, I thought, entranced; the soul approaching heaven must see a sight like this, the light of God glancing off a thousand thousand angel wings. Had Jacob passed this way, I wondered, and watched the birds take flight?

The man led us along a road in the sands only he could see. He pointed to slick channels which, he said, were not there yesterday and would be gone again tomorrow. Elsewhere the sand looked sound enough but he showed us how, if you stepped on it, it billowed like cloth. Takes years, he said, to know how the water wicks below the skin of mud and chart it, here – he jabbed a finger at his head. He'd been taking folk across the sands, here and Lune-sands all his life, and his father before him, when they weren't cockle-picking or fishing. 'The land hereabouts is all water-wash,' he said, 'and the tidal sleck and the crusted ooze with all the dainty birds tripping at their ease is no more sound than the trumpery players put on to fool folk with their stories.'

We crossed the Cocker again; on the bank the horses sank so far into the sand their noses dipped into the water. This would be a death for a devil I thought, sucked slowly into the mud and sand, destroyed by your own struggle to be free.

'It's not the mud that kills you, often as not,' the man said, 'it's the tide. It has a hunger in it when it comes in that it can't slake, no matter how fast it swallows.'

He took us as far as Cockersand Abbey, where the land juts out with only a wide channel between it and the point across the water where winds of every compass blow the sere grasses.

'I have never seen the sea before,' I said to Talbot.

'How could you have?' he answered, 'Now you have seen it, what do you think of it?'

I gazed out at the immeasurable horizon. Light danced on the water as though tickled by the sun, but I was not fooled. It rocked with the rhythm of the moon and stars and held us at naught. Only the wind, the breath of God, or His angels, could ruffle its surfaces. Beneath the blue dazzle monsters lurked; my father had told me tales of the whale, that the shipwrecked took for an island in the fog only to be pulled down into the green deeps; of the selkies, who sang in human voices and combed their weed-strewn hair, and of the mariners who hearing them could never be at peace again, but must stand in the shallows craning towards the waves, or hold a shell on their pillow all night for the hush of the sea in their ear. The water was blue as the leaves and fields are green, which is to say the colour dissolved and remade itself in a hundred different hues. Near us it was silver, but further out it slid towards the bright blue of the Virgin's gown, or of my dead father's eyes, that yearned always towards the promise in the furled sails of the tall ships that came up the Severn in his boyhood. At the horizon the rim was darker still and in the heat a haze was gathering; I could just see the white sails of a tall merchant ship. If I were a man, I would not hesitate, I thought. Who would not want to feel the heave of the waves beneath their feet and lean towards the rim of the blue world over a dipping prow, bound for the jewelled cities of the earth?

I turned back to Talbot and swept my arm across the bay. 'It is too big for thought,' I said. 'It yields to us and defies us all at once.'

'Looks fair enough from here,' the guide said, turning his pony back, 'you'd best get on now, there'll be a storm afore dark I shouldn't wonder.'

We turned inland along the sands that edge the Lune river, past ragged saltmakers at the sands' edges, and over the mouth of the Conder. A string of brown geese like a loose arrow flew over our heads inland. It seemed a good sign. Only two or three miles further on lay Lancaster.

Soon enough, the grim brown castle came into view; all the immense hewn power of dukes and kings. Somewhere behind the walls, perhaps in the great squat tower, was the county gaol. The town was hidden behind. What do I do now? I thought. After so long, we were here. Crows wheeled round the castle walls. I felt so sick with fear that Juno, sensing it, came to a halt beneath me.

'Haste yourself,' Talbot called back, 'the clouds gather and we need lodgings.'

I urged Juno to a trot and tried to smile away all my foreboding and ignore the thickening air. At the city gates a lunatic man mopped and mowed, wearing nothing but breeches. I could not help but stare at him; he leered madly back at me and lunged for Juno's bridle, but Talbot struck him and he fell away.

'Christ, but you're a fool for every clapperdudgeon and feigning Abram-man you meet, Jabez.'

He was not feigning, there was frenzy in the man's eyes. I shuddered with the thought that had made me pause. Could Jacob have become like him, struck from door to door, nameless, mouthing at the air? What would I find now I was here at last?

I took a breath; whatever it might be I would face it. 'If you are above ground. Jacob,' I said silently, 'I will find you; however you have fallen, my heart's darling I will bear you up – but don't be dead, not dead I beg you.'

I passed under the stone arch and on into the city.

28

The evening air was soft and close; then, in the thick twilight, the sky ripped brightly open. Thunder rolled down from the fells above the city as though a giant were toppling peaks. We scurried for shelter to an inn that Talbot knew. All evening the storm continued; I had to put off trawling the taverns for news. Rain fell in torrents and the torrents flowed over gutters and cobbles, sluicing the town of its dirt and its ghosts.

The morning was clear and gusty, with the heat washed out of the streets. Talbot hailed me outside the inn. He was in conversation with a boy who'd walked from Wigan with a basket of cannel coals on his back. 'Put a candle to them,' he said, 'and they burn straight off, any which way they are held, and they are not greasy like ordinary coal, but slick and shiny.' Talbot picked out a piece bigger than a duck's egg and declared he would go at once to get it polished.

The boy nodded, 'It will show your face back to you better than a mirror.'

'Aye,' Talbot said, cradling it, 'it will show that and more. Come Jabez, we have much to do.'

I shook my head at him, 'I have my own business today,' I said, walking off before he could answer. All along the street he called after me, but I flung up my arm in farewell.

All I knew was that Jacob had been stabbed in an alley, near to a tavern. I'd thought I could simply say I was the dead man's cousin, wishing to visit his grave as I passed through, but I was met with bafflement, or polite condolences – or memories as windblown and devoid of colour as last year's leaves. They remembered the scuffle and resented the hasty departure of the young lords – it was a tragedy, with the party so fine and free in its spending, though Master Croft could swear the devil blue. As for the knifing, it was rogues come up from Bowland; it was a Bury thief; they'd heard it was started at a cockfight past St Leonard's Gate; it was over some rogue's doxy; it was the bed-broker whose girl he hit; it was that he'd refused to pay; it was her brother – and whether rogue, pander, or brother, the murderer was always gone – to Liverpool, to London, over the Irish sea. Even the place was disputed – it was on Kelne Lane, no surely Penny Street, they'd heard it was the row below the Weary Wall. One by one the tavern keepers shook their heads and named each other as the house where he was laid. Even the sexton disavowed him; the parish clerk could show me the register if I'd like – he'd heard he'd been taken to be buried in a parish further north, or was it south, he was not sure, now he came to think of it – at any event, it was not here.

Sometimes when I poked at the memories they blew off like chaff, and sometimes it was as if I poked a bruise and eyes grew hard and blank as polished metal.

'What do you expect?' said Talbot that night, when I recounted the day to him. 'You, a stranger, scratching at dirt that has been trod down safe so that respectable people can walk on it and not get their boots smeared. An' if there was lying, and money paid down, all the more reason to resent any raking.'

'If I were to offer money?'

'Aye offer money. Pay enough and a mob will swear on the Bible they have seen him in the moon.'

'Then will you scry for me?'

He took my hands and looked at me. It was clear to me he was struggling within himself. At last he nodded, sighing, 'Though lately I have not felt the spirits whispering at my ears – but for you my little Jabez, tomorrow I shall try.'

We borrowed a mirror from the inn and set it so that the light falling through the casement would spring into the room. Neither one of us took breakfast, but spent the hours from dawn on our knees. When the sun was strong, Talbot drew a circle round us both and said the words and waited. Nothing. The surface reflected the sky. I was afraid in case I saw a crow fly across it, but there was only a vacancy. At last Talbot shook his head.

'I am sorry Jabez-Jane. I am become so used to you I dread you finding your pigman. Perhaps it is that. Or perhaps the fairies are angry that I am making gold without them. Or it might be, of course, that he is not to be found.'

After he'd gone I sat on the bed. For a while I wept as though all hope was lost, but then I collected myself. Talbot couldn't help me, but I could help myself. If he were no longer here there were people who knew what happened, who might be persuaded to say where he had gone. Someone would let something fall.

In all my imaginings I had only to gain Lancaster to find him. He was either on the road as it led north or waiting for me in the city. Sometimes, when my courage failed me, it was the fresh mound of his grave that haunted me, with its wooden cross. But never this quicksand of sympathetic rumour and untruth. Perhaps he had indeed gone mad and forgot himself and me. I spent the day enquiring of healers, apothecaries, cunning women. No one had been called for, nothing procured, no one paid to nurse him.

Talbot sighed impatiently. 'Leave off your moping. You ask too many questions, go back to your taverns,' he went on, 'buy ale and wait and listen.'

I did as Talbot said and haunted the taverns and alehouses hour on hour, sliding greetings into talk with strangers. My master, I let slip, liked to be rid of me till evening. I was friendly, I asked about trade, about the harvest; I shared my jug of ale. I did not speak of Jacob any more, but occasionally made a mention of Sir Thomas, Edward Croft. I did not speak to women, neither the potgirls nor the wenches who sidled in when the sun began sinking; they looked at me too closely.

It surprised me a little, how easy I took to dissembling, how I could look in a man's face and smile and lie. It surprised me too, how eager men were, finding me quiet, to hint at the dark corners of their lives. One day, I found myself thinking, if I ever earn my bread through offering physic I will remember this. Gently, I would nudge them away from their own concerns and back to talk of the trouble at Easter. Very slowly, like bits of a picture showing though white-wash, I learned things I had not known.

29

While I was about my business Talbot pursued his. It was not honest, I could tell that much, although I never knew the whole of it. There were title deeds – the gift of a suppressed friary near Kirkham, other houses, made out in the Preston lawyer's name and in Talbot's own name too.

'Do you suppose anyone would be such a sot as to allow you to usurp ownership with these?' I asked him.

'Why not?' Talbot smiled. 'It happens every day. But that is not, quite, what I am after, at present. These will be security for loans, that's all. You are not too nice for that, are you Jabez-Jane? With your dead men's rings stitched in your drawers?'

The people at the inn treated him, I saw, with an exaggerated respect. Even I was bobbed and bowed to. A sly rumour had begun he was a wastrel cousin of George Talbot, the Earl of Shrewsbury. After luncheon one afternoon he appeared with a lawn ruff and a fancy velvet doublet that hung down to his thighs, so thick in the July afternoon he looked basted for the spit. For me he brought a fine blue jerkin.

'Don't get a speck on it, or the hiring will cost double,' he grunted, thrusting it at me.

That evening he took a private room. I was weary of sitting alone for bits and scraps from strangers and agreed to join him. After all, it was part of my story that I had a master to serve. We were gamesters, ale-knights, gallants – at least to those beyond the locked door. Before the potboy and the girl with the ale jug, Talbot was a gentleman losing great sums at cards. I drank more ale than I was used to, although by now I could stomach a bellyful. Near midnight I glanced into my bowl and saw a gaunt shock-headed boy grin back at me. He had wobbled into pieces before I knew him for myself.

My mind was unsteadied, but not only by the drink. When I was Jacob's wife, I knew the names of things and their shapes. My secrets were the simples I gathered from the woods and fields. I had long since buried my wayward past. Jacob had walked into my trial and proved me not a witch but a wife, and when I took his hand and stepped out into the sunlight the world steadied beneath my feet and ceased its whirling changes. There were the seasons, the rise and fall of the sun, the properties of flowers, the day's work, and, as present as breath, the promise of his body beneath his lockram smock, the scent of it.

Those were the years of the sun, of Jacob's golden hair. Since losing him I felt I had fallen back towards the inconstant moon, that is now a curved blade and now a hanging pearl, but ever the moon still. I was a boy and a thief and I slapped thighs and threw curses and slept each night next to a conjurer of daemons. How could I once again be Martha, walking through the wet dew with Jacob? I tried to summon my old face into the ale-pot, but she would not come.

By the dark middle of the night I found I was on my bed with a candle burning and my thoughts still eddying like the water at Cockerham sands. I thought of my book – I had long since stopped calling it the Steward's – with its gods and girls and heroes flowing into new forms as water flows around an obstacle. A girl became a cow, a tree, a spider. Was that what Talbot was after too; a friary became a scroll became a bag of gold? In my half sleep I saw the rushing tide at the Lune's mouth, the turbulent roll of it, making new patterns of the bay. I was the grinning boy in the beer bowl laughing with the surge, and then I was the tossed foam on its back, fizzing into sea mist.

High in the curtains of the bed sat a crooked spider. In the book spiders were the daughters of Arachne, the girl cursed because she dared to talk back to the gods. On the chair beside me hung Talbot's borrowed velvet, hunched round a man of air. How dare you hire new faces, it seemed to say, you and that farting hoaxer beside you, what right have you to put on borrowed clothes; it is against the laws of man and heaven to create yourself anew. Arachne was a poor man's child; she could weave better than Minerva, but what did her skill weigh against Minerva's power? The goddess simply twisted her into a crooked, creeping thing. That was honesty's reward – as though heaven's lords and ladies, and her fat burghers, would allow a fair fight – and with a woman, too!

When day broke through the slats my head ached, but I didn't feel subdued or guilty. If Arachne had learned how to play a part she would never have had to scuttle and hide so. She deserved better. Only when a dew-spangled web caught the slant light of morning did we catch our breath at her skill. The world was set against clever women; it was no sin to trick it if you could.

Or think of it this way, I thought. Every second parish had a tale of the devil being cheated of a soul. At Cockerham sands our guide, learning that Talbot was in the way of a diviner, told us a story of a local cunning man. No cleverer man had ever walked the banks of the Lune, he said. So of course, when the devil came to Cockerham the people begged his help. He stepped onto the sands and drew a summoning ring and the Fiend in all his fiery wickedness stood before him. 'I'll leave this place in peace,' Satan said, 'if you can pose me a task I cannot answer; three chances you'll have, and if you fail, I'll take your soul.' First off the wizard asked him how many raindrops hung on the hedgerows between the sands and Ellel. 'Thirteen,' cried Old Nick. 'All the rest were shaken free by the wind I raised in coming here.' 'Count how many ears of corn grow in Tithepig's field.' the wizard said; before he could draw a breath the Old Enemy answered him and though the number was beyond count he felt in his bones that the devil had it right. 'One task left,' said the devil. 'Look how the jaws of hell slaver for you.' So the wizard looked out at the sea, sore afraid, thinking he might be seeing it for the last time. He dug his toes into the cool sand and felt how it shifted as the water passed through it. 'Twist a rope of sand,' he said, 'and wash it here, in the Cocker, without losing a grain.' Well, the devil screamed at that and quivered and kicked, but there was nothing he could do. He was beaten.

The devil could not hook your soul if you were wilier than he, not if you stepped ever so near, not so long as you watched the world closely and did not overreach.

The carousing that night set the pattern. Talbot let his reputation bubble through the town and then he followed after, enquiring for loans, with the deeds in his satchel as surety. He was very careful to borrow discreetly, so that each lender believed himself the only patron, the deeds he held the only mortgaged property. I gave him the rings I had left to pawn alongside. The men who lent to him – three in all – were bloated with greed and gold, and congratulated themselves for lifting property so lightly from a noble fool. Talbot himself had fits of conscience, alternately jubilant at the sound of gold or on his knees in church, wringing God for forgiveness for sins he would continue to commit tomorrow, but I held myself a hardened wretch, and did not have a qualm that I was party to deceit.

30

One night in a low-roofed tavern in Butchers Street I fell into talking with a grizzled, burly man who said he was a cooper. He showed me where he had lost two fingers to a burn. The skin was pink and smooth still, knotted up like peeled wood. I helped him to ale and nudged him into talk of scandal. I'd lately come, I said, from the Marches; there was open fighting in Shrewsbury between my lord Croft's men and his brother knight Thomas Coningsby. Talk was they'd quarrelled here in Lancaster, round Easter time.

He nodded, he remembered them. A great to do there was. The party had been here almost a week, at the manor at Highfield, when the lords quarrelled and Croft took rooms at the Blue Boar. He brawled through every tavern, lined the pockets of every card player in the town. It was as though he held a grudge against peace itself. There were rumours he had a harlot stripped and made to stand against a wall so that he and his men could throw their daggers between her thighs. Almost any other man's son and he would have been pinned in the castle – but his father had long fingers in the north. Then a man was murdered and he left – cantered off at dawn like the wind was after him.

I nodded and raised my cup to cover my face a moment. His words stirred a memory – the party of horsemen cantering through the wood on Easter Eve, when Meg and Mary and I were gathering flowers. One, in front, grimacing into the wind on a fine black courser. How could I not have recognised Edward Croft? By this time I had learned to recover myself quickly. It was as though the story were not of Jacob but of some other man. I looked over the lip of my beer and drew up my brows for more, batting away a red-lipped doxy who had hovered about me all evening like a fly. You could make of that what you wished, my companion said, dropping his voice, and glancing just enough towards the jug for me to know to pour it, only you'd better not be making too much of it if you didn't want an accident one night when the fog was thick enough to make the watchmen and the constables forgetful.

Soon after, as I picked my way out, through rushes sticky with beer and spit, I found the girl was on my arm. I tried to shrug her off. I was used to jades – half the alehouses were stews on the side and I was not such a fool as I had been when the girl in Worcester had set about selling me to her friends.

'Leave me be,' I said, as gruffly as I could. 'I'm not for you.'

'No,' she said, drawing me into the shadow by the door, 'I've guessed that much, duckie, you've no yard, unless it be buckram. But I don't mind that, not if there's silver nesting where your prick should be.'

The room felt suddenly distant. I tried to appear scornful, but her eyes were too clever, there was no practising on them. I tried to push past her to the door, but there she was before me. I watched her glance merrily at the room behind me and for a moment I was afraid. If she were to denounce me, here, before this rabble? But she didn't denounce me, instead she took my head in her hand and pulled me into a long kiss, so that the men behind us cheered and stamped. 'Better let her pluck your cherry, lad, 'fore some carrion bird makes off with it.'

Her lips were soft and sweet and I felt nothing at all, except a desolating loneliness.

She took me by the hand and drew me into the street then, leaning her back against a wall and pulling me close by my shirt. 'There,' she said, 'did you like that?'

'No,' I said. We were the same height, more or less; the same age too I'd guess. Her face still had a softness to it beneath the paint, but her expression was sharp – she had given over coquetry and was all over shrewdness, 'What do you want?' I said. 'Money?'

She smiled. 'You like secrets, don't you? Costly things, they are. How much will you pay for a secret, I wonder?'

'To have one kept or to have one told?'

'Well,' she said, leaning in to me as a man walked by, 'You'll be needing the first, if t'other's to be any good to you. Come with me.'

I followed her along Butchers Street to a damp alley off Fish Market where a door stood ajar and a candle burned in the casement, flickering over the gutter that ran beside the flagstones. A cat wheedled against my legs. Jacob's knife was in my belt, but I knew it would be of little use – if this was a trap I could not cut my way out. There was a parlour of sorts on the first floor, with gaudy hangings and a bird in a cage. A farmer was snoring on a couch with his head on the lap of an old jade who was picking at her nails. She looked up as we came in.

'Got yourself a fine colt for breaking in, have you Betsy?' she said with a wink, then turned to me. 'You'll be wanting wine sir? And pie? Sarah!'

A small girl appeared from behind a painted cloth.

'See to the gentleman's shoes, girl. And bring him wine.'

'No!' I said, as she bundled herself at my feet and began unlacing me. 'No, thank you.' My voice sounded ridiculous, leaping higher than the candle. The old punk exchanged a glance with Betsy, but so smoothly it passed with a gutter of the flame.

Betsy led me up dark stairs to a further room, ripe with the smells of the market, even now that the moon was rising. She lit a pair of candles and I caught my breath, for the place was hung with bits of coloured glass stitched into lace, ribbons, strips of lawn. The walls glinted like a church.

'You're fortunate,' she said, 'I don't show everyone. When the sun is just so, it throws colour petals all across the room.'

'How did you come by it all?

'Found some, was given some. Folks know I like it. Some call me the glass girl. Some say I summon spirits with the lights.'

I turned to her; she must have thought me disapproving, for she went on. 'I ain't no devil-dealer. *God is light*, it says so in the Gospels.'

'All the same,' I said, 'you should take care. The gallows get hungry. I was called a witch once.'

'And were you?'

'No more than you,' I said.

'Is that why you feign to be a boy?'

There was a knock at the door and the small girl came in with the wine I didn't want and a great hunk of pie. Her coming broke into what had begun to feel like an openness between us. I was glad – I should have learnt by now to be more careful.

The room was thick with heat. I unbuttoned my jerkin and leaned out of the casement in my shirt. The roofs overlaid each other like a pile of planks. Not far off a dam rat and all her young softly picked their way across the tiles.

'No,' I said, 'that's not the reason. I'm looking for someone. Petticoats get attention on the road. People say he was stabbed here, the week before Easter.'

'Your leman, was he?'

I turned and looked at her and despite all my resolutions a sob rose in my throat. 'I have been to every pigswill brewhouse in the city and all I hear is that he's cold. It's said there were knives drawn over a girl, but I don't believe it. He was – he is – truer than the morning.'

She was sitting on the bed, idly circling the rim of her goblet with her finger. 'You don't know much of men, do you?'

'What do you mean?'

She patted the bed next to her for me to sit down. I was minded to stand, indignant, at the window, but she did not laugh and I was too tired for resentment. I sat down a little awkwardly and she put her goblet down and reached her arms round me, pulling my head onto her shoulder. She was almost as skinny a wretch as I was, but for a moment I could have believed myself with Sally; it was so long since a woman had embraced me. I missed it so.

'It en't the same. The world don't hold it's false for a man to dally when he's away from home, not if he's heart-whole. They can no more keep from it than shitting. But you think he's living still?'

'He's not dead.' I sobbed out, 'Nobody could show me to his grave.'

She stroked my hair while I wept and then she let out a long sigh. 'There now. You're a nesh fool, you are, you're like a ballad, tramping heath and hollow to find your lover. Look how you've made my face run in sympathy. What will you pay me to learn a little more?'

I pulled back abruptly at that and stood and wiped my eyes. There was no comfort from strangers, only pursuit of gold. She had played me better than a pipe. A little show of pity and I'd spilt like a cracked cup. To look for honesty from a spotted whore!

'Oh, look at you,' she said, 'stiffer than a puritan at prayer. Do you think I don't eat? I could be sitting on a butcher's knee nibbling my way to a silver shilling, if I hadn't pitied you. You never touched a bit of gold with dirt on it? Is that it? I should call you out, you and that swindling dissembler you're confederate with. He's no more a gentleman than you are a squire.'

She was right. Who was I to judge her stratagems and play the puffed-up cock? 'I'm sorry sister,' I said, and reached out for her hand, which after a moment she let me take. I sat back down on the bed. 'Please,' I said, 'tell me what you know and I promise I'll pay you better than the butcher.'

She sniffed a little and trimmed the candle. 'There ain't that much. There was a girl working at the Saracen's Head, hadn't been there long. Fresh sweet thing she was, the landlord's niece, although that only came out later. One of your lordings took a fancy to her and as the devil willed it came across her late when he went to take a piss. Only the work of a minute, and a sovereign flung at her and all done, but the poor wretch screamed and bit his hand before he had his pizzle out.' She paused and took both my hands. 'Your young man, if that's the one, happened to be running into the alley. Perhaps it was a foggy night; perhaps the shadow was too thick, or perhaps he was as rash a niddicock as you are – he stepped in front of the girl and took his master's dagger in his belly.'

My breath had stuck in my chest while she talked. I saw it all – Jacob pushing Croft back from the terrified girl; Croft's disbelief – this man, half a head taller, stronger than he was, defying him, was one of their own servants. A cur from Coningsby's stables! I doubted he said a word, I doubted he paused at all, but simply reached for the blade and stuck it. I nodded. 'So,' I said, forcing my voice level, 'is he dead indeed? Did he bleed to death in the gutter?'

'All I know is, he was believed dead and his body taken back to the Saracen's, but the girl sat vigil beside him and bound him as well as she could. Towards dawn she declared a stir of life in him. Then he was gone. Some said he was slipped away by the other lord, some said Croft had paid men to see him well buried on the moors. Then an agent of Croft's father turned up and made it understood that no one must say anything at all. The girl was sent to another house.'

I sat silent a long while and then I nodded and thanked her and gave her a whole reckless angel from my purse. I wanted to hoard and count over what she had told me alone.

'Tell me,' I said, as she took me to the stairs, 'did you know me at once a girl? I had almost given over fearing discovery.'

'Don't fret. You are barely a girl at all; there's few would wonder enough to make you out.'

'Yes,' I said, nodding, 'I've learned how little people care to look at their fellows. But you knew, straight.'

'For us it pays to be attentive. Any whore could tell you that. The sots down there in the marketplace, they see the world as their wishes reckon it – as it appears in their looking glass. We know that's all just dazzle and reflection – bits of truth and broken shards and splinters.'

31

Two days later I left Lancaster with Talbot for Hornby Castle. After meeting Betsy I had spent a day loitering round The Saracen's Head, but even my attempts to bribe were fruitless. I was impatient. By the afternoon nobody would speak to me and finally the landlord stepped out from his barrels and kicked me onto the street. As I limped off a boy pulled at my breeches and whispered he'd been sent to say I'd better leave, or maybe I'd be made a present of my tongue. It could be the landlord sent him, I don't know, but I was frightened. I skulked back to the inn glancing into alleys for a man with a knife. There seemed little I could do more in the city anyway. Wherever Jacob was, it was not here.

My own reasons for leaving aside, I was anxious about Talbot's activities. As we'd drawn north he'd grown ever more reckless and now, just as he neared his lady patron, he appeared heedless of risk altogether. He had paid for our hired clothes and bought fine collars and even after this had too much gold to sew into our seams, but it was not his cozening that worried me so much as the rumours that had spread about his sorcery. He had had dealings at the inn with men who had sold him a pouch of red dust and a scroll inscribed with magical signs that he loudly declared contained wonders, and must not be spoken of. His candle coal had been polished to a beautiful round stone that could give a man back a picture of himself; Talbot spoke of it with awe quite openly, said it would lead him to the company of angels. A little magic might be safe for a dissolute gentleman, but that ruse could scarcely last and then our situation would be dangerous. A man might go to a scryer to find his goods, or his wife, but he'd join the mob against a conjurer.

He had evidently sent ahead, for we were expected; the horses were led off and our luggage carried by servants to fine lodgings near to the tower itself. The Lady Elizabeth, we were informed, would give Talbot an audience in an hour, after we had eaten.

'Are you afraid?' I asked Talbot, when the servant came to fetch us.

Talbot gestured at the grey looming tower, with its high windows, 'Of this?' he asked. 'Yes, a little. Of course. I'm not a fool, Jabez. But a new world is coming and the old will fall. For now this tower rises above us with all its power and we are creatures who creep about at its base, but when the last days begin I shall be golden.'

I glanced at him. He had left the counterfeiter behind and was all prophet now, but I didn't have his faith or confidence. The last time I tried to enter a great house I had been chased away and handed to a mob who clawed the skin off my back. My hands sweated at the thought of it. I glanced at Talbot – how little he knew me; how little we knew each other! We were ushered into the hall itself where a fire roared despite it being harvest.

I had expected an old woman, laden with jewels that mocked her loose, thin skin, but the Lady Elizabeth was not old, although she was pale enough, with a way of throwing her hand up to her forehead to feel the heat or the moistness of it. For a second I thought what it might be to approach her with my bag of simples – to gauge the pinkness of her eyes and the smell of her sweat and mix her up remedies – but I was not such a simpleton as to think I could safely physic a body like hers. She and I and Betsy of the stews would all be worms' meat soon enough, but till then, her silks and velvets deterred any healer who could not read Greek. She gestured us to sit.

'What branch of Talbot are you? Worcestershire?'

Talbot inclined his head.

She smiled. 'I am told the county grows good pears. I have some property near, or is it Herefordshire – I forget – there's a moated grange among it, mostly a ruin now, there is some story attached, I recall. I thought it might be a pretty present for you; very pleasant country they tell me, and softer than here. But never mind that. I am told you have rare gifts, Edward Talbot, that you can see things, like the magician of the tower in the story. Is it true?'

'It is, ma'am.'

'Is it?' She craned forwards towards him and her eyes flamed, but perhaps it was borrowed brightness from the burning logs. 'Tell me how it started. Did a devil come to you? I am dying you know; you must tell me the truth and not waste time.'

She wore a cross about her neck; it was crusted with stones and every now and again the afternoon sun or the fire sparked it; what good is it there on her chest, I thought, where she cannot catch the gleam of it and has only the weight. I noticed that she did not touch it once. Her eyes flitted with a kind of desperate energy, as though she was stood on a brink.

'There is a cloth before our eyes, that blinds us to the celestial world,' Talbot said, meeting and steadying her eyes. 'For ordinary men, only when they dream does it grow so gossamer thin that they see beyond. But I was born with different eyes. Even as a child I sensed at times the air thick with spirits. Standing by a pool or staring in my cup visions grew unasked for from the surface of the water.'

'Ministers of the Church say these are devils, sent to deceive us and drown our souls in sin.'

'There are devils madam, it is true – and many times I have had to cast them from me in the shape of rats and monkeys. Other times I've known them take on pleasing shapes – a soft young girl offering me a chain of daisies – mild-seeming as the flower, but an adder in your hand. Such visions test me, they rip my soul apart; I call on God and all the angels to take away my eyes, but He has made me a door. I cannot help but look. I become the veil itself, men look through me to the spectral world. But I swear to you on that holy cross you wear at your heart that mine is a holy quest; I help clowns find the coin they dropped or their wandering pig, but I know I can find a greater prize, for I know there is a treasure hid in a field which is of more worth than all else besides.'

'One precious pearl. Yes.'

No wonder she believed him, I believed him myself. Owl-eyed, stub-thumbed, he looked more suited to manage a bearpit than to discourse with a peer's daughter, yet there was a power in his words that compelled. His voice, too, was rich and warm, plain but educated. Don't be afraid, it seemed to say, see how I open your eyes to wonders. I'd told him once that his voice, when he wasn't crabbed, was his one beauty. 'Yes,' he said, 'but note how I keep it a notch below gentlemanly when I talk to my betters, so as not to unsettle their pride.' He was a counterfeiter and a gamester, but he could draw spirits from the air.

'I confess,' Lady Elizabeth said, 'I have been curious for a long time. I have read a little; perhaps you would be surprised a woman would read so much. I know Hermes Trismegistus, who walked the earth with Moses, when God spoke directly to His people. I am persuaded a divine magic is accessible to man.'

'And a godhead too – as Mirandola has written – our souls are a cluster of seeds and what in our lives we cultivate will grow, whether it be to the state of a cabbage, or a sensual beast or the angel that perceives by intellect – or even greater than this – to withdraw into the unity of our own spirit, one with the solitary darkness of the Maker.'

There was a solemn silence after he spoke. I was afraid he had gone too far – from the corner of my eye I caught a servant, out of his mistress's eye cross himself – but Lady Stanley was nodding, a hand at her temple, her eyes glistening with tears.

'I should like you to scry for me, now, Talbot.'

A gentlewoman I had not noted came forward. She must have been seated in a window; she swept past both of us with a look of faint disgust before turning to her mistress.

'My Lady,' she said, 'you are tired. The excitement is not good for you; you must eat now. This can wait until tomorrow, surely?'

Lady Elizabeth sighed and nodded. 'You are right, as always, Mary, but my husband might return tomorrow and then there would be no scrying for me at all. I am sure Mr Talbot will not vex me. Do you need more candles?'

Mary hovered for a moment, with her mouth full of words, and then pressed her lips together and stepped back, glaring at Talbot as though she would dearly like to kick him.

'Yes, more candles,' Talbot said, 'and begging your leave, madam, I must go apart for some minutes to pray.'

We were led into the chapel. Talbot flung himself before the Virgin and began his mutterings. I bent my head and pressed my palms together, but my soul clammed up and fell to bargaining – lead me to Jacob, Lord, I thought, and I will peel myself open even to the heart, if you desire it.

At last Talbot heaved himself up and we were led back. With the shutters closed one half of the hall was in shadow, but at the further end constellations of lit sconces picked out the gallery. Talbot approached Lady Elizabeth and asked for cushions that they might both kneel. When they had done so he solemnly pulled from his bag the candle coal showstone, placing it on a cloth of velvet before him. She gasped. It was indeed beautiful – smooth as water and black as though it were darkness itself made stone. Talbot called it obsidian stone, forged out of fire. If she knew, I wondered, that a ragged boy had chipped it from the earth near Wigan and sold it for pennies! A little to the side, Lady Elizabeth's gentlewoman stood, her nose uptilted like a watchful hound. I took up my position behind Talbot likewise.

If I were her, I thought, I should doubt too. I would note how my lady's hands twitched in yearning and damn Talbot for a parasite, a prowler, a practiser upon the weak. I thought him so myself quite often, but not in this. A solemn magic hung round him and his eyes were lit by spirit fires. We all of us sought God's ear every day, we looked and found His warnings and blessings in the fields or in the clouds, why should He not send His angels to talk to us directly?

'In nomine Patris filii et Spiritus Sanctus Amen,' Talbot said, making the sign of the cross, and uttering the words I had learned to mouth along with him. 'On, Ell, Eloy, Eley, Messias, Sother, Emmanuel, Sabaoth.'

We waited in silence for him to continue. The room grew very quiet. It seemed to me that the air shimmered. I would not have been surprised to see it part like a curtain and a spirit or a fairy enter. Then all at once the candle flames, each and every one, sputtered and bent low as though from an unseen breath. Even Mistress Mary gasped. Talbot began to speak in a low, chanting tone. 'I see a spark of fire; it spins and grows; it blazes, it steps free from the stone. It is a man tall and lustrous in a pilgrim's cloak, with a staff in his hand. Who are you that is called to the crystal?'

'I am Azarias,' he answered in a different voice, 'who travelled with Tobiah, Tobit's son and you know me as Raphael, who stirred the waters of Bethesda to heal the sick. Look now at what I shall show you.'

Then Talbot leaned back and looked up towards the great rafters of the hall, where shadows cast by the candles dimly flickered. He threw his arms wide. 'I will,' he said, and stood, gesturing to Lady Elizabeth to stand with him. He stared into the darkness of the roof space.

'Behold,' he said in Azarias's voice, 'A wide plain with a long empty road across it that leads to a stretch of shining silver water. It laps a range of mountains like a moat. The dawn begins behind the peaks – look how the cloud flushes pink with welcome. And now there is a multitude upon the road; men and women of every station and degree.'

Talbot paused and looked round at us with unseeing eyes. 'Do you follow?' he asked in Azarias's voice still.

We nodded, struck with the vision which seemed to hang before us like a cloth, painted out of air and candlelight.

He went on, 'After the people, although they know it not, trail jewelled serpents on their bellies in the dirt. And soon the serpents reach those who straggle last – the lame and the halt, the old and the very young; but them they pass by. And soon they reach the body of common folk, men and women each with the sign of their trade or manor upon them and some of these glance at the jewel-crusted serpents with desire and are hobbled at the ankle with a bite; but these too are soon passed by. Then the snakes pass among brave fellows – fine ladies in carriages, bishops and princes and these stoop for the gold and the bright gems on the serpents' backs and pick them up to hang round their necks or twist them into rings about their fingers. Hung about with vipers they dazzle through the afternoon.'

We saw it all, the degrees of men and women, the gentry and

nobility with vipers curling at their necks. He paused. Lady Elizabeth was paler than a winding sheet, staring at Talbot with feverish eyes. Her gentlewoman laid a hand upon her shoulder, signalling him to stop, but he went on.

'In the evening all approach the silver water and plunge in over their heads. And those who the serpents passed by emerge from the water as birds who fly up to the mountain, but those hung about by snakes are held down by the weight of them and their new feathers flap like weeds in the moving depths and cannot help them and the worms begin to writhe and feed upon their flesh.'

Talbot stopped speaking, but we did not move at once, for his eyes had fallen back towards the stone. After a moment he shook himself. 'Azarias walks away,' he said, in a voice so quiet I think I alone could hear it, 'but wait, he pauses, and throws another vision like a coin to a begging man. It is the moon and the devil has built a bridge across it. A lame swan flies through the darkness pecking stars; it crosses the bridge. On the farther side stands a man with a limp, holding a spirit child by the hand. He takes a ring from his hand and throws it to the swan and the bird becomes a woman.'

Then Talbot's eyes returned to us and he nodded and crumpled to the floor. I thought him in a fit, but when I took his head in my hands he opened his eyes and murmured quietly.

'All is well,' I said to Lady Stanley who had started forwards as though she too might fall, 'It is only that the visions exhaust him.'

'Yes, yes,' she said, taking my hand. 'He must rest. I am moved beyond all thought. Tomorrow we must continue.'

Her eyes looked afraid and lonely. I almost forgot her greatness and squeezed her smooth white hand, but caught myself in time; she was in a tower and locked in velvet. I bowed low and helped Talbot to his feet. With one arm across my shoulders and the other across a servant we half walked, half dragged him out.

'I hope you weren't impressed by that charade, Elizabeth,' I heard the lady Mary say behind me. 'You should have them whipped.'

'Peace, Mary,' her mistress answered. 'Don't presume to tell me what I should believe. I don't care what he is. An angel spoke through him. I'm sure of it.'

It was still only five o'clock. Servants brought meat and pottage and wine to the table but Talbot could not eat. He turned and groaned on his bed, crying out that his spine was being ripped apart and his entrails burned. More than once he commanded me to look and tell him whether or no he was on fire. There was an angel and a devil wrestling for his soul and he would go barefoot and beg his living in a blanket if he could only be rid of their wrangling and this cursed gift. I am sure he meant it, too. If he was a cozener, as the lady Mary said, then it was not only the great ones that he deceived but me, his companion and, as I thought, his friend; I was sure Azarias's last crumb had been for me. What it meant, however, I had no idea. I bit my tongue and waited.

He slept all evening and into the night. I dined and lay down early, puzzling the story of the bridge and the moon. It made little sense to me. When we had visited the pool he had simply shown me Jacob, smiling with his arms open in welcome. This was another kind of seeing altogether, fraught with riddles.

In the dark middle of the night I took the stone from Talbot's bedside and taking a candle sat down with it upon my knee. I knew the words to say. If Azarias had spoken to Talbot perhaps he would speak to me. Softly, I began. The candle flame danced on the shining surface of the stone and then, as I watched, it seemed to enter. It was drawing me towards it. A terrible dread engulfed me. I gasped and covered the stone with my nightshirt. Not yet, I thought, not now.

32

The following morning, a bright warm sun clamoured at the shutters; Talbot was not there. At first I was concerned, given his transports the night before, but as soon as I ventured out I heard him, loudly declaiming to a gardener on the pruning of roses. As soon as I can be alone, I thought, looking at the gardener, I shall talk to all the people here to find out what they know. I will pay a boy to tramp to all the villages about. Jacob was near death, he cannot have been taken far.

On seeing me advance Talbot stepped forward and, to my astonishment, grasped my arms and clasped me to him, kissing me on the lips. I released myself as swiftly as I could and studied him for signs of madness, taking in, too, the gardener's surprise that a master should embrace his servant so heartily.

'Are you well, sir?' I asked.

He hesitated, then grinned, and taking me by the elbow, walked me aside among the little paths of the knot garden, pausing however, in full sight of the gardener, to pluck a pink rose and thread it in my shirt.

'Oh Jabez-Jane,' he said, 'I am struck with wonder. You saw it happen. An angel walked with me. This dross earth will turn to gold beneath my feet; it will pour riches upon me. I tell you, it blasted my soul to see the seraphim, flaming red, step out of the stone and open up the mind of God on earth.'

'You lay on your bed, after, crying that a demon and an angel tussled for your soul. You did not seem so certain then it was a holy vision.'

'It was holy. I saw nothing against His word, all was in praise of God. I tell you a music flowed through me as I slept which pacified the roaring in my head; it was an angel singing; pearl-soft, pearl-pure, it wrapped a dream of peace round my gritted heart.'

'I'm glad of it,' I said.

We passed by a pretty summerhouse and through a gate. Before us reared a hedge maze. I knew of them, there was one at Hampton Court, although I had never approached it. Talbot entered. I paused a moment, then followed after him between hedges that were higher than my head. Talbot turned a corner and the paths branched and I couldn't see him although I knew that he was near, by the rustle of the leaves. The paths thwarted me; they folded back upon themselves, or turned aside or stopped dead; above me the sun grew high and hot and soon there were no more sounds of Talbot. I began to be a little afraid – at first out of dread that one of the household should chance upon me – that I would turn a corner and see the Lady's young son and his nurse perhaps, or worse, Mary, the lady-in-waiting. Lord Morley himself might have returned! I began to run, skidding at the turns, taking whatever path I thought was new. I felt foolish to be caught in so silly a trap and more foolish that I was afraid. Why had I not waited among the roses? At the centre was a tower; time and again I came close to it, only a hedge between us, but then I would be thrown back to an outer ring. It was not like being lost in a wood – where the sun and the sound of water and the fall of the land were signs to be read; the maze was the puzzle of a man's mind, the dead-ends, the frustrations were human-made.

Half an hour, more, had gone by and I had advanced and regressed in turn, now attempting to reason out the pattern, now choosing blindly with panic in my throat. All at once I heard Talbot's voice above me. I looked up, he was standing on the roof of the central tower, leaning on the balustrade and grinning.

'How far you have travelled from your village, Jabez-Jane, and to so little purpose.'

'Damn you Talbot, tell me the way to the centre.'

'And your tongue grown so rough; it will give you whiskers yet.'

'Which way?'

'Do you know the story of the Minotaur, Jabez-Jane? Pasiphae's bastard son – half man, half bull - that they imprisoned in a labyrinth? Of course you do, it's in your little book.'

It must have been almost noon; the sun bore down on me and the hedges trapped the heat. I was tired of his games.

'I think your bumpkin, your hob-clunch husband is probably rather a bull-man, isn't he, Jabez? Great bull shoulders and hairy arms? That way will lead you nowhere.'

My heart beat in fear that he should broadcast me a woman so publicly. I stopped and glared up at him, took the rose he had given me and ground it under my shoe. He stopped his grinning and glared back at me in turn.

'Is he hung like a bull, Jabez?'

I swallowed and said nothing.

'Will you go back to your byre and lie on your back for an unlettered boor? A lobcock, a rustic that chews the cud and spits?'

I reached a choice of ways and turned away from the centre, and found it. Talbot had come down to the foot of the tower. I pushed him aside, but he caught my arms.

'And when you find him, if ever you do, will either of you have the wit to get out? You'll be stuck in the labyrinth for ever. Do you think you will be happy, Jabez, buried in a muck-strewn hamlet, with pigs and peas your only conversation?'

'Enough.' I said. 'You have abused me enough. Stop now or I shall hate you.' I tried to pull myself from him, but he pressed me against the tower wall.

'Marry me,' he said. 'The vision last night. The final one. You are the swan, the bird of the sun, who must cross back over the moon, the male and female conjoined. Only when I, the man with the limp, capture you with a golden ring will you recover your true shape. In union with you I will join what is sundered and conceive the royal child; the devil will be defeated. It is so clear. Last night when you stood behind me I felt a greater power in my sight. You are called to be my wife.'

'No,' I said, 'No.' A chill seized me despite the noon sun and the warm wall at my back. 'It can't be what was meant. It can't be. The man was Jacob.'

'You have looked under every stone in Lancaster. He is not here. He is lost. The man you are called to unite with is me. An angel came to me. You felt its presence.'

I looked at his face; he was in earnest. A horror began to seep through me – that he was right – that it was him, not my own sweet Jacob I was travelling towards. I too had felt the presence of the angel. Was that why I'd been tempted to look into the stone?

He shook my arms a little and then smiled, taking my silence for consent. His eyes were bright with excitement, but they didn't move me. God's word or no I would not do it. I could not marry him, even if I risked hell in refusing.

'Even if what you say is true – which I do not grant – you do not love me Edward Talbot and I don't love you.'

He laughed. 'Earthly love, what's that? We can give each other animal satisfaction, Jabez. Love might come, and if it doesn't, what then? I – we – are destined to soar high above this corrupted midden, to become purified, golden. I shall find the stone.'

'No,' I said. 'I will love you as a friend. No more.'

He released my arms and stepped back. I watched shutters close on the gleam in his eyes, leaving only a malicious glint. His lip curled. 'You prefer your peasant and a hovel life to me. Think girl! I could teach you Latin, take you with me to the courts of princes, lead you even into the company of angels – your sight sustaining mine.'

'Then I would be your familiar,' I said, 'not your wife. You are a devil to tempt me with learning. Leave off this talk; you frighten me.'

I turned to enter the tower, but he caught my arm. 'Unsexed wretch. Your blood is congealed ice.' He brought his face so close I could almost feel the sweat on his cheeks. 'I could force you,' he said. 'I should have done it days and days since. I could do it here, now, at the heart of the maze; that would be fitting don't you think?'

I shook his hand away. 'You would not,' I said. 'That is not what I meant. I am not afraid of you in that way. It's your ambition makes me tremble. I don't doubt your gifts, Edward Talbot, but you would eat Satan's apple and chew the pips, yes and send me to the highest branches to pick you more, if you believed that it would serve your purposes. Listen to yourself, boasting of angels and threatening rape. You are the bull, Talbot, not Jacob.'

For a moment he held my gaze, but the thrill of violence was gone. He passed his hand over his eyes then and fell to his knees and groaned. 'Forgive me,' he said. 'I think there is a demon in me still. I almost have it crushed, but it is like a worm in the soft matter of my brain; its channels divert the proper course of my thoughts.'

It went through my mind to lay my hand on his hat; I am sure he meant me to do it – to absolve him as though I were a priest. My hand hovered, but then I turned and leapt up the stone stairs of the tower. Let him feel some pangs. From the top of the tower the maze was laid out before me with all its angles and threads like a cobweb. How easy to find one's direction when raised up above the jostle of blind circumstance. No wonder the nobility were fond of the game. As I leant on the rail Talbot came up beside me, easy as though nothing had happened between us.

'I believe Lady Stanley will make me rich,' he said, 'I have great hopes of it.'

'You'd better be going down, then,' I said. 'She may call on you early.'

This he ignored, turning back from the view towards me. 'She mentioned the legend of the tower. Do you know it?'

I shook my head.

'Long ago, in the East, a magician built a tower upon which he set a mirror whose properties were such that it could show if any enemy approached. In time its secret became known to the wizard Merlin, who crafted another, more wonderful yet, that revealed – however distant – how a man fared, who he dealt with. Men came to it to ask after their wives, girls their sweethearts, merchants to spy across the seas for pirates, the King to look into the intrigues of his court. It was round and smooth and could hold a world within it.'

'Very like your showstone.'

'Yes, but my glass exceeds it, for these showed the workings of men, but yesterday I called an angel.' He pulled the stone from the bag on his shoulder and made it flash with sunlight. 'I can command wonders. Not only what is, but what will be. A minister of heaven, Jabez. Think of that.'

'I do. I am afraid of it. I believe you saw an angel. But if an angel can speak through the stone, why not a devil? Are you strong enough to bear such visions?'

'I am stronger when you stand behind me,' he said miserably, but then held up his hand, 'don't worry, I have done. I'll not speak of it again until you ask me to.'

'I never will,' I said, stepping down the stairs to leave.

If things were not resolved, at least they were quiet between us; we prepared for the second audience and as the hour approached Talbot grew nervously excited, praying urgently upon his knees, then taking out the stone and wiping it over and over with a piece of silk, talking of the great canvas of redemption he had been shown the day before, spelling out to me its meaning. He broke off only when he reached the final pictures, the angel's gift to me and here he begged I would forget his conduct, that he didn't understand it himself, I was nothing other than a boy to him – indeed he liked me better as a boy – it had been the vision, its seeming command that had moved him.

His contrition upset me almost more than his violence; it attested more than threats could ever do that he read the moon and the bridge and the limping man sincerely. I looked out of the casement and wondered if it was time now to go on alone. Tomorrow, I thought, I would ask Juno of Talbot and leave. And if the angel were right and to leave was to act against God, well then, I would take the punishment.

We waited and nobody came. Talbot began to pace the room. At last he declared we should present ourselves without a summons, but at that moment a servant knocked.

The Lady Elizabeth, the man informed us, was indisposed. If Talbot could attend her tomorrow she would be pleased to consult with him again. He should know that she held him to be gifted beyond the ordinary measure of mankind and was of a mind, if he consented, to engage his services forthwith. As a pledge of her good faith she sent this ring and out of her unparalleled munificence, this – he extended a scroll, frowning some displeasure as he did so – the deeds to a property, a moated grange with a couple of acres of land, from her father's holdings near the border of your own county. And to prevent all disputes she had added with her seal a letter that it was freely given. I listened while Talbot offered up dishes of gratitude for the man to carry back.

As soon as the servant had gone however, he fell to cursing. The ring and scroll he flung from him as though they were slick with dung. 'I am cursed, cursed. A ruin, she said it was a ruin, and no land! I am being paid off. That hag Mary is behind it. And I can feel the spirits tugging at my eyes. I could have shown her marvels.'

I picked the ring up and unrolled the parchment. The grange was in a parish called Mathon; I had no idea where that was. The ring was a band of gold with a small green stone. I tucked them both away.

'There is tomorrow,' I said. 'This is already generous.'

'Perhaps,' he said. 'I tell you, Jabez, I cannot wait. There are spirits at my shoulders pushing me to revelation. I burn with starlight. You must let me scry for you. Now.'

'No!' I said, more loudly than I meant to. 'You are not my master, Edward Talbot.'

To avoid further discussion I left him and went to the stables, to ride until my head was clear. I did not want to hear more now from yesterday's angel nor any other. I would never marry Talbot, but the world he offered plagued my peace. The dread I had felt when I looked into the stone was for what I might see – Jacob dead, or lost to me – but it was not only for that; I had seen the light begin to grow and felt a hunger for knowledge, for revelation, that fright-

ened me. It would do me no good, all that. The image I must cling
to was the one I had seen in the pool – Jacob with his arms wide in
welcome and the moor rising up behind him. It was like Satan
himself to tempt me so, to hold the wide world open before me. I
clattered out, repeating the words from Matthew as I went: "'Again
the devil taketh him up, into an exceeding high mountain, and
sheweth him all the kingdoms of the world, and the glory of them;
And saith unto him, All these will I give thee, if thou wilt fall down
and worship me.'"

33

When I returned that night Talbot was not there. Good, I thought, a ride will calm him as it did me. I ate the supper that had been left out for us alone and went to bed, glad to be rid of him for a few hours. At midnight I drifted out of sleep to the sound of the bell tolling the hours and saw that his bed was empty. When I called his name there was no reply.

Something was wrong, I was sure of it. He had taken the showstone. I pulled on my breeches, reproaching myself. I should not have left him, distracted, goaded by voices, as he was. Yet all might be well; the apprehension I felt merely the flutter of my own unease. Juno was surprised by the lantern, but I stroked her and talked to her gently and she let herself be saddled up. Softly, softly, I led her out of the yard. The village was silent, puddled in darkness. I took the road towards Lancaster, for no other reason than it seemed the better track. We picked our way slowly; I held up the lantern – in part to light the road and part in fear that I might find him strewn senseless on the ground. There was a heavy silence, broken only by the odd sheep and the constant rushing of the river.

I passed a village and then another; nobody marked me but a

chained dog that startled Juno with its barking. All the lights were tamped. More than an hour had passed; I began to chide myself for taking on such a fool's errand. He did not need a nurse! When I returned I would find him sack-sopped, snoring. And anyhow he might as well have taken the road north. Then at last I saw lights ahead of me. I looped Juno's bridle round a branch and put out my lantern so that I could approach unseen. It was an inn, with a bar room well lit, but no one, it seemed, within. The door was ajar and there was a jug of ale on a table with half-full tankards and chairs pushed back.

A little further on, where the black shape of the church rose up, I heard men's voices. There were half a dozen or so, huddled in the churchyard. I climbed the wall at a distance and trod gently up behind them, so close I could smell the beer on their breath. For their part they were intent on peering forwards; they did not notice me. Then the jostle shifted a little and across from me, in the lamp-light, I saw Talbot, at the foot of an open grave.

He was on his knees, hatless, rocking slightly back and forth in prayer. Drunk. His right cheek was black with blood and when he extended his arms over the grave his hands too were bloody. On the lip of the pit lay the showstone, lit all round by candles.

I scarcely dared breathe. This was no calling of angels. What madness had entered his soul? Kneeling beside him was a tall man, with a boy beside them holding the lantern high. All at once, in a strong clear voice, Talbot's voice rang out.

> You charms, enchantments and thou earth, whose
>   herbs
> Have furnished wizards at their greatest need,
> You elves, fairies, spirits of hills, brooks, woods
> Approach me now. For I by charms have made
> the calm seas rough and made the rough seas plain

I've raised such winds the very mountains shook
The bowels of earth have thrown forth stone and
    trees
And dead men have come walking from their
    graves.

The simple men beside me trembled with wonder but I knew the verses, they were mangled from Ovid, words the witch Medea used to summon her awful magic.

I pushed through, calling his name, but he did not appear to hear me. He was caught in his own drunken spectacle, mountebanking magic; the whites of his eyes gleamed in the lamplight. Two men took me by the arms and half flung me over the stone wall so that I sprawled on the yew-rich earth. Behind me a man cried out.

'Rise and talk,' Talbot said, 'I command you, speak to me, if you are not a fiend of hell. There are questions you must answer.'

I felt stick to my stomach and crawled away. Let him damn himself, I thought, I have done with him. A pink dawn was weakly glowing by the time I had settled Juno in her stall; I threw myself down in my clothes and let an uneasy sleep take me.

It seemed barely an hour later that a servant came knocking with my breakfast and a message. Mistress Mary, Lady Elizabeth's lady-in-waiting, had requested Talbot's presence. I was thinking how to respond when the door opened to the lady herself. She swept a glance round the room.

'He is not here,' she said.

'Mistress,' I said, 'he is gone out to pray. It is his custom.'

She laughed and poked a finger in my face. 'I know you for a pair of charlatans. Your master, I am told, is famous in Lancaster as a gamester and a drunk. I am here to tell you that you are to leave. The Lady Elizabeth was taken ill in the night; she is like not to recover. Her husband is expected daily and although he is as big a fool as she, I will see to it he does not welcome you.'

I bowed. 'Of course, ma'am, if we are not welcome, we will leave.'

'At once,' she said, turning on her heel to go. Then she threw up her hand. 'Wait,' she said, without turning. 'You were given a ring, yesterday. My lady is not well, she did not mean to part with it. You must return it to me.'

'I believe,' I said, 'that the ring was freely given to my master. He has it now about him. I shall tell him it has been asked for.'

She wheeled round and slapped my face. One of her stones cut a line across my cheek. 'Slave!' she said. 'What is your name?'

'Jabez Foxe,' I said, looking straight into her small blue eyes.

'Return the ring,' she said quietly, 'or I shall swear you stole it and the people here will affirm it on the Bible. I shall prevent your leaving. I shall seize your horses. I shall let you rot in Lancaster castle until the noose or the fever take you.'

For a moment I played at defiance still, feeling the blood prick along the cut and drip down. Then I went into our chamber and retrieved the ring. I placed it in her open palm.

'Be gone by noon,' she said, 'and do not tarry in the town, Jabez Foxe. It may not be convenient to ruin your master. Nobody will notice if I ruin you.'

Talbot had crossed the country to reach this place and we were cast out after a single audience. Perhaps he would have tried to brazen it out. I doubted it. Lady Stanley was bound tight in her linen sheets, with leeches and nurses about her bed, priests hovering in the shadows. I packed away both our bags and pitied him a little. He had come so close to a position; a nest under the house eaves like the swifts that flew in and out under the roof above the casement. Poor Talbot, he was like the swift, the martlet; rest-

less, never able to pause, yearning for heaven, even as he fed on
flies.

* * *

The stablehand was only a boy, open-faced and curious and easy with
the horses. He could almost have been Jacob a dozen years ago. I fell
into conversation with him as I helped him brush Juno down and strap
the bags to her back. The manner of our departure made me wary, but
he was eager to talk. It was not often a stranger came to the parishes
hereabouts I asked? No, he said, not often, outside fair times, unless
they were pedlars or visitors to the castle. Had he heard of a wounded
man being tended in a village a few months back – a southern man,
stabbed in a brawl in Lancaster? He paused a while, long enough for
my heart to lift and my breath to catch, but he was only sifting for an
answer and at length he shook his head. There was no one like that, he
said. I turned my face to Juno's flank. Except, he brightened, catching
my arm so that despite myself I sparked again, a cousin of his mother's
in Westmorland had just married a stranger, a taverner, they said he
was, from London. He was keeping the tavern now for her father,
doing no end of business. They were in a fair way to being rich. I
nodded, feeling my eyes brim. Perhaps I was out of practice with disap-
pointment, perhaps it was the foolish sense that here, in a stableyard
so like the Court at home, I was more likely to hear of him, but for a
moment I had felt such hope. As it sank the flame of it scorched.

A rider came into the yard behind us and the boy hurried out,
leaving me to lean into Juno. I would grow old, I thought, with looking, the wound growing a little harder, the pain familiar month by
month, until I barely remembered my unscarred self, or what it was
I longed for, unless it was the innocence we'd shared. We had loved
each other, Jacob and I, long before we knew our proper selves. All

our youth was twined together, like the rings of rushes that we used to weave to slip on one another's hands. And yet it struck me that if I did not find him I would go on living and build a life that he would never know. Already, impossible as it seemed, I was forgetting him – how could I think this ruddy uncouth stablehand, gabbling to a stranger in the yard, resembled him at all? For almost the first time I tried to picture the days that would come after I found him and felt afraid that what we had might have unravelled.

The boy was running back with a mouthful of news; I took Juno's bridle and began to lead her out in hopes of forestalling him, but he skidded up to me.

'It's a rider from Caton,' he said. I frowned, the name meant nothing to me. 'You'd best be off. Your master's been taken to Lancaster gaol. There's others coming here; they say he has magic books, that he's a sorcerer, they'll take them and you, too, if the mistress don't prevent it.'

'She won't prevent it,' I said, thinking of Mistress Mary. 'Can you help me? Show me a different road.' I saw him hesitate. 'I'll give you a shilling.'

He nodded and gestured to me to follow him. 'I didn't let on you were still here,' he said, smiling at his cunning. 'I'll take you out Gressingham way, only to the river mind – you can take the Kirkby Lonsdale road back.'

After we had gone on a while he stopped. 'It ain't true what they said, is it?'

'What did they say?'

'That he's a conjurer, that he calls up devils, that he made a dead man speak.'

'No,' I found myself saying, but more perhaps to myself than to the boy whistling at my knee, 'that isn't it. He's not a bad man. It's natural, holy magic that he's after. He sees the threads that bind us to the spirit world, the strings of light, and he seeks to pluck them as a man might pluck a lyre to make music. He thinks we've fallen off from the golden light of God and wants to make us pure and gold again.'

The boy was staring at me, his mouth hanging open. As soon as I am out of sight, I thought, he'll cross himself and pray and pick himself a whip of thorn and place nine notches in a rowan stick to guard against the wizard's boy he aided. We had reached the desolate ruins of a castle where the road crossed the Lune, all gravel and shallows.

'This is the way,' he said, beginning to pace back already, 'Go west a mile then take the road south and west to Lancaster. You can't go wrong and if you do there'll be plenty of folk on the road.'

The day had not fulfilled the promise of the dawn; I passed miles of drizzle-dull pasture, enclosed with piled stone walls. It was too bleak for much in the way of crops until I dropped down towards Lancaster, but then there were plenty of people coming and going. They greeted me with friendly indifference and many of the men touched their forelocks in respect and the women half bobbed and in truth, it barely felt strange at all to sit above them, with the wide green horizon open to me. I felt at ease in breeches astride Juno, the reins in my hand; I was no longer lame and poor. He left in March, I thought and now the summer is almost gone. It has been half a year; I am not who I was then.

At a distance post four miles from the city, before the road fell to the river, there was a stand of trees. It looked an unfrequented spot. I slipped from Juno's back and led her across to them and tied her where she could not be seen. Further on, in the crook of the dell, hidden from the road and the river both, I came across all that remained of a two-roomed house. The walls were low and mossy now, mounded up with leaves and briars. At one end, where the hearth had been, was a wide flat stone. There was nobody about. I heaved it up. The earth beneath was dry as new ashes. I made a hole and lined it roughly with loose stone until I had made a shallow chamber. Every few moments I paused and listened and waited, but there was only the birds and below, the gurgle of the river. Wrapping them in his leather bag I set down Talbot's books, half of his money and his letters – all but the title deeds. Those I tucked in my doublet. Carefully, I scattered more stones above them and put the hearth stone back. It was as good a hiding place as any.

34

Near St Leonard's Gate I found a quiet tavern and stabled Juno. It was already past two in the afternoon and so I refused the landlord's offer of a meal and went straight into town to the dirty alley by the market and the open door of the whorehouse.

She was in the parlour on the first floor, half asleep on the couch with her head resting on the old jade's shoulder. The place looked more shabby by daylight, the hangings frayed and faded, the air ripe with stale sweat, ale and shit. A fly had settled on Betsy's painted cheek. The old woman did not recognise me; she bustled up at my approach to begin her patter, but Betsy raised a hand to silence her.

'Good day, sister,' she said.

My first thought had been to pay Betsy to visit Talbot in the gaol and enquire if Jabez too, was looked for, but her greeting brought me back to my true self.

'Good day.' I said. 'My master has been taken to the castle. Have you woman's clothes I can pay you for the hire of?'

'No end, no end of fine clothes,' the old jade said, cackling. 'We'll have you back a goodwife in no time.'

We were of much the same size, Betsy and I. She brought me a bodice and heaped skirts and petticoats on her bed. I slipped off my doublet and hose and became a woman again.

'You make a better youth than you do a woman. Wait, you need a cap too, to hide your straggle of a thatch. Look at you, with your legs flung wide like an apprentice. It's something when a whore must teach you modesty. Why do you bother with him, this master of yourn, does he owe you money or do you love him as well as the other one, your bonny truelove?'

'No,' I said, 'neither one nor the other, but I'll help him if I can. I owe him that.'

'An' if you're known or he names you? You'll be taken along with him, you know that?'

'I'll take the risk.'

'What is he accused of, swindling?'

'I think of conjuring. He is a scryer and an alchemist. He has a showstone; he drew down an angel for Lady Stanley.'

'Could he draw down a duke for me?'

'You mock,' I said, 'but if you could hear him you would believe. It was as though we saw what he saw, we too heard the angel talking. It cast a vision for me, too, I am sure of it. I believed it was leading me to my husband, but Talbot reads it differently. He says it is commanding us to marry.'

She patted my hand. 'Are you sure he does not play you? He knows what tune to play. What was this vision?'

'The moon. The devil flings a bridge above it and a lame swan crosses over to a limping man. He throws her a ring. When she reaches him she turns into a woman. I am the swan. Talbot my master has a limp. He believes it is sent by God.'

'It sounds a child's game to me. You are well rid of him. I'll look after your men's things for you. I doubt you'll be out of them long, you'll feel quick enough how skirts keep you trailing dirt. Have you nothing else you wish me to keep?'

I smiled and shook my head. I liked Betsy well enough, but I knew better than to trust her with Talbot's gold. 'I'll not be long,' I said.

* * *

When I had seen him last his face had run with blood. There was no time for me to prepare simples myself and so I found an apothecary's shop on Market Street and bought a paste of elderflower, horsetail and lavender. In case of greater pains the man directed me to a bottle of dwale, the concoction of spirits, belladonna and bryony, that surgeons use to dull men's senses for the knife. Outside the castle a gypsy woman was selling herbs. I bought a sprig of rosemary and held it to my nose.

It took all my strength to ask to step inside the dark walls of the castle and then to follow the gaoler through stinking corridors to Talbot's cell. The air was sour with old piss, and rang with the clank of metal on stone. For a second I was back there, in Ludlow, awaiting trial. I pinched the rosemary hard between my fingers till the keen scent of it revived me.

I gave the gaoler a silver coin I could not spare, and a plum cake from the market, telling him I was of Lady Elizabeth's household, that she lacked a smooth black stone the man Talbot had in trust from her, that he would earn my lady's favour if it was returned to me. It was too easy. The man was all obsequious bluster, rushing off at once to retrieve the stone in its pouch and restore it. I wondered whether he would have handed me the prisoner himself if I had asked for him in my lady's name.

'What is there against him as a conjurer?' I asked.

'As to that, I'd say in truth there en't much,' the man said. 'Some fools said he was raising of the dead and speaking in charms, but he denies it and there en't no one who will swear they was present at the act. There was a fight at the alehouse in Caton. He broke a man's nose and there's talk that he had a book of spells and magic instruments, but your lady's gentlewoman had the room he lodged in searched and nowt was found, not the book, nor the youth who worked alongside him. Then there was a message it weren't to be followed no further. I b'lieved your lady had washed her hands of him, so to speak.'

'She has indeed, but there must be no scandal. If the man could be quietly let go, it would be best.'

'Ah,' he said, rubbing one hand over the other, 'if it was up to me, I'd say just that, just that. Let the fellow go with just a bit of a kicking. But it ain't quite so easy I'm afraid. There's a complaint been lodged that he forged a document, a set of title deeds, borrowed money on it. Won't touch your lady, that, praise God. It's from his time in t' city.'

I nodded. 'May I see him?' I asked. 'My lady has requested that he be treated decently, and given some comfort. No pains are to be used against him.'

I was shown into the cell. The straw was greasy with dirt and there were maggots in the brimming shit pail. Against one wall there was some planking for a bed and on it Talbot was huddled, his head on his knees, only his owl eyes staring.

I held a handkerchief against my nose. 'Oh horrible, horrible,' I said, as though such sights were new to me. I pointed at the pail. 'Please, good sir, that must be emptied. And he must have a jug of water and clean straw. My lady asked particularly about the straw.'

The man hesitated; I wondered if I had gone too far, but I placed a quarter-angel in his palm and he shuffled off to 'see about it straight.'

Talbot raised his head. 'Mistress Jabez,' he said quietly. 'You took your time. I suppose you are going to berate me now. Have you hidden my things well? I thought I was lost. You must find Babcock – the man who says I cozened him – and pay him off. He lives on the corner of Penny Street and Chennell Lane.'

In the thin light from an arrow slit he looked grey; all the mad blaze was gone from his eyes. One indeed was swollen to a slit and the gash on his forehead was wide and sore. I set about cleaning and pasting it.

'Why do you do it Talbot?' I said as I worked, 'Why do you venture your soul, your freedom like this? When all is so nearly won? Each time. You ride a hundred miles and more to reach here, then risk all in gaming and false papers. You take an angel by the hand and then instead of throwing yourself down and thanking God for His high gift you go roaring to the gates of hell.'

He patted the cut approvingly and leant back against the wall behind him. 'Do you see,' he said, 'how here and there the rough stone has worn itself to a shine from the rubbing of men's hands?'

I snorted with impatience and held his good eye until he shrugged and sighed.

'I don't know why, Jabez. I cannot rest. You said once that I was like Phaeton, Apollo's son, who begged to drive his father's golden chariot. To feel beneath him the horses of the sun. Imagine such power pulling at the reins. I think there is a dragon that spurs me on to burn all that I hold. When you left me yesterday I was all fire. I could have set light to the moon. I shouted philosophy to the empty road and every empty-headed rustic that I met. Drink did not begin to douse the burning in me, not even the blows I roused some clowns to batter me with.'

'I saw you, at the grave.'

'The days are coming Jabez. That is what the angel meant. "There shall be no more death, neither sorrow, neither crying, neither shall there be any more pain, for the former things are gone.'"

I heard the gaoler rattling at the end of a corridor with a pail. 'Even if I allowed that what you did was lawful, which I do not,' I said, 'why did you risk a branding or worse with your gambling, your counterfeiting?'

He shrugged. 'Your little loot had nearly all gone, Jabez; we needed gold.' It was not a good answer, and he knew it as well as I, for he fell silent. Then he sighed. 'Very well, for sport then. I cannot plod out my life. I cannot drudge. When I see the chance I must always take the reins, I must always attempt to grasp at the sun and fly above the mud.'

'Phaeton was a fool.' I said quickly, listening to the gaoler getting closer. 'He did not have the strength he thought he had. The horses were too wild. He scorched half the world and burned himself to death. At least they will not hang you, it is not a hanging offence.'

'I might never see the sun again. I might be branded, mutilated, pelted by the multitude.'

I did not know what to say, I had no comfort to offer and the gaoler was bundling through the door. I remembered the dwale and thrust it with some money into his hands. 'This—' I said.

He interrupted me, 'I know what it is woman, I was an apothecary, remember?'

I turned, shielding Talbot with my skirts. They were good for this at least. 'When is he to be tried? I asked.

'What is it, Tuesday? Be next Monday I reckon. No reason for delay, we're none too busy, not likely to be busy till St Bartholomew's Day and the harvest drunks. Clerk is taking depositions tomorrow. Trial Monday, branding Tuesday eh?' He tried a laugh.

Talbot had slunk back into a crouch. I nodded at the gaoler to be let out. The air in the street was so sweet I stood a long while breathing and then I turned south down Chennell Lane to blunt Babcock's ardour.

At first he would not admit me; then he called me Talbot's whore. He shouted that it was too late; he had taken the false deeds to the justice. Talbot must be a prisoner for life, he must be branded, face the pillory, lose his ears. I waited while he stormed himself out and then I asked him if he wished to recover any of his gold. He was not such a fool as to refuse outright. Within an hour he had agreed to urge clemency; to say he understood that Talbot had himself been duped; to acknowledge he had been repaid.

By the time I reached the bawdy house I felt wrung out with weariness. Betsy was not at home. The old beldame, leering, offered to collect my things and give me a closet to 'peg my pizzle back on' but I said I'd wait and eat. I sat myself on the couch and directly fell asleep. I woke with a start that spilled my undrunk wine. A man's fingers were working their way beneath my bodice. I turned to him in horror and he gave me a drunken smile, but did not remove his hand until I seized his lace-cuffed wrist and flung it off. The room was warm with candles; I remembered where I was just as the old woman came in.

'Oh no, Master, she's not in the profession. Or not yet. Are you, dearie?' She frowned, needing an answer.

'No.' I said. 'I was here to see Betsy. Is she back?'

Oh yes. Hours since. She has a gentleman at present. I might go and see for you if she could spare a minute?'

A little later Betsy appeared, half-dressed. She beckoned me to follow her to her own room.

'I can't be long,' she said a little crossly. 'This one likes me to be there when he wakes. Here are your clothes. That's sixpence.'

It was a relief to pull on my breeches, but as she gathered up the petticoats I thought how I might soon have need of them. She was happy enough for me to buy them off her, and when I barely haggled she pecked me on the cheek, all bright again, her sleepiness shrugged off like a drab coat.

'What will you do, now?' she asked, 'will you stay in town?'

'No,' I said. 'It's a few days till he's tried. Until then I'll try my search east and north a little.'

'I hope you find your leman.' She paused, looking me up and down. 'I fear it'll go hard with you, to hold a distaff and to bob again, even to a husband. Do you love him dearly?'

'Yes,' I said. 'Dearer than life, Betsy.'

She nodded and then a man's voice called her name and she bustled me from the room and onto the narrow stairs, pausing at a door just off the parlour.

'Farewell, sister. Come and see me,' she said.

I nodded and hugged her, breathing in her scent of lavender and rosemary and sweat. As she turned to go into the room she suddenly paused. 'Oh yes,' she whispered, 'that magic dream – the devil and the bridge. Laugh at me if you will – I am not learned like you or your foolmonger, but there is a bridge they say the devil threw up across the Lune outside Kirkby Lonsdale. You might try there.'

35

It was dawn by the time I reached Juno at the tavern. It had rained overnight and the road glistened but I felt there was a heat waiting above the mist. Betsy's last words had set my blood racing like a wheel that spills from its axle and whirls and bounces faster, faster downhill. My hands shook dreadfully, so I spent some time brushing Juno down, letting the wide sweep of the bristles against her flank calm me. It struck me that I had not thought to ask Talbot what had become of Erebus. Well, no matter, I had done what I could for now. No doubt the horse had been seized in lieu of charges or stabled at a fee.

Betsy could be wrong, of course; it was her reading of a picture made of air. And it could be the devil that sent it, but of all the wisps and whispers I had followed this had to me the simple ring of truth. 'I would let myself believe, Juno,' I said to the mare, 'perhaps today, perhaps tomorrow, I shall see him. I will hold him in my arms.' I set off on the road I had come from Hornby and was soon climbing into cloud. At the highest point I was wrapped in a white mist that glowed as the sun breathed upon it. I could barely see the road ahead, but it didn't matter. My mind was full of better visions.

Perhaps I would chance upon him in the street, turning a corner or ducking out of a shop. Perhaps I'd be directed to a house where he lay sick, but mending. Yes, I thought, that was more likely, for if he was hale why would he be here?

I urged Juno to a sharp trot. The mist had damped the harvest off and after Halton other travellers were few; luminous silence enfolded me round until a man, or a lumbering cart shadowed the haze and then grew into colour. Beside us the grasses were beaded heavily with dew, spiked here and there by yellow asphodel. It seemed that every seed, every stalk and stone gleamed with expectation.

Then the road fell, passed the turn for Gressingham and led on into new country. At Arkholme the mist drew apart and faded; the world waked into bright warm certainty, with all its strangeness gone and the road ahead flecked with people. For five more miles we barely paused. Juno, sensing my eagerness, pushed herself to a canter wherever the road was level and clear. I wanted badly to arrive and yet the nearer we came, the more my chest tightened with mistrust. If he had left already? I might have missed him on the road by an hour, a day, a week! Oh it would be too much, too much to bear. But why, if he could walk, would he be here still? The question kept returning. He must be sick almost to death. Round and round my thoughts raced, till my lungs hurt with the pain of breathing, but always, at the last, they returned to this. Perhaps he was disfigured, or ashamed at what he had become and thought to let me have a better life without him. 'No,' I said aloud. 'As long as you have life, Jacob, I will tend you, and if relief is to be found then I will find it. I have as much skill in my fingers as any London physician. I know as much as they.'

At last, round about noon, I came to a forking of the ways. Kirkby Lonsdale, I was told, was to my left, to the right the Devil's Bridge. I hesitated, then turned Juno to the right. Perhaps it was fear prompting me, but it seemed important to visit the bridge first, before I attempted the town.

It was a fine spot, with the river wide beneath the vast, ancient bridge. I led Juno to the shingles to drink and there being no one by, stripped off my hose and breeches and my doublet too to stand with her in the cool flood and calm my nerves. Sunlight played on the underside of the arches in echo of the rippling water. I watched the swallows swoop and sip from the surface and listened to Juno drink.

'Hulloa there, traveller,' a man's voice shouted. I started and looked up, he was leaning over the parapet of the bridge. 'Best be careful there – another step or two and you'll be over your neck.'

He was right. I chided myself that I had not seen. A few paces further off and the shingle fell into deep dark pools. It was lucky Juno was on my left side. The man appeared behind me as I stepped back.

'A fair few bones lie round this bridge,' he said. 'For a second I took you for a swan, in your shirt and your arms so white. Then I saw the horse.'

'A swan,' I said, staring at him stupidly, scrabbling to retrieve and fasten my doublet.

He laughed and clapped me on the back. 'Eyes aren't so good these days. Come for tomorrow's market, have you? Course I've lived in Kirkby man and boy, but I still say there's no better place to trade, not north or south, east or west. Honest people you'll find us, lad, and our girls are fresher than daisies.' He nudged me in the ribs.

'Looks like they must live off milk and butter,' I said sweeping my arm vaguely towards the pastureland beyond the bridge. 'I've rarely seen such fine cattle. Where would a stranger find a welcome, friend?'

'Well, there's a question. No end of choice. The Bull is a fine hostelry, but to my mind you could do no better than The Sun, top of Main Street. Honest food and good ale and the young man who's got the run of it now knows horses better than any, though he's a southerner like yourself.'

Somehow I forced an answer. 'A southerner you say?'

'Aye, somewhere or other. A few months back. Old Jack the landlord brought him up from Lancaster. Taken the care of him after he took a blade in the belly; but he's mended good and proper. Fixed for good now, he is.'

I felt myself grow giddy and staggered pulling on my hose to cover my buckling knees. 'That was a Christian act, to nurse a stranger.'

'You could call it payment,' the man said. 'Word is the lad stepped between his master and old Jack's youngest daughter, prevented her being forced, and her a slip of a thing, fourteen years old.'

I nodded, unable for the length of a breath to speak. 'God bless them both,' I said, at last, pulling at my voice to keep it low and steady and fussing with the points of my doublet to keep him from noticing the blood rush to my face.

'Aye, they've been blessed in it, all round. Right, well, I must leave you. Promised my sister in Leck I'd be with her these two hours. My name is Roger, Roger Alderson. Find me in town tomorrow and I'll stand you a pot of ale.'

'Jabez Foxe, your servant. God b'ye,' I said. 'And thank you for your good counsel.'

After he had gone I sank down on the stone beach. So it was true; he was here, only a mile away. Soon, so soon, all this would be over. Tonight I would sleep with his warm body laced with mine. How should I greet him? How find him out alone? Should I put on my woman's garb or be a boy a little longer? I began to undo my pack to pull out the kirtle, but then I checked myself. The thought of hobbling into town in Betsy's trumpery, game for laughing boys, decided me – I did not want a stir; I got back up on Juno's weary back.

Soon enough the road became a street; workshops where men paused to watch the mounted stranger. I felt too visible, drawing eyes as a horseman is bound to do, clattering along in the dozy August heat. I got back down, gripping Juno's bridle as though it were a candle in the dark. Main Street. He could step before me at any moment; he could stride out of a shop, like this ironmonger's just beside me; he would know at once the roll of my walk. My guts knotted, I could not breathe, I could not think, not clearly. What would he do, what would he say – and I myself? He was well-mended the man had said. Good. And yet he had not stirred to find me. A thousand meetings played out through my head; there were people all about and I did not dare to look. Then, too soon, I reached a junction and a boy was hovering at my side. Could he take the mare? 'Look sir, here, the stableyard of the Sun, she would be well looked after, no better yard in town.' I nodded dumbly, took my bag and watched him take Juno through the gates. He glanced back and gestured to the inn door.

36

The hall was dark after the glare outside; for a moment I stood dazed, then I made out a large long room, with barrels at the back and a burly grey-haired man among them tapping ale. There were two tables of men; they looked up as I entered and nodded friendly-wise. The place smelt of ale and fresh rushes and herbs strewn in the rushes. I sat down at a table by the street door, pushing myself into the shadows.

'There's a man come in wants ale, Alice!' one of the customers called out and from beyond the barrels a young woman emerged. She drew a jug of ale and approached me. There was a lightness to her walk, as though she was ever on the edge of dancing.

'Welcome stranger,' she said smiling. 'Have you come far? Will you be wanting a room?'

'Your pottage, if you please,' I said. She was about my age, or younger; soft-cheeked and bonny, with bright red hair. 'And yes, I've come a long way.'

'Well stay a while, friend,' she said, 'you look traiked, you're as pale as whey.'

I took courage from her gentleness.

'I've been told,' I said, 'a Jacob Spicer works here.'

She stopped smiling and stepped back at once; her voice when she answered was guarded, sharp. 'Who are you? What do you want with him? You've his southern tongue, the exact same. He's not Jacob Spicer here. He's Jacob Cockshoot. If you've brought another letter you can keep it, he's been plagued enough. Near lost his mind after the last one.'

This made no sense. I shook my head. 'No,' I said, 'no letter. I ... a greeting only, nothing to harm him. Please, give him this,' I pulled a sprig of rosemary from my pocket.

She did not take it. 'If you ask me, he's done all the remembering he needs to do. The past should stay home.' She sighed. 'But you don't look as you mean ill. Give it to him yourself, he'll be here presently. I'll fetch your pottage.'

A table called her and then she left through the door at the back, leaning to whisper to the old man. I did not want to ponder what she'd said, not yet, and I did not have time to. Another door opened; for a second a man was framed in light in the doorway, then he stepped through. He carried a small barrel on his shoulders and was turning his head to shout to someone behind him. He limped slightly. His curls were the colour of ripe corn.

Jacob.

It was him: he was here, across the pipe smoke and the chatter. He lightly placed the barrel down and stood a moment.

I felt intensely aware of his every movement, his every breath, every thread of his shirt or rush-stem at his feet and yet I could no more have spoken or stood than flown. I was like the fox or the otter that scents the hounds and freezes, hair upstaring, poised. The ale cup was hard in my hand. One of the customers hailed him and he came forward and clapped him on the shoulders, laughing. My Jacob, laughing. Life was this moment; here, now, nothing else. To have it stay so, I would forego heaven. I gripped the ale and pressed myself into the wall. Then the old man tossed a word to him and he looked up, and looked across to me, still laughing, and slowly the laughter slipped and was gone. He frowned and shook the frown off and took a step towards me, his eyes seeking out my own. All other sounds and details fell away. I looked into the fierce puzzle in his eyes; he walked towards me. A man called his name and he put up his hand to forestall him. He moved round a table, he was halfway here, his lips were forming to a name; I found my legs again and bolted for the door.

The street was busy with people; I stared at them wildly and shrank into a dark alley opposite to quiet myself. What had I been thinking? Why was I still in breeches and hose? It could not be in there, among the ale-bibbers, that we found one another again. I could not bear an audience. The inn door opened; he walked into the road, shielding his eyes to look in each direction in turn. Oh God, the sight of him there, before me. I closed my eyes and hauled in a breath, and stepped out into the sun.

A laden cart had lumbered between us. I couldn't see over it. When it had passed he was gone. Then I saw him, turning into the stables. I followed. The boy was nowhere about. Did he hear my footfall on the stone behind him? I used to say that he could hear the landing of a sparrow on a twig. He did not look, but I felt how his hands and shoulders tensed. He opened Juno's stall. Still he did not look.

A strange calm possessed me; time held its breath. There was only he and I in all the world. Why had he not turned at once when he felt me behind him? But no matter, it was only a few paces. He was there, caught where sunlight fell into shadow, on one knee, tenderly feeling Juno's leg for swellings. My shadow fell across him.

'You have ridden her too hard. See? A windgall.' His voice was low and choked; he leant his head against Juno's flank. I tried to focus on his hands – so familiar, so gentle on the horse's leg. There, the pale sickle scar on his right thumb. I reached out and let my right hand hover over his, and he turned his head to watch it. I let my palm draw closer till the thrill of our almost touch rippled through me, through us both; with a long slow indrawn breath he watched as I placed my hand on his, on his rough warm skin.

'Jacob,' I said.

At once he twisted his hand about mine, then gripped my wrist hard and pressed my palm against his cheeks, his brow, his mouth, as he stood up, slowly, stiffly – how different from the easy grace I'd known! – keeping me still behind him so that I could not see his face.

'I was not sure,' he said. 'There's a boy there says he knows you, Jack said, and I looked and I thought you were a spirit.'

I leant my head against his back and he shuddered at the touch. I could hear the fast beating of his heart. 'Look at me Jacob. I am no spirit. I am your own true wife.'

'I cannot!' I did not understand – his voice was harsh. Then he said more gently, 'I cannot look at you, Martha.'

He clasped my wrist so hard it hurt me; I did not want to pull away. The stable boy appeared in the glare of the yard. 'Jacob, I've mucked out and set down fresh straw and seen to all the beasts. The mistress wants to know if you're coming in and if there's aught else I should be doing.'

'No,' Jacob said. 'Go in Thomas.'

The boy hesitated, glancing at where Jacob held me fast. 'Is all well?'

'Go in,' Jacob said, 'all is well. Tell Alice I'll be back shortly.'

The boy ran back. We were alone in the close gloom of the stall. At last he turned to me, with the sun all behind him, flaming the tips of his hair. I searched out his eyes; there was something wrong; there was a horror waiting for me just beyond my vision, like a night hag glimpsed at the edges of a dream. If I could only make him look at me and draw him close surely I could blink it gone, this creeping dread. I raised my free hand to his face but he threw his head back askance. So strange and so known at once – to be here, close to him and at odds.

'I had a letter,' he said. 'Why do you think—' and he raised his free hand to wave towards the tavern. 'How did you travel? Alone, poor, how did you get money? And these?' he plucked at my breeches, 'What led you to dress up like a man, your legs stripped to every brazen stare on the high road?'

'What?' I said, 'You challenge me? After the road that I've come to find you!' I pulled away from his grasp but he would not let me go and so I leaned in and spat my words into his face. 'How do you think? I turned a trick with every man I met. And when there were none willing I pulled on a codpiece and followed an upright man, sometimes his doxy, sometimes his thief.'

As I spoke I saw the fury gather in his eyes, I felt it burn in mine; then he was kissing me, hard, insistent and I was drained of anger. There was only his soft mouth and his tongue and the rough wood of the stall behind my back. He pulled his fingers through my shorn hair and across my breasts and I lifted his shirt and kissed the muscles of his chest, his ribs, the strange new rope of a scar.

'Oh dear God, my heart's darling,' he said kissing my neck, my ears, the tears that wet my cheeks. 'I near died for want of you.'

I smiled, 'I have found you, Jacob, it's over, all's well.'

He pulled heavily back and drew my hand away. 'No,' he said and groaned, 'I don't know. What's to be done?'

I frowned, and the night hag crept back from the dark corner where I had banished her.

'What do you mean?' I said, but Jacob had turned, there were footsteps in the yard and a woman's voice rang out.

'What business is it keeps you? Is he here still? If he is a friend, bring him to the parlour.'

It was the red-haired woman who had served me. She was still more pretty in the sunlight; as Jacob stepped out to greet her she smiled and touched her belly lightly and I understood.

I had no words, no breath for words. The night hag had me by the throat and choked me. There was only shock and darkness and a need for air.

'Wait,' he called back to me, 'wait a moment and I'll come with you. Please. I'll come. Just a moment, I beg you.'

37

He hesitated and looked back as he ducked into the inn behind her, but I had pressed myself into the shadows. My only thought was to get out, to be somewhere with only stone and crows for company, where I could allow myself to face the horror that pressed up at me. It was real – I would not believe it – I had seen it with my eyes. I felt at once wildly agitated and separate from myself. It did not take long to saddle Juno up, to fix the bag and roll and loop the bridle over her head. I left a coin for the boy on the stall door and walked her out of the gates to the mounting block. Over and over the picture returned, her hand touching her belly, her familiar smile. A hundred yards down Main Street I heard him shouting after me, but the road was near empty and I squeezed Juno to a trot.

I did not take the road for Lancaster but crossed the bridge and blindly headed east, towards the high fells that brooded in a line above the town. Where a likely track branched steeply off the road I met a cowman driving a dozen cattle. I opened the field gate he was headed to and the beasts lumbered through to the fresh grass. It would be a good fine afternoon, he said, and a clear night too, God willing. I pointed to the track and asked where it led.

'It's the fell road,' he looked at me quizzically, 'don't lead nowhere, mostly.'

I nodded and took it. Here in this wilderness, I could begin to think. Soon the hill was bare of trees and farms and the lane grew rougher, steeper and I slid from Juno's back, remembering she was already weary with the morning's ride. So long ago that seemed! When all seemed good and happy! Like a world made out of cloud that a child might point to and say, 'look Mother, Father, a church spire, a castle in the sky.' She was with child, his child. Again and again I saw the way her hand reached to her belly, the way she smiled at him. *The past should stay home,* she had said. How had I been so slow to piece it? I remembered the Hornby stablehand: *a cousin of my mother's in Westmorland has just married a taverner.* The fellow at the bridge too, as good as spelt it out: *Fixed for good, now, he is. Blessed all round.*

How could the sun shine boldly in the sky and he be false to me? So soon, only half a year since he had left! How long before he swived her, two months, three? All his vows forgotten, all our life, kicked like so much rubbish in a ditch, stepped over. Was I forsaken already when I left Hope? I had been afraid of a thousand thousand endings, but never this. I thought we had exchanged hearts, he and I, that my blood pulsed to his. A kind of numb bewilderment enveloped me. I knew a sharper suffering would engulf me soon, but as yet all I felt was a hollowness. I had seen a woman once whose house was burning. She opened her mouth to scream, but no sound came, although her body shook with terror. I was caught like her, waiting for the scream, for the roof of heaven to crush me with the thought of what was lost.

The fells were empty of people. I could be as lonely here as I could wish. As I climbed higher the grass was mingled with mountain heather, already turning the heathland purple. High above a lark delicately twirled and sang. The track curled beneath a knoll where a twisted birch tree hung over a beck. Suddenly I knew that I could walk no further. I led Juno to the stream to cool her leg and then I crushed and wrapped wild thyme about the gall for want of other herbs and tied her loosely to the birch tree so that she could graze. The tussocked grass was soft when I lay down. I let my mind pour into darkness.

When I woke the dew was falling and the western mountains were mantled red and orange. At first I felt the weight of sorrow but could not remember what it was and then, remembering, I tried to close my eyes again as though the knowledge of it would recede in darkness, but it did not go. All was as it was, or almost all – I sat up with a start. Someone had draped a cloak about me.

He was a few feet off, kneeling and blowing on a small flame that trembled and seemed to die and then took heart and rose up stronger. He glanced across and nodded. How often at our hearth had I watched his breath stroke flame into the kindling? It was a workaday sight, so tenderly common that I felt the great grief begin to brim and swallowed hard to hold it back.

'A cowherd down the way told me a strange boy had ridden up here. He was afraid he meant to do himself some mischief. Did you, Martha?'

His voice had lost the choked harshness it had before in the stables; it was almost gentle again, almost the voice I was used to wake me in the dawn when he rose to work, or that spoke to me in the night when we lay softly knotted on our bed. Its edge was one I had not heard for years, not since I was a girl and he was torn between wanting me and thinking me a witch. We seemed to have come so far, I thought, but the wheel has turned and we are back where we began. Worse, he has forsaken me.

'No.' I said as harshly as I could. 'I'm not the giddy chit you fished from Pentaloe ponds. You have broken my heart, husband, but I'll not die of it. Or if I do, it will be far away from here. How long did you wait before you fucked her?'

He winced and the flames bent towards his sharp inbreath. His voice grew harder. 'It was after I learned that no sooner had you heard that I was dead – not one month after – than you were on your back, a circlet of daisies on your head, letting yourself be ploughed by some sweat-seamed oaf. And profitably too. You were with his child, the letter said. What, did you lose it? Did he cast you over for a passing jade?'

The light was furring into night; the distant hills were smudged grey. For a second I felt again the kick that cracked my belly open. I dug my fingers into the thin earth and felt that I was sinking into it – I was like Eurydice when Orpheus looked behind too soon, when they had almost reached the upper world with its good fresh air. It had been a kind of death when he did not come home and now, when all had appeared restored, all found again, life had crumbled into dust. Not even dust, but a stinking midden heap. I could not speak; there was a fist of sorrow at my throat that choked me.

The near and distant hills, and the great arching vault of heaven grew into night all round me; black and vast forever. How could my Jacob, my dear one, who I'd defied the world to find, how could he speak like this? I tried to tell myself I was not here, but in some other place, where Jacob had smiled and clasped me to him, but here was only darkness and the cruel delighted flames of the small fire; they played across his face, flashed in his angry eyes. 'You don't deny it. By Christ I should hate you Martha. I believed I hated you.'

I rubbed the spiny grass with my flat hands. 'You were a fool.' I said. 'A letter. From the Steward, no doubt, and you believed it, every word. You didn't write to me. You didn't come. What happened to you Jacob? How could you doubt me? You – who withstood your mother and your lord and even God's minister – to stand beside me and to swear me honest.'

He stood up, too quickly; his hand went to his side in pain. 'It wasn't only the letter, though that was enough. The man who brought it, Rhys his name is, a good Leominster man, warned me that it brought bad news. He'd a cousin who said that you'd been tramping the parish peddling salves, that a rich man had taken a liking to you and you weren't likely to refuse him. All the parish were tattling how he'd knocked you up. I know how men looked at you, how little you understood how to guard against it. You were always wild.'

There was enough truth in his words to make me bite back the sharp answer on my lips.

'I was not false, Jacob.'

'I turned the tables over; I pounded the walls until my fists bled. "Forget her," old Jack said, "women are as hard to hold, as changeable as water till they have a baby at the breast."'

His face was a mask of shadow. I had thought it the map of my own heart, but I could no more see it than discover what lay in the dark star gaps. I stared at the absence where his face should be.

'I was never false to you.' I said again.

I walked over to him and took his face between my hands and turned it to the fire. He would not look at me, but he did not take my hands away.

'I healed the Steward's leg and then he hounded me until I ran away. Look at me.'

At last, stiffly, he turned and looked. There was fury and confusion in his gaze; I held it. We did not speak. I felt it, felt how his soul searched mine. Slowly, slowly the anger in his eyes gave way to horror.

He took my hands in his. 'Dear God, what have I done?' he said, so quietly I could barely hear. Then he pulled away and walked off, gripping his head. 'It drove me mad, the thought of another man's lips, of you permitting ... I think my brain was addled from the fever. Now I can hear you, touch you ... it was not true, was it? It seemed so certain. Oh God! I have ruined us both.' He sank to his knees and ripped at the turf and groaned.

I came and knelt before him and he lifted his face to mine. 'Oh Martha, my coney, my heart's truth, what shall I do? I cannot lose you twice.'

I placed his head on my shoulder and wrapped my arms about him, tight. I had no good answer, but for now the dark held tomorrow at bay. For a long while we clung like that together and the fire folded back to embers and all round us the still night opened to the stars. Then I stood and took the blanket roll from Juno's back and laid it down. He blew on the embers and fed them twigs until the fire revived. We lay down gently side by side. He took my hand and kissed it, gently.

'They made me swear,' he said. 'When I came to myself, at the inn, Coningsby's man was there. I had committed a terrible crime, he said, Lord Croft was inclined to have me hanged or kill me out of hand, but my lord, out of the regard that he had held me in and his great clemency, had wrought on him so that, if I agreed to be dead to my wife and village, to bide here in the north under a new name, I could be allowed to live. Better, my lord would pay the good family of the inn to have me tended till I recovered from my wounds, if that was God's wish. You would be afforded a living, allowed to keep the cottage. If I did not swear then I must suffer all the penalties of ingratitude. No protection from my lord and no provision for my wife at home. I must be thought dead to all. I must swear it.'

He raised himself on an elbow to look at me. 'Understand, Martha. I was at the brink of death. My shirt was black with blood, I could feel my life was ebbing from me – as the man talked the inn-room shrank to the pale moon of his face, growing and receding.

Only his voice was clear. I was already dead and this my last act –
that you would be provided for. I swore.'

I could not bear his face so close, his eyes searching mine, his
lips so near. If I touch your lips, I thought, if they brush against my
cheek, I will be lost. 'Lie back,' I said. 'Please. You did right, Jacob.
You had no choice.'

He lay back. 'Jack Cockshoot brought me here; it was his
younger daughter Lizzie in the alley that night. Alice sat by my bed
hour on hour, defied the priest and her father when they said that
she should give up hope.'

I swallowed. The stars were bright and hard above me. 'Then I
must bless her for that.'

We were both silent. Both uncomfortable with what must come
next. It was a while before he began again. 'It was Ascension. I was
hale enough to walk the bounds a little. Oath or no I was preparing
in my head to leave, to come to you, even at the cost of my neck and
your safety. It would be a sore blow to old Jack, I knew, and a sorer
one for Alice. Their hopes in me gave me more urgent cause to go –
but I owed them both my life. I could not just up and leave without
a farewell, like a thief.'

Oh, I thought, if you had only gone. It's your gentle heart that
undid you, Jacob, you saw the pain that you would cause and put it
off; if you had thought more how every day I grieved and hoped; if
you had known how Boult worried at me.

'Every day,' he said, as if in answer to my thoughts, 'every hour
of every day I thought of you, stricken, alone, unprotected. More
than once I had borrowed Jack's nag and tried to see how far I could
get - only for my wound to stop me. There was to be a church ale.
The whole town was making ready. I would go the day after, I
decided, whether I was fit enough or no. Then Rhys came bearing
money, and the letter. I was so glad to see a face I knew, hear a
Marches voice. I pumped him for news of home, if he'd heard aught

of you. He was no rumourmonger, Martha; he did not want to speak. It was like breaking walnuts with your teeth to make him open. And then the letter, confirming all. The words burned me, Martha. Boult wrote he had been working for my return, but that a new misfortune had befallen me. The words seemed writ in sorrow – there was money wrapped in the paper.'

They told me you were dead, I thought, and I had far less cause to doubt, and I would not believe it. I said nothing, for what good was it to fight, now, with the sun wheeling towards dawn?

'What an ass I was, led by the nose! A credulous fool. But remember – Rhys thought he was honest. I saw no cause for the Steward to lie and I was barely mended from a fever that had shivered my body and my mind into pieces. The letter sent me mad. I raged – a day, a night – I did not know I had such anger in me. Against my horns, the pig's breath whoreson who rode you, against you. Jack said they were afraid they'd need the ropes. "She thinks you dead," they told me, "it's no wonder that she took another." Then Alice quieted me, with honeyed mead and coyings and...'

He paused and I waited, hoping for a better reason. At last he sighed. 'I don't know, Martha, I don't know why I lay with her. All through the pain and fever I dreamt that you were there, mopping my brow, singing to me, but when I came to it was Alice. When she came to me, after the ale, I made believe her to be you.'

He was silent again. I remembered how for a second, just a second, in Bewdley, I had been tempted by the thought of comfort.

'And yet,' he began once more, 'that's not it either, or not all. I think it was despair. To find that you had cast me off like a used shift. I hated you. My life was drained of hope or light. She and the ale offered comfort of a kind and damnation too. I wanted that.'

He turned on his side again to look at me, to see how far I understood, if I could forgive him. 'It was only that once, Martha.

That one night, until July, when she told me she was carrying my child.'

The embers cast a pale glow across his face, the strong line of his cheekbones, his full lips. 'Oh Jacob,' I said, and he was kissing my mouth, a long slow kiss that went beyond words. Tears ran into my hair.

'No,' he said, at last, 'I cannot bear it' and his kiss became more urgent; he leaned into me, drawing me to him. I pulled away.

'You have to bear it, Jacob. We both do. It can't be undone. She is going to have your child. I will survive. I am much wiser to the world now. One day, God willing, we will find each other again.'

He threw himself back with something like a roar. 'Damn Edward Croft and the Steward too. I will find them out and kill them. I will take Boult's jowled neck and twist it till I hear it snap. With these hands I'll do it.'

'No,' I said. 'Don't damn yourself for him.'

I offered him a kiss for a book of tales, I wanted to say, *I thought it would be nothing, but he put his fat wet tongue in my mouth and his fat hands squeezed my breasts.* I opened my mouth to speak, but though the dark was gentle I felt how the words would eat at him. Like a worm in the guts. For now he would seek to destroy it by turning to me again and fiercely claiming back what had been taken and perhaps this time I would not stop him, but instead I'd pull him into me, the sharp pain blossoming into pleasure. And perhaps then we would not part in the morning, but go down, hand in hand, to a life somewhere. But afterwards, he'd feel the worm again. It would take months, years perhaps to die and it would whisper to him that I set Boult on.

Better, far better that we parted loving, forgiving one another. If I wrought on him to stay with me this would be lost. More and more his thoughts would turn to the child growing up without him and perhaps too to the simple-hearted girl who'd trusted him. And

I, I would know that I had torn him from a child that he yearned for with every breath, and from a good living, all for a woman at ease astride a horse in hose and doublet, who ravelled pagan tales in her dreams.

I took his hand and pressed it and he put his head on my breast and I stroked his curling hair and neither of us slept. I think that night that we were closer than we had ever been before, threaded together like woven cloth.

Slowly the east began to pale and the stars dimmed. The sun flecked the sky pink and lavender blue. I cursed it. What would I do, where would I go, now? I would carry this loss in my heart forever; I could not endure it. And yet I knew too that I would. I would find a way to live; I held my fortune in my fingers and my wits.

We ate the bread and meat he'd brought by the ruins of the fire, without speaking, but when I began to rise he seized my hands and put his arms about me. I could not bear to think this was the last time. I buried my face in his chest.

'I will leave her. She has kin, she's young. Don't hide your face, Martha. Kiss me again. I will not, I cannot let you go.' He said the words, but there was resignation in his voice.

'You must,' I said. 'Do you love her, Jacob?'

'No!' he said, then, 'No. Or not as I love you. She's good and kind and she loves me and…' his voice trailed off.

'And she carries your child,' I said. I would not look at him. There was a grey rock in the stream, grown over with liverworts, grey and grey-green and yellow, like interlocking hands or a flat pattern of land and water. I willed myself stone. If you ask again, I thought, I shall not be able to refuse.

He did not ask. Instead he took a ring, the ring I had given him so long ago at our handfasting and handed it to me. I looked down at it and shook my head but then I took it. How like a knife love was, how like a blade in the heart!

'What will become of you?' he said.

'I will go south.' I was glad he could not see how my eyes brimmed.

38

I watched my husband slowly ride away. When he reached the valley road he stopped and looked up. Come back, I thought. Oh, turn back to me, don't leave me here. I even flung my arms out towards him, but I doubt that he could see me in the heather, and the next moment I dropped them to my sides and simply stood and watched. He had no choice but to go; I had no choice but to let him. We craned to look, with the steep mountainside between us; at last he turned his horse's head and rode away. I watched him dwindle between the hedgerows – till he was small as a blown leaf, till he was gone.

I sank down to the heather next to Juno then and sobbed till I was wracked and dry. I have lost him, I thought, I will have to find a way through this world without him. All this way north I had the hope of him; in his strong arms, I thought, all I've lost will be restored; in them I'll find a home again, I'll know myself again, and God willing one day perhaps we'd have a child. No more. 'I am my own guide now,' I said aloud to Juno. I would help Talbot if I could, and then I would set out alone. How big the world was! Near and far the slopes were brushed with purple, but just next to me a clump bloomed white. My grandam brought me white heather once from the market, I remembered, for the luck it gave. Keen and fresh it smelt, just as this, when I pinched a woody stem. Where were you yesterday? I thought bitterly, I had no luck then. I picked some now, nonetheless. God knew, I still had need of it; I had nothing else. I was like the children in my grandmother's stories who set out on the road. Youngest sons, but girls too, odd times, and what was I but a mixture of the two? If they were clever and good they got three gifts to help them. I twirled the heather in my fingers. Maybe I was like them in that too, a little. I had my simples and the book; the skills I had in both could bring a living. Who knew but a third gift might come?

Sometime before noon a boy ambled past with a dog and a flock. He was playing on a pipe. When he saw me he started back – I must have looked a ragged sight – but I hailed him and he came and sat beside me. He had no shoes. I gave him a penny to play some more.

'What's that one called?' I said when he finished an air.

'En't got a name. I made it up. You can give it a name if you give me another penny.'

I smiled at his cheek. 'Call it "Martha's Farewell",' I said, 'and play if for me again.' When he'd finished I clapped his shoulder. 'It's a good tune. You must play it at the inns and ales in Kirkby Lonsdale. Will you do that?'

'I will,' he said grinning, 'I'll say a fairy boy came out the hill and gev it me.'

'Good. And be sure to say its name, there's another penny for your promise,' I said. 'You play your pipe well. It'll make your fortune for you.'

'Aye,' he said, grinning, and whistling the dog to be off, 'I'll be a gentleman by and by, see if I en't.'

I unlooped Juno and led her to the road to follow him, tucking the heather in my doublet as I went. The hills and valleys rolled down before me, threaded with choices.

* * *

Talbot's trial was set back and I was half grateful, for it put off the end I knew was soon coming. It was harvest and there was work for any hand that asked it, despite most of the land being given up to pasture; I tarried at a place in Arkholme; the farmer would give me only 2d a day 'being so slight a lad', but I got food and a space in a barn to sleep and stabling for Juno. As soon as the sun had dried the yellow corn in the morning, the reapers advanced with a long slow slice of the sickle, curling round the field to its centre, but my hands were nesh and unpractised and an hour after the men had left at the day's end I was still there, binding the sheaves and stacking them. The stems cut welts and ridges into my palms; my back was a stiff board. I was glad of it; the pain pushed back my desolation. At night I took the jug that was offered and drank it down and drank it down again. Only briefly, in the moments before I pitched into a black sleep, and the moments when the bell woke me, was I forced to look my sorrow in the face; day by day I bound it, tighter than the wheat and rye.

I worked a week binding and a week on the threshing floor and that was good, too, flinging the flail behind my head to pound the grain loose, then working the winnowing fan. When I needed to talk I did, but mostly I was silent. After the first night, when I was told I thrashed and groaned in my sleep, the people let me alone, deciding I was a little touched, and that suited me so well I let myself, more than once, be heard muttering.

I thought of home, of Hope, where we had arrived at harvest time and been accepted. Had the last day of reaping come already? Were Meg and the other little ones chasing through the stubble for the gleanings? At home, on the last day, a stand of corn was left, tied together from four bunches like the legs of a mare and the best reapers would fling a sickle to cut it. Hours it took, sometimes, and the harvest supper waiting. Sally said she'd grown up with a man, Thomas Bengry, who could stand with his back to the corn and still cut it, clean off, from fifteen paces, but I thought it skilful enough to do it face on, to hurl a blade and catch her crown and slash it free. Back and forth the men called then. 'I have her.' 'What hast thee?' 'A mare, a mare, a mare.' By the time they came to eat they'd all be hoarse with shouting, but the man who'd cut her would sit opposite Boult, or Sir Thomas if he was at home, at the head of the table. They did not cry the mare here. I was relieved; it felt to me I should be cried out too.

I did not visit Talbot. I knew the date of the trial; until then I lied to myself that he did not need me. It was not true, of course; in my heart I knew that the dank blackness of the prison would be eating at his soul; that he might be ill; that he would surely be hungry; but I clung to the sun and air to preserve me; the almost silent companionship of strangers; the oblivion labour offered. In the sun and in labour I felt closer to Jacob. The chaff was winnowed off for the beasts, but the good grain we poured into sacks so that it was dry and tight.

I thrust a hand into the warm seed. Talbot would say that it was made of light and so it was, of course; conceived of earth and sun, cut only so it could be born again. Jacob, I thought, there is something to be held to in this, what we shared, the kernel – something to be grasped, to keep from canker.

'I like to do that, too.' It was the farmer himself, come up behind me. He scooped a handful of grain in his palm. 'It's been a good year.'

I nodded, suddenly grateful for some talk. He was an old man, thickened but strong. I had seen him pick up a bumble bee and watch it crawl across his palm, and gently brush the pollen from its velvet back with his finger. My hand was too much a woman's beside his.

'I was thinking of the corn,' I said. 'How it dies to be reborn, as our Saviour did.'

He looked at me a touch more closely, and I was afraid I'd been too open. '"The ploughman, be he never so unlearned,"' he said, evidently quoting, '"shall better be instructed of Christ's death and passion by the corn that he sows in the field, and likewise of Christ's resurrection, than by all the dead posts that hang in the Church" – a bishop said that, and I believe it.'

I smiled, but I said nothing. I had believed him a papist, like most people here, in their hearts, but often openly, too, even before foreigners.

'You're a strange one, Jabez,' he went on, 'folks say you're witless, that they've seen you jabber to the moon, but I've seen the players and I think you act the part. And she's too fine a mare for a common hand.'

'I was not always poor—' I began, but he held up his hand to stop me.

'Oh, don't worry, I'm not about to pry. You work hard and keep quiet, that's enough for me. There'll be work here again next harvest if you want it. Spring too, if the winter keeps the parson busy.'

I left soon after, in part because I felt I should be discovered if I had not been already, and in part because my unease grew at my neglect of Talbot. It felt good to be astride Juno again, with the green dairy land giving way to sheep and heather as we climbed towards Lancaster, but the hollow in my chest ached like an unset bone and I was glad that it was Juno who had the task of placing one leg and then another forward on the road. My heart had a blade in it. It would be like this for me always now, I thought. I could not imagine ever being happy. The best I could hope was to learn to breathe round the pining misery I felt. If only I could throw the vision of him off; he unsettled me moment by moment – how he looked in waking, the imagined process of his day. The words of the old song haunted me:

> Lully, lullay, lully, lullay,
> The falcon hath borne my love away ...
> And she weeps both night and day;
> Lully, lullay, lully, lullay ...

Over and over the lines came and I did not care that they were meant for the love of God not man. The bleak hills wobbled through my tears.

The tavern outside St Leonard's Gate had no rooms when I arrived, which suited my pocket, since they were happy to lodge Juno. At length, although the tapster made a show of being loath to lodge a gentleman so meanly, he dealt with me for a space in the loft above the stable. The rats were not so bad, he said, and I could take his cat Barbel, if I was afeared. I did not care so much about the rats, but I took her. She was large and stippled grey with yellow eyes and when I buried my face in her warm fur she hummed. She made me think of another cat, long ago, before Hope, when I was called a witch and thrown in a makeshift cell above the stables, with old Ruth Tranter and the cat they said was her familiar. Poor brave Ruth, whose only crime was pity. She combed my hair and sang to me and it saved my soul. It was as Talbot said, or like my reckoning of it, the world was threaded like a lyre, and in the harmonies our spirits purr one with the other, allaying sorrow.

Dawn was barely wisping in the east when I donned a bonnet and limped through St Leonard's towards the market where the pillory had been set up, on a kind of stage. Talbot had been sentenced the day before. He looked thin and grey in the courtroom, but had brightened when I came in. The justice noted it.

'That's a pretty vessel to leak tears for you, Talbot,' he said. I bent my head and clasped my hands piously together on my skirts. 'And to pray for your soul, I warrant.'

He was lucky, the justice said. Since Babcock had attested that the debt was paid there need be no further imprisonment. There was no mention of scrying, of Hornby Castle, of spirits raised from the dead. One day of punishment for his counterfeiting, and he would be free to go. He should fall on his knees and praise God for the leniency shown him. Talbot hung his head and said nothing. He was led away. They would not let me in, but for a price the gaoler – a new man, far less obliging than his fellow – said that he'd pass on the vial I had brought.

The day before had been blazing and to walk into the courtroom was to duck into darkness; the heat and ceremony closed about you, with only the dust-specked shafts of sunlight and the mooning flies offering relief. The night, however, had brought rain; the gutters that ran through the middle of the cobbles gurgled and spilled and the streets were puddled. At first all we women held up our skirts and stepped daintily enough, but the barrows and carts and running boys soon mocked our efforts and most of us abandoned our hems to the dirt. I watched the market setting up and waited.

I felt his arrival as a prickle of excitement in the air. A couple of boys ran past me westwards to where the road led to the castle, hooting; the maids and matrons, lads and men left off their haggling and turned to look, a gleam in their eyes despite the lowering sky. There was Talbot, shackled, with a board about his neck declaring him a forger. He mounted the pillory with a set face, glancing round a little, and I drew close enough to see his owl eyes were glassy. So either the gaoler was honest, or Talbot had saved what I brought when I saw him first.

The crowd drew a little closer, grinning, jostling one another.

'Where's all your art, now, dog-leech?' a man cried as the board descended on his neck and wrists.

'Jarkman!'

'Dungshark!'

'Look how his tongue droops like a spent prick!'

A man pointed, 'It's the conjurer!'

'Aye!' another answered. 'Him with the devil's looking glass – where are your spirits now, where are your demons?'

'Heretic!' a pretty woman screamed at my elbow. 'What's he doing in the stretchneck, it's the gibbet should have him.'

All about her people who had been intent on chipping pennies off a weaned pig, or testing the weave of a basket, or deciding between pies, found that they were angry beyond measure, in proportion to their righteousness. Then the sheriff's man raised an arm and they fell silent like the dogs they were, open-jawed, for the treat. He took a nail from his pouch and nailed Talbot's ear to the board; the second took longer for he dropped the nail and, swearing, had to scrabble for it at Talbot's feet, but then that too was hammered in. Blood trickled from the iron and at that moment the sun shone out of the clouds lighting it scarlet. A cheer went up from the crowd, the officer stepped back and a pile of muck landed on Talbot's head. It was like a signal to the crowd; the air was thick with the festering waste of the market.

I nudged the young man at my elbow. 'What did he do?' I asked, 'I cannot read the writing.'

'Why,' he said to me, 'and nor can I, but that's no matter. I'm told he draws circles for the fairies and guides them to the cribs of bairns to take them in the night. There's a woman out at Caton who was left a changeling in her child's stead. Screeched night and day it did, unnatural. Her neighbours were praying for the crows to come.'

'Aye and there's worse,' a woman near him said, 'they say he has a book of magic that the devil himself gave to him, but his boy ran off and there's nobody been able to find him – or the rope would have had them and good riddance.'

I made the sign of the cross to quiet them and then I saw that he had seen me and I brought my hand before my lips and looked back, so that only he could see I blew a kiss; his eyes half smiled. My intention had been to drug him. I had made a paste so that he would scarcely feel the hours or the refuse and worse, that the rabble would throw, but I saw now that was no good. When his head drooped the pain of the nails jerked it back upright; to sleep would be to rip his ears across. It struck me I had done him a disservice with the dwale.

A man stepped up to Talbot with a cup, turning to grin at the crowd as he did so.

'Here,' he said, 'you must be thirsty, brother.' He tipped the cup at Talbot's mouth and hooted. 'Drink piss, earwig.'

Talbot cried out as he snatched his head away and a fresh welt of blood dripped from the board, but his eyes grew more focussed. I bustled forward with my bottle.

'Here's more for you,' I shouted, climbing the platform. I tipped the ale to his lips. 'What can I do?' I whispered.

His right eye was too bruised to open, but his left swivelled up to mine. 'Marry me,' he said, 'pillow my head on your soft breasts, salve my hurts with your sweet cunt. The gallows are more kind than this.'

The day grew hot, but heavy, so that the warmth felt like a threat. Over the fells dark clouds would be piling. Perhaps Jacob would be securing shutters at the tavern, talking softly to the horses. The crowd was looser now, people came and went between shopping and jeering. The flurry of dirt, eggs, fish heads, cock's combs, offal, slacked and started more wearily, like the waves of an ebbing tide. I did what I could; I weaved in front of boys with onions, carrots, bones, stones; I lay my arm round the neck of a man who caressed a flint in his fingers, leering up at his black teeth, his plague-sore mouth, until he dropped the stone.

A rumbling began from the east and a thunder wind scurried at skirts and caps, rattled the shutters of the houses. The traders made haste to close and bundle up. People began to think of shelter. Talbot was not due to come down for another hour or more, but the officer was glancing at the sky. A large drop plashed and burst on the platform; there was a moment while the clouds breathed in and held their breath; large drops fell singly here and there, cooling upturned faces, spattering the dust; then, like a curtain, the downpour.

'Here, you!' the sheriff's man was calling me. 'What are you, his cockatrice? Take him.'

He drew out a blade and deftly, as though cutting stems of corn, sliced through the tops of Talbot's ears and threw them to the ground for the dogs to find. Then he lifted the board and pushed his body so that he crumpled like a child on the platform, his ears bleeding into the pooling rain. I bound his head tightly with a scarf and with his arm round my shoulder somehow hoisted him upright.

It was not far to the alley off Fish Market, but I barely made it; his legs buckled every second step. At first Betsy would not let me in.

'What kind of business is this?' she said, pointing at Talbot. 'Did your lover let you down? I warned you. Very well, but a few minutes only. I'll not be a harbourer of rogues and felons.'

I bought good wine to mollify her and revive Talbot and then I left through the rain to rid myself of my clogging skirts and to harness Juno so that I could fetch him back to the tavern.

40

Juno was badly named – she was nothing like the jealous queen of heaven; she was the sweetest-tempered mare that ever lived. Talbot was mad with pain and wine and fury as she bore him back; he beat her about the neck as he cursed and spat until I could stand it no longer and pitched him into an open trough, threatening to leave him there unless he could be gentle with her. Even after this she stood by while I hauled him again into the saddle.

The rain fell without stint. It plastered our hair to our heads and our clothes to our backs. It spewed out from the gutters and the drains, till all was slick with mud and the only colours in the world were grey and brown. The tavern was emptier now; the night before I had taken a room for us both that was reached round the back, with only the ancient one-eyed servant to see how we came and went. It was nothing to him if a woman was in my room, just so long as he was tipped. Nothing to him either if I had to haul my companion, cursing to his bed.

'Liquor had his legs has it?' he said. 'It's a terrible thing, a liking for swill. Want me to look out a skeel in case he throws it?'

'Yes,' I said, 'and a kettle of hot water, Tom, if you would. My friend's fallen and I have to clean the hurts.'

I could scarcely manage him; he threw himself, filthy as he was, on the bed and I thanked myself for stripping the linen and laying sacking down. When I tried to come near to undo his filthy doublet he flung his arm at me and called me an iron-papped scrat, unnatural, a man-woman.

'I will not let you die, Edward Talbot.'

'I want to, damn you. I am ruined, maimed. Every bald-rib starveling, every hollow-cheeked scrag and stick-legged ragged brat in every street will point at me and mock. I will be stoned out of the meanest middenstead as a branded man, a rogue, a cozener. I, Edward Kelley, who could have held in his hand the flower of the sun.'

'So you are plain Edward Kelley now?'

'What is it to you what I am? I need more wine. Never be a woman, Jabez, it doesn't suit you. You have the heart of a toad. A woman's gentle soul could not bear the weight of such a conscience as yours. To cast me off for a muck-shoveller! I offered you my learning, my bared soul.'

'It was your body, chiefly, I refused. Not your mind, although lately that's grown rank enough.'

There was nothing to be gained from this. I left him on the bed to go in search of wine and the promised kettle of water. When I returned he was snoring, but already beginning to shiver in his wet clothes. Without care the wounds would soon fester. I mixed the wine with enough hemlock to quiet him a little and spooned it into his mouth and then I stripped him of his wet clothes and piled blankets on him. Afraid they would not warm him quick enough, I picked up my faithful Barbel and settled her at his side.

His wrists and neck were swollen from the boards and there were open sores where he had been shackled. I worked from the feet, wrapping the bruises with comfrey and applying yarrow and garlic and woundwort to the sores. A week since I had gone to the moors to collect the bog moss that grew there and now I had it dry and clean. The Queen herself would not get a better dressing, unless there were London cures that I knew nothing of. He twitched a little but slept on as I worked and the cat purred with the rise and fall of his raw-boned chest. As soon as I was done, I thought, I would have pottage sent up; he was all shrunken and gaunt. Then I turned to his head, and all the thrown mullock of the market that had crusted and cut it. A gash above his right eye I stitched with waxed thread. I thought he would wake at that, but he merely threw an arm feebly to the sky and mumbled a curse. At last I unwrapped the cloth to attend to his mutilated ears. It is good you had a goblin face, I said to him as he slept. There is less to lament.

I sent the clothes to be laundered and ordered the food. Then I sat by the bed, waiting to see if he fell into a fever while the pottage grew cold and night slowly gripped the street close and then slowly released it, scooping day from the east. At some point I must have dozed for I woke to find him watching me out of his one good eye.

'What rat hole is this Jabez?' he said when he saw I was awake.

'One that I have paid for, to save your ingrate life,' I said, testily enough. There was a limit to the pity he could wring from me; some I needed for myself.

He put a hand up to his ears. 'What did you use? Bog moss? Was it clean or did you buy it off some piss pedlar? It is not enough by itself. You should have asked me how to make a poultice.'

'Talbot,' I said, standing over him, 'do not make me the butt of your anger.'

He hauled himself up and nodded and my heart felt for him as he shuffled his swollen neck and the bile in his gaze softened to misery. 'Forgive me Jabez,' he said. 'Each day in that foul place I prayed that the door of the cell would open and you would come. It was so dark, Jabez, foul and dark every inch, so airless. The stone walls ran with sweat. I began to lose faith in the sun itself. Even your ploughboy would have been welcome.'

I stood up and went to the casement. 'I found him,' I said without turning round. 'He's mine no longer; there's a bonny girl with a child in her belly.'

'Ah,' he said. I leaned at the window, twisting my hands, waiting for barbs, all basted about with cruelties, to fall, but he said nothing and I blessed him for it. When I looked back he was eating last night's pottage, wincing as he swallowed.

'We have not done so well, you and I,' he said gently when I took the empty bowl. 'All is lost. All. My books they told me were burned at Hornby and the stone, Jabez, that brought me angels: it was seized. Each time I asked for it I was told I should rejoice it had been returned to Hornby and could not be used to damn me as a sorcerer.'

'Here,' I said taking the stone from the bag where I had placed it. 'I had it from the gaoler. And the books too, are safe. Buried, with what is left of your gold, not far from here. All is saved, but what I used to pay Babcock – that and the Hornby ring; Lady Elizabeth's companion made me give that back.'

The stone lay like an egg in his hand, black and deep as the vault of heaven where angels step out of the stars.

41

Talbot healed quick enough in body, with my tending, but his mind remained dejected, pious and melancholic or restive and cursing in turns. He did not stir from the room, but would pray for hours on his knees on the bare boards, berating himself for his pride and greed then bargaining with God for favour as though it were an apple and Christ a costermonger with a barrow in the street. I feared he would never go out again. I have lost more than you, I thought, but I said nothing. My ache for Jacob was my own. Every day cost me more money. I told the landlord he was brainsick and had food sent up.

In the evenings, when the shadows began to web the four walls, he saw spirits, elves and fairy people, or the wraiths of the dead. 'There,' he would whisper, 'the little people, in the hearth again,' and I would look and see nothing but unswept ash. I held his hand, then, to keep his mind from stepping through. Sometimes he believed his visitors were spawned by hell, that they were demons trying for his soul; other times he swore it was simply that his mind was worn so thin it was like a piece of wafting gauze – the spirit world passed through it as easy as light or water. The showstone lay unused beside the bed; although he often laid his hand on it he would not use it. He had told me once that only God's ministers, only angels could be summoned to the stone; I urged him to pick it up and question if these were indeed devils that beset him, but he was afraid. He had failed the angel in the stone, he said and dared not face it.

'Very well,' I said, one evening, 'I will look. You say most scryers use a boy to do their seeing. I am almost a boy.'

I sat on the bed next to him and picked it up. It had frightened me before, when I feared the vision it sent, of the bridge and the swan and the limping man, that it was commanding me to marry Talbot, but the riddle had been truer and more simple and more sad. My heartache left no room for other fears. Even towards death and the thought of death, I felt only numbness. The stone was round and smooth as an egg. I had felt it begin to open for me once; perhaps its black depths could open my eyes again to wonder.

Talbot had twisted away from me in peevish misery but now he turned back and moved the candle to draw the light; dipping his finger in the wax drew a cross on my forehead. *'On, Ell, Eloy,'* he chanted, *'Eley, Messias, Sother, Emmanuel, Sabaoth,'* and I said the words after him.

'You must say what you see, exactly,' Talbot said. 'You are the scryer now.'

I cradled the stone in my palm and let my mind play across its emptiness. To begin with there was only blackness, nothingness, but then it seemed to me this nothing folded itself back and back until I looked into the abyss of night itself. I reeled at the horror of such unending space. I think I would have dropped the stone, or hurled it from me if Talbot had not grasped my shoulders.

Slowly, a fog rolled across the darkness and swirled to a point of light that extended and became a dazzling scene of noble men and women, gilded towers, feasts and dancers; they dissolved as if they

were made of water, of drifting cloud. Through the mist appeared a
golden man – more beautiful than any I had ever seen. 'Look,' he
said, and he scooped a handful of the red clay at his feet and fash-
ioned from it a figure, a shining child who looked up at the stars,
who became a labourer, a woman with child, a courtier, a king;
round him lions ranged, bears, a deer, a mouse, a salmon river-leap-
ing, a blackbird at its morning song – all the creatures of the earth
and sky ravelling and unravelling. And the king crumbled back into
the clay and became a scholar, a lawyer, a wild rogue, a one-toothed
beggarwoman. Then, nothing – the stone was a black lump in my
hand and my brain was giddy with pain and confusion.

When I ceased talking and looked up, Talbot was rocking
slightly; his eyes gleamed.

'Do you see, Jabez? The golden man, the shining child, the
fallen fabric of creation. It is a message for me to learn the language
of heaven, to thread back to the golden world. You and I, Jabez, we
will conceive the royal child; all the courts of Europe will be open
to me.'

I did not see at all, but I was glad the vision brought him hope. He
was soon asleep. I laid the stone down and went to my own bed. How
could so small a rock hold a universe within it? It made me shudder. I
had hoped that it would show me Jacob – that I would see him
thinking of me. I prayed to God to protect him and as I prayed images
of the vision came back to me more gently; Talbot had misconstrued
it all. What was it but the delicate glory of creation spun out of earth
and falling into it again, as a bird threads the air with song that stays a
while in the ear and then dissolves back into air. I picked up my book
and turned to the story of Prometheus, fashioning man out of the
earth and teaching him to gaze up at the heavens and 'mark and
understand what things were in the starry sky'.

After the scrying Talbot began to recover his self-love and his trust in his great destiny. It was a trial, he said, of his strength and faith. Did I know the story of Pythagoras, who first taught that the planets moved by numbers, making music? The mob set upon him to tear him limb from limb; they set alight his house and he was forced to crawl away to die of hunger and despair. Or Socrates, convicted for challenging the pieties of fools? I let him talk on; it was foolish bragging, but there was some truth. The crowd had pelted him for conjury not for counterfeiting.

When the light failed his apprehensions returned. Night after night he begged me to lie next to him and hold him to keep him safe from the night hag who gripped his throat and choked his dreams with horrors, and night after night I refused, till he said that I was colder than Diana and the moon and deserved to die alone in my barren bed, that when we were married he would roll off me in the heat of my lust till I cried for him to come to me. In truth I was not afraid of mischief; at times I even felt myself that I was cruel, denying him comfort. It was that when I lay alone in the darkness, I felt again Jacob's head on my breast as we lay wrapped together on the fell, Jacob's body warm against mine, and all the sorrow and the closeness of that night.

After two weeks of this I went to a milliner's and bought him a fine close cap, all stitched about with stars about the base.

'Look,' I said, holding up the stone for a mirror so that he could see himself, 'not a whit of your injury shows. You may go abroad again without any fear of mockery.'

He made a show of wincing at my using the stone for vanity, but I could see he was delighted, puffing out his chest as he used to do, smoothing his owl feather brows.

'We must collect your books, Talbot, and your gold. I buried them well, but the damp of Autumn may find them out if we leave it too long.'

'You go. I hate to walk. Children mock my gait. It would be more than I can stand, at present.'

'I hobble as much as you. It is scarce four miles, but you might ride Juno if you wish.'

I had to draw him out into the world again before I could leave him and I felt the bargain that I had to strike with him must be made in the open air. To my relief, he nodded.

'And you must put on petticoat and kirtle, Jabez-Jane. I will not have my wife in breeches.'

'I am nobody's wife, Talbot. And it would look strange, don't you think, to have a woman hold her husband's bridle?'

* * *

It was a fine September day and the low morning mist had risen from the fields. The leaves had the dark leathery look of late summer but there were flowers enough by the road and in the meadows – loosestrife, devil's bit, selfheal. The hedges were clotted with blackberries and gaggles of children picking them. A small boy held me out a handful, grinning with purple teeth.

'Never eat them,' Talbot said, checking his cap, when I offered some up.

'You're like the old women in my village, who forbad them, said the trail of the serpent had passed over them. My father scorned their ignorance at refusing nature's bounty.'

'And what was he, your father, an educated man?'

'He knew Latin when he was young, but...'

'But what?'

I said nothing; Talbot had already turned away to watch a kestrel that hovered like a hanging stone, then wheeled away towards the heather. How long was it since I had thought of my dead father, how he'd raged for years against our narrow valley and the tavern walls and never left them? I remembered a day suddenly, an afternoon; I was lurking in the hedge afraid to go home because Robert Tanner had caught me scrumping apples at the Hall and had sworn he'd tell my father, that there'd be a beating in it. I watched a beetle crawl across my hand in all its glossy armour as I sucked at the salt tears that ran onto my lips. Then a shadow moved across the light and I looked up to see my father looking down at me. He reached out with his big hands and pulled me out and put me on his shoulders like a queen. 'Don't be afraid Martha,' he said, 'they can spare an apple. The trick is how to take it.' And he pulled from his pocket a bright pippin and passed it up to me. I was high, high, with the tall clouds above me and the sweet, crisp joy of the apple in my mouth.

The peas and beans were still being picked, but the fields were shorn of wheat and barley.

'You've missed the harvest,' I said, as we began to climb up from the valley floor.

'No, Jabez' he said, venturing a grim smile, 'I've been well cropped.'

I found the distance post easy enough. We waited a little way off while a pedlar and his pack passed by, wishing him a good day, and then we turned off to the trees. I tethered Juno out of sight as before and pointed towards the dell. I could see Talbot weighing up in his mind whether to chastise my choice, but he let it be.

A woodpecker flew before us. My grandmother called them yekkels, she'd point to their dipping flight: 'There'll be rain,' she'd say, but it was hard to believe now, with the sun splashing light through the leaves and rippling the wood loam like moving water.

'Look,' I said to Talbot, pointing to the light and shadow, 'your gold has spilled onto the forest floor.'

He took my arm, grinning. 'What children we shall have, Jabez!'

We had reached the ruined cottage, and I sat down, weary. A

robin on an alder tree nearby was singing its autumn song. I
fancied there was a sadness to its chirping, now that nesting was
done with. I remembered another ruined house, when I fled the
mob with Jacob and we lay down together and a blackbird sang,
full-throated, for the spring.

'No,' I said. 'I will not marry you. I told you already.'

I had half expected the fury he had shown me in the maze, but
he too was weary. He sat down on a stump of stone, facing me and
his face looked puzzled. 'You said so, but surely,' he said, 'now you
have been cast off – all's changed? What else is there for you? We
are to have a child. I have such power in me, Jabez – you have seen
it. I need a mate who can assist me, scribe for me. You may even
scry for me; it has to be, you must see that.'

'No,' I said. 'I don't want it. You shouldn't marry. Not yet. You are
scarcely begun. How would you keep a wife? You need to find a
patron. You must be unencumbered; think what work you have to
do – what teaching – all the creatures, all the matter of the world
strung together in becoming; the earth conceiving these birch trees
and their leaves falling into earth again. Or this robin, spinning the
air into song.'

He smiled. 'That is the trouble with women. However clever,
they mistake the whole for the parts – you have forgot the purpose,
Jabez, how all things strive towards light, the material to the airy
spirit, base metal yearning to become pure gold. I seek redemption.'

'We differ,' I said. 'I don't want perfection in this world. I like
creation as it is.'

'Mortal, decaying. Impure.'

'Changing shapes as the clouds do. I will not marry you. You
have a fierce fiery mind, Edward Talbot. You have taught me not to
be afraid to think. I say I won't go with you.'

Yes, I thought, as he snorted his contempt and threw up his
hands, you are like a wildfire. I would be fuel to you. He said

nothing for a while, but stared at me with his owl eyes, 'You know I never loved you as a woman,' he said at last.

I nodded.

He sighed. 'Very well, let's fetch my property and my gold. What will you do now, Jabez?' His voice sounded almost gentle.

I swallowed. 'I wish to go south again, to the grange given you by Elizabeth Stanley, and build it up and live there.'

He frowned again. 'But you said you wouldn't marry me. And I'll not live there. A ruin in a wood, with pigs and peasants for neighbours.'

'I want to live there alone, as a widow. I want you to give me the deeds.'

'What?' His shout sent crows cawing to the fields. He had sprung up and was lowering over me. 'You brazen bitch! Never!'

'Very well.' I stood up and began to walk back towards Juno.

'Where are you going?'

'Back to the tavern.'

'And my gold, my property?'

'Find it yourself,' I said.

It took an hour to make terms. More than once he fingered the knife at his belt, as though tempted to bring the blade to the argument, but I had no fear of that. He was like a torch that flares and does not last long. All I had to do was wait. He knew what he owed me. By the time we got back to Juno he was clapping me on the back and laughing at the trick I'd played him. I made him promise that on the morrow he'd come with me to a lawyer to have the transfer made just and tight.

42

Early, just before it is light, I whistle my dog Jack from his heavy sleep beside the fire and walk up the steep horseshoe curl of the valley to the ridge. This is soft country, where the land rolls in waves towards the Marches. The sides of the valley are wooded, but the gentle hollow at its heart is pasture. My neighbour has made me a present of three ewes; in the spring I will buy more. Today, each blade of grass is feathered with ice and the trees have branches of white bone. I am alone, but for Jack, but I have my ghosts about me – Jacob, my lost child. Is his son born yet, I wonder, his tender daughter? Does he hold her in the crook of his arm and look out on the dawn-flushed snow?

Jack whines. He has scented a vixen and is eager to be off, but I put my hand on his head and hold him. He sniffs about my skirts in the dew. I am a woman now, mostly; I tell myself I have done with gadding, but I keep my doublet and hose and breeches in my chest and more often than I ought I saddle Juno and canter through the lanes, skittering the indifferent mud. Beside my bed, beneath the Bible, I keep my book of transformations.

The house was not such a ruin as Lady Stanley said, or at least not all of it. I arrived in the golden twilight of an October evening and plucked myself an apple from a tree that hung over the yard. There was an old woman, Jennet, living there. At first she thought to curse me out, or scare me with stories, but when at last she trusted that I did not mean to throw her on the parish, she taught me how to read the place, which boards were rotten, where to net rabbits.

There was no moat, old Jennet told me, it had been filled in by order of the church, to appease the ghost. Nobody had been in the old stone tower, not since he was a living man. It was a terrible tale she said. After the dissolution of the abbey that owned it the farm had been sold to its master, but he lived too well and took to thieving to pay his debts – a gentleman by day but by night a masked man on the highway – till a friend of his, riding back from Worcester, drew his sword and severed the wrist that had seized the bridle. What a homecoming was that, finding a mangled hand in his reins and on its finger his dear friend's ring. As for the master, he died from loss of blood on the road. Ever since then he was forever coming home, leaping into the tower and over it, into the moat.

The tale kept people away. I think she half believed it herself, but I broke the locks with an axe and went in, frighting a ghost owl from the upper landing, where an open casement gaped. There was a pelt of dust, and cobwebs, and rat litter in the corners, but the walls were stone and the timbers hale and the oak dresser laden with plate as though waiting its master's return. Nobody in the village would help me to clear it, even for money, until the minister came to pray with me and bless it clean.

At Christmas I will have a visitor. My little Owen, who I have not seen since he was eight years old, who is now a student of divinity in Oxford. Owen, who was buried with me in the clay and, like me, found. Is his hair still white, I wonder?

I parted with Talbot in Lancaster; he declared he had business in Richmond and headed north and east across the moors. He said that he would write to me, if only to tell me how I could have laced my hair with gold and rode in carriages to the courts of kings. 'Do,' I said, 'write to me when you are famous, when you are sought by kings and emperors, when her majesty pleads with you to return to her from Poland and Bohemia.'

'And to whom should I write, Jabez-Jane, what name?

'Martha,' I said, choosing, 'Martha Stone, Widow.'

HISTORICAL NOTE

Many of the people and places in the book are real. Martha's journey north and her perceptions of places she goes through echo John Leland's travels (mostly undertaken in 1539) in his *Itinerary*, and follow the great Tudor maps of the counties of England by Christopher Saxton and John Speed, with their detailed charts of principal towns and cities.

Ovid brightened up the lives of Elizabethan school children who spent hour on hour translating Latin back and forth. I've used Arthur Golding's wonderful verse translation of the *Metamorphoses*. It was published in the 1560s and is still available as a Penguin Classic.

Thomas Coningsby and Edward Croft are historical figures – eldest sons of families that vied for dominance in Herefordshire; from the late 1570s the rivalry grew increasingly violent, with skirmishes in Leominster, Hereford and even London. At least one man was killed. Hampton Court Castle in Herefordshire (which is well worth a visit), where the book opens, was inherited by Thomas Coningsby when a boy. He toured Italy with the poet Sir Philip Sidney, saw action as a soldier and acted as High Sheriff of Here-

fordshire. Towards the end of his life he founded a hospital in Hereford for veterans and servants. Edward Croft was the eldest son of
James Croft of Croft Castle (now run by the National Trust). He
appears to have been an unstable character. In the late 1580s he was
charged with engaging a conjurer to bring about the Earl of Leicester's death. Not long after he fled to the Netherlands to escape debt.
He was disinherited by his father and did not return to England.

Elizabeth Stanley was the heiress of William Stanley of Hornby
Castle, but far less is written about her than about her male rela-
tives; her son William Parker, Baron Monteagle, was involved in the
discovery of the Gunpowder Plot. In 1582 it seems John Dee sent
Edward Talbot to obtain books held by her husband Lord Morley
after her father's death.

Edward Talbot was indeed born Edward Kelley. Little is known
of his early life, except that he was born in 1555 in Worcester and
probably trained as an apothecary. He may have studied (as Talbot)
in Gloucester Hall, Oxford. He is believed to have had his ears
cropped in Lancaster around 1580 for forging title deeds or counterfeiting coins. There are other, wilder stories – he was indeed said to
have attempted to raise a corpse. Then, in 1582, as Edward Talbot,
he was introduced to John Dee, mathematician, philosopher and
astrologer for Elizabeth I. Dee was involved in a spiritual quest; he
used crystal gazers – scryers – to call and talk to angels. The Neo-
Platonist and Hermetic ideas I give to Kelley/Talbot are close to
those of Dee; the image of the world as a lyre comes from Dee's
Propaedeumata Aphoristica, published in 1568 in English, which
Kelley might well have read. In Kelley, at last, he found a scryer up
to the task. 'Dee was a fool and Kelley was a knave,' A.F. Pollard
wrote in his chapter on Kelley for Thomas Seccombe's *Lives of
Twelve Bad Men* in 1894, but over the last few decades historians
have taken Dee's alchemical researches more seriously and, noted

the brilliance and consistency of Kelley's visions, which Dee meticulously recorded in his diaries.

The men worked in a close and fraught partnership for years. Dee's diaries show Kelley to be a complicated man; a bully, a brawler and a charmer, given to intense fits of doubt, but also intensely ambitious. Perhaps at his instigation he and Dee left England for Bohemia and spent itinerant years talking with angels and haunting the courts of princes. He married, but reportedly hated his wife, even convincing Dee that the angels had instructed them to swap spouses. He believed, however, in educating women equally, hiring a distinguished Latin tutor for his stepdaughter Elizabeth Jane Weston, who became a celebrated neo-Latin poet. She regarded him as a 'kind stepfather'.

At length Kelley broke away from Dee and turned to practical alchemy through which he acquired great wealth and fame, even becoming a knight of Bohemia. Increasingly, it was he and not Dee who became sought after across Europe – Lord Burghley petitioned him to come home to make gold for Elizabeth. Perhaps to keep him Rudolph II, Holy Roman Emperor, imprisoned him twice in a castle in Bohemia. Dee's son Arthur reported that he died after falling from the castle walls, attempting to escape.

The poor, like Martha, or like Jacob, are, of course, not so well chronicled; all we have are songs and plays and stories.

BOOK CLUB QUESTIONS

- How does Martha change across the novel?
- What do you think are the key turning points for her? Do you think she makes good decisions?
- What do you think of Kelley/Talbot? How much sympathy do you have for him?
- In Martha's world, superstition and the supernatural were very much part of everyday reality – is this still at all true for you?
- Kelley/Talbot is a real historical figure who is believed to have had his ears cropped around 1580. Do you like fiction to weave in real historical people and events? How far is it important to be accurate?
- As a man Martha has a level of freedom – of movement and of speech – that she could never have as a woman. How far is this still true today?
- If Jacob had never left do you think Martha would have been content to stay in the village?

- Do you recognise any of the herbal remedies which Martha uses? Do you use any?
- Alchemy was as much a spiritual quest as a quest for gold. Kelley/Talbot's words – 'whatever is in the universe has order and harmony in relation to everything else' comes from John Dee, Elizabeth I's astrologer. The idea of the universe as a lyre is also Dee's: 'The entire universe,' Dee wrote 'is like a lyre tuned by some excellent artificer, whose strings are separate species of the universal whole.' What do you think of these ideas?
- Martha is drawn to Kelley/Talbot's idea that identities aren't fixed, but where he pursues golden perfection, she accepts earthy realities. Where do you stand?
- The journey Martha covers opened up new worlds to her. The distance between the Welsh Marches and the north is nothing today, but do real differences remain?
- Do you think Martha will ever see Jacob again? Will he be happy, do you think?

ACKNOWLEDGMENTS

A great many people helped me write this book and I am grateful to all of you. Firstly, my friends and family for their patience and support; most of all my parents, Sarah Porter, Sarah Eisner, John Porter, Steve Roser, Tara McCullough, Kathleen Woodhouse, Jane Greenwood, Ros McCarthy and Sarah Warren. Thank you to my lovely agent Peter Buckman and the brilliant team at Boldwood. Particular thanks to Clare Mockridge for reading an early draft and improving my horse lore; to Lily Xia for trying to teach me not to splice commas; to Joe Xia, my first reader; to my fellow Scribblers Olivia Levez, Sarah Dukes, Mike Woods, Cathy Knights and Mel Dufty. Thanks ever so much to William Edmundson and Vicki Hunt (and Jack) for the space and warmth and friendship that restored us all this plague summer and gave me room to write. And most of all and always, thank you to Chris; for everything, but especially, this year, the shed.

Martha's travels follow the beautiful, detailed early modern maps of Christopher Saxton and John Speed. For the life of Kelley/Talbot and his theories of alchemy I drew particularly on Deborah Harkness's scholarship on John Dee; the lectures that introduced the Royal College of Physicians 2016 exhibition: *The lost library of John Dee*; Christopher Whitby's PhD thesis: *John Dee's actions with Spirits*; *The Diaries of John Dee* edited by Edward Fenton and Benjamin Woollet's biography of Dee: *The Queen's Conjuror*. For the history of scrying I drew on Theodore Besterman's: *Crystal Gazing: A Study in the History, Distribution, Theory and Practice of Scrying*. The *Dictionary of National Biography* was, as always, a great first source for all the historical figures in the book.

For Martha's herbalism I culled Maud Grieve's: *A Modern Herbal* (1931). I'm grateful to all the local tourist, history and folklore sites I trawled through to understand Martha's journey – particularly when lockdown made real travel impossible.

MORE FROM ELEANOR PORTER

We hope you enjoyed reading *The Good Wife*. If you did, please leave a review.

If you'd like to gift a copy, this book is also available as an ebook, digital audio download and audiobook CD.

Sign up to Eleanor Porter's mailing list for news, competitions and updates on future books.

http://bit.ly/EleanorPorterNewsletter

Explore Martha's first adventure in *The Wheelwright's Daughter*.

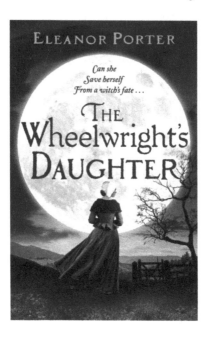

ABOUT THE AUTHOR

Eleanor Porter has lectured at Universities in England and Hong Kong and her poetry and short fiction has been published in magazines.

Follow Eleanor on social media:

- facebook.com/ellie_porter_author
- twitter.com/elporterauthor
- instagram.com/eleanorporterauthor
- bookbub.com/authors/eleanor-porter-f4eb18af-c78e-430c-9d1e-24b0bcfdb562

ABOUT BOLDWOOD BOOKS

Boldwood Books is a fiction publishing company seeking out the best stories from around the world.

Find out more at www.boldwoodbooks.com

Sign up to the Book and Tonic newsletter for news, offers and competitions from Boldwood Books!

http://www.bit.ly/bookandtonic

We'd love to hear from you, follow us on social media:

facebook.com/BookandTonic

twitter.com/BoldwoodBooks

instagram.com/BookandTonic